Praise for
LISA JACKSON

"When it comes to providing gritty and sexy stories, Ms. Jackson certainly knows how to deliver."
—*Romantic Times BOOKreviews* on *Unspoken*

"Provocative prose, an irresistible plot and finely crafted characters make up Jackson's latest contemporary sizzler."
—*Publishers Weekly* on *Wishes*

"Lisa Jackson takes my breath away."
—*New York Times* bestselling author Linda Lael Miller

Cold Blooded

"*Cold Blooded* grabs you by the throat from page one and does not let you off the edge of your seat for a moment after that."
—*Romance At Its Best*

"Taking up where last year's phenomenal *Hot Blooded* left off, *Cold Blooded* is a tight, romantic, edge-of-your-seat thriller."
—*Romantic Times BOOKreviews*

"*Cold Blooded* is an exciting serial–killer thriller... an entertaining tale."
—*BookBrowser*

"Crisp dialogue, a multilayered plot and a carefully measured pace build suspense in this chilling read that earns the WordWeaving Award for Excellence."
—*WordWeaving.com*

LISA JACKSON

HIGH STAKES

HQN™

ISBN 13: 978-0-373-77274-2
ISBN-10:   0-373-77274-2

HIGH STAKES

CONTENTS

GYPSY WIND   9

DEVIL'S GAMBIT   251

Dear Reader,

When HQN Books asked me about repackaging some of my books together, I helped my editor pair those that had similar themes, and in the case of *High Stakes,* I picked *Gypsy Wind* and *Devil's Gambit,* as I *loved* writing both those books. The novels were written around the breathtaking world of horse racing, a high-energy, dangerous sport involving some of the fastest and most beautiful creatures on the planet.

Then there are the people involved. Some with lots of money, some greedy, some honorable, some pure evil. The world of horse racing makes for an incredible backdrop to a love story, especially for an animal lover like me.

The characters of Brig Chambers and Becca Peters in *Gypsy Wind* came to me as if I'd known them forever. Their reunion story is passionate and hot, the line between love and hate blurred as they rediscover each other.

As for Tiffany Rhodes and Zane Sheridan, they have preconceived ideas about each other, and though Tiffany knows she shouldn't trust Zane, she can't fight her burning attraction for him.

Also, as a footnote, my youngest son is intrigued with the reissuing of some of my books and he's always saying, "Hey, Mom, let me know when *Devil's Gambit* will be released again." It was his little joke, as the book was written when he was really young. He liked the title and now when he asks, I can tell him it's on the stands!

I hope you enjoy both stories in *High Stakes!* Let me know what you think of the book by e-mailing me at lisa@lisajackson.com.

Enjoy,

Lisa Jackson

GYPSY WIND

CHAPTER ONE

THE SMALL DARK ROOM WAS AIRLESS and full of the familiar odors of saddle soap, well-oiled leather, and stale coffee. It began to sway eerily, as if the floorboards were buckling. Becca knew that her knees were beginning to give way, but she couldn't steady herself and she had to clutch the corner of the desk in order to stay on her unsteady feet. Her throat was desert dry, her heart pounding with dread as she stared in horror at the small television set across the room. The delft blue coffee cup slipped from her fingers to splinter into a dozen pieces. A pool of murky brown coffee began to stain the weathered floorboards, but Becca didn't notice.

"No!" she cried aloud, though no one else was in the room. Her free hand flew to the base of her throat. "Dear God, no," she moaned. Tears threatened to pool in her eyes and she leaned more heavily against the desk, brushing against a stack of paperwork which slid noiselessly to the floor. Becca's green eyes never left the black-and-white image on the television but fastened fearfully on the self-assured newscaster who was tonelessly recounting the untimely death of oil baron Jason Chambers.

Flashes of secret memories flitted through Becca's mind as she listened in numbed silence to the even-featured anchorman. Her oval face paled in fear and apprehension and she felt a very small, very vital part of her past begin to wither and die. As the reporter reconstructed the series of events which had led to the fatal crash, Becca vainly attempted to get a grip on herself. It was impossible. Dry wasted tears, full of the anguish of six lost years, burned at the back of her throat and her breath became as shallow and rapid as her heartbeat. *"No!"* She groaned desperately. "It can't be!" Her small fist clenched with the turmoil of emotions and thudded hollowly against the top of the desk.

Hurried footsteps pounded on the wooden stairs, but Becca didn't notice. She couldn't take her eyes off the screen. The door to the tiny room was thrust open to bang heavily against the wall, and a man of medium height, his face twisted in concern, rushed into the office.

"What the hell?" he asked as he noticed the defeated slump of Becca's shoulders and the stricken, near-dead look in her round eyes. She didn't move. It was as if she hadn't heard his entrance. "Becca?" he called softly, and frowned with worry when she didn't immediately respond. He took in the scene before him and wondered about the broken cup and the brown coffee which was running over a scattered pile of legal documents on the floor. Still Becca's fearful eyes remained glued to the television set. "Becca," Dean repeated, more sharply. "What the hell's going on here? I was on my way up here when I heard you scream—"

Becca cut him off by raising her arm and opening her palm to silence him. Taken aback at his sister's strange behavior, Dean turned his attention to the television for the first time since entering the room. The small black-and-white set was tuned into the news and the story which held his sister mutely transfixed was about some light plane crash in the Southern Oregon Cascades. No big deal, Dean thought to himself. It happened all the time; a careless pilot got caught in bad weather and went down in the mountains. So what? Dean shifted from one foot to the other and searched Becca's stricken white face, searching for a clue to her odd actions. What was happening here? Becca wasn't one to overreact. If anything, Dean considered his younger sister too even-tempered for her own good. A real cool lady. Becca's poise rarely escaped her, but it sure as hell was gone today.

While still attempting to piece together Becca's strange reaction, Dean leaned over to pick up some of the forgotten legal documents. It was then that the weight of the news story struck him: Only one man could break his sister's cool, self-assured composure, and that man, if given the chance, could cruelly twist Becca's heart to the breaking point. It had happened once before. It could happen again, and this time it would be much worse; this time that man had the power to destroy everything Dean had worked toward for six long years.

Silently Dean's thin lips drew downward and his icy blue eyes slid to the screen to confirm his worst fears. He waited while the sweat collected on his palms. A faded photograph of Jason Chambers was flashed onto the screen and Dean's pulse began to jump. It was true! Jason Chambers, head of one of the largest oil companies in the western United States, was *dead*. Dean swallowed back the bile collecting in the back of his throat.

The news of Jason Chambers' death didn't fully explain Becca's outburst. Dean wiped his hands on his jeans before straightening and then listened to the conclusion of the report. He hoped that the reporter would answer the one burning question in his mind—perhaps there was still a way out of his own dilemma. He was disappointed; the question remained unanswered. Dean's jaw tightened anxiously. When the news turned to the political scene, Dean turned the set off.

Becca slumped into the worn couch near the desk and tears began to run down her soft cheeks. She wiped them hurriedly aside as the shock of the newscast began to wear off and the reality of the situation took hold of her. Her hand, which had been raised protectively over her breasts, slowly lowered.

"Are you all right?" Dean asked, his voice harsh despite his concern. He poured a fresh cup of coffee and handed her the mug.

"I… I think so…" Becca nodded slowly, but she had to catch her trembling lower lip between her teeth. She accepted the warm mug and let its heat radiate some warmth into her hands. Though the temperature in the stifling office had to be well over eighty degrees, Becca felt chilled to the bone.

The silence in the room was awkward. Dean shifted his weight uncomfortably. He was angry, but he didn't really know whom to blame. It was obvious that Becca was caught in the web of memories of her past, memories of Brig Chambers and his tragic horse. Dean's lips pursed into a thin line as he paced restlessly in front of the desk while Becca stared vacantly at the floor. A silent oath aimed at the man who had caused his sister so much pain entered his mind. Brig Chambers could ruin everything! Dean coughed when he leaned against the windowsill and looked across the spreading acres of Starlight Breeding Farm. Brig Chambers, if he was still alive, had the power to take it all away!

Dean asked the one question hanging between his sister and himself. "Was there anyone with Jason Chambers in that plane?"

Becca closed her eyes as if to shield herself from the doubts in her mind. "I don't know," she whispered raggedly.

Dean frowned and rubbed his hands over his bare forearms. He pushed his straw Stetson back on his head, and his reddish eyebrows drew together. His blue eyes seemed almost condemning. "What did the reporter say?"

"Nothing…the accident had only happened a couple of hours ago. No one seemed to be sure exactly what caused the crash…or who was in the plane. The reporter didn't seem to know too much." Becca moved her head slowly from side to side, as if to erase her steadily mounting fear.

"The station didn't know who was in the plane?" Dean was skeptical.

"Not yet," she replied grimly.

Dean ran a hand over his unshaven cheek and pressed on. "But surely someone at Chambers Oil would know."

Becca sagged even deeper into the cracked leather cushions and toyed with her single, honey-colored braid. It was difficult to keep her mind on her brother's questions when thoughts of Brig continued to assail her. "The reporter said that there was a rumor suggesting that Jason might have had a couple of passengers with him," Becca admitted in a rough whisper. Hadn't Dean heard the story? Why was he pressuring her?

"Who?" Dean demanded. His blue eyes gleamed in interest.

Becca shrugged and fought against the dread which was making her feel cold and strangely alone. "No one seems to know for sure. I told you it's only speculation that anyone is with Jason…no one at Chambers Oil is talking."

"I'll bet not," Dean muttered, unable to hide the edge of sarcasm in his words. His eyes turned frigid.

"Maybe they just don't know."

"Sure, Becca," he mocked. "You of all people know better than that. If Chambers Oil isn't talking, there's a good reason. You can count on it."

"What do you mean?"

Dean looked his sister squarely in the eyes and the bitterness she saw in his cold gaze made her shudder. His scowl deepened. "What I mean is that we, you and I, don't know if Brig Chambers is alive or dead!"

Becca drew in a long, steadying breath as she met Dean's uncompromising stare. Her brother's harsh words had brought her deepest fear out into the open and she had to press her nails into her palms in order to face what might be the cruel truth. *He can't be dead*, she thought wildly, grasping at any glimmer of hope, but fear crawled steadily through her body, making her blood run cold and wrenching her heart so savagely that it seemed to skip a beat in desperation.

She wouldn't allow the small gleam of hope within her to die. "I think that if Brig had been on the plane, the television station would have known about it."

"How?"

"From the oil company, I guess."

"But they're not talking. Remember?"

"I…just don't think that Brig was on the plane." Why didn't she sound convincing?

"But you're not sure, are you?"

"Oh God, Dean," she whispered into her clasped hands. "I'm not sure of anything right now!" As quickly as her words came out, she regretted them. "I'm sorry… I didn't mean to snap at you. It's not your fault," she confessed wearily. "It's all so confusing." Silent tears once again ran down the elegant slopes of her cheeks.

"What are we going to do?" Dean asked, not moving from his haphazard position against the windowsill. Anxious lines of worry creased his tanned brow.

"I don't know," Becca admitted as she faced a tragedy she had never before considered. *Was it possible? Could Brig really be dead?* Her entire body was shaking as she drew her booted feet onto the edge of the couch and tucked her knees under her chin. As her forehead lowered, she closed her eyes to comfort herself. No matter what had happened, she vowed silently to herself that she would find a way to cope with it.

Dean watched his sister until the anger which had been simmering within him began to boil. His fist crashed onto the windowsill in his frustration. "I told you that we should never have gone back to old man Chambers," he rebuked scornfully. "It was a mistake from the beginning to get involved with that family all over again. Look what a mess we're in!"

"Not now, Dean," Becca said wearily. "Let's not argue about this again."

"We have to talk about it, Becca."

"Why? Can't it wait?"

"No, it can't wait, especially now. I told you that going back to Jason Chambers was a mistake, and I was certainly right, wasn't I?"

"I had no choice," Becca pointed out. "*We* had no choice."

"*Anything* would have been better than this mess you managed to get us into! What the hell are we going to do now?"

Trying futilely to rise above the argument, Becca attempted to pull the pieces of her patience and shattered poise into place. "For God's sake, Dean, Jason Chambers is dead! For all we know, other people might have died in that plane and all you can think about is the fact that we owe Jason Chambers some money."

"*Some money?*" Dean echoed with a brittle laugh. "I wouldn't call fifty thousand dollars 'some money.'"

Becca could feel herself trembling in suppressed fury. "The man is *dead*, Dean. I don't understand what you're worried about—"

"Well, then, I'll enlighten you, dear sister. If Jason Chambers is dead, we're in one helluva mess. I don't pretend to know much about estates and wills or anything that happens when a guy as rich as Jason Chambers kicks the bucket, but any idiot can figure out that all of his assets and liabilities will become part of his estate. You and I and the rest of Starlight Breeding Farm are part of those liabilities." Dean took off his hat and raked his fingers through the sweaty strands of his strawberry-blond hair. "There's only one man who is going to benefit by Jason Chambers' death: his only son, Brig. That is, if the bastard is still alive."

"Dean, don't…" Becca began. She was visibly trembling when she rose from the couch, but in her anger some of the color had returned to her face and a spark of life lightened her pale green eyes.

"Don't you dare come to the aid of Brig Chambers," Dean warned. "Any praises you might sing in his behalf would sound a little hollow, wouldn't you say?"

"Oh, Dean…all of that—"

"That what? Scandal?" Dean suggested ruthlessly.

"I don't want to talk about it."

"Why not? Does the truth hurt too much? Don't you remember what happened at Sequoia Park?"

"Stop it!" Becca shouted irritably. In a more controlled voice, she continued. "That was a long time ago."

"Give me a break, will ya, Becca? Brig Chambers nearly destroyed your reputation as a horse breeder, didn't he? And that doesn't begin to touch what he did to you personally. Even if your memory conveniently fails you, I've still got mine." Dean wiped a dusty layer of sweat from his brow with the back of his hand before striding to the small refrigerator and withdrawing a cold can of beer. He dropped into a chair, popped the tab of the can, and let the spray of cool white foam cascade down the frosty aluminum. After taking a lengthy swallow, he settled back into the chair and cradled the beer in his hands. His cold eyes impaled his sister, but he managed to control his temper. Calmly, he inquired, "You're still carrying a torch for that bastard, aren't you?"

"Of course not."

"I don't believe you." Another long swallow of beer cooled Dean's parched throat.

"Oh, Dean, let's not argue. It's so pointless. What happened between Brig and me is part of the past. He took care of that."

Dean noticed the wistful sigh that accompanied her argument. "Then why did you run back to Brig's father when you needed the loan?"

Becca's full lips pursed. "We've been through this a hundred times. I had no other choice. No bank in the country would loan me ten thousand dollars, much less fifty thousand."

"Exactly. Because Brig Chambers ruined your reputation as a horse breeder." His knowing eyes glittered.

Becca ignored Dean's snide comment. "Jason Chambers was my only chance...*our* only chance."

Dean drained his beer and crushed the can in his fist. He tossed it toward the wastebasket and missed. The can rolled noisily across the floor to stop near the worn couch. "Well,

Becca, you had better wake up and face facts. Our 'only chance,' as you refer to old man Chambers, is *dead*. And now, for all we know, his son, or whoever's still alive, practically owns our Thoroughbred. The only thing we've got going in our favor is that no one knows about the loan or the horse. That is right, isn't it? Jason Chambers was the only person who knew about Gypsy Wind?"

"I think so. He's the only one at Chambers Oil who would have been interested."

"Good! I guess we can count ourselves lucky that the local press hasn't shown much interest in her. Maybe we'll get a break yet. If our luck holds, the attorneys for Chambers Oil will be too busy with the rest of the Chambers empire to worry about our note for the fifty grand. Maybe they won't even find it. The old man could have hidden it."

"I doubt that."

"Why? He wanted to avoid the publicity as much as we did."

"That was before he died. I don't know what you're suggesting, Dean, but I don't like it. There's no way we can hide that horse and I wouldn't want to try. The Chambers family has to be advised that the collateral for that note is Gypsy Wind. That's only fair, Dean."

"That's not fair, Becca, it's damned near crazy! How can you even think about being fair with the likes of Chambers? What's going to happen is that we'll lose our horse! The last six years of work will go down the drain! Take my advice and keep quiet about the Gypsy."

"I can't! You know that. Keeping quiet would only make things worse in the long run. Sooner or later someone in the Chambers family is going to find the note and realize that we owe that money. And what about the horse? Even if I wanted to, I couldn't hide Gypsy. For one thing, she's insured. Soon she'll start racing. One way or another the Chambers family is going to find out about her."

Dean muttered an oath to himself. "Okay, Sis, so where

does that leave us? Back at square one? Just like we were six years ago? What the hell are we going to do?"

The headache which had been building between Becca's temples pounded relentlessly against her eardrums. To relieve some of her tension, she tugged at the leather thong restraining her hair and pulled the thick golden strands free of their bond. Absently she rubbed her temples and ran her fingers through her long, sun-streaked tresses. "I wish I could answer you, Dean, but I can't. Not right now. Maybe later—"

Dean ground his teeth together. "We can't wait until you pull yourself together, damn it! We haven't got the time!"

"What do you mean?"

"I mean that we have to find out if Brig Chambers is still alive! You've got to call Chambers Oil—"

"No," Becca blurted. "I...can't."

Dean bit his lower lip and shook his hands in the air. "You have to, Becca. We've got to know if Brig was a passenger on that plane. We have to know if he went down with his father."

"*No!*" Becca's face once again drained of color. Caught in the storm of emotions raging within her, she dropped her forehead into her palm. "We'll find out soon enough," she murmured.

"What are you afraid of?"

Becca's green eyes, when she raised them, pleaded with her brother to understand. "I'm not ready, Dean. Not yet. I don't know if I'll ever be...able to face the fact that Brig might be dead," she admitted.

"So I was right. You are still in love with him." Dean's mouth pulled into a disgusted frown. "Damn it, Becca, when are you going to realize that Brig Chambers is the one man responsible for nearly ruining your life?"

The tears which Becca had been struggling against began once again to pool, but she held her head proudly as she faced her reproachful older brother. Why couldn't Dean understand the pain she was going through? How could he remain so bitter? Her voice was low when she replied. "I know better than anyone what Brig did to me, and it hurt for a very long time. But I cared for that man, more than anything in my life…and I can't forget that. It's been over for a long time, but once he was everything to me."

"You're dreaming," Dean said icily.

"Just because it's over doesn't mean it didn't happen."

"Why are you telling me all of this?" Dean demanded as he stretched and paced restlessly in the confining room.

"Because I want you to know how I feel. I was bitter once and it's probably true that I should hate Brig Chambers, but I don't. I've tried to and I can't. And now that he might be dead…" her voice broke under the strain of her churning emotions.

For a moment sorrow and regret flashed in Dean's opaque blue eyes. It was gone in an instant. "There's no way I can understand how you still feel anything for that louse, and I think you had better prepare yourself: Brig might already be dead. As for Gypsy Wind, I think we have ourselves one insurmountable problem." His face softened slightly and for a fleeting moment, through the shimmer of unshed tears, Becca once again saw her brother as he had been during her childhood, the adolescent whom she had adored. The calloused and bitter man had faded slightly. His expression altered and she could feel him closing her out, just as he had for the past few years. Now, when she needed him most, he was withdrawing from her. "Come on, Sis," he said tonelessly. "Buck up, will you?"

He opened the door to the office, and as quickly as he had burst into the room over the stables, he was gone. Becca heard his boots echoing hollowly against the worn steps. Slowly she followed her brother outside. She stood on the weathered landing at the top of the stairs. Holding her hand over her eyebrows to shade her vision, Becca watched the retreating figure of her brother as he sauntered to his battered pickup, hopped into the cab, engaged the starter, and roared down the dry dirt road, leaving a dusty plume of soil in his wake.

THE LATE AFTERNOON SUN WAS BLINDING FOR Northern California at this time of the year, and the wind, when it did come, was measured in arrid gusts blowing northward off Fool's Canyon. The charred odor of a distant forest fire added to the gritty feel of weariness which had settled heavily between Becca's shoulder blades.

He can't be dead, she thought to herself as she remembered the one man who had touched her soul. She could still feel the caress of his fingers as they outlined her cheek or pushed aside an errant lock of her hair. She closed her eyes when the hot wind lifted her hair away from her face, and she imagined Brig's special scent: clean, woodsy, provocatively male. Idly she wondered if he'd changed much in the last six years. Were his eyes still as erotic as they once were? It had been his eyes which had held her in the past and silently held her still. Eyes: stormy gray and omniscient. Eyes that could search out and reach the farthest corners of her mind. Eyes that understood her as no one ever had. Eyes that touched her, embraced her. Eyes which had betrayed her.

"He can't be dead," she whispered to herself as her palm slapped the railing. "If he wasn't alive, I would know it. Somehow I would know it. If he were dead, certainly a part of me would die with him."

Slowly she retraced her steps back into the stuffy office and reached down to pick up the remains of the coffee cup. Her movements were purely mechanical as she straightened the papers and placed them haphazardly on the corner of the desk. She wiped up the coffee, but her mind was elsewhere, lost in thoughts of a happier time, a younger time. Though she sat down at the desk and attempted to concentrate on the figures in the general ledger, she found that the mundane tasks of keeping Starlight Breeding Farm operational seemed vague and unimportant. Images of Brig kept lingering on her mind, vivid pictures of his tanned, angular face and brooding gray eyes. Becca recalled the dimple that accompanied his slightly off-center smile and she couldn't help but remember the way a soft Kentucky rain would curl his thick, chestnut hair.

Deeper images, strong and sensual, warmed her body when she thought of the graceful way he walked, fluid and arrogantly proud. Her cheeks burned when she imagined the way he would groan in contentment when he would first unbutton her blouse to touch her breasts.

"Stop it!" she screamed as she snapped the ledger book closed and pulled herself away from the bittersweet memories of a love that had blossomed only to die. "You're a fool," she muttered to herself as she pushed the chair backward and raced out of the confining room. She had to get away, find a place in the world where traces of Brig's memory wouldn't touch her.

Her boots ground into the gravel as she ran past the main stables, across the parking lot, and through a series of paddocks, far away from the central area of the ranch. She stopped at the final gate and her clear green eyes swept the large paddock, searching for the dark animal who could take her mind off everything else. In a far corner of the field, under the shade of a large sequoia tree, stood Gypsy Wind. Her proud head was turned in Becca's direction, and the flick of her pointed black ears indicated that she had seen the slender blond woman leaning against the fence.

"Come here, Gypsy," Becca called softly.

The horse snorted and stamped her black foreleg impatiently. Then, with a confident toss of her dark head, Gypsy Wind lifted her tail and ran the length of the back fence, turned sharply, and raced back to the tree, resuming her original position. Dark liquid eyes, full of life and challenge, regarded Becca expectantly.

A sad smile touched Becca's lips. "Show off, are you?" she questioned the horse.

Footsteps crunched on the gravel behind Becca.

"I thought I might find you here," a rough male voice called as a greeting to her.

Becca looked over her shoulder to face the rugged, crowlike features of Ian O'Riley. He was shorter than she, and his leatherish skin hid nothing of his sixty-two years. Becca managed a thin smile for the ex-jockey, but nodded in the direction of the spirited horse. "How did the workout go this morning?"

The bit of straw that Ian had been holding between his teeth shifted to one side of his mouth. "'Bout the same, I'd say."

Becca sighed deeply and cast a rueful glance at the blood-bay filly. As if the horse knew she was the center of attention, she shook her dark head before tossing it menacingly into the air.

"There's no way to calm her down, is there?" Becca asked her trainer.

"It takes time," Ian replied cautiously, but his words were edged in concern. "It's hard to say," he admitted. "She's got the spirit, the 'look of eagles,' if you will…but…"

"It might be her undoing," Becca surmised grimly.

Ian shrugged his bowed shoulders. "Maybe not."

"But you're worried, aren't you?"

"Of course I'm worried. History sometimes has a way of repeating itself." He noticed the ashen pallor of Becca's skin and thought that he was the cause of her distress. He could have kicked himself for so thoughtlessly bringing up the past. He wanted to caution Becca about the Gypsy, but he had to be careful not to disillusion her. In Ian's estimation, Becca Peters was one of the finest horse breeders in the country, even if her brother was worse than useless. Ian attempted to ease Becca's mind. "Gypsy Wind just needs a little more work, that's all."

Becca wasn't convinced. "She does have Sentimental Lady's temperament."

"The spirit of a winner."

"It was Lady's spirit that was her downfall."

Ian waved dismissively and his face wrinkled with his comfortable smile. "Don't think that way, gal. Leave the worrying to me, that's what you pay me for."

"If I paid you for all the worrying you do, I'd be broke."

Laughter danced in Ian's faded blue eyes and his grizzled face showed his appreciation for Becca's grim sense of humor. "Just leave Gypsy to me. We'll be ready, come next spring."

"Ready for what?"

"Whatever the competition can dish out. Surprise them, we will. Even the colts."

"You think she can keep up with the colts?" Becca was clearly dubious and a cold chill of apprehension touched the back of her neck. The last time she had put a filly against a colt, the result had been a nightmare. Becca had vowed never to repeat her mistake.

"Of course she can. Not only that, she'll outclass the lot of them. Just wait and see. Remember, we have the element of surprise on our side."

"Not much longer. The first time she runs, the press will be there, digging up everything on Sentimental Lady."

"Let them. This time will be different," he promised. Ian gave Becca a hefty pat on the shoulders before he sauntered back toward the brood-mare barn.

Becca's gaze returned to the fiery horse. She wanted to be unbiased when she appraised the blood-bay filly, but Becca couldn't help but compare Gypsy Wind with her full-sister, Sentimental Lady. Gypsy was built similarly to Sentimental Lady, so much so that it was eerie at times. Though slightly shorter than Lady, Gypsy Wind was heavier and stronger. Fortunately, Gypsy's long, graceful legs were stouter than Sentimental Lady's, capable of standing additional weight and stress. Her coloring was identical except that the small, uneven star which Lady had worn so proudly was missing on her sister.

Doubts crowded Becca's tired mind. Maybe she had made

a foolish mistake in the breeding of Gypsy Wind. The question haunted her nights. How was she supposed to know that the offspring of Night Dancer and Gypsy Lady would produce another filly, an uncanny likeness of the first?

As she watched the dark horse shy from a fluttering leaf, Becca wondered what Brig would think if he saw Gypsy Wind. She had asked herself the same question a thousand times over and the answer had always been the same. He would be stunned, and afterward, when the initial shock had worn thin, he would be furious to the point of violence. Still, Becca had hoped to someday proudly show off the Gypsy to Brig. New tears burned in Becca's throat as she watched the dark horse and realized that Brig might never see Gypsy Wind. Brig Chambers might already be dead.

Becca let loose of the emotional restraint she had placed upon herself and cried quietly, feeling small and alone. She lowered her head to the upper rail of the fence and let out the sobs of fear and grief that had been building within her. Why had she never swallowed her stubborn pride and told Brig Chambers just how desperately she still loved him? Why had she waited until it was too late?

CHAPTER TWO

THE FIRST GRAY FINGERS OF DAWN FOUND Becca still awake, lying restlessly on the crumpled bedclothes. She snapped off the radio that had been her companion throughout the long night. The endless hours had been torture. There had been no broadcasts during the night to relieve her dread. She was numb from the reality that the only man she had ever loved might be lost to her forever.

The night had seemed endless while she stared vacantly at the luminous numbers on the clock radio, listening above the soft static-ridden music to the sounds of the hot summer night. Even in the early hours before dawn, the mercurial temperature hadn't cooled noticeably, making the night drag on even longer. Though the windows of her room had been open, the lace curtains had remained still, unmoved by even the faintest breath of wind. Trapped in a clammy layer of sweat, Becca had tossed on the bed, impatiently waiting for the dawn. When she had finally dozed, it was only to be reawakened by nightmares of an inferno, a disemboweled Cessna, and the haunting image of Brig's tortured face.

It was nearly six o'clock when her silent vigil ended. The familiar sound of a throbbing engine pierced the solitude as it halted momentarily at the end of the drive. At the sound, Becca rolled out of bed and quickly slipped into a clean pair of jeans and a T-shirt. She pulled on her boots as she ran from her room, flew down the stairs, and raced like a wild-woman to the mailbox.

Her heart was thundering in her chest and her fingers were trembling as she opened the rolled newspaper. Anxiously her eyes swept the headlines, stopping on a blurred photograph of a ragged, weary-looking Brig Chambers. *He's alive,* her willing mind screamed at her while her eyes scanned the article to confirm her prayers. Slowly the fear and dread which had been mounting within her heart began to ebb. "Thank God," Becca whispered in the morning sunlight as she crumpled into a fragile mound at the side of the road and let the tears of joy run freely down her cheeks. "Thank God."

It was several minutes before she could collect herself. She stood up and hastily rubbed the back of her hand over her eyes to stem the uneven flow. A tremendous weight seemed to have been lifted from her shoulders as she half-ran back to the house. She reread the article several times before finally opening the kitchen door. A wistful smile crossed her lips. She still felt sadness at the death of Brig's father, but the relief in knowing that Brig was alive warmed her heart.

The newspaper article indicated that Chambers Oil was not, as yet, making a statement concerning the crash, although the rumor that there had been passengers on the plane was confirmed by a company spokesman. The names of the persons accompanying the oil baron on his tragic journey were being withheld until the next of kin had been notified.

Becca stared at the picture of Brig and wondered how he was. His relationship with his father had been close, if sometimes strained. No doubt Brig was immersed in grief, but she knew that he would survive. It was his way.

The aroma of fresh-perked coffee greeted Becca as she entered the roomy old-fashioned kitchen. "What are you doing up so early?" she asked Dean as she reached for a mug of the steaming black coffee.

"Couldn't sleep," Dean grumbled. He sat at the table, his

forehead cradled in his palms. His sandy hair was uncombed and he had two days' worth of stubble on his chin. It looked as if he had slept in his dusty jeans and T-shirt.

"You got in late last night," Becca observed quietly. "I didn't expect to see you till midafternoon."

"I guess I've got things on my mind," he replied caustically. He raised his bloodshot eyes to stare at his sister, and in an instant he knew that Brig Chambers was still alive. It was written all over Becca's relieved face. "You got the paper?" he asked gruffly.

Becca nodded, taking a sip from her coffee as she sat down at the small table. Because Dean was being irritable, she purposely goaded him. "Do you want the sports section?"

Dean's eyes darkened. "Not this morning." He reached for the paper and began skimming the front page. Mockingly he added, "I'm glad to see you're back to normal."

"A pity you're not."

"All right, all right, I admit it. I've got one helluva hangover...Jesus Christ, give me a break, will ya?" His eyes moved quickly across the newsprint. "So Brig wasn't in the plane with his father!"

Was Dean relieved or disappointed? Becca couldn't guess. Her brother was becoming more of an enigma with each passing day. "Thank goodness for that," she sighed.

Dean shook his head slowly from side to side, trying to quell the throbbing in his temples and attempting to concentrate. "Okay, so now we know exactly what we're up against, don't we?" His eyes narrowed as he ran his thumb over his chin. "The question is, what are we going to do about it."

"I haven't quite decided—"

Before she could continue, Dean interrupted with a shrug and an exaggerated frown. "Maybe we won't have to worry about it at all."

"What do you mean?"

"I mean that it might be out of our hands already. Once Brig finds out about Gypsy Wind *and* the fifty grand, he might make his own decision, regardless of what we want."

"You think so?"

"What's to prevent him from taking our horse? After all, his old man practically bought her."

"I doubt that Brig would want the filly...you know that he gave up anything to do with racing—"

"Because of Sentimental Lady?" Dean asked bluntly. "Don't tell me you're still suffering guilt over her, too."

"No..."

"Just because Brig blamed you for—"

"Stop it!" Becca got up from the table and went over to the counter. For something to do, she began cutting thick slices of homemade bread. She didn't want to remember anything about the guilt or the pain she had suffered at Brig's hand; not now, not while she was still bathing in the warmth of the knowledge that he was alive. Realizing that she couldn't duck Dean's probing questions, she addressed the issue in a calmer voice. "I think the best thing to do is to wait, until sometime after the funeral. Then we'll have to talk to the attorneys at Chambers Oil."

"They'll eat you alive."

Becca sighed audibly. It was impossible to get through to Dean when his mind was set. Sometimes she wondered why he was so defensive, especially whenever the conversation steered toward Brig. After all, it was she whom Brig had blamed, not Dean. She placed the bread on the table near an open jar of honey. "We can handle the attorneys...but if you would prefer to talk to Brig—"

"*What?* Are you out of your mind?" Dean's skin whitened under his deep California tan. "I have *nothing* to say to Chambers!"

Becca assumed that Dean's ashen color and his vehement speech were caused by his hangover and his concern for her. She dismissed his hatred of Brig as entirely her fault. Dean knew how deeply she had been wounded six years ago, and her brother held Brig Chambers solely responsible. Dean had never forgiven Brig for so cruelly and unjustly hurting his sister. But then, Dean never did know the whole story; Becca had shielded him from part of the truth. Patiently, she forced a smile she didn't feel upon her brother. "I'll go and talk to Brig myself."

"Becca!" Dean's voice shook angrily and it made her look up from the slice of bread she was buttering. "Don't do anything you might regret…take some time, think things over first."

"I have."

"No, you haven't! You haven't begun to consider all of the consequences of telling Brig about the loan or the horse! Don't you see that it will only dredge up the same problems all over again? Think about what a field day the press will have when they learn that *you* and the money you borrowed from Chambers Oil have bred another horse, not just any horse, mind you, but nearly an exact copy…a twin of Sentimental Lady! It may have been six years, Becca, but the press won't forget about the controversy at Sequoia Park!" Dean's pale blue eyes were calculating as they judged Becca's reaction.

"Gypsy Wind is going to race. We can't hide her or the note."

"I'm not asking you to," Dean hastily agreed as he noticed just a tremor of hesitation in Becca's voice. He tried another, more pointed tack. "Just give it time. Brig Chambers has a lot more problems—important problems—than he can handle right now. His father was killed just yesterday. If you bring up the subject of Gypsy Wind now, it will only burden him further."

"I don't know…"

Dean pressed his point home. "Just give it a little time, will ya? Of course we'll tell him about the filly, when the time is right. Once she's proved herself."

"She won't race for another five or six months."

"Well, maybe we'll have sold her by then."

"Sold her?" Becca repeated, as if she hadn't heard her brother correctly. "I'll never sell Gypsy Wind."

Dean's lips pressed into a severe frown. "You may not have a choice, Becca. Remember, when Brig Chambers finds that note, for all practical purposes, he owns that horse."

"Then how can you even suggest that we sell her?" Becca asked, astounded by her brother's heartlessness and dishonesty. Sometimes she didn't think she understood her brother at all. She hadn't in a long while.

"It might be that the horse is worth more now! For God's sake, Becca, we can't take a chance that she'll get hurt when she races. Think about Sentimental Lady! Do you want us to run into the same problem with Gypsy Wind?"

Becca was horror-struck at the thought. Her stomach lurched uneasily. Dean's chair scraped against the plank floor. He raked his fingers through his hair impatiently. "I don't know what we should do," he admitted. "I just wish that for once you would thing with your head instead of your heart!"

Becca's green eyes snapped. "I think I've done well enough for the both of us," she threw back at him. "As for listening to my heart—"

"Save it!" Dean broke in irritably. "When it comes to Brig Chambers, you never have thought straight!"

Before she could disagree, the screen door banged against the porch, announcing Dean's departure.

TEN DAYS HAD PASSED AND THE ARGUMENT between Becca and Dean was still simmering, unresolved, in the air. Although they hadn't had another out-and-out confrontation, nothing had changed concerning the status of Starlight Breeding Farm and its large outstanding debt to Chambers Oil. In Dean's opinion, no news was good news. To Becca, each day put her more on edge.

Becca had considered calling Brig and trying to explain the situation over the telephone, but just the thought of the fragile connection linking her to him made her palms sweat. What if he wouldn't accept the call? Did he already know about the note? Could he guess about the horse? Was he just waiting patiently for her to make the first move so that he could once again reject her? Though the telephone number of Chambers Oil lingered in her memory, she never quite got up enough nerve to call.

Excuses filled her mind. They were frail, but they sustained her. Brig would be too busy to talk to her, now that he was running the huge conglomerate, or he would be attempting to sort out his own grief. Not only had he lost his father in the plane crash, but also a friend. One of the persons on board the ill-fated plane was Melanie DuBois, a raven-haired model who had often been photographed on the arm of Brig Chambers, heir to the Chambers Oil fortune. Her slightly seductive looks opposed everything about Becca. Melanie had been short for a model, but well-proportioned, and her thick, straight ebony hair and dark unwavering eyes had given her a sensual provocative look that seemed to make the covers of slick magazines come to life. Now Melanie, too, was gone. Dead at twenty-six.

On this morning, while packing a few things into an overnight bag, Becca tried not to think of Melanie DuBois, or the young woman's rumored romance with Brig. Instead, she attempted to mentally check all of the things she would need for a weekend in Denver. Knowing it might be impossible to get hold of Brig at the office, Becca had vowed to herself that she would go back to the Chambers mountain retreat and find Brig if she had to. She had visited it once before when she was forced to borrow the money for Gypsy Wind from Brig's father. Becca was willing to do anything necessary to keep Gypsy Wind. That was the reason she was packing as if she would have to stay for weeks in the enchanting retreat tucked in the slopes of the Colorado Rockies. Wasn't it?

"I don't suppose there is any way I can talk you out of

this." Dean said as he leaned against the doorjamb of Becca's small room.

"No." She shook her head. "You may as well save your breath."

"Then you won't begin to listen to how foolish this is?"

Becca cast him a wistful smile that touched her eyes. "Save your brotherly advice."

"When will you be back?"

"Monday."

Dean's bushy eyebrows furrowed. "So long?"

"Maybe not," she replied evasively. She snapped the leather bag closed. "If I can get everything straightened out this afternoon, I'll be back in the morning."

"Uh-huh," Dean remarked dubiously. "But you might be gone for the entire weekend?"

"That depends."

"On what?"

"Brig's reaction, I suppose," Becca thought aloud. Her heart skipped a beat at the thought of the man whom she had loved so desperately, the man she had once vowed never to see again.

"Then you really are going to tell him about our horse, aren't you?"

"Dean, I *have* to."

"Or you *want* to?"

"Meaning what?"

Dean strode into the room, sat on the edge of the small bed, and eyed his younger sister speculatively. How long had it been since he had seen her look so beautiful? When was the last time she had bothered to wear a dress? Dean couldn't remember. The smart emerald jersey knit was as in vogue today as it had been when Becca had purchased it several years ago, and her sun-streaked dark-blond hair shone with a new radiance as she tossed it carelessly away from her face. Becca looked more alive than she had in months, Dean admitted to himself. "Examine your motive," he suggested with a severe smile. He started to say something else, changed his mind, and shook his head. Instead he murmured, "Whatever it is you're looking for in Denver, I hope you find it."

"You know why I'm going to see Brig," Becca replied calmly. She hoisted her purse over her shoulder, but avoided Dean's intense gaze. Unfortunately, she couldn't hide the incriminating burn on her cheeks.

"Yeah, *I* know," Dean responded cynically, while picking up Becca's bag, "but do *you?*"

THE CEDAR HOUSE SEEMED STRANGELY QUIET without the presence of his father to fill the rooms. Though it was still fastidiously clean and the only scent to reach Brig's nostrils was his father's favorite blend of pipe tobacco, the atmosphere in the room seemed...dead.

It's only your imagination, he chastised himself as he tried to take his solemn thoughts away from his father. It had been nearly two weeks since the company plane had gone down, and it was time to bury his grief along with the old man.

In the past twelve days Brig had come to feel that his life was on a runaway roller coaster, destined to collide with any number of unknown, intangible obstacles. There had been the funeral arrangements, the will, the stuffy lawyers, the stuffier insurance adjusters, the incredibly tasteless press, and now, unexpectedly, a wildcat strike in the oil fields of Wyoming. It appeared that everyone who remotely knew Jason Chambers had a problem, a problem Brig was supposed to handle.

Damn! Brig ran his fingers under the hair at the base of his head and rubbed the knot of tension that had settled between his shoulder blades. In the last week he hadn't had more than two or three hours sleep at a stretch and he was dog-tired. The last thing in the world he had expected was for his robust father to die and leave him in charge of the corporation.

Brig had worked solely for Chambers Oil for the last six years, and in that time his father had trained him well. Brig

had become the best troubleshooter ever on the payroll of
Chambers Oil. No problem had seemed insurmountable in the
past, and usually Brig flourished with only a few hours of
sleep. But not now—not tonight. In the past the problems had
come one at a time, or so it seemed in retrospect. But since
Jason Chambers' death, the entire company appeared to be
falling apart, piece by piece. Somehow, Brig was expected to
hold it steadfastly together. A sad smile curved his lips as he
now understood that maybe his father had only made running
the company seem simple. "I've got to hand it to you, old
man," Brig whispered as he held his drink upward in silent
salute to his father.

Maybe I'm just not cut out for this, he thought to himself
as his lips pulled into a wry grimace. *Maybe I just don't have
what it takes to run an oil conglomerate.*

As he sat in his father's favorite worn chair, his elbows
rested on the scarred wooden desk, the same desk he remembered from his childhood. Brig took a long swallow from his
warm scotch. It was his third drink in the last hour. He rubbed
the back of his neck mechanically and rotated his head before
tackling the final task of the day. His frown deepened as he
stared at the untidy stack of papers banded loosely together
in the bottom drawer of the desk. A few moments earlier Brig
had discovered that this drawer, and this drawer only, had been
kept locked. So this was where Jason Chambers had kept all
of his personal records—the transactions that were hidden
from the disapproving eyes of the company auditors and the
disdainful glare of tax attorneys. Brig had suspected that the
papers existed, but he had always figured that they were the
old man's business, no one else's concern. He smiled sadly
to himself and silently cursed his father for the reckless,
carefree lifestyle which had ultimately taken his life. "You
miserable son-of-a-bitch," Brig whispered fondly. "How
could you do this to me?"

His gray eyes lowered to the first scrap of paper in the

stack, a yellowed receipt from a furriers for a sable coat. Brig couldn't help but wonder which one of the dozen or so women his father had dated over the last few years had ended up with the expensive prize. With an oath of disgust, leveled for the most part at himself, Brig tossed the papers back into the drawer, slammed it shut, and locked it. He was too tired to think about his father or the string of women who had attracted Jason Chambers since his wife's death.

"If I had any sense I'd burn those blasted papers and forget about them," he muttered to himself; to open that portion of his father's life seemed an intrusion of the old man's privacy. Unfortunately, the inheritance tax auditors didn't see things from the same perspective. He dimmed the desk lamp, picked up his drink, and walked to the window to draw the shade. Flickering lights in the distance caught his attention and he left the shade open. He narrowed his eyes and squinted to be sure just as the twin beams of light flashed once again. Headlights. Someone was coming. *Who?* Brig's thoughts revolved backward in time to earlier in the afternoon. He was certain he had ordered his secretary to keep his whereabouts under wraps. Hadn't Mona understood him? He didn't want to be disturbed. He needed this weekend alone.

Don't get crazy, he told himself as the car drove up the long gravel road. Brig Chambers couldn't hide, not since he took command of Chambers Oil. If someone wanted to find him badly enough, it wouldn't be hard to do. It didn't take a genius to guess that he would be spending a quiet weekend in Jason's rustic cottage in the mountains. Brig had hoped that the two-hour drive from Denver would discourage most people interested in contacting him. He had the foresight to take the phone off the hook, and he hadn't expected to be interrupted. From the looks of the strong headlights winking through the trees, he'd been wrong. Perhaps it was critical business. He checked his watch. Why else would someone be coming to the cabin at nearly ten o'clock at night?

The car rounded the final curve in the driveway and Brig strained to get a glimpse of the driver. Who the hell was it?

BECCA'S HEART WAS RACING AS RAPIDLY as the engine of the rental car she had picked up at the airport. All of the confidence she had gathered at dawn had slowly ebbed with the series of problems she had encountered during the day. It was almost as if she were fated not to meet Brig again. To start off her day the flight had been delayed, then there was a mixup in her hotel reservation, not to mention that the rental car which was supposed to be waiting for her had never been ordered, according to the agency's records. It had taken an extra four hours to get everything straightened out. To top off matters, when she had finally managed to arrive at Chambers Oil, she had been politely but firmly rebuked. The efficient but slightly cool secretary had informed Becca that Brig Chambers was gone for the remainder of the day and wasn't expected back into the office until Monday morning. If no one else could help her, then Becca was out of luck. No, the silver-haired woman had replied to her query, Mr. Chambers hadn't left a telephone number where he could be reached...if Becca would kindly leave her name and number, Mr. Chambers was sure to get back to her early next week. Becca had declined. It had seemed imperative at the time that she see Brig in person. Right now, she wasn't so certain.

After cresting the final hill and following the road around an acute turn, Becca stepped lightly on the brakes of the rented sedan. In front of her, silhouetted against a backdrop of rugged, heavy-scented pine trees, stood the rustic cedar cabin of Jason Chambers. Soft light from the paned windows indicated that someone was inside. Becca swallowed with difficulty as six abandoned years without Brig stretched before her. After all of the pain, would she be able to see him...or touch him? There was no doubt in her mind that he was in the house; she only hoped that he was alone and that he would see her. The angry years apart from him dampened her spirits and she wondered fleetingly why she had decided to come to the lonely cabin to seek him out. She had even brought her overnight bag with her. Was it an oversight or had Dean been right all along?

Before the questions which had been nagging at her could steal all of her determination, Becca switched off the ignition, opened the car door, and stepped into the night.

As Brig sipped his scotch he watched the idling car sitting in the driveway. The engine died and Brig strained to identify the driver. When the car door opened and the interior light flashed for a second, he caught a quick glimpse of a woman stepping from the car. Brig's jaw tensed. This wasn't just any woman, but a tall, graceful woman with a soft mane of golden hair which shimmered in the moonlight. He didn't catch sight of her face, but he knew intuitively that she was incredibly beautiful. The pride with which she carried herself spoke of beauty and grace. Hazy, distant clouds of memory began to taunt him, but he savagely thrust aside his cloudy thoughts of another striking blonde, knowing that she was lost to him forever. Though she still occupied his dreams, he denied himself conscious thoughts of her. Why did she still haunt him so? And why could he remember every elegant line of her face with such breathtaking clarity? He was a damned fool when it came to Becca Peters. He always had been.

Brig cocked an interested black eyebrow as he stared voyeuristically at the well-shaped stranger hurrying to the porch. What *woman* would be looking for him in the middle of the night, at this secluded mountain home? An expectant smile lit his face only to withdraw into a suspicious frown when he realized that the gorgeous creature now rapping upon his door was probably another one of his father's mistresses, coming to claim what she considered rightfully hers. Brig drained his drink as he advanced toward the door. He hoped to hell that the blonde wasn't wearing a sable coat.

In the past week Brig had secretly dealt with one of his
father's mistresses. Nanette Walters was a calculating bitch
who was ready to spill her guts about her relationship with
Jason Chambers to any interested gossip columnist for the
price of a one-way ticket to the Bahamas. Fortunately, Brig
had gotten to her first. The thought of Nanette's aristocratic
beauty and easily bought affections soured Brig's stomach
and he clenched his jaw in determination as he steeled himself
against what would certainly be another cold, expensive
demand by one of his father's latest women.

Every muscle in Brig's body had tensed in anticipation by
the time he reached the door. The insistent rapping had stilled,
but the woman was persistent. Brig hadn't heard her restart the
car and leave. He jerked the door open and let the light from
the interior of the house spill into the night. The pale lamplight rested on the long, tawny hair of the woman standing on
the porch and a familiar scent hung in the night air. Brig felt
himself waver. He couldn't see her face; her head was bent over
her purse and she was rummaging through it as if she were
looking for something. Disgust forced a smile of contempt to
Brig's lips when he understood: the blonde obviously had her
own key to his father's private retreat.

The stranger lifted her bewitching green eyes and Brig's
breath caught in his throat. Memories of making love to her
in a fragrant field of spring clover clouded his mind. Was she
an illusion? As his stunned gaze met and entwined with hers,
Brig couldn't help but slip backward in time. It was as if six
long years of his life had suddenly disappeared into the
darkness. He damned himself for the stiff drinks. *It couldn't
be Becca, not after six unforgiving years.*

"Rebecca?" he whispered, not believing the trick his mind
was playing on him. He must have had more to drink than he
thought. A thousand questions surfaced as he stared at her and
just as quickly those questions escaped, unanswered. It had
to be Rebecca—the resemblance was too perfect for it to be

unreal. What was she doing here, at his father's private cabin in the middle of the night?

Wasn't it just yesterday when they had made love in the rain? Couldn't he still taste the warm raindrops on her smooth skin? He closed his eyes for just a moment—to steady himself—and his dark brows knitted in the confusion that was cutting him to the bone. Why the hell couldn't he think straight?

THE SOUND OF HIS DISBELIEVING VOICE whispering her name moved Becca to tears. Her answers caught in her swollen throat. Why hadn't she sought him out sooner? Why had she waited so long? Was pride that important?

A wistful smile, full of the memories they had shared together, touched her lips. He looked so tired...so worried. Her lips trembled when she realized that he, too, might be vulnerable. He had always been so strong. Without understanding the reasons behind her actions, she reached up and touched his rough cheek with her fingertips.

His eyes flew open. They were as she had remembered them: deep-set and steely gray. They touched her as no other eyes had dared. They held her imprisoned in their naked gaze, encouraged rapturous passion.

"Brig," she murmured, her voice raw. "How are you?" Her hand still caressed his cheek.

He studied her for an endless second, but ignored her concerned inquiry. His eyes probed deeply into hers, asking questions she couldn't hope to answer. "What are you doing here, Rebecca?"

"I came to see you."

It was so simple and seemed so honest. For an instant Brig believed her. He needed to trust her. Perhaps it was the look of innocence in her round, verdant eyes, or maybe it was the effect of more than one too many drinks. But that didn't entirely explain his feelings. More than likely it was because, in the past few weeks, he had felt so incredibly alone.

Whatever the reason, Brig couldn't resist the look of naive seduction in her eyes. "God. Rebecca, why did you wait so long to come back?"

CHAPTER THREE

HE DIDN'T THINK ABOUT THE PAST AND GAVE little considera-
tion to the future. Instead, Brig took Becca into his arms and
crushed her savagely against him. He couldn't let her vanish
as quickly as she had come. His lips captured hers almost
brutally, as if he could reclaim in a single kiss what had been
lost to him for so long.

Becca's knees weakened in his embrace and she wound her
arms possessively around his neck to cling to him in silent desperation. She returned the fever of his kiss with the same
passion she felt rising in him. Tears of joy ran unashamedly
down her cheeks and lingered on her lips. He tasted the depth
of her longing in the salt of her tears.

Becca didn't resist when he lifted her from the porch and
carried her inside the cabin. Instead she held him more tightly
than before and wondered if she would feel the ecstasy of
dying in his arms.

The room into which Brig took Becca was shadowed in
darkness. There was the slight hint of an expensive blend of
pipe tobacco in the air which reminded Becca of Brig's father
and her reason for seeking him out. She knew she should tell
Brig about Gypsy Wind now, before things got out of hand.
But she couldn't. It felt too right being held by the man she
loved. She couldn't tear herself from his embrace.

A thin stream of moonglow pierced through the skylights
and gave the room some visibility. As Becca's eyes became

adjusted to the darkness, she realized that she was in a bedroom: Brig's bedroom.

Brig walked unerringly to the bed. He dropped Becca on a soft down comforter and let his weight fall against her body. He crushed her to him, holding her fiercely to him. His lips brushed hers in tender kisses flavored with scotch and warm with need. His hands pressed intimately against the muscles of her back and through the light jersey fabric of her dress, Becca could feel the heat of his fingertips. They sparked fires in her she had thought dead and rekindled a passion she had buried long ago.

He tasted just as she remembered and the roughness of his unshaven face reminded her of lazy mornings spent waking up in his arms, arousing desires smoldering from the night. His kisses were the sweetest pleasure she had ever known.

"Rebecca," Brig moaned, tortured by the demons playing in his mind. "Rebecca… God, how many nights has it been?" His warm breath fanned her face.

"Since what?" she prodded, her breath torn from her throat.

"Since we made love?"

She swallowed the lump in her throat. "Too many," she admitted. His fingers entwined in the strands of her honey-gold hair. She couldn't read his expression in the darkness, but she could feel his unchallenged sincerity. Slowly, she touched his lips and felt the hard angle of his masculine jaw. His hand reached up and covered hers and he kissed it.

"Why did you wait to come back?" he asked.

"I don't know… I was afraid, I suppose."

"Of me?"

"No!" She tried to think, tried to explain what she felt, but she couldn't.

"You had the right to be." He pulled his head away from her hand, putting a little distance between them. He let go of her hand and rolled away from her. Why was she here? Why now?

"Don't!" she cried, refusing to release him. Her arms

wrapped around his back and she whispered against the back of his neck. "It was my pride…. Let's not talk about it. Not here. Not now."

He tried to disentangle her arms. "Rebecca. Don't you think we should talk things through?" He tried to keep his wits about him, attempted to think logically, but he couldn't. The feel of her breasts crushed against his back and the warmth of her arms around his chest made his blood begin to race.

"Please, Brig. Can't we just forget…just for a little while?" Her heart was pounding so loudly she knew he could hear it. Her breath was barely a whisper, a small plea in the middle of a clear mountain night.

"Dear God, woman. Don't you know how you torture me?" he asked raggedly. Becca let the air out of her lungs. He was about to deny her, again…she could feel it. "I wish I could forget you," he said as if she weren't listening. The bed sagged as he shifted again. He loomed over her in the darkness as he planted one hand on either side of her body. "Do you know what you're asking?"

"Yes," she said.

Cold suspicion had begun to form in his mind, but as he gazed down upon her his doubts fled. The moonlight caressed her face in its protective radiance and her eyes took on a heavenly silver-green purity that begged him to believe her. As she lay upon the bed staring trustingly at him, he knew her to be the most beautiful and beguiling woman he had ever had the misfortune to meet.

Becca couldn't see the pain in Brig's gray eyes, couldn't hope to read his expression, but she knew that he was gazing down upon her, trying to find the strength to pull away again. That knowledge was a dull silver blade twisting slowly in her heart. He wanted to love her, but was denying himself.

"Why did we let it go sour?" he asked, his fists clenching in the restraint he was holding over his body. Dear God, she was beautiful. His question was rhetorical; he didn't expect an answer.

"We made mistakes..."

"Like tonight?" he asked cruelly.

"Does this feel like a mistake to you, Brig?" If only she could look into his eyes. If only he would let her.

"Nothing has ever felt wrong with you," he conceded as he lowered his head and his lips met hers in a kiss that spanned the abyss of the six lonely years separating them. The warmth of his lips filled her and she let them part to encourage more intimacy. Everything felt so right with him; it always had. As his mouth claimed hers it was as if all the doubts and fears she had furtively harbored had disappeared. *He wanted her.* Her heart clamored joyously and her blood began to run in heated rivulets through her veins. The love she had chained deep in the shadowy hollow of her heart became unbound in the knowledge that he wanted her. She wrapped her arms around his neck and enjoyed the comfort of his caress.

His tongue slid familiarly through her teeth, touching hers and mating with it in a passionate dance once forgotten. He explored her mouth, groaning softly in pleasure at her heated response. "I've missed you," he admitted roughly, drawing his head away from hers for a moment. He brushed back the silken strands of her hair and kissed her forehead lightly before letting his lips trail down her cheeks to recapture her mouth. "Let me love you."

The jersey dress buttoned on the shoulders. Brig's fingers slid the pearl-like fasteners through the holes and the soft fabric parted to expose her neck and shoulders. He kissed the white column of her throat, nuzzling gently against her neck. Without thinking she tilted her head, letting her sun-streaked hair fall away from her throat and offering it to him willingly. His moist tongue pressed against her skin and he tasted the bittersweet tang of her perfume—the same scent she had worn in the past. It was a fragrance he would never forget.

Once he had been with a woman who was wearing Rebecca's fragrance; he had left that woman before the evening had begun. The perfume had evoked too many unwanted memories and destroyed any possible attraction he may have felt for the poor woman.

But tonight was different. Tonight he would drown in the gentle fragrance of wildflowers that filled his nostrils. Tonight in the dusky bedroom, the scent that clung to Rebecca's hair fired his blood and summoned a passion in him he had thought was lost long ago. No other woman had reached him the way Rebecca had, and he had vowed that none would. No other woman had dared enrage him so dangerously. Her soft moan of pleasure encouraged him. He felt her body trembling beneath his persuasive hands.

With a gentle tug the dress slid lower on her body. Lace from a cream-colored slip partially obscured the swell of her breasts and highlighted the hollow between them. He moved over her and his mouth moistened that gentle rift.

"Brig," she whispered, closing her eyes and letting him touch her soul. His hands slid over the silky fabric of her slip, arousing in her aching breasts a need that seemed to consume her in its fire. The satin fabric teased her nipples into hard, dark points that strained against the lace. His warm lips touched the gossamer cloth and Becca moaned her gratitude as the moist heat of his mouth covered her nipple.

Dizzy sensations of a lost past whirled in her mind. Images of a moonlit night and a cascading waterfall filled her thoughts. "I'll always love you," she had heard him say, but that was long ago, in a time before treachery and deceit had ripped the two of them so ruthlessly apart.

His tongue moistened the lace and his lips teased her breast through the gentle barrier of silk and satin. Slowly, he turned their bodies, pulling her over him so that her breasts would fall against him and he could take more of her into his mouth. He groaned in satisfaction when the strap of her slip slid down her shoulder and her breast became unbound. She wore no bra to encumber her, and as the rosy-tipped breast spilled from the slip, Brig captured it in his lips and let his teeth tease the engorged nipple.

"Please love me," she gasped, praying that he understood her needs were not only physical. She wanted to relive the happiness they had shared. She needed to claim again the time when he was hers.

His hands were warm as they pressed between the slip and her ribcage. So slowly that it seemed pure agony, he pushed the fabric past her hips and onto the floor. He disposed of each piece of her clothing as if it were a useless piece of cloth, used only to impede him in his quest to claim her. When at last she was nude, lying trembling in his arms, he took her hands and guided her to the buttons of his shirt.

With whispering softness he brushed kisses over her eyelids as she opened his shirt and slid her hands under the oxford fabric. Her fingers touched him lightly at first, gently outlining each of the muscles of his chest. His groan of satisfaction as she traced each male nipple made her more bold and she slid the shirt over his shoulders, letting her fingers glide down his arms and trace each hard, lean muscle. When his shirt dropped to the floor he gripped her savagely, pushing her naked breasts against the furry mat of his chest. His lips rained liquid kisses of pulsing fire over the top of her breasts before returning to her mouth. Once more his tongue pushed insistently through her teeth to capture and stroke its feminine counterpart. Becca wanted to blend with him and break the boundary that separated his body from hers. She wanted to become one with him, to feel his heart beat in her blood. An ache, deep and primal, began to burn within her, igniting her blood until she felt it boil in her veins.

Brig had never stopped kissing her and his hands hadn't halted their gentle, possessive exploration of her body, but he had managed to remove his pants. She didn't know the exact moment when he had discarded his clothes, but rather became slowly conscious of the fact that he was naked, lying under her and matching her muscles with the rock-hard flesh of his own. His hands moved in slow circles over her back and his lips left none of her untouched as he caressed her.

She felt herself tremble at the familiarity of his touch, the intimacy of his skin on hers. A flush of arousal tingled her skin and she felt the warm glaze of his sweat mingling with her own.

His hand passed over her thigh and her body arched against him, pleading for more of his touch. He wrapped his arms around her and rotated both of their bodies on the comforter, so that once again he was leaning over her, looking at her eyes, misty in moonglow.

Words of love threatened to erupt from her dry throat, but before she could utter them, his knee wedged between her thighs and took her breath away in a rush of desire.

"Becca," he moaned into the tawny length of her hair, "are you sure this is what you want…really sure?" All of his muscles had become rigid with the restraint he placed upon himself. Beads of sweat, tiny droplets of self-denial, formed on his upper lip as he awaited her response.

In answer, she threaded his dark hair between her fingers and pulled his head down on hers. She kissed him with the fervid desire so long repressed. Six years she had waited for him. Six years she had yearned for his caress.

He groaned in relief as he gently came to her and found that portion of her no other man had touched. She seemed to melt into him, joining him in a pulsating rhythm that they alone had explored in the past and had now rekindled in the darkness of his bedroom.

The sweet, gentle agony began to build in her as she captured every movement of his body. The fire within her burned more savagely with each persuasive strove of love, until she felt herself erupt. When he felt her release, he exploded with a passion that shook both of them and left him drained

of the frustration that had been with him for the past few
weeks. He held her tightly, softly pressing his lips to her hair.

"Stay with me tonight," he coaxed.

She sighed in contentment, warm in the cradle of his arms
and the luxury of afterglow. It was moments later, when the
beating of her heart had slowed, when the reality of what she
had done brought her brutally back to the present. Brig's
breathing was regular, but he wasn't asleep. When she attempted to free herself of his embrace, he tightened his grip
on her, imprisoning her against him.

"Brig…I think we should talk," she whispered, hoping to
find the courage to bring up her reasons for seeking him out.
She felt him stiffen.

"Later."

"But there are things that I—"

"Not now, Rebecca! Let's wait, at least until the morning."
Her resolve began to waver. She closed her eyes and tried to
content herself by resting her head against his chest and listening to the steady beat of his heart.

The image of a dark horse, racing dangerously along the
ocean's shore, hoofbeats thundering against the pale sand,
formed in her tired mind. Lather creamed from the horse's
shoulders and foam from the sea clung to the speeding legs.
Sentimental Lady ran with the wind. The image of the horse
compelled Becca—she had to tell Brig all of her secrets. He
had to know about Gypsy Wind.

"Brig, we *have* to talk."

"I said not now!"

"But it's important. Remember Sentimental Lady?"

"How could I forget?" His voice was coated in contempt.
He made a derisive sound in the back of his throat. "Let's just
leave this conversation until later."

"I can't."

"We've waited for six years, Becca. One more night isn't
going to make much difference."

"But you don't understand—"

"And I don't want to!" His voice was stern, his eyes flashed anger. She felt herself tense at his cutting reprimand.

"I just want to talk to you. Don't treat me like a child. It didn't work before, and it won't work now," she whispered.

His voice softened. "Look, Becca, the past couple of weeks have been a little rough. I'm only asking that you put whatever it is you want to talk about on hold—until the morning." He knew what it was she wanted to discuss, but he was too tired to go through the argument of six years past. He didn't want to think about her deception, nor the ensuing scandal, didn't want to be reminded of how deep her betrayal had been. All he wanted was to hold her and remember her as she had been before all of the damned controversy. His arms bound her tightly as he tried to forget the lies and anguish. "If you really want to talk about anything right now, of course I'll listen…" Brig pressed his lips to her eyelids and he felt her begin to relax. If only he could concentrate on anything other than that last hellish race.

For the first time that night, Becca realized how much Brig had aged. The years hadn't been kind to him, especially now, right after the death of his father. Her confidence began to waver.

"I want to talk to you about your father."

Brig's arms tightened around her and in the moonlight Becca could see his eyes opening to study her. "What about my father?" he asked.

Becca sighed deeply to herself, but it wasn't a moan of contentment. It was a sigh of acceptance: Brig would never love her, never trust her. She could feel it in the firm manacle of his embrace, read it in the skepticism of his gaze. The tenderness she had once found in him was buried deeply under a mound of suspicion and bitterness. "I owe your father some money."

No response. Her heartbeat was the only noise in the room. The seconds stretched into minutes. Finally he spoke. "Is that why you came here tonight, because of some debt to my father?"

"It was the excuse I used."

His gray eyes held her prisoner. "Was there any other reason?"

"Yes," she whispered.

"What was it?"

"I wanted to see you, touch you…feel for myself that you were alive. When I first heard about the plane crash I thought you might be dead." It was impossible to keep her voice even as she relived the nightmare of emotions which had ripped her apart. Even with his powerful arms about her, she could feel her shoulders beginning to shake.

"So you waited nearly two weeks to find me."

"I didn't want to intrude. I knew things would be hectic—the newspapers couldn't leave you alone. I didn't want to take any chance of dredging everything up again, not until I'd talked to you alone."

"About the money?" His voice was cynical in the darkness.

"For one thing."

"What else?"

"I needed to know that you were all right…"

"But there's more to it, isn't there?"

She nodded silently, her forehead rubbing the hairs of his chest. All of his muscles stiffened. Her voice was steady when she finally spoke. "I had to borrow the money to breed another horse."

"So you came to the old man? What about the banks?"

"I didn't have enough collateral—the stud fee was a fortune."

"You could have come to me," he offered.

"I don't think so. You made that pretty clear six years ago."

"People change…"

"Do they?" She laughed mirthlessly. "It took all of my courage to come to you now…. It would have been impossible three years ago. I didn't even want to approach your father, but it was the only solution. Even Dean agreed, although now he's changed his mind."

"Your brother? He was in on this?" The softness in Brig's

voice had disappeared and was replaced by disgust. "I would have thought that by this time you would have gotten enough sense to fire that useless bum."

"Dean was there when you weren't," she reminded him, a touch of anger flavoring her words.

"I wasn't there because you shut me out."

"You weren't there because you chose not to be!" she retorted, shifting on the bed and trying to wiggle free of his embrace.

"After all these years, nothing's changed, has it? You're still willing to believe all the lies in the gossip tabloids, aren't you?" He gave her an angry shake and his eyes blazed furiously.

"Dean was there."

"Dean lied."

"Dean lied and the newspapers lied?" she repeated sarcastically. "What kind of fool do you take me for?"

"A woman who's foolish enough not to be able to sort fact from fiction or truth from lies."

"I didn't come here to argue with you."

"Then why did you come?" His thumbs slid slowly up her ribcage, outlining each delicate bone as it wrapped around her torso. "Did you come here to seduce me?"

"No!"

"No?" His fingers inched upward until they touched the underside of her breast, teasing the sensitive skin.

"I came here to explain about the money—and about Gypsy Wind."

"The horse?"

"Yes—please, don't touch me. I can't think when you touch me."

"Don't think," he persuaded, his lips and tongue stroking the flesh behind her ear. Her breath became ragged as much from desire as from the frustration she was beginning to feel.

"But I want you to know about the money… I want you to understand about Gypsy Wind… I want…"

"You want me."

How could she deny what her body so plainly displayed? Her nipples had hardened, anticipating his soft caress, her skin quivered beneath his touch and the fire in her veins was spreading silently to every part of her body. "Oh, Brig, of course I want you," she said. "I've wanted you for so long…"

Desire lowered his voice. "I don't care about the money and I don't give a damn about your horse—"

"But you will. In the morning, when you're sober—"

"I am sober and the only thing I care about is that you're with me. I don't care how you got here, and I'm not all that concerned with why you came. It only matters that you're here, with me, beside me…alone. Just let me love you tonight and tomorrow we'll discuss whatever you want to."

"I just wanted you to know why I had to see you."

"It doesn't matter. What matters is that you did." His lips touched her familiarly, softly tracing the line of her jaw, the curve of her neck. His hands gently shaped her breasts, feeling anew the silky flesh beneath his fingertips. He wasn't hurried when his mouth descended to her nipple. It was as if the slow deliberation of the act increased its intensity and meaning. Becca turned her head and groaned into the pillow as his lips molded over her breast.

"Just love me, Brig!" she cried desperately as his hands slid leisurely down her backside to rest on her buttocks.

"I will, Rebecca," he vowed, moving his body over hers and gently parting her legs. "I will."

CHAPTER FOUR

BRIG HAD LONG SINCE FALLEN ASLEEP, BUT BECCA was restless. She had tried to unwind in the comfort of Brig's embrace, but found it impossible. Continuing doubts plagued her. Though she had tried to tell him about Gypsy Wind, she was sure that she hadn't really gotten through to him. In the morning, when the scotch he had consumed wouldn't cloud his mind, he would see things in a different light. Nothing would change. If anything, the doubts he felt for her would only be reinforced. He wouldn't forget the agony of the past, nor would he be able to rise above his long-festering suspicions of her. The night had only softened the blow slightly. Under the light of a new day his old doubts would resurface.

Becca shuddered as she anticipated his response to the fact that she owed him more than fifty thousand dollars for a horse which would remind him of the tragedy of Sentimental Lady. The fact that Becca had planned Gypsy Wind's conception and borrowed money from Brig's father to have her conceived would feed Brig's gnawing doubts. Becca closed her eyes and tried to drift off to sleep, attempted to be lulled by the sound of Brig's rhythmic breathing. But sleep was elusive; her fear kept it at bay.

Her love for Brig was as deep as it had ever been, his just as shallow. If Becca had hoped to find a way back into his heart, she had destroyed it herself. Gypsy Wind would become the living proof of Becca's deceit, a reminder of the grim past.

Tears of frustration burned hotly behind Becca's eyes and slid silently over her cheeks.

Sleep refused to come. Becca was still awake when the first ghostly rays of dawn crept into the room and colored it in uneven gray shadows. Slowly she extracted herself from Brig's arms, careful so as not to disturb him. She reached for a blue terry robe hanging on a nearby chair and pulled it over her shivering body. Without the warmth of Brig's arms around her, the room seemed frigid and sterile. She rolled up the sleeves of the robe, cinched the tie around her waist, and walked across the thick, ivory pile of the carpet to stand at the bay window. After pulling the heavy folds of cloth around her neck, she sat on the window ledge and stared vacantly out the window to watch the sunrise.

The sun crested the horizon and flooded the mountainside with golden rays that caught in the dewdrops and reflected in the snow of the higher elevations. Becca restlessly ran her fingers over the moisture which had collected on the panes of the windows. How many nights had she dreamed of falling back into Brig's arms? How many unanswered prayers had she uttered that she would find a way back into his heart? And now that she was here, what could she do to stay in his warm embrace? Brig's words of the night before came back to taunt her: *"Why did we let it go sour?"* If only she knew. How had something so beautiful turned ugly? Becca smiled grimly to herself as she reconstructed the events which had drawn Brig to her only to cruelly push him away.

THE PARTY HAD BEEN DEAN'S IDEA, A WAY TO gain more national press coverage for his sister and the filly. Until that night, not much attention had been given the tall girl from California with the small stables and what was rumored to be the fastest Thoroughbred filly ever bred on California soil. The wiser, more sophisticated breeders in the East had considered Becca Peters and Starlight Breeding Farm much the way they did with any new, West Coast contender: a lot of California hype. Until the untried filly had proved herself, few gave her much notice, with the one glaring exception of Brig Chambers.

When Becca had received word that Brig Chambers, himself a horse breeder of considerable reputation, wanted to see Sentimental Lady, she had agreed and Dean had suggested the party. Dean's arguments had included the fact that news coverage would be good business for the Lady as well as Starlight Breeding Farm. He had also mentioned that Brig Chambers, part of the elite racing social set, deserved more than a smile and a handshake for flying across the continent to see Becca's horse. Becca had reluctantly agreed.

The celebration had taken place on a private yacht harbored in San Francisco Bay near Tiburón. The owner of the yacht, a rich widow of an insurance broker and friend to the California racing set, had been more than delighted to host the gala event on her late husband's gleaming white vessel. Brig Chambers wasn't often on this side of the continent, and rarely accepted invitations to posh gatherings, but this night was different.

Becca caught her first glimpse of him when he was ushered through the door by Mrs. Van Clyde. The short woman with the perfectly styled white hair and sparkling blue eyes looked radiant as she escorted Brig through the crowded, smoke-filled salon. He was taller than Becca had imagined…with a leanness that Becca hadn't expected from the spoiled son of an oil baron. In his sophisticated black tuxedo, Brig Chambers looked more than a pampered only son of wealth; he seemed *hungry* and *dangerous*, exactly the antithesis of the image he was attempting to portray in his conservative black suit. Becca had heard him referred to as "stuffy"; she didn't believe it for a moment.

Nina Van Clyde, in a swirl of rose-colored chiffon, introduced him to each guest in turn, and though he attempted to give each one his rapt attention, Becca noticed a restlessness in his stance. It wasn't particularly obvious, just a small movement such as the tensing of his jaw, or his thumb rubbing the edge of his first finger, but it clearly stated that he wasn't comfortable. His smile was well-practiced and charming, a brilliant, off-center flash of white against bronze skin, but his eyes never seemed to warm to the intensity of his grin.

Becca studied his movements over the rim of her champagne glass. He reminded her of a caged panther, waiting for an opportunity to escape, watching for just the right prey. He definitely intrigued her, and when his dark head lifted and he met her unguarded stare, the corners of his mouth turned downward in amusement.

After a brief apology to Mrs. Van Clyde, he advanced on Becca, ignoring any of the other guests.

"You're Rebecca Peters," he said coldly.

"And you're Mr. Chambers."

"Brig."

Becca inclined her head slightly, accepting the use of first names. Perhaps he didn't like to become confused with his famous father.

"I guess I should thank you for all this," he stated, cocking his head in the direction of the other guests and the well-filled bar.

"It was my brother's idea."

He seemed to relax a bit, and his gray eyes softened. "You may as well know, I'm not crazy about this sort of thing."

Becca's full lips curved into a smile. "I could tell."

He answered her smile with one of his own. "Shows, does it?"

"Only to the practiced eye."

"Were you watching me that closely?" His eyes traveled over her face, lingered in the depths of her green gaze, before trailing down her body and taking in all of her, the way the sea-blue silk dress draped over one of her shoulders to hug her breasts before falling in soft folds of shimmering fabric to her ankles.

Becca felt the heat of her embarrassment burn her skin. "Of course I was watching you," she admitted. "You're the center of attention."

As if to give credence to her words, several men Becca recognized as San Franciscan breeders came up to Brig and forcefully stole his attention.

Becca wandered through the crowd, politely conversing with several other California breeders. She sipped lightly at her champagne, never once losing her feel for Brig's presence in the room. Presently he was talking with a reporter from a San Francisco newspaper. Though Becca didn't openly stare at him, she knew where he was in the throng of elegantly dressed people dripping in jewels.

The music from a small dance band was nearly drowned in the clink of glasses and chatter of guests. A hazy cloud of cigarette smoke hung in the salon where knots of people congregated while sipping their drinks from the well-stocked bar. Becca was alone for the first time and she took the chance to escape from the stifling room.

Once on the deck, she took in a deep breath of sea air and tried to ignore the muted sounds of the party filtering from the salon. A breeze caressed her face and lifted the wisps of hair that had sprung from their entrapment in a golden braid pinned to the back of her neck. Water lapped against the sides of the slowly moving vessel, and Becca could see the glimmering lights of San Francisco winking brightly in the moonless night.

She leaned her bare forearms against the railing and smiled to herself, glad to be free of the claustrophobic crowd in the main salon. She felt Brig's presence before he spoke.

"I should apologize for the interruption of our conversation," he announced, leaning next to her on the railing. He didn't look at her, but rather concentrated on the distant city lights and the sounds of the night.

"It wasn't your fault," she replied with a sincere smile. "I'm willing to bet it will happen again."

"I don't think so." He sounded sure of himself and his opinions.

"You underestimate the persistence of we Californians, especially the press."

"I'm used to dealing with the press."

"Are you?"

Brig smiled and clasped his hands together. "I've already had the...pleasure of meeting a few reporters tonight. Were they your idea?"

Becca shook her head and her smile faded.

"Don't tell me," Brig continued. "Your brother has something to do with that, too."

Becca was intrigued. "How did you know?"

"Lucky guess," was the clipped reply.

"Dean thought the publicity would be good for the stables and Sentimental Lady. I didn't see that it would hurt."

Brig's hand reached out and touched Becca's wrist. He forced her to turn away from the view to look into his eyes. "There's a subject I've been wanting to discuss all night. I'd like to see your horse. She's the reason I'm here."

Becca tried to manage a smile. "I know," she replied, wondering if he was going to release her wrist. He did.

"Then you'll show her to me?"

"Of course. We can drive there tomorrow."

"Why not tonight?" he demanded.

"It's a three-hour drive," she responded before she began to think clearly. Was he serious? "Besides, it's late...and then there's the party. Mrs. Van Clyde would be offended if we left. That is what you're suggesting, isn't it?" Becca wasn't really sure she had understood him correctly.

"That's exactly what I'm suggesting."

"I don't know..." The night wasn't going as she and Dean had planned.

"Don't worry about Mrs. Van Clyde. I can handle her."

"But my brother..." Becca was grasping at straws, but things were moving too fast. There was an arrogant self-assurance to Brig Chambers which unnerved her. And then there was Dean—he had wanted to talk to Brig in private about a job with Chambers Oil.

Brig's smile became cynical. "I'm sure your brother can take care of himself." His hand touched her bare elbow, guiding her toward the door to the salon and the noisy crowd within. "Make your apologies, get your coat and whatever else you brought here, and meet me on the starboard deck."

"What about transportation? We've got to be more than a mile out."

His gray eyes stared at her as they reentered the room and the din of the party made it impossible to converse. Brig leaned over to whisper into her ear. "I've already managed it. Trust me."

For the first time in Becca's twenty-six years, she wanted to trust a stranger, completely. She found Dean leaning over a well-endowed brunette, and pulled him aside to tell him of the change in their plan. Dean wasn't pleased and had trouble hiding his anger, but he didn't argue with Becca. He couldn't. He was smart enough to realize that Brig Chambers was used to doing things his way. Any argument would fall on deaf ears and only serve to anger the son of one of the wealthiest men in America. Dean could afford to be patient.

A motor launch was waiting and took Brig and Becca over the cold water to the dock, where Brig's car was parked. The drive through the dark night should have taken nearly four hours, but was accomplished in less than three. Becca should have been nervous and restrained with the enigmatic driver of the car, but wasn't. Their conversation flowed naturally and the only fragments of tension in the air were caused by the conflicting emotions within Becca. The man driving so effort-lessly through the winding, country roads was a stranger to her, but she felt as if she had known him all of her life. She had never felt so daring, nor so trusting.

His laughter was rich and genuine, yet there was a danger-

ous glint in his gray eyes that made Becca tremble in anticipation. How many of her thoughts could he read in her smile?
She couldn't dismiss the awareness she felt for his masculinity. It was a feeling that entrapped her and sent shudders
of expectation skittering down her spine.

Throughout the long drive, she had managed to keep her
poise intact and tried to ignore the voice of femininity that
begged her to notice Brig Chambers as a man. But as the sleek
car began to twist down the rutted lane toward the farm, she
felt all of her composure beginning to slip away. The headlights flashed against the white buildings near the paddock and
Becca's pulse jumped. The disrepair of the little farm seemed
glaring. Perhaps it was better that Brig had come at night.
Perhaps he wouldn't notice what was so painfully obvious to
her: rusty gutters, wooden fences mended with baling wire,
chipped paint which was peeling off the boards of the barns.
She swallowed back her embarrassment. It was all worth it.
Money that should have gone to renovation and repair was
well-spent on Sentimental Lady and her training. Becca knew
deep within her heart that all of the money used on the horse
would come back a hundredfold once the filly began to race.

Becca attempted to disregard her hammering heart. She was
home; that thought should calm her, but it didn't. The fact that
she was virtually alone with a stranger, a pampered rich boy
of the socially elite, unnerved her. He would walk through the
barns and into her life, scrutinizing it under the same standards
of the Kentucky breeders. Starlight Breeding Farm was a far
cry from the glamorous blue-grass establishments of the East.

The tires ground to a halt on the gravel, and Brig cut the
engine. He reached for the handle of the door, but Becca
reached out to restrain him. "Wait."

Brig's hand paused over the handle. "Why?" He turned to
face her. She could feel his eyes upon her face in the dark interior.

"This isn't... I mean, we don't handle things the same
way you do."

"Pardon?"

"I mean we don't have the facilities or the staff to…"

His fingers touched her shoulder. "I just came here to look at your filly, Rebecca. I'm not here to judge you."

"I know…. Oh, damn! *Why* are you here?" The question that had been teasing her for the past week leapt to her lips.

"I told you, I came here—"

"I know, 'to see the horse.' That's what has been bothering me," she admitted. Was it her imagination, or did his fingers tense over her shoulder?

"Why?"

"This doesn't make much sense, at least not to me."

He removed his hand and Becca felt suddenly cold. "What doesn't make sense?"

"The fact that you came here. No one, not even Brig Chambers, flies more than two thousand miles to 'look at a horse,'" she accused. Her words were out before she had a chance to think about them.

Brig leaned back against the leather cushions of the Mercedes and touched her cheek lightly. He hesitated and frowned. "Someone might if he thought the horse was a threat to one of his own."

"Is that why you're here?"

His hand reached out in the darkness and his fingertips caressed her cheek. Becca took in a deep breath and he dropped his hand, as if suddenly realizing the intimacy of the gesture.

"It's one reason," he conceded. His voice seemed deeper. "I have a pretty decent stable of two-year-olds. I'm sure you already know that."

"Who doesn't? Every racing magazine in the country has run at least one article on Winsome." What kind of game was Brig Chambers playing with her, Becca wondered. He wasn't being completely honest, Becca could feel it. She hadn't earned her reputation at twenty-six without some degree of insight into the human psyche, and she knew intuitively that there was more to Brig Chambers than met the eye. He hadn't flown across the United States to "scope out the competition." The owner of a Thoroughbred the likes of Winsome didn't waste valuable time.

"Are we going to look at your Lady?" Brig asked.

"If you level with me."

She could see the gleam of his white teeth in the darkness as he smiled. "You're not easily fooled, are you?"

"I hope not," she shot back. "Is that what you're trying to accomplish?"

"No. But there is another reason why I'm here," he allowed. "If I like the looks of Sentimental Lady, I'm prepared to offer a good price for her."

The bottom dropped out of Becca's heart, and angry heat rushed through her veins. "She's not for sale." As quick as a cat, Becca opened the car door, stepped outside, and slammed the door. She picked up her skirt and began to march to the house.

Brig had anticipated her move and was beside her in three swift strides. "Is there a reason why you're so angry?" he asked as he grabbed her arm and turned her to face him. In the dim light from a shadowy moon, he saw the glint of determination in her wide eyes.

"I loathe deception." She tried to pull her arm away from the manacle of his grip, but failed. "Let go of me!"

"I didn't deceive you." His fingers dug into the soft flesh of her arm.

"Bull! Dean set this up, didn't he? He's wanted to sell Sentimental Lady from the moment she was born."

"No!"

"Liar!"

Brig's eyes narrowed as he looked down upon her fury. Even enraged, she was gorgeous. "Your brother mentioned that you might be interested in selling—nothing more."

"Well, he was wrong! She's not for sale!"

"That's too bad," he said softly.

"I don't think so." Her anger began to ebb. There was something about him that soothed her rage. She knew he was going to kiss her and she knew she should stop him, but she couldn't. When his head bent and the fingers of his free hand wrapped around her neck to cradle her head, she began to melt inside. And when his lips brushed hers in a tender kiss that promised a night of unbound passion, she had to force herself to pull away from him.

"Was this part of Dean's plan, too?"

His jaw tensed and the corners of his mouth turned down. "Your brother had nothing to do with this."

Her silent green eyes accused him of the lie. He dropped her arm with a sound of disgust. "You don't know the truth when it stares you in the face, do you? I came out here to see your horse, and perhaps offer to purchase her. Period. Yes, it was your brother's suggestion, but I did know a little about Sentimental Lady, and if I hadn't already been interested, I wouldn't have come, and that's the end of it."

He took a step away from her before continuing. "I put up with that ridiculous party and talked to a crowd of people I hope to God I'll never have to face again. And then I arranged for transportation out here, wherever the hell we are. Now you turn paranoid on me. You asked for the truth, Rebecca, and I've given it to you. If anyone's scheming to take your horse away from you, it isn't me!"

"Didn't you just say you planned to buy her?"

"Only if you're willing to sell! I might consider making an offer on her, *if* I like what I see." He stopped his tirade to take in a deep breath. "Look, Rebecca, I don't know what problems you've been having with your brother, and frankly I don't want to get involved in family disputes. If it's too much trouble for me to look at your filly, then forget it. I think I can find my way back to civilization."

He turned on his heel and began to return to the car. "Wait," Becca called. Brig stopped. "If you want to see Sentimental

Lady, I'll take you to her." He followed her to the largest of the buildings surrounding the paddocks.

The door creaked when she opened it and there was a restless stirring when Becca flicked on the lights. A few disgruntled snorts greeted her as she passed by the stalls of the awakened horses. Becca murmured soothing words to the animals and stopped at Sentimental Lady's stall. "Come here, girl," she called to the dark filly and made soft clucking sounds in the back of her throat.

Sentimental Lady's nostrils flared and she backed up distrustfully as she eyed Brig. She stamped her foot impatiently and flattened her dark ears against her head. "She doesn't like strangers," Becca explained to Brig before softly coaxing the high-spirited horse to come forward.

Brig's gray eyes never left the horse. He studied the filly from the tip of her velvet-soft nose to her tail. Lady tossed her near-black head and snorted her contempt for the man appraising her.

"Is she as fast as she looks?" Brig asked.

"She's fast." Becca found it impossible to put into words how effortlessly Sentimental Lady ran, how rhythmically her black legs raced, or how fluidly her muscles worked. The horse was a study in grace when she lengthened into her stride.

"Is she sure?"

Becca snapped off the lights and closed the door. "She's strong."

"And big," Brig murmured. He rubbed his thumb pensively over his jawline. "She's one of the tallest fillies I've ever seen. What's her girth?"

"Seventy-five inches."

Brig shook his head and scowled. "Have you had any trouble with her legs?"

Becca was a little defensive. "We've had to watch her ankles."

"She's too big," was Brig's flat, emotionless statement. "Her legs won't be able to carry her the distance."

"Because she's a filly?" Becca shot back.

"Because she's a *big* filly. Her girth is over an inch larger than Winsome's and his legs are stronger."

"You haven't seen her run," Becca whispered as they walked toward the house.

"I'd like to."

"Why? I told you she wasn't for sale."

Becca placed her hand on the doorknob, but Brig took hold of her arm, catching the warm flesh and forcing her to turn and look at him. "I came all this way. I'd like to see her run." His eyes touched hers and in the darkness she could read more than interest for a horse in his gaze. Passion burned deep within him, Becca saw it as clearly as if he had whispered, "I want you." Becca managed to unlock the door and it swung open, inviting them both into the comfort inside.

Her pulse was racing and her lips desert dry. She tried to think calmly, but found it impossible. Her smile trembled with the confusion that was overtaking her. "Sentimental Lady has a workout scheduled for tomorrow morning…" Was he listening? He was looking at her lips, but Becca doubted if he had heard a word she said. "You could come and see her then." She began to retreat into the house, but felt the muscles in her back press up against the doorjamb. "She…runs at six."

His hands captured her bare shoulders. His face was only inches from hers and his clean scent filled her nostrils. "It's already after two."

"I know…"

His lips pressed hotly against hers and the delicious pressure of his fingers on her shoulders increased. His warm breath fanned her face as he pulled his head away from hers to look into her eyes. "I can't go back to the city tonight. It will be nearly dawn when I get there," he pointed out.

Becca's senses were swimming and she found it impossible to think clearly. "But…" *What was he asking?*

His fingers touched the hollow of her throat and her pulse

jumped. He gazed down upon her through heavy-lidded eyes. "Let me stay with you," he suggested throatily, and softly nuzzled the inviting column of her neck. She had to fight the urge to collapse into him.

She pressed her palms against his chest. Her eyes searched his face. "I find you very attractive," she admitted.

"Why do I expect the word *but* to preface the rest of your response?" He smiled, and in the pale light from an uneven smattering of stars, Becca returned his grin.

"Because I don't know you..."

His fingers toyed with the neckline of her dress, rimming the silken fabric. "Tell me you don't want me," he commanded, softly, before pressing a kiss to her bare skin above the edge of the dress.

"I can't," she conceded breathlessly. Why did she feel that the edge of her soul was exposed to his knowing gaze?

"Why not?"

"Because I do want you," she replied honestly.

The corners of his mouth quirked.

"But that's not enough."

"There's nothing wrong with physical need."

The stillness of the night seemed to close in on Becca. Brig's touch was warm and inviting. It seemed as if they were alone in the universe: one man and one woman. His lips once again brushed hers, caressing her with a passion she had never known, promising a night of rapture and warmth, if only she would take it. She had been lonely so long. "Physical need is important," she agreed quietly. "But there has to be more."

"What is it you want, Rebecca? Are you waiting to fall in *love?*" he asked contemptuously.

"I'm not *waiting* for anything. It...it just has to be right for me."

He took his hands off of her and planted them firmly on either side of her head, bracing himself on the doorjamb. His gray, brooding eyes forced her to hold his unwavering gaze.

"I'm not asking for anything you're not willing to give. I would never push you into anything you don't want. Believe it or not, I know that this isn't easy for you."

"Do you?" She wanted to believe him, needed to hear that he understood her.

"Of course I do. It's written all over your face."

"It's not that I'm a prude."

He smiled. "I know. And I'm not looking for a one-night stand. If that's what I wanted, I could have stayed in San Francisco, or New York, for that matter. The truth of the matter is that you intrigue me, Rebecca Peters. Just who are you?" His finger came up to trace her lips. Shivers of anticipation traveled hurriedly down her spine. "I've read about you and your farm out here. A beautiful young woman with an impoverished breeding farm somehow has the brains to breed Night Dancer, one of the greatest racing studs of all time, to a little-known mare called Gypsy Lady and ends up with perhaps the fastest Thoroughbred filly ever bred. I want to know about you, Ms. Peters, all about you."

"And that includes sleeping with me?" she asked. "Are you stupid enough to think that you could possibly understand me by sleeping with me?" She knew she should feel outraged, but she didn't.

"I had no intention of sleeping with you when I came out here. I was only interested in you because of business."

"But?" she coaxed, lifting her elegant eyebrows.

"But you happen to be the most intriguing woman I've ever met." His hand slipped under her head, and he deftly removed the clasp that held her hair restrained. With one quick movement of his fingers, her golden hair spilled down past her shoulders, still wound loosely in a thick braid. "Trust me," he pleaded as his lips met hers in a kiss that was bold rather than tender. His mouth found the moistness of hers and he held her against him hungrily. "Let me love you, Rebecca," he whispered.

"Oh, Brig… I…" His lips stilled her response and the heat

of passion began to race through her veins. She gasped when his hands found the clasp of her dress and the blue silk fabric parted, leaving her upper shoulder bare. His lips were warm and moist where the fabric had once been, and Becca felt her bones beginning to melt. She couldn't think, couldn't stand. Before she swayed against him, Brig reached down and captured her sagging knees with the crook of his arm. He lifted her off her feet and touched his lips to her forehead as he carried her inside the old farmhouse.

Becca's heart was racing, but she didn't protest as he carefully mounted the stairs. When he hesitated on the landing, she encouraged him by indicating the direction of her room. He didn't turn on the light and Becca's eyes grew accustomed to the shadowy light cast by a cloud-covered moon. Carefully, Brig set her on her feet and let the elegant blue dress slip into a puddle of silk on the floor. His hands moved downward over her body, as if he were memorizing each soft contour of her muscles, every rib in her ribcage. His groan was primal when he cupped her breast and felt the weight of it in his hungry palm. Her answering sigh of expectation fired his blood and his lips, hungry with unsatisfied desire, pressed forcefully against hers. She felt the tip of his tongue press through her teeth to touch the inner reaches of her mouth.

His lips devoured her, spreading a trail of demanding kisses across her cheeks, inside her ear, and down the column of her throat. His tongue touched the delicate bones surrounding the hollow of her throat and drew lazy, wet circles of delicious torment that forced her to cling desperately to him, hoping the sweet agony would never stop.

"Love me," she whispered, her hoarse voice breaking the stillness of the night. She entwined her arms possessively around his neck and let the tips of her fingers delve below his collar. Her eager hands encountered shoulder muscles tense with desire. "Touch me, sweet lady," he pleaded. Deliberately he forced her onto the bed with the weight of his body.

The mattress sagged as their combined weight molded together. Impatiently he discarded his clothes, damning the frail barrier holding them apart.

His body was damp with perspiration. The beads of sweat collected on his forehead and ran down his spine. A gentle breeze lifted the curtains and whispered through the pine trees to scent the room, but it did nothing to cool the passion storming between them.

Heated torment inflamed Becca's veins and pounded in her eardrums. The dim light from a pale moon let her see the man she was about to love, let her read the fire in his eyes, let her witness the rising tide of his emotions.

His hands slid possessively over her body, molding his skin to hers. The sweat that clung to his body blended with hers as he moved his torso over hers, claiming her body. Becca moaned when he took her breast into his mouth and teased the nipple with his tongue and teeth. Her fingers dug into the muscles of his back as she gave in to the sweet ecstasy of his caress.

His eyes were glazed in barely restrained passion when he took her face between his hands and stared into her soul. "I want you," he whispered. "Please let me know that you want me."

"Oh, Brig, please…" She didn't have to finish; her eyes pleaded with him to take her.

"May this night never end," he whispered savagely before once again molding his swollen lips to hers.

He braced himself so that he could watch her face as he found her. She gasped with satisfaction at the moment they became one, feeling a delirious triumph at the union of their flesh. The ache within her began to ebb and the words of love forming on her lips died as he slowly urged her to sensuous new heights of passion. They moved as one, together in rapturous harmony, blending flesh to flesh, skin to skin, muscle to muscle until the tempo began to quicken and the pressure within Becca's body began to thunder and echo in her heartbeat.

She felt the fires within her begin to flare and Brig's answering shudder of surrender.

"I love you," she whispered, while tears of relief filled her eyes. "I know it's irrational, but I think I love you."

"I know," he murmured, kissing the wet strands of her sun-streaked hair and holding her trembling body as if life itself depended on it.

CHAPTER FIVE

WHEN BRIG OPENED HIS EYES, he noticed that his body was covered in sweat, evidence of his recent nightmare—the vivid and brutal dream that had interrupted his sleep repeatedly during the last six years. The nightmares had become less frequent, but being with Rebecca again had triggered the ugly, painful dream. He lifted his arm to touch her, to find comfort in the softness of her body and to convince himself that his memory of making love to her hadn't been part of the dream, hadn't been conjured by his imagination. His hand touched the crumpled sheets, cold from the morning air. The bed was empty.

Brig's eyes flew open with the realization that she was gone. He lifted his head from the pillow too quickly, and a ton of bricks pressed on his skull in the form of a hangover. Then he saw her—as beautiful as he remembered. It wasn't part of his dream. Rebecca was really here, in his father's cabin in the foothills of the Rockies. She was huddled in his favorite blue robe, her fingers drawing restless circles on the window ledge where she sat as she stared out the window. She appeared absorbed in thought. Pensive lines of worry marred the smooth skin of her forehead. Her honey-blond hair was unruly and tangled as it framed her delicate face. Her green eyes stared, but saw nothing. What was she thinking?

He started to call her name, but withheld the impulse as he recalled the first time he had seen her. Dressed elegantly in shimmering blue silk, her hair coiled regally upon her head,

Rebecca had combined beauty with grace. She had been refined and yet seductive.

Brig hadn't fallen in love with her then. It had come much later when the feelings of respect and trust had grown into love. They had worked together side by side, day after day, in the sweat and grime of training a headstrong bay filly to become the racing wonder she was. With Rebecca's fiery Thoroughbred and Brig's money, they had formed a partnership intent on taking the racing world by storm. They planned to shake up the elite world of horse racing with Sentimental Lady, a filly who could outdistance the colts.

At the thought of the elegant horse, Brig's stomach turned over and the taste of guilt rose in the back of his throat. For the first time in his life, Brig had allowed himself to be shortsighted. Perhaps his clear thinking had been clouded with love, but nevertheless it was a poor excuse for letting his emotions override his logic. He had known from the moment he laid eyes upon Sentimental Lady that her legs weren't strong enough to carry the weight. If only he'd used his head instead of trusting a woman with beguiling green eyes!

His nightmares were a surrealistic replay of the events that had shattered his life. It was always the same. He was with Rebecca in a crowd of thousands of cheering people. The track was dry and fast—Sentimental Lady's favorite. The warm California sun glistened on the flanks of a blood-bay horse as she nervously pranced toward the starting gate. The other horse in the match race, Winsome, had already won top honors as a three-year-old. His list of victories included two of the three jewels of the triple crown and now he faced an opponent he had never previously encountered. Although Sentimental Lady had stormed into the racing world as a two-year-old, and at three had won all of her starts, including the Kentucky Oaks, the Black-eyed Susan, and the Coaching Club American Oaks, she hadn't raced against the colts. She had shattered several world records, and was clocked faster than Winsome. The press and the fans demanded a match race of the two most famous three-year-olds of the season: Sentimental Lady challenging Winsome.

There was another side to the story, an interesting twist that headlined the gossip columns. The filly, renowned favorite of the feminist fans, was bred and owned by Rebecca Peters, a young woman making her way in a man's world. The colt belonged to the stables of Brig Chambers, heir to an oil fortune and rumored to be romantically involved with Ms. Peters. It was a story the press loved, a story which extended the bounds of the racing world and included the romantic glitter of the very rich. Pictures and articles about the famous couple and their rival horses were flashed in both racing tabloids and gossip columns alike. Reporters couldn't get enough information on the horses or their owners. Speculation ran high on the future mating of Sentimental Lady to Winsome.

As the world saw it, Brig Chambers had it all: a beautiful, intriguing woman and two of the fastest horses ever run. Nothing could go wrong, or so he was told. So why then did he argue against the race, and when he finally relented, why did doubt keep filling his mind as he watched a lathered Lady being led into the starting gate? Why was there an uneasy sense of dread? Where was the exhilaration, the excitement? The false sense of security he had felt earlier in the week began to crumble. The race was a mistake—a terrible mistake.

Winsome, veteran of many victories and known for his calm temperament, was led into the starting gate. The crowd roared its approval and Sentimental Lady spooked at the sound. She skittered across the track and shied as her jockey attempted to urge her toward the gate. Nervous sweat lathered her withers and she tossed her head in apprehension.

"She's too nervous," Brig muttered, but his words of concern were lost in the approving roar of the crowd as Sentimental Lady sidestepped into the starting gate. The gate closed and Lady reared, striking her head. It was too late. The door opened with the ringing of bells and shouts from the crowd. An empty track stretched out before her and Sentimental Lady bolted. Brig yelled at the officials, but his voice was drowned in the jumble of noise from the fans.

"No!" Brig shouted at the jockey, watching the race between colt and filly in silent horror.

Winsome was ahead, but Sentimental Lady seemed to get her footing. She was astride the black colt before the first turn. The speed of the race was incredible and Sentimental Lady finished the first quarter faster than she had ever run. Winsome liked to lead and was known for crushing his opponents early in the race, but Sentimental Lady hung on, holding her own against the powerful black horse.

The blood drained from Brig's face as he watched the horses, racing stride for stride, heartbeat for heartbeat. "This is a mistake," he screamed at Rebecca. "She's not going to make it…"

"She will!" Rebecca disagreed, her eyes shining in pride at the way the Lady was running. The crowd seemed to agree, roaring, urging the horses onward in their blinding pace.

"We've got to stop the race!" Brig shouted, shaking Becca.

"It's too late—"

"We've got to! Lady hit her head in the gate. Her stride's off!"

"You're crazy," Becca screamed back at him, but a flash of doubt clouded her green eyes. "Look at her—she's running with the wind!"

Sentimental Lady was a neck ahead of the colt, but he was pushing her, driving her to greater speeds, forcing her to run faster than she ever had.

The horses were halfway down the backstretch, their legs pounding the track furiously, their dark tails trailing behind. Nostrils distended, they ran, neck and neck, stride for stride, eyeball to eyeball. The white fence inside the track hampered Brig's view, but still he saw the misstep as clearly as if he had been astride her rather than on the sidelines.

The blow to the leg came with a sickening snap that Brig imagined rather than heard. It was the brittle crack of bone as nearly twelve hundred pounds of horse came crushing down on fragile legs.

For a moment Brig stood transfixed, watching in sickened dread. "She broke down," he yelled at Rebecca, who had witnessed the fateful step.

Winsome pressed on, and Lady, her spirit and courage refusing to be extinguished, continued to race on her three good legs. The jockey fought desperately to pull her up, knowing that her competitive fires would carry her on and further injure her. Each stride pushed her tremendous weight on the shattered bone, further pulverizing the bone into tiny fragments ground into tissue, dirt, and blood.

Brig didn't see Winsome finish the race. He ran across the track to the site of the injury, where the jockey was trying to calm the frightened animal. The veterinarian arrived and tried to soothe the horse, while attempting to examine the break. Lady reared and Rebecca, with frightened tears running down her face, softly called to the horse, hoping to somehow forestall the inevitable.

"Good girl. That's my Lady," she said tremulously. "Let the doctor look at you, girl."

The frightened horse reared. Blood was smeared on her regal white star, and her right foreleg was a twisted mass of flesh and bone. The whites of her dark eyes showed the fear and pain.

Rebecca reached for the horse's reins but Sentimental Lady reared again. The injured leg glanced Becca's shoulder, leaving her ivory linen suit stained with blood and her shoulders bruised.

"Get away from her," Brig shouted, pushing Becca away from the terrified horse.

"I can't...oh, Lady...Lady," Becca called as she backed away. "Calm down, girl, for your own sake..."

The veterinarian looked grimly at Brig. He nodded toward

Becca. "Get her out of here." He spoke rapidly as he placed a clear, inflatable cast over the horse's damaged leg. It quickly turned scarlet with blood.

"It's all my fault," Becca screamed as Brig put his arms around her shaking shoulders and led her away from her horse.

"Don't blame yourself."

"It's all my fault!" she cried over and over again, hysterical. "She should never have run. I knew it—I knew it. Damn it, Brig, it's all my fault!"

Brig hadn't understood her overwhelming sense of guilt. He dismissed it as an overreaction to a tragic event, until twelve hours later Sentimental Lady was dead and the results of the autopsy proved Becca right. Only then did he understand that she was, indeed, responsible for the courageous horse's death.

Brig rubbed his hands over his eyes and tried to dispel the brutal apparition that destroyed his sleep. How many nights had he lain awake and wondered how he could have prevented the gruesome tragedy; how many days had he tried to find a way to absolve Rebecca of the guilt? How much of the guilt was his? He should never have agreed to the match race; it was a devil's folly. Even if the tragedy hadn't occurred, there was the chance that the beaten horse would never have been the same.

As it was, a beautiful animal had been ruined unnecessarily, a waste due to the poor judgment of humans. If that wasn't enough to torture him, the truth he had learned after Sentimental Lady's death should have kept him away from Rebecca Peters forever. And yet, last night, without thinking of any of the horrors of the past, Brig had made love to her as if the deception had never existed.

Brig wanted to hate her. He wanted to curse her in the darkness and throw her out of his life forever, but he couldn't. As he watched her staring vacantly out the window, the sadness in her eyes touched his soul. How had she ever been caught in such an evil trap? Why had she drugged her own horse in an expensive attempt to quicken Sentimental Lady's speed? His stomach soured at the thought. Why did she seem so innocent and honest, when he knew her to be a liar? She was a dichotomy of a woman, beguiling and treacherous.

"Rebecca?"

Brig's voice called to her from somewhere in the distance. "Rebecca, are you all right?"

Becca cleared her mind and found herself staring out the bay window of Jason Chambers's mountain cabin. Brig's concerned voice had brought her crashing back to the present. How long had she been daydreaming about a past that was so distant? She cast a quick glance at Brig. He was still in bed, propped up on one elbow and staring intently at her. He seemed anxious and didn't appear to notice that the navy blue comforter had slid to the floor. How long he had been watching her, Becca couldn't guess.

She shivered and wrapped her arms around herself, to build her courage rather that create warmth. "I guess I was just thinking," she replied evasively. She turned her head away from him and hid behind the thick curtain of her hair, where she brushed aside a lingering tear which had formed in the corner of her eye. She had loved him so desperately and the bittersweet memories of their past caught her unprepared to meet his inquisitive gaze.

His dark hair was rumpled and a look of genuine concern rested in his unguarded stare. "What were you thinking about?" he asked. He didn't attempt to hide the worry he felt for her.

Her lips trembled as she attempted a smile. "Us."

"What about *us?*"

Her voice was frail, but she forced her eyes to remain dry as she found his gaze and held it. "I...I was thinking about how much love we had, once," she admitted.

"Does that make you sad?"

She had to swallow to keep her tears at bay. He couldn't

understand, he never had. She averted her gaze and stared sightlessly out the window. "It's just that I loved you so much," she admitted raggedly.

His brows knit in concentration as he drew his knees beneath his chin and studied her. Why was she here, opening all the old wounds? What did she want? "I loved you, too," he said.

"Not the same way." It was a simple statement of fact.

"You're wrong."

"You still don't understand, do you?" she charged, as she whirled to imprison him with her damning green stare. "I wanted to spend the rest of my life with you. I wanted to share all of the expectations, the joys, even the disappointments with you." Her voice caught in the depth of her final admission. "I wanted to bear your children, Brig. I wanted to love them, to teach them, to comfort them when they cried… Dear God, Brig, don't you see? I wanted to be with you forever!"

"And I let you down?"

"I… I didn't say that…"

His gray eyes challenged her from across the room. The silence was heavy with unspoken accusations from a distant past. With an utter of vexation, Brig fell back against the bed and stared, unseeing, at the exposed beams in the ceiling. "I wanted those things, too," he conceded.

"Just not enough to trust me."

"Oh, Rebecca…don't twist the truth." He felt raw from the torture of her words. "I asked you to marry me, or have you conveniently forgotten that, too?"

"I remember," she whispered.

"Then you can recall that *you* were the one who couldn't make a commitment. *You* were the one who had to prove yourself to the world." The rage which had engulfed him six years before began to consume him once again and he had to fight to keep his temper under control. How many times would he let her deceive him? His fingers curled angrily around the bed sheet.

"I needed time."

"I gave you time, damn it!" He sat upright in the bed and his fist crashed into the headboard. "You asked for time, and I gave it to you!" His ghostly gray eyes impaled her, daring her to deny the truth.

"But you couldn't give me your trust, could you?"

"Do you blame me?" Pieces of their last argument pierced Brig's mind. His accusations, her violent denials. If only she could have told him the truth! He didn't wait for her to respond to his rhetorical question. Instead he grabbed his clothes and stood beside the bed. He was still naked and Becca could see the tension in all of his rigid muscles. His voice was uneven, but he managed to pull together a little of his composure. "Look, Rebecca, this argument is getting us nowhere. I'm going to take a shower and get cleaned up. I drank a little too much last night and I'm paying for it this morning. When I clear my head, we'll talk."

He turned toward the bathroom, but paused at the door and faced her once again. His voice was softer and his smile wistful. "I'm glad you're here," he admitted, wondering why he felt compelled to explain his feelings to her.

She didn't move from her seat on the window ledge until she heard the sound of running water. Once she knew he was in the shower and she had a few minutes to herself, her tense muscles relaxed and the tears burning at the back of her eyes began to flow in uneven streams down her cheeks. She pinched the edge of her thumb between her teeth and tried not to think about the love they had found, only to lose.

Was it her fault, as Brig insisted, or was it fate which held them so desperately apart? If only she hadn't been so blind when it had come to Sentimental Lady, if only she had listened to Brig's wisdom. Perhaps they would still be together, would have married, and would share a child. Perhaps Sentimental Lady would still be alive. But Becca had been young and hell-bent on making a name for herself as a horse breeder. Sentimental Lady had been her ticket to success. How was

Becca to know that Brig's prophecies would be proven correct, that Sentimental Lady's legs were too weak for her strong body? Not even her trainer had guessed that Lady would break down. And how was Becca to know that someone would inject her horse with an illegal steroid, a dangerous drug that alone might have permanently injured her horse? In the end, Becca had not only lost the fastest horse she had ever owned, but also the trust of the one man she loved. Was it her punishment for being overly ambitious, for fighting her way to the top in a man's domain?

Becca stiffened her spine and tried to ignore the unyielding pain in her heart. Perhaps she was overreacting. Last night Brig hadn't been overly upset when she had tried to explain about the horse; maybe she was blowing the problem out of proportion. But then again, last night Brig had been drinking and was shocked to see her. Everything that had happened between them was somewhat unreal, an unplanned reunion of two lovers suffering from the guilt of the past. This morning things were different. Gone were the excuses of the night, the passion of six lonely years, the feeling of isolation in the mountains. Today, the world would intrude and the mistakes of the past would become blindingly apparent.

She had decided to accept Brig's decision concerning Gypsy Wind and the money. She realized that, legally, she had virtually no say in the matter. If Brig demanded repayment, she would have to sell the Gypsy. Nothing she owned even approached fifty thousand dollars. However, she would try her damnedest to made Brig understand what the horse meant to her, what Gypsy Wind represented. Before her resolve could waver, she went to her car and grabbed the overnight bag she had stashed in the backseat. She cleaned herself in the guest bath and changed into her favorite forest green slacks and soft ivory blouse. The outfit was a little dressy for the rugged mountains, but this morning Becca wanted to look disturbingly feminine. She wound her hair into a gentle twist and pinned it loosely to the back of her neck before touching a little color to her pale lips and cheeks.

Without consciously listening, she knew the exact moment when the shower spray was turned off. Apprehension rose in her throat. She had to keep busy and hold her thoughts in some sort of order, because like it or not, she knew that she and Brig were about to become embroiled in one of the most important arguments in her life. She planned her defense while putting together a quick breakfast from the sparse contents of the refrigerator. By the time she heard the bedroom door opening, the hasty meal was heated and the aroma of freshly perked coffee mingled with the scent of honey-cured ham to fill the rustic kitchen and dining alcove.

She thought she heard Brig coming, but his footsteps paused, as if he had entered another room in the house. She waited and then heard him continue toward the kitchen. She was just sliding the eggs onto a plate when he strode past the dining alcove and through the door. She was concentrating on her task and didn't look up.

"What's this?" he asked, just as she set the plates on the table.

"What does it look like? It's breakfast." She turned to face him and found that he wasn't looking at the table. Instead he was staring intently at her, as if he were trying to put together the pieces of a mysterious puzzle. He looked more like the man she remembered from her past. Clad only in jeans and an old plaid work shirt, he seemed younger. His head was still wet from the shower and his jaw cleanly shaven. The slight hint of a musky aftershave brought back provocative memories of living with him in a rambling beach house overlooking the moody Pacific Ocean.

"I'm not talking about the food," he replied cautiously. His eyes turned steely gray. "Your clothes, did you bring them with you?"

Her eyes met his and refused to waver. "Yes."

"Wait a minute. Are you saying that you *intended* to spend

the night with me? Don't you have a hotel or something?" When she didn't immediately respond, he grabbed her arm and his fingers tightened painfully. Suspicion clouded his gaze. "Just what's going on here?" he demanded.

"What do you think?"

"I *think* that you planned last night."

"I only planned to find you…not seduce you, if that's what you're implying. I didn't even know if you would see me. I had no idea that we would end up making love."

His grip tightened on her arm. "Then why the change of clothes?"

She couldn't help but blush. "I really didn't know where I'd be spending the night. I only guessed that you would be here, and I knew that it was too late to head back to a hotel in Denver."

"And what if you hadn't found me? Did you plan to sleep in the car?" He couldn't hide the sarcasm in his voice.

"I don't know."

"I'm just trying to understand you." He sighed, releasing her arm.

"I tried to explain everything last night, but you wouldn't listen."

"I'm listening now." He crossed his arms over his chest and leaned against the counter.

Becca took a deep breath before she began. "I told you that I owed your father some money…fifty thousand dollars to be exact." She watched his reaction, but he didn't move a muscle, stoically waiting for her to continue. "I needed the money to breed a horse."

"And I assume that your mare conceived and now you have yourself a Thoroughbred."

Becca nodded.

"Colt or filly?"

She met his gaze boldly. "Filly. Her name is Gypsy Wind." Brig's jawline hardened. "You told me that much last night.

But you neglected to tell me that she's a full-blooded sister to Sentimental Lady."

Becca hid her surprise. "I tried to tell you everything last night. You weren't interested."

In frustration, Brig raked his fingers through his hair. He shifted his eyes away from Becca for just a minute. "I can't believe that you would be so stupid as to make the same mistake twice, *the same damned mistake!*"

"Gypsy Wind is no mistake."

"Then why are you hiding her?"

"I'm not."

"Come on, Rebecca. Don't deny it. If you'd let out the word that *you* were breeding another horse, a full sister to Sentimental Lady, the press would have been on you like fleas on a dog. That's why you hid her, came to a private source for money."

"I came to your father as a last resort."

"Sure you did," was Brig's contemptuous response. "I bet the old man really ate it up, didn't he? He never could pass up the opportunity to pull one over on the press." The smile that tugged at the corners of Brig's mouth didn't touch his eyes. There was a sullen quality, a bitterness, that made his features seem more angular.

Becca's chin lifted and a defiant glimmer rested in her round eyes. "How did you know that Gypsy Wind is Sentimental Lady's sister?"

"Because I knew there was more to the story than what you admitted last night." His raised palm stilled her protests. "And I admit that I didn't want to discuss anything with you last night, including your horse or the money you owed my father." Brig noticed that the defensive gleam in her eyes wavered. "But you did pique my interest, and after my shower I went into the old man's den. That's where I found this." He extracted a neatly folded document from his back pocket.

"The note," she guessed aloud, staring at the yellowed paper.

"That's right." He tossed the note onto the table and it slid across the polished oak surface to rest next to Becca's mug. The figure of fifty thousand dollars was boldly scrawled on the face of the document; Becca's signature attested its authenticity.

As Becca reached for the paper, Brig's words arrested her. "Check out the back." Becca turned the note over and saw Jason Chambers' notation. *Proceeds to be used for breeding of Night Dancer to Gypsy Lady.*

"When did you plan to tell me about her, Becca?"

"I did—"

"Because my father died! What if he hadn't?" Brig's voice was deadly. "How long would you have waited? Until she began racing?"

"I don't know," she whispered honestly.

Brig reached for a chair, turned it around, and dropped into it. He straddled the seat and rested his arms against the back while his eyes impaled her. "Why don't you tell me all about it," he suggested, ignoring the now-cold breakfast. "We've got all weekend, and I can't wait to hear why you took it upon yourself to flirt with tragedy all over again."

CHAPTER SIX

WHILE BECCA TRIED TO COLLECT HER THOUGHTS, the meal was started and finished in suffocating silence. All of her well-rehearsed speeches, all of her defenses for breeding Gypsy Wind fled under Brig's stony gaze. The tension in the air was difficult to ignore, although Brig tried to appear patient, as if he understood her need for silence.

When they finished breakfast, Brig opened one of the French doors in the small alcove and quietly invited Becca to join him on the broad back porch that ran the length of the cabin. Becca carried her cup of coffee, cradling the warm ceramic in her palms as she stepped outside into the brisk mountain air. She couldn't help but shiver. It was still early in the morning and a chill hung in the mid-autumn air. Becca took a long sip from her coffee, hoping it would warm her and give her the strength to face Brig with the truth concerning Gypsy Wind. There was little doubt in her mind that Brig would be angry with her and she half-expected him to push her out of his life again and this time keep the horse.

Brig followed Becca onto the porch. He leaned his elbows on the hand-hewn railing and his gray eyes scanned the secluded valley floor. A clear stream curled like a silver snake along a ridge near the edge of the woods. Already the aspens were beginning to lose their golden leaves to the soft wind. Brig's gaze followed the course of the creek and a wistful smile pulled at the corners of his mouth. It was in that stream where he had caught his first native brook trout. He hadn't done it alone. His old man had taught him how to cast and watch for the fish to strike. God, he missed that cuss of a father.

Abruptly Brig brought his wandering thoughts back to the present. He turned to face Rebecca and caught her watching the play of emotions on his face. He had hoped that in the morning light, without the blur of too many drinks, Rebecca Peters would lose her appeal to him, but he had been wrong. Dead wrong. Even the condemning proof of her treachery, the note to his father, couldn't mar her beauty. He supposed that if anything, it had added to her intrigue. Becca had always been a woman of mystique. The six years he had been away from her had given a maturity to her expressive green eyes which made her captivating. He knew that he shouldn't be susceptible to her, that he should outwardly denounce her, but he couldn't. Instead he tried a more subtle approach. "I guess I should apologize for last night."

"Why?" she asked, observing him over the rim of her cup. Dread began to inch up her spine as she wondered which way the conversation was heading.

"It's been a long week. A lot of problems. I didn't expect to see you last night and I had no intention of getting so carried away."

Why was he apologizing for something so right as making love? "It's all right…really."

"I didn't think you would come here."

She shook her head and the sun glinted in the golden strands of her hair. "I know. Look, everything's okay."

"Is it?" A muscle began to jump in his jaw. "Is spending the night with a man so easy for you that you can shrug it off?"

Her gaze hardened. "You know better than that."

"Did you plan last night?"

A hint of doubt flickered in her eyes. "I don't really know," she said honestly. "I…I don't think so."

"I'm not usually so easily seduced." His voice was cold.

"Neither am I."

For the first time since she had come to him, Brig allowed himself the fleeting luxury of a smile. It was just as she had remembered, slightly off-center and devilishly disarming. "I know," he admitted begrudgingly. He hoisted himself onto the railing and stared at her. His eyes pierced her soul. "Why don't you tell me about your horse."

"She's the most beautiful animal I've ever bred."

"Looks don't count. Remember Kincsem, an ungainly filly who won all fifty-four of the races she entered."

"Gypsy Wind is fast."

"Sentimental Lady was fast."

"But she's stronger than Lady—"

"She'll have to be." Brig's eyes implored her. "Good Lord, Becca. What I can't understand is why you want to put yourself through all of this again. And the horse. Jesus, Becca... what about your horse? The minute she begins to race the press will be all over her. And you can bet that they won't forget about Sentimental Lady, not for a second! Damn it, the entire nation was affected by Lady's last race." His voice had increased in volume and he could feel the splinters of wood imbedding into his palms as he curled his fingers around the rough wood of the railing. His eyes were angry as he remembered Sentimental Lady. "I just don't understand you, Rebecca Peters... I don't know what you're trying to prove." His voice was softer as he added, "Maybe I never did."

Despite Brig's violent display of emotion, Becca remained calm. It was imperative that he understand. "Rebreeding Gypsy Lady to Night Dancer was a logical move," she stated softly. "Hadn't you ever considered it?"

"Never!"

"Your father understood."

Brig's gray eyes flashed dangerously. "My father understood only two things in the past few years: How to make a helluva lot of money and how to spend it on a pretty face."

"You know that's not true."

Brig laughed humorlessly. "Maybe not, but I can't understand for the life of me why he agreed to loan you so much money—just to see it thrown away on some fiasco."

Becca could feel her anger starting to seethe. "Gypsy Wind is no fiasco, Brig. She's probably the best racing filly ever bred."

"You said the same thing about Sentimental Lady."

"And I believed it."

"You were wrong!"

"I wasn't! She was the best!"

"She broke down, Becca! Don't you remember? She couldn't take the pressure—she wasn't strong enough. Her leg snapped! Are you willing to put another horse through that agony?" Brig's eyes had turned a stormy gray.

"It won't happen," she whispered with more conviction than she felt. Something disturbing in Brig's gaze made her confidence waver.

"You said that before."

Becca's stomach was churning with bitter memories of Lady and the grueling, treacherous race. "In that instance, I was mistaken," she admitted reluctantly.

"And what makes you so sure that this time will be any different?"

"Gypsy Wind is not Sentimental Lady." Becca's voice was thin but determined. Brig recognized the pride and resolve in the tilt of Becca's face.

"You just admitted your mistake with Sentimental Lady."

"We aren't talking about Lady. If we were, I'd probably agree with you. But Gypsy Wind is an entirely different horse."

"A full-blooded sister."

"But she's stronger, Brig, and fast—"

"What about her temperament?" Brig demanded.

For the first time that morning, Becca hedged. "She's a winner. Ian O'Riley is training her. You know that he wouldn't bother with a horse if she didn't have the spirit."

"That was Lady's problem: her spirit. Ian O'Riley should

know better than anyone. After all, as her trainer, he paid the price."

"For the last time, we are not talking about Sentimental Lady!"

Brig was pensive as he sat on the railing, his hands supporting his posture. Becca's large green eyes were shining as she talked about the filly. She was proud of Gypsy Wind, sure of her. Brig found himself wanting to believe Rebecca, to trust her as he once had. If only he could. Instead he voiced the question uppermost in his mind. "So why did you come here to tell me about her—why now?"

"I wanted you to know. I didn't want you to hear it from someone else."

"But the old man knew. What if my father hadn't died?"

"I would have come to you."

"When? If that horse is as good as you say she is, why didn't you start her as a two-year-old?"

She avoided his gaze for a moment. "I didn't think she was ready. I don't know when I would have come to you." When she looked up and her eyes met his, they were once again steady. "It would have been soon. I wouldn't have allowed her to race until I had told you about her. I just wasn't sure how to approach you. When I found out that Jason had been killed, I knew I had to see you, as much for myself as for the horse. I wanted to know and see with my own eyes that you were all right."

"You knew that much from the papers."

"I wanted to touch you, Brig, to prove to myself that you were unhurt. I *had* to see for myself. Can't you understand that?" Her honesty rang in the clear air and Brig had to fight the urge to take her into his arms and crush her against his chest.

"Now that you're here, what do you expect of me?"

Becca drew in a deep breath, forcing herself to be calm and think clearly. "I want you to let me race the horse. I'm going to be honest with you, Brig, because I really don't know how else to handle this. I don't own a lot in this world, and most of what I do have is mortgaged to the hilt. But I do own Gypsy Wind, and I'd stake my life on the fact that she's the finest two-year-old alive. When she begins to race, I'll be able to repay you, but not before."

"Are you asking me to forget about the note?" His dark eyes watched her, waited for any emotion to appear on her face.

"No. I'm only asking that you hold on to it a little longer. You can't possibly need the money."

"Do you really think I would try to take your horse away from you?"

She swallowed with difficulty. "I hope not."

His eyes clouded. "You never have understood me, have you?"

"I thought I did once." Becca's throat began to tighten as she looked at him. Why did she still love him with every breath of life within her?

"But you were wrong?" he prodded.

"I never thought you would…crucify me the way you did."

"Crucify you? What are you talking about?"

She couldn't hide the incredulous tone in her voice. "You tried to destroy me six years ago."

"I had nothing to do with that—"

"Don't deny it, Brig. Almost single-handedly, you ruined my reputation as a horse breeder."

"No one can tarnish another's reputation. What happened to you was a result of *your* own actions," he spat out angrily.

Becca felt the insult twist in her heart like a dull blade. All these years she had hoped that Brig's condemning silence wasn't what the newspapers had made it. Her hands were shaking and she had to set down the cup of coffee for fear of spilling it. "You really thought I drugged Sentimental Lady?" she asked, her voice barely audible in the still mountain air. Her green eyes accused him of the outright lie.

"I think you know who did."

Becca couldn't resist the bait. "I have my own suspicions," she agreed.

"Of course you do. Because it had to be someone who had access to the horse before the race, someone you employed. Unless of course you injected her yourself."

"You don't believe that!" she cried, desperately holding on to a shred of hope that he could still trust her.

"I didn't want to."

"Then how can you even suggest that I would purposely harm my horse?" Bewilderment and the agony of being unjustly accused twisted her features. Brig lifted his body from the railing and stepped toward Becca. He was so close that she could feel the warmth of his breath against her hair.

"Because I think you know who did, Rebecca, and with your silence, you've become an accomplice to a crime too grotesque and inhumane to understand." Her eyes flashed green fire, but he persisted. "Whether you actually injected Sentimental Lady or not, you were responsible for her well-being and should have protected her against the agony she had to suffer."

Becca reacted so quickly, she didn't have time to think about the result of her actions. Her hand shot up and she flexed her wrist just as her palm found Brig's cheek. "You bastard!" she hissed, unable to restrain her anger.

Brig grabbed her wrist and pulled her roughly to him. "I'm only reminding you of what happened."

"You're twisting the truth to suit yourself."

"Why would I do that, Rebecca? It doesn't make any sense."

"Because you knew that she'd been drugged. Weren't you the one who wanted the race stopped just after the horses were out of the gate?"

"Because Lady hit her head."

"Because you had second thoughts!" she accused, the words biting the cold air.

He jerked her savagely, as if he would have liked to shake her until she began seeing things his way. "Second thoughts?"

he repeated, trying to understand her damning stare. His dark eyes narrowed. "What do you mean?"

"I mean that you don't have to lie anymore, Brig. Not with me. There's no one here but you and me, so you may as well confess. Your secret will remain safe. Hasn't it for the last six years?"

The fingers digging roughly into the soft flesh of her upper arms slowly relaxed. A quiet flame of fury burned in Brig's eyes, but the ferocity of his anger ebbed and he slowly released her. His whisper was rough and demanding. "What secret?" he asked. To his credit, he was a consummate actor. The confusion flushing his face seemed genuine.

Rebecca could feel tears pooling in her eyes, but she blinked them back, reminding herself not to trust this man who had passed his guilt on to her.

"What secret?" he asked again. A portion of his anger had returned as he guessed the twisted path of her defense.

She pleaded with him to be honest with her; her eyes begged for the decency of the truth. "You know that I didn't do anything to Sentimental Lady, Brig, and you also know that no one employed by me would have dared to harm that horse. The reason you know it is that you were the one who paid someone to inject her."

"*What?*" he thundered.

"There's no reason to deny it."

"You're out of your mind!"

"Not anymore. I was once, when I thought I could trust you."

His anger faded into uncertainty. "You've actually got yourself believing this, haven't you?"

"It's the only thing that makes any sense—"

"You mean it's the only way you can absolve yourself of the guilt."

Becca's slim shoulders sagged, as if an insurmountable weight had been placed upon her. The reasoning she had hoped would prove false came easily to her lips. "You were the one who had invested all the money in Sentimental Lady's training, and you were the one who received the lion's share of the insurance against her," Becca pointed out. When Brig tried to interrupt, she ignored him, allowing the truth to spill from her in an unbroken wave. "If Sentimental Lady hadn't broken down, but gone on to win that race, you knew that she would be disqualified because of the drugs. They would have shown up in the post-race urine sample. Winsome would have come out the victor. Either way you won. Once again, the stables of Brig Chambers would have come out on top!"

"You scheming little bitch!" he muttered through tightly clenched teeth. "You've got it all figured out, haven't you? It may have taken you six years to come up with an alternative story, but I've got to give you credit, it's a good one."

"Because it's true."

It was difficult to keep his anger in check, especially under the deluge of lies Becca had rained on him, but Brig Chambers was usually a patient man and he forced himself to remain as calm as possible under the circumstances. He told himself to relax and with the exception of a tiny muscle working in the corner of his jaw, he seemed outwardly undisturbed. He watched Rebecca intently. Damn her for her serene beauty, damn her for her quick mind, and damn her for her pride; a pride which couldn't suffer the pain of the naked truth. He hoped that he appeared indifferent when he spoke again.

"You've convinced yourself that this story you've fabricated really happened."

"It did."

"No way. If I wanted Winsome to come out a victor, I wouldn't have spent so much money on Lady."

"And if you hadn't spent so much time with her, with me, there wouldn't have been all of the hype. The press and the public might not have demanded a match race."

"What good was the race to me? I had the best three-year-old colt of the year. If it was money I was after, I could have sold Winsome to a syndicate and put him out for stud, instead of gambling on another race."

"But he wouldn't have been nearly as valuable."

"What if he had lost?"

"You made sure that he didn't." Her voice was cold and nearly convincing.

"I didn't touch Sentimental Lady—"

"But you know who did," she cut in quickly, sensing his defeat. "You paid them off." Her eyes, lifted to his, were glistening with tears.

For a moment his fists doubled and he slammed one violently against a cedar post supporting the roof of the porch. Startled birds flew out of a nearby bush. He stopped, and restrained his fury before walking back to her. When his hands lifted to touch her chin, they were unsteady, and when his thumbs gently brushed one of her hot tears from her eye, she thought she would crumble against him. She wanted to tell him nothing mattered, that the pain of the past should be forgotten; but pride forbade her.

"Don't twist the truth and let it come between us," he pleaded, his voice as ragged as Becca's own fragile breath. He gently took her into his arms and folded her tightly against his chest. "It's kept us apart too long."

Pressed against him, Becca could hear the steady beat of his heart. She could feel the comfort and strength of his arms around her, shielding her from the pain of the past. She understood his need to be one with her, but she couldn't forget what had held them so desperately apart. Perhaps it was because she had been so young and vulnerable. Maybe she hadn't had the maturity or courage to handle the situation surrounding Sentimental Lady's death.

When Brig's uncompromising silence had condemned her for allowing someone to drug her horse, she should have been more vocal in her denial. When the press had hounded her for the truth, she should have held a press conference to end the brutal conjecture about the accident. If she had, perhaps the newspapers wouldn't have had such a field day with the coverage of the tragic incident. As it was, it had taken months for the story to die down and even after the investigation, when Ian O'Riley had proved by a preponderance of evidence that he made every reasonable effort to protect the horses in his care from any foul deed, the reporters wouldn't give up.

If Becca had been stronger, she might have been able to deny, more vehemently, any knowledge of the crime. As it was, with the death of the great horse and the pain of Brig's accusations, Becca had taken refuge from the public eye. Her brother Dean had helped her piece together her life and slowly she had regained her courage and determination. The gossip had finally quieted. She and Dean had survived, but Brig's brutal insinuations hung over her head like a dark, foreboding cloud.

The worst part of it was that Brig knew she was innocent. He had to. As Becca's tired mind had sifted through the evidence of those last painful days before the race, it became glaringly apparent that Brig Chambers was the one who would most benefit by drugging Sentimental Lady. Only one reasonable solution could be deduced: Brig Chambers paid someone to inject the horse.

In the first few weeks after the race, Becca thought she would die from the torture of Brig's deception and accusations. She hadn't been interested in anything in her life when she realized that Brig, or someone who worked for him, had purposely set her up. Because she had been so devastated by Brig's ruthlessness, and because she didn't know how to defend herself, Becca had unwittingly taken the blame for the deed by her silence. There hadn't been enough evidence to indict anyone in the crime, but the scandal and mystery of Sentimental Lady's accident remained to cripple Rebecca's career. If it hadn't been for her brother Dean and his care for her, Becca doubted that she would have ever gathered the courage to return to horse racing and the life she loved.

As she stood in the shelter of Brig's arms, she knew that she should hate him, but she was unable. Her bitterness toward him had softened over the years, and then, when for a few lonely, wretched hours she had thought him dead, she finally faced the painful truth that she still loved him. As she gazed upward at him, wondering at the confusion in his brow, she agonized over the fact that he had treated her so callously. How could he have abused her? After all, she had held her tongue and when the press had accused her unjustly, she hadn't defended herself by smearing his name. Despite the silent rage and humiliation, she hadn't lowered herself to his level nor dragged his famous name through the mud. Meticulously, she had avoided fanning the fires of gossip as well as steadfastly refusing to give the columnists the slightest inklings of her side of the argument. It was no one's business. Her affair with Brig had been beautiful and intimate. She wasn't about to tarnish that beauty by making their personal lives public. Her dignity wouldn't allow it. Instead she had gone home and licked her wounds with the help of her brother. Dean was right; by all reasonable standards she should loathe Brig Chambers for what he did to her.

Why then did the feel of his arms around her give her strength? Why did the steady beat of his heart reassure her? Why did she secretly long to live in the warmth of his smile?

They stood holding each other in the autumn sunlight, as if by the physical closeness of their bodies they could bridge the black abyss of mistrust which silently held their souls apart. They didn't speak for a few breathless moments, content with only the sound of their hearts beating so closely together and the soft whisper of the cool breeze rushing through the pines.

"I've never stopped loving you," Brig whispered in a moment of condemning weakness. The muscles in his arms tightened around Becca with his confession. He hated himself intensely at that moment. For six years he had ignored his feelings for Rebecca, hidden them from the world and from himself. In one night of revived passion, she had managed to expose his innermost secrets.

Becca's knees sagged. So long she had waited to hear those words of love from this proud man. She had yearned for this moment, and when it was finally hers, she grasped it fleetingly only to release it. The words sounded too hollow, a convenient excuse for a night of passion. "I don't think we should talk about love," she managed to say, though her throat was unreasonably dry.

His hands moved upward to her chin and tilted her face to his. Dark eyes, gray as the early morning fog, gazed into hers. "Why not?"

"Because you and I have different meanings for the word. We always have."

His dark eyebrows drew pensively together. "I suppose you might be right," he reluctantly agreed. "But I can't believe that you're denying what you feel for me."

"I've always known that I'm attracted to you and I thought that I loved you once...sometimes I think I still do."

"But you're not sure?"

She wanted to fall back into his arms and reassure him, to pledge the love she felt welling in her heart, but reason held her words at bay. "I'm just...trying not to get caught in the same trap I fell into before."

A fleeting expression of pain crossed his face, but was quickly hidden beneath the hardening of his rugged features. "Is that what I did to you—'trapped you'?" The thin thread of patience in his voice threatened to snap.

"I trapped myself."

"And you're not about to let it happen again."

Her attempt at a frail smile faded. "I try not to repeat my mistakes."

"With the one glaring exception of Gypsy Wind."

Becca pursed her full lips. "If there's one thing I'm sure of in this world, it's that Gypsy Wind is not a mistake."

"What about your feelings, Rebecca? Can't you trust them?"

"About horses, yes."

"But not men?" He cocked an angry black brow.

"They're more difficult," she admitted.

He stepped back from her, leaned insolently against the railing, and crossed his arms over his chest. "They? I'm not talking about the other men in your life, Rebecca. I'm just trying to sort out how you feel about me…about what happened last night."

She drew in an unsteady breath. "That's not easy."

His eyes narrowed and the gray pupils glittered like newly forged steel. Every muscle in his body tensed. "So what you're attempting to say is that you have become the kind of woman who keeps all of her emotions under tight rein. Everything you do is well thought out in advance."

"I mean that I try not to see the world through rose-colored glasses anymore—"

He cut her off. "So you've become a bitter, calculating woman who works men into her life when it's convenient, or when she needs a favor."

It took every ounce of strength in Becca's heart to rise above the insult. "I hope not."

Again he mocked her as he continued. "The kind of woman who can hop into bed with a man as part of a business deal."

Her face flushed with anger. "Stop it, Brig. I'm not like that. You know it as well as I do."

"I don't think I know you at all. Not anymore. I was hoping that what we did last night meant something more to you than a quick one-night stand."

"It does."

"What?" he demanded. His voice was low, his eyes dangerous, his jaw determined.

"It would be easy for me to excuse what we did last night as an act of love."

"Excuse? For God's sake, woman, I'm too old for excuses!"

"Brig, what I feel for you is very strong and sometimes I delude myself into believing that I still love you," she began hesitantly. "What happened last night happened because of a set of circumstances and the fact that we care for each other—"

"Care for?" he echoed. "What the hell is that supposed to mean? 'Care for' is something you do for an elderly aunt!"

"Don't insult me, Brig. I said that I care for you. It means exactly what it implies."

Brig ran his fingers impatiently through his dark hair. Hot spurts of jealousy clouded his thinking. "Tell me this, Becca, just how many men have you *cared for* in the last six years?"

Becca's eyes flashed dangerously. "Is that what you want to know? Why don't you come straight to the point and ask me how many men I've slept with?"

"One and the same," he threw back.

"Not necessarily."

"Okay, then, how many men have you slept with?" He watched the disbelief and anger contort her even features. Wide eyes accused him of being the bastard he was. The thought of another man kissing those lips or touching her golden hair made his stomach knot.

"That's none of your business, Brig. You gave up all of those possessive rights when you threw me out of your life."

"You walked away."

Her lower lip began to tremble, but she held back her hot angry tears. "I had to, Brig. Because you thought so little of me that you honestly contended that *I* destroyed Sentimental Lady. Even with everything we had shared together, you never trusted me. In my opinion, without trust, there is no love." Her voice cracked, but she continued. "Just who the hell do you think you are? You have no right to ask me about my love life."

"I'm just *someone who cares for you*," he mocked disgustedly.

Becca felt her entire body shake. "You really can be a bastard when you want to be."

"Only when I'm pushed to the limit."

"It's reassuring to know that I bring out the best in you," she tossed out heatedly. She could feel her anger coloring her cheeks. "I think this discussion is over. We don't have much to say to each other, do we?" She pivoted on her heel and started toward the door. As quick as a springing cat, Brig was beside her. His grasp on her arm forced her to spin around and face the rage contorting his chiseled features. His lips were thin, his eyes ruthlessly dark.

"You'd like to run out on me again, wouldn't you? After all, it is what you do best."

"Let's just say that I don't like to waste my time arguing with you. There's no point to it."

"Counterproductive, is it? Not like sleeping with me?"

She slid her eyes disdainfully upward. "Let it go, Brig. We have nothing more to discuss."

Angrily, he jerked on her arm and she lost her balance. She fell against him and her hair came forward in a cloud of honey-colored silk. "I've never met a woman who could infuriate me so," Brig uttered through his clenched teeth. For the most part his anger was leveled at himself for his weakness.

Becca tossed her hair out of her resentful green eyes. "And you've met your share of them, haven't you? What about Melanie DuBois? Didn't she ever 'push you to the limit'?" The minute the jealous implication passed her lips, Becca knew she'd made a grave error in judgment. The rage in Brig's eyes took a new dimension, one of piteous disgust.

"You really know how to hit below the belt." Brig released her as if holding Becca was suddenly repulsive. She rubbed her upper arms in an effort to erase the pain he had caused.

"I'm sorry," she whispered. He had walked away from her,

putting precious space between their bodies. "I had no right to say anything about her." Becca detested anything as petty as jealousy, and she realized that her remark about the dead woman was not only childishly petulant, but also deplorable and undignified. She had to make him understand. "Brig—"

He waved off her apology with the back of his hand. "Don't worry about it." His jaw hardened and his lips thinned as he pressed his hands into the back pockets of his jeans.

"I just didn't mean to say anything that mean." Her animosity faded. "I...I don't want to argue with you and I don't want our discussions to deteriorate into a verbal battlefield, where we just try and wound each other for the sake of some shallow victory." She took a step toward him, wanting to touch him, but holding her hands at her sides.

His voice was coldly distant. "You didn't wound me, if that's what you're afraid of."

"What I'm afraid of is that I look like a hypocrite."

He arched his eyebrows, silently encouraging her to continue.

"I didn't want to discuss my...past relationships with men, and then in the next moment I brought up one of the women in your life."

He shrugged. "Forget about it."

"But I know that you and Melanie were close—"

"I was never close to that woman," he cut in sharply.

Becca was taken aback. "But I thought—"

Again he interrupted, this time more harshly. "You thought what the rest of the world thought, what Melanie DuBois wanted the world to think. If you would have had the guts to come to me before my father was killed, before your back was up against the wall, you would have realized that everything in those cheap gossip tabloids was a hoax. A carefully arranged hoax."

"You never publicly denied it."

"Isn't that a little like the pot calling the kettle black? Besides, why would I? Any statement or contradiction I might have made would only have worsened an already bad situation. I decided it just wasn't worth the effort." Brig read the look of doubt on Becca's elegant face. "I can't deny that initially I was attracted to Melanie. Hell, she was a beautiful woman. But it didn't take me long to figure out what she was really after."

Brig paused, but Becca didn't interrupt, afraid to learn more than she wanted to know about the glamorous woman romantically linked to Brig, and yet fascinated with Brig's denials. A severe smile made him appear older than his thirty-five years.

"Anything you read about Melanie DuBois was precisely engineered by Ms. DuBois and that snake she called an agent." Brig leaned more closely to Becca. He withdrew his hands from his pockets and captured her shoulders with the warmth of his fingertips. She felt the muscles in her back begin to relax. "Don't tell me you believe everything you read in the papers." His gaze was coldly cynical.

Becca cocked her head and eyed him speculatively. Her hair fell over his arm. She knew he was referring to her vehement denouncement of the press coverage of Sentimental Lady's last race. "Of course not," she whispered.

"Then trust me. I have never had anything other than a passing interest in Melanie DuBois."

Her wistful smile trembled. "I'm sorry I made that stupid remark and brought her up. It was…unkind."

Brig recognized the flicker of doubt that darkened Becca's green eyes. "You still don't believe me, do you?"

"I'm just trying to understand, Brig. If Melanie had no connection with you, why was she in the plane with your father?"

For a moment he returned her confused stare. She seemed so vulnerable, so genuinely perplexed. He brushed aside an errant strand of her blond hair, pausing only slightly to rub it gently between his fingers. "Do you want me to tell you all about Melanie?" he asked softly.

She hesitated only briefly. "No." It wouldn't be fair. Hadn't she just told him that her love life was none of his business? She had no right to his.

"What if I told you it was important to me that you know?" His eyes moved from the lock of hair he had been studying and gazed intently into hers. He pushed the golden strands back into place.

"I'd listen," she sighed.

His intense gray eyes didn't leave hers. "I met Melanie at a cocktail party in Manhattan. It was one of those sophisticated affairs which everyone dreads but still attends."

"Not exactly your cup of tea."

"That's right. But I was forced to go. Business. Melanie was there. After I'd made the proper appearance and taken care of the Chambers Oil business, I got ready to leave. Melanie came up to me and asked me to take her home. I complied."

Becca's throat became dry, but something in his gaze reassured her. A sick feeling took hold of her as she realized she didn't want to hear about the other women in Brig's life. "I understand," she murmured, hoping to close the subject.

"No, you don't."

"I don't want to hear what happened, Brig. It's your business and I don't want to know about any of your affairs."

"Yes, you do," he persisted. "The business deal had gone sour, and I was dead tired from a flight earlier from the Middle East. That night I had no interest in Melanie."

"But there were other nights."

"Not with her."

Becca shook her head. "Brig, just let it alone. The woman is dead and I don't want to hear about it. Not this morning."

"It's important, Rebecca, because I never did sleep with Melanie."

"I find that hard to believe."

"That's understandable. She was a gorgeous woman... desirable, I suppose, but I just wasn't interested."

"Why not?"

"There wasn't any chemistry between us. Do you understand that?" His fingers touched her neck, stroking the soft skin familiarly. It was a warm caress shared only by lovers.

"Yes," she admitted. How many times had she dated wonderful, kind, intelligent men and found that she felt no passion for them. It was as if she was cursed to love only Brig. Only Brig had been able to catch her soul. He looked into her eyes as if he could see into the darkest corners of her mind.

"At first I made the mistake of thinking that Melanie was all right. She was a little vain, but I chalked that up to her being a model. We dated casually, but it wasn't anything serious. The papers got wind of it and blew it out of proportion, but I really didn't care. Not until I understood what it was that Melanie really wanted."

"Which was?"

"My father." Brig let the full impact of his statement settle upon her before continuing. "As a model, Melanie was hot, starting to climb toward the pinnacle of her profession. But she wasn't getting any younger, and modeling is a young woman's game. Melanie was smart enough to realize that her career would only last a few short years at best. She liked the good life. Even with the money she earned, she was always in debt. It takes a lot of cash to keep a townhouse in New York, a condo in L.A., and a cabin in Aspen. That woman could spend money faster than the treasury department could print it."

"And so she became romantically involved with your father," Becca guessed with a sickening feeling of disgust.

"More than that. She was pressuring Dad into marrying her."

"But the press…why didn't they know? This sounds like something the gossip columnists would get wind of."

"Melanie had to be patient. Dad insisted on it." Brig looked away and squinted against the rising sun. "Patience wasn't Melanie's long suit, but she played her cards right. When she knew I wasn't interested in her, she moved in on

Dad. He was probably her target all along. Anyway, Melanie had to wait in line."

Becca understood. "Because he was involved with Nanette Walters."

Brig frowned and shook his head. "I can't for the life of me understand Jason's choice in women, not since Mom died. But there it was. And even though Nanette was just one in a long succession of women, my father cared for her." Brig's hands slid down Becca's spine and he pulled her close to him. "Jason made sure that all the women in his life were…comfortable. He gave Nanette her walking papers along with a sizable gift of jewelry."

"Why are you telling me all of this?" she asked, aware of the soft touch of his hands against the small of her back.

"I wish I knew," he admitted, kissing the top of her head.

CHAPTER SEVEN

NOTHING WAS RESOLVED, AND, FOR THE MOMENT, it didn't seem to matter. Becca accepted Brig's silent invitation to stay with him for the remainder of the weekend. Upon his suggestion, she donned her jeans and sneakers and they hiked together through the leaf-strewn trails of the lower slopes, holding hands and flushing out a frightened doe and twin fawns who quickly bounded out of sight and into the protection of the dense woods. Brig held her hand warmly in his and with the other, pointed out secret treasures from his boyhood. The abandoned tree house he had unskillfully crafted at twelve was missing more than a few of its floorboards. It looked weathered and discarded in the ancient maple tree. The bend in the path where he had discovered a broken arrowhead was now overgrown. The deep pool in the mountain stream was as crystal clear as it had ever been, though it had been twenty years since he had last caught a native trout in it or swum naked along its bank.

Becca felt that Brig was showing her a secret side to his nature. A dimension she had never before been allowed to see. It warmed her heart to think that he would share his fondest memories with her. She walked with him until her muscles ached, and they laughed into each other's eyes as if they were the only man and woman in the universe. They were alone, male and female, basking in shared affection, afraid to call their feelings love.

When twilight began to darken the hillside, they raced

back to the cabin. Becca lost by a miserable margin, and Brig's gray eyes danced with his victory. She pretended wounded anger, but he saw through her ruse and as she attempted to brush past him into the cabin, his hand shot out and captured her waist. Her head tilted backward and her golden hair fell away from her face, framing her twinkling green eyes in tousled, tawny curls. Her cheeks were pink from the cool fresh air and her lips parted into a becoming smile more sensual than any Brig had ever seen.

"You love to win, don't you?" she asked.

"I love to be with you," he responded, his eyes darkening mysteriously.

Her arms entwined around his neck. "I can't think of another place I'd rather be."

"That, Ms. Peters, is an invitation I can't ignore," he replied, tightening his grip on her waist and bending his head to mold her chilled lips to his. She closed her eyes and let the taste of him linger on her lips. She savored every moment she shared with him. Too long she had waited for the intimate pleasure of his touch.

His fingers spanned her waist to grip her possessively. His tongue slid between the serrated edges of her teeth to explore the warmth of her mouth. He groaned when the tip of her tongue found his. The pressure of his mouth against hers hardened with the passion that fired his blood.

When he lifted his head, it was to smile wickedly into her passion-glazed eyes. "Sometimes I wonder if I'll ever get enough of you," he mused against her ear.

"I hope not," she breathed fervently.

They walked into the cabin silently, arms entwined, bodies barely touching. While Brig started the fire, Becca managed to put together hodgepodge sandwiches from the dwindling supply of food in the refrigerator. Together they drank chilled wine, nibbled on the sandwiches, and warmed their bare feet near the glowing embers of the crackling fire. The tangy scent of burning pitch filled the air. Sitting on the floor, her head nestled against Brig's shoulder, Becca felt more at home than she had in years.

She watched him as he finished the last of his wine. The firelight sharpened the lines of his face, but even in the hard light, the charm of his smile was undiminished. The last six years had added a rugged quality to his masculinity. He was as lean as he had ever been and his hair was still near black with only the slightest sprinkling of gray.

He turned his gaze to her and found her staring intently at his profile. His eyelids lowered and his smile became provocative. "You're an interesting woman, Rebecca," he whispered hoarsely. With his finger he traced the line of her jaw and let it lower to the column of her neck. His finger stopped its descent at the hollow of her throat where it began drawing sketchy, lazy circles. "I'm not sure I like what you do to me."

Her eyebrows raised, prompting him onward. She couldn't find her voice, it was lost in the soft swirl of emotions generated by his feather-soft touch.

"I'm not in control when I'm around you, not in complete command of myself."

His fingers found the top button of her blouse, released it, and toyed with the edge of her collar. Becca closed her eyes and she felt her body warming from the inside out, heard the ragged sound of her uneven breathing as he unhooked another button and then another. She had to draw in her breath quickly when his hand slipped under the soft fabric of her bra to lovingly cup a breast.

"Oh, Brig," she sighed, turning her body, twisting in his arms in order to move closer to him. She felt her nipple harden, and moaned in contentment when his head lowered and he took her breast in his mouth. The soft movements of his tongue and lips comforted her and helped increase the thundering tempo of her heartbeat.

Slowly he undressed her and then when she was naked, he

discarded his own clothes. He lowered himself beside her, letting the hard length of his body mold against the soft tissues of hers. His arms wrapped around her, his hands kneaded the soft muscles in her back. "You're mine," he whispered roughly against her neck. His lips warmed a trail of hungry kisses down her throat, over the hill of her breasts, around her navel. "You've always been mine."

The possessive sound of his voice made her blood thunder in her ears and the moist warm heat from his swollen lips ignited her skin. She ached to be a part of him. The void within her yearned to be filled with the depth of his passion. She began to yield with the persuasive touch of his hands on her buttocks.

"Stay with me," he pleaded. Heavy-lidded eyes held hers in a heated gaze that promised a lifetime of love. If only she could believe those eyes.

"Forever," she whispered, pushing aside her doubts and letting herself become swept up in the tide of rising passion. She felt the weight of his body as he shifted to part her legs and claim once again what had always been his.

SUNDAY AFTERNOON CAME FAR TOO QUICKLY. Isolated in the cozy mountain cabin, Becca had felt secluded from the rest of the world. She had forced herself to forget the pain of the past and the brutal anger of her argument with Brig concerning Gypsy Wind. Now it was time to face the truth and unwrap the shielding cocoon of false security she had willingly used to cover herself from the pain of past deceits.

From her vantage point in the kitchen, she could look out the window and see Brig. He was sitting on the porch steps, gazing intently across the valley floor. He rested his elbows on his knees and cradled a cup of steaming coffee in his hands. His wavy hair was rumpled, and despite the fact that he had shaved earlier, already there was evidence of his beard darkening his hard jawline. He squinted past the rising fog and his breath misted in the crisp autumn air.

He must have heard her footsteps as she approached. Though he didn't turn his head to look in her direction, he spoke. His eyes remained distant. "You've come to tell me that it's time you left," he stated flatly.

She sat down next to him, wedging her body between his and one of the strong supports for the roof. "We can't hide up here forever." She huddled her arms around her torso. Though wearing a moss-colored bulky knit sweater, the chill in the air made her shiver.

"I suppose not." Again his voice was toneless. He took a long scalding sip of his coffee.

"It would be nice to spend the rest of our lives up here," she mused aloud while watching the flight of ducks heading southward.

"But impractical."

"And irresponsible."

His mouth quirked downward. "That's right, isn't it? We both have pressing responsibilities."

She tilted her head and studied his features. This morning he seemed suddenly cold and distant. "Is something wrong?"

"What could be wrong?"

"I don't know…but you look as if something's bothering you."

"Any guesses as to what it might be?"

Her smile faded. "Gypsy Wind."

"That's a good start." Brig's lips compressed into a tight, uncompromising line.

Becca's heart missed a beat. "What do you want to do with her?"

"Nothing."

"Nothing?" she repeated.

"I don't want you to race her, Becca. I don't want you to go through all of that pain again."

"A race doesn't have to end in pain and death."

"You're tempting fate."

"Don't tell me you believe in that nonsense. I've never thought of you as a man who put stock in fate or destiny, or whatever else you might call it."

"Not usually. But we're not dealing with a usual set of circumstances here." He set his cup down and grabbed her by the shoulders as if he intended to shake some sense into her. "Damn it, Becca. You don't have to prove anything to me or the rest of the world. There's no need to try and purge yourself of this thing."

"I'm not," she argued, her face tilted defiantly. "I'm only attempting to do what any respectable breeder would if he were in my shoes. I'm trying to race the finest filly ever bred."

"Forget it!"

Becca's anger flashed in her eyes like green lightning. Her fingers dug into her ribs. "Just what is it you expect me to do?"

The severity in his gaze faded. "I want you to hang it up," he implored. His fingers were gentle on her shoulders as he tried to persuade her. "Sell Gypsy Wind if you have to, or better yet, keep her, but for God's sake and hers, don't let her race!"

"That's crazy."

"It might be the sanest thing I've ever suggested."

"It's impossible. Gypsy Wind was bred to run."

"She was bred to absolve you of Sentimental Lady's death."

The insult stung, but she didn't let go of her emotions. "There's no point in arguing about this," she stated, attempting to rise. His hands restrained her.

"There's more." His voice was low.

More to what?"

"I want you to stay with me."

"Oh, Brig," she said, thinking of a thousand reasons to stay. "Don't do this to me. You know I want to stay with you…" Tears began to gather behind her eyes.

"But you can't?"

She shook her head painfully, thinking of Starlight Farm, her brother, Dean, and Gypsy Wind. She had worked six long,

tedious years to get where she had, with no help from Brig
Chambers. In the beauty of one quiet weekend, he expected
her to change all of that. "I've got to go home."

He struggled with a weighty decision. His eyes grew dark.
"Stay with me. Make your home with me. Be my wife."

The tears that had pooled began to spill from her eyes and
her chin trembled. "I wish I could, Brig," she said. "But it's
just not possible. You know it as well as I."

"Because of Sentimental Lady."

"Because you lied to the press. You accused me of killing
the horse—"

"I knew that you didn't intend to kill her. I never for a
moment thought that you intended to hurt her."

"You know that I didn't hurt her."

"But someone who worked for you did."

"Is that what you're doing? Trying to convince me that it
was one of the grooms…or maybe Ian O'Riley…or how
about my brother, Dean, or the vet? You know who did it, Brig.
Don't point the finger somewhere else. I might have been
gullible enough to believe you once, but not any longer."

"Becca, I'm telling you the truth. Why can't you accept that?"

His eyes were steely gray, but clear, his expression exasperated. Becca longed to trust him. She wanted to believe anything
he told her. "Maybe because you never came after me."

"Only because you didn't want to see me."

"That's a lie."

"I called, Rebecca. You refused to speak to me."

Becca shook her head, trying to dodge his insulting lies.
"You never called. Don't start lying to me, Brig. It's too hard
a habit to break."

The pressure on her arms increased. "I did call you, damn
it. I talked with your brother once and that old trainer O'Riley
a couple of times. I even talked with your cook, or housemaid,
or whatever she is."

Doubt replaced her anger. "You talked to Martha? When?"

"I can't remember exactly."

"But she's been gone for over five years."

"I spoke to her about six months after the accident," Brig replied thoughtfully. "It was the second call I'd made."

Becca drew in her breath. "No one told me that you'd phoned."

Brig's eyes narrowed suspiciously. "And that's why you didn't phone me back?"

"I couldn't very well return what I'd never received."

"Then someone—no, make that everyone in your house is lying to you."

"Or you are," she thought aloud.

His fingers carefully cupped her chin. "Why would I? What purpose would it serve? As soon as you go back to California you could check it out."

"I don't know."

"Face it, Becca. Someone is covering up. Probably the same person who drugged Sentimental Lady."

"It just doesn't make any sense. Why would anyone working with me to make Sentimental Lady a winner want to throw the race?"

Brig got up and began pacing on the weathered floorboards of the porch. He ran his fingers thoughtfully through his hair. "I don't know," he said quietly. "Unless someone had it in for you. Did anyone have an ax to grind with you? It could be something that you might think insignificant like… an argument over a raise…or the firing of a friend."

Becca rested her forehead on her palm and forced her weary mind to go backward in time, past the ugly race. It was futile. She shook her head slowly.

Brig was desperate. He came back to her and forced her eyes to meet the power of his gaze. "You've got to think, Rebecca. Someone deliberately tried to keep us apart, probably for the single reason of keeping the truth of the race secret. As long as we suspected each other, we wouldn't think past our suspicions. We wouldn't be able to find the real culprit, even if he left a trail of clues a mile long."

"But the racing commission...certainly its investigation would have discovered the truth."

"Not necessarily—not if the culprit were clever. And remember, the commission was more concerned about Sentimental Lady's recovery than the drugging. By the time all of the havoc had quieted, the culprit could have covered his tracks."

She wanted to believe him but couldn't think past the six lonely years she had spent in the shadow of that last damning race without Brig's strength or support. "I don't know," she whispered. "It all seems so farfetched."

"Not more so than your half-baked accusations that I had something to do with it!"

"But why? Why would anyone want to disqualify Lady?"

Brig closed his eyes for a moment and tried to clear his head. Nothing was making any sense. "I don't know." His eyes snapped open. "But you must. Think, Rebecca, think!"

"I have, Brig. For the past six years I've hardly thought of anything else. And the only logical answer to the question of who injured Sentimental Lady was you."

"But you don't believe that anymore, do you?"

Her smile was thin. "I don't know what to believe. But if it's any consolation, I never wanted to think that you had anything to do with it."

"But you still have doubts."

She looked bravely into his eyes. "No."

For the first time that morning, the hint of a smile lightened his features. He took her into his arms, and held her body close to his. The power of his embrace supported her. "Then you'll stay with me?"

"Not yet," she said, dreading the sound of her own voice.

The arms around her relaxed and Brig stepped away from her. "Sometimes I don't think I know what you want, lady, but I assume this has something to do with your filly. You still

intend to race her, don't you, despite what happened to Sentimental Lady."

"I have to." Couldn't Brig understand? Gypsy Wind had
more than mere potential for winning races—she was a
champion. Becca would risk her reputation on it.

"No one's holding a gun to your head."

Becca put her hands on her hips and tried a different
approach. "Why don't you come to the farm and see first
hand what it is that makes Gypsy so special? Come and watch
her work out. See for yourself her power, the grace of her
movements, the exhilaration in her eyes when she's given her
head. Don't judge her before you've seen her."

Brig tossed the idea over in his mind. His work schedule
was impossible. He had no time for horses or horse racing.
He'd ended that folly six years ago. But Rebecca Peters was
another thing altogether. He wanted her. More than he had
wanted her six years ago. More than he had ever wanted
anything. He saw the look of pride on her face and he noticed
the defiant way she stood as if ready to refute anything he
might say. Thoughtfully, he rubbed his thumb slowly under
his jaw. "What if I disagree with you?"

"You won't." Becca wondered if she looked as determined
as she sounded.

Brig cocked his head but didn't argue. "If I do decide to
go to California and I think that Gypsy Wind is unsound, will
you promise not to race her and give up this foolish dream?"

"Not on your life." Her eyes glittered with fierce determination.

"And you're not afraid that someone might do to her what
was done to Sentimental Lady."

"I've been racing horses ever since Sentimental Lady's
death. The incident hasn't recurred."

Brig's voice was edged in steel. "Then I guess we're at
an impasse."

"Only if you want to be." Her hand reached out and her

fingers touched his arm. "Don't shut me out, Brig. Not now. I don't think I'm asking too much of you. Please come and see my horse. Reserve your judgment until then. If you think she's not as fine as I've been telling you, we'll work something out."

"Such as?"

"I'll find a way to repay your loan within the year. Is that fair?"

"I suppose so. Now, what about my proposition? Will you marry me?"

"Give it time, Brig. We both need time to learn to love and trust each other again. Six years is a long time to harbor the kinds of feelings we've had for each other. You can't wash them away in one weekend in the mountains."

"Nor can you prove to the world that you're one of the best Thoroughbred breeders in the country. I was wrong about you, Rebecca. You haven't changed at all. You're still giving me the same flimsy excuse you did the last time I asked you to marry me. I'm not a man who's known for his patience, nor am I the kind of man who gets a kick out of rejection. I've asked you twice to marry me, and I won't do it again."

Becca struggled with her pride. When she spoke her voice was strangely detached and the words of reason seemed distant. "I didn't come to you to try and coerce a marriage proposal from you, Brig, nor did I intend to have another affair with you. All I wanted was to know that you were safe and to tell you about Gypsy Wind. I've done those things and I've also told you that I intend to repay my note to your father. Business is done. My plane leaves in less than four hours from Denver. I have to go."

His face was a mask of indifference. "Just remember that you made your own choices today. You're the one who will have to live with them."

CHAPTER EIGHT

THE TRIP BACK TO STARLIGHT BREEDING FARM was uneventful, and Becca had to force herself to face the realization that she had no future with Brig Chambers. If ever she had, it was gone. She had thrown it away. Becca knew that Brig cared for her, in his own way, but she also knew that he didn't trust her and probably never would. The best thing to do was to forget about him and concentrate on paying back the debt to him as quickly as possible. She frowned to herself as she unpacked her suitcase. Forgetting about Brig and what they had shared together was more easily said than done. In the last six years she had never once forgotten the tender way in which he would look into her eyes, or his gentle caress.

"Cut it out," she mumbled to herself. The last thing she should do was brood over a future that wasn't meant to be. With forced determination, she pulled on her favorite pair of faded jeans and started toward the paddock. The first order of business was Gypsy Wind.

Becca clenched her teeth together as she thought about training Gypsy Wind to be the best Thoroughbred filly ever raced. She may have already made a monumental mistake by not racing the filly as a two-year-old, and if she were honest with herself it had something to do with Brig and the fact that, at the time, he didn't know about Gypsy Wind. At least the secret was now in the open, and Becca vowed silently to herself that she would find a way to make Gypsy Wind a winner with or without Brig's approval.

She found Ian O'Riley in the tack room. His short fingers were running along the smooth leather reins of a bridle last worn by Sentimental Lady. He turned his attention toward the door when Becca entered.

"I heard you were back," he said with a smile.

"Just got in a couple of hours ago."

Ian's smile faded. "And how did it go…with Brig, I mean?"

Becca tossed her blond braid over her shoulder and shrugged. "As well as can be expected, I guess." She took a seat on a scarred wooden chair near the trophy case. The award closest to her was now covered with dust, but Becca recognized it as belonging to Sentimental Lady for her record-breaking win of The New York Racing Association's Acorn Stakes. Absently, Becca rubbed the dust off the trophy.

"What does he think of Gypsy Wind?"

"Not much," Becca admitted. "Oh, Ian, he thinks I was foolish to breed her. He accused me of trying to absolve myself of her death."

"He thinks that's why you did it?"

Becca nodded mutely.

"And he's got you believing it, too."

Becca shook her head and put the trophy back in the case. "No, of course not, but he did make me question my motives. He even suggested that I didn't race her as a two-year-old because I was afraid of his reaction."

"Nonsense!" Ian's wise blue eyes sparked dangerously. "He knows better than that—or at least he should! Sentimental Lady's legs weren't strong enough, and I'm not about to make the same mistake with Gypsy Wind. That's the trouble with this country! In Europe many Thoroughbreds never set foot on a racetrack until they're three. And when they do, they run on firm but yielding turf.

"Gypsy Wind's legs won't be fully ossified until she's three, and I'm not about to ask her to sprint over a hard, fast track. It's a good way to ruin a damned fine filly!"

Becca smiled at the wiry man's vehemence. "I agree with you."

Ian's gray eyebrows raised. "I know…and I'm proud of you for it. It would have been easier to run her this year and make a little extra money. I know you could use it."

"Not if it hurts Gypsy Wind."

Ian's grizzled face widened into a comfortable grin. He winked at Becca fondly. "We'll show them all, you know. Come early next year, when Gypsy Wind begins to race, we'll have ourselves a champion."

"We already do," Becca pointed out.

"Have you given any thought to moving her to Sequoia Park?"

The smile left Becca's face and she blanched. "I was hoping that we could keep her somewhere else."

Ian put a gentle hand on her shoulder. "It holds bad memories for me, too, Becca. But it's the closest to the farm and has the best facilities around. I thought we would start her in a few short races locally before we headed down the state and eventually back East."

"You're right, of course. When would you want to move her?"

"Soon—say, right after the holidays."

Becca felt her uncertainty mount, but denied her fears. "You're the trainer. Whatever you say goes."

Ian paused and shifted the piece of straw that was forever in his mouth, a habit he'd acquired since he'd given up cigarettes. "I appreciate that, gal. Not many owners would have stood up for a trainer the way that you did."

It was Becca's turn to be comforting. "Don't be ridiculous. We've been over this a hundred times before. You and I both know that you had nothing to do with what happened to Sentimental Lady. I never doubted it for a minute."

"She was my responsibility."

"And you did everything you could do to protect her."

His wizened blue eyes seemed suddenly old. "It wasn't enough, was it?"

"It's over, Ian. Forget it."

"Can you?"

Becca smiled sadly. "Of course not. But I do try not to brood about it." She stared pointedly at the bridle Ian held in his gnarled hands. "Is there something else that's bothering you?" It wasn't like Ian to be melancholy or to second-guess himself.

Ian shook his gray head.

"How did the workout go this morning?" Becca asked, changing the subject and hoping to lighten the mood of the conversation.

Ian managed a bemused smile. "Gypsy Wind really outdid herself. She wanted to run the entire distance."

"Just like Lady," Becca observed.

"Yeah." Ian replaced the bridle on a rusty hook near a yellowed picture of Sentimental Lady. He stared wistfully at the black-and-white photograph of the proud filly. "They're a lot alike," he mumbled to himself as he turned toward the door. "Got to run now, the missus doesn't like me late for supper."

"Ian—"

His hand paused over the door handle and he rotated his body so that he could once again face Becca.

"After the race at Sequoia…"

Ian pulled his broad-billed cap over his head and nodded to encourage Becca to continue.

Becca's voice was less bold than it had been and her cheeks appeared pinker. "After all the hubbub had died down about the horse, did you ever take a call from Brig…a call for me that you never told me about?"

Ian's lips pursed into a frown. "He told you about that, did he?" Ian asked, pulling himself up to his full fifty-four inches. "I figured he would, should have expected it." Ian rubbed the silver stubble on his chin. "Yeah, Missy, he called, more than once if I remember correctly."

"Why didn't you tell me?"

Ian leaned against the door and had trouble meeting Becca's searching gaze. "We thought about it," he admitted.

"We?"

"Yeah, Martha, Dean, and I. We considered it, talked a lot about it. More than you might guess. But Dean, well, he insisted that we shouldn't bother you about the fact that Brig kept calling—said that after all you'd been through, you didn't need to talk to him and start the trouble all over again." Ian shifted his weight from one foot to the other.

"Someone should have asked me."

Ian nodded his agreement. "That's what Martha and I thought, but Dean disagreed. He was absolutely certain that anything Brig might say to you would only…well, open old wounds."

Becca lifted her chin. "I was old enough to care for myself."

The old man flushed with embarrassment. "I know, Missy. I know that now, but at the time we were all a little shaken up. Martha and I, we never felt comfortable about it."

"Is that why Martha quit so suddenly?"

Ian's faded eyes darkened. "I don't rightly know." He considered her question. "Maybe it helped her with her decision to move in with her daughter. Leastwise, it didn't hurt."

"Did Dean speak with Brig?" Cold suspicion prompted her question.

Ian thought for a moment and then shrugged his bowed shoulders. "I can't say for certain—it's been a long time. No, wait. He must have, 'cause right after he told me he'd taken care of Brig, we didn't get any more calls."

"How many calls were there?" Becca's heart was thudding expectantly. Brig hadn't lied.

"Can't recall. Four—maybe five. Dean was afraid you might take one yourself."

"So he told me not to answer the phone, in order that he could 'protect' me from nosy reporters," she finished for him.

"Is that what he told you?"

Becca nodded, her thoughts swimming. Why would Dean lie to her? "So Dean was the one who made the final decision."

"Yeah. Martha and I, we agreed with him."

"Why?"

"He was only looking after you…" His statement was nearly an apology.

"I know," Becca sighed, trying to set the old man's mind at ease. "It's all right."

Ian gave her an affectionate smile before leaving the tack room and shutting the door behind him. Becca bit at her lower lip and stared sightlessly into the trophy case. Why would Dean hide the fact that Brig had called?

Swallowing back the sense of betrayal that was rising in her throat, she tried to give her brother the benefit of the doubt. Surely he had only wanted to protect her, in his own misguided manner. But that had been six years ago. With the passage of time, Becca would have expected him to tell her about the calls. Why not tell her after the shock of the race had worn off? Was he afraid she would relapse into her depression? For a fraction of a second Becca wondered if there were other things that Dean had hidden from her. Was he responsible for the money missing from petty cash? And what about the roofing contractor he had suggested, the bum who had run off with her down payment for a new roof on the stables.

"Stop it," she chided herself. She was becoming paranoid. Though she didn't understand her brother at times, she couldn't forget that he had been the one who had helped her put her life back together when it had been shattered into a thousand pieces six years ago at Sequoia Park.

Still troubled about the fact that Dean had purposely lied to her, Becca left the tack room and tossed aside the fears that were beginning to take hold of her. She made her way upstairs to the office and tried to concentrate on the books. Though she had been gone for little over three days, she knew that the bookkeeping would be far behind, as it was near the end of the month. It was time to start organizing the journal entries for month-end posting. She opened the checkbook and realized that several checks were missing. What was happening? No entries had been made for the missing checks. A new fear began to take hold of her. Was someone at the farm stealing from her? But the checks were worthless without a proper signature: Rebecca's or Dean's.

"Dear God, no," she whispered as the weight of her discovery hit her with the force of a tidal wave. She sat down at the desk, her legs suddenly too weak to support her.

The sound of a pickup roaring down the drive met her ears. She recognized it as belonging to Dean. She waited. It wasn't long before his boots clamored up the stairs and he burst into the room, smelling like a brewery and slightly unsteady on his feet. His boyish grin was slightly lopsided.

Becca thought he looked nervous, but mentally told herself that she was just imagining his anxiety.

"Hi, sis. How was the flight?" he asked casually as he popped the tab on a cold can of beer, took a long swallow, and dropped onto the ripped couch.

"Tiresome, but on schedule," she replied, watching him with new eyes. He settled into the couch, propped the heels of his boots against the corner of the desk, and let his Stetson fall forward. Balancing the can precariously on his stomach between his outstretched fingers, he looked as if he might fall asleep.

His voice was slightly muffled. "And good ole Brig, how was he?"

Becca hesitated only slightly, carefully gauging her brother's reaction. His eyes were shadowed by the hat, but there appeared to be more than idle interest in his gaze. Becca supposed that was to be expected, considering the situation. "Brig was fine."

Her noncommittal response didn't satisfy Dean. "And I suppose you told him about the horse," he said sarcastically.

"You know I did."

His boots hit the floor with a thud, and beer slopped onto his shirt before he could grab the can. He stood to his full height and looked down upon her with his ruddy face contorted in rage. "Goddamn it, Becca! I knew it! You didn't listen to one word of advice I gave you, did you? I don't know what the hell's gotten into you lately!"

"Precisely what I was thinking about you," she snapped back.

"I'm only trying to look out for your best interests," he proclaimed.

"Are you?"

"You know I am." He took another swallow from the beer, but it didn't begin to cool the anger in his steely-blue eyes. He shook his head as if to dislodge a bothersome thought. "I knew it," he said, swearing under his breath. "Damn it! I knew that if I let you go to Denver you'd come back here with your mind all turned around."

"If you let me?" she echoed. "I can make my own decisions, Dean, and there's nothing wrong with my mind!"

"Except that you can't think straight whenever you're near Brig Chambers!"

"You and I agreed that Brig had to know about the horse—there was no other way around it."

"We didn't agree to anything. You went running off to Denver with any flimsy excuse to look up Brig again."

"And you decided to tie one on, after taking a few checks from the checkbook."

For a moment Dean was stopped short. Then, with a growl, he dug into his pockets and threw two crumpled checks onto the desk. "I was a little short—"

"Where's the other check?"

"I cashed it. Okay? So sue me!"

"That's not the point."

"Then what is, sis? And what happened while you were in Denver? Unless I miss my guess, you started to fall in love all over again with that miserable son of a bitch, and then he threw you out on your ear."

Becca rose from the desk. She had to fight to keep her voice from shaking as badly as her hands. "That's not what happened." Her green eyes deepened with her anger.

"Close enough." Dean took a final swallow of beer and drained the can before he crushed it in his fist. "So what did he tell you to do—sell the horse?" Dean's knowing blue gaze bored into Becca's angry emerald eyes.

"We considered several alternatives."

"I'll just bet you did," Dean agreed with a disbelieving smirk.

Becca swallowed back the hot retort that hovered on the end of her tongue. Trading verbal knife wounds with her brother would get her nowhere. "I've decided to keep the horse. I told Brig that we'd pay him back within the year."

"Are you out of your mind? Fifty grand plus interest?" Dean was astounded. "That'll be impossible! Even if Gypsy Wind wins right off the bat, it takes a bundle just to cover her costs. You're going to have to stable her at a track, hire an entire crew, enter her in the events—it will cost us a small fortune."

"She's worth it, Dean."

"How in the world do you think you can pay off Chambers?"

"She'll win."

"Oh God, Becca. Why gamble? Take my advice and sell her!"

"To whom?"

"*Anyone!* Surely someone's interested. You should have listened to me and sold her at Keeneland when she was a yearling. It's going to be a lot tougher now that she's racing age and hasn't even bothered to start!"

"And you know why," Becca charged.

"Because you didn't have the guts to let Brig Chambers know about the horse, that's why. I don't know how you've managed to keep so quiet about her, or why you'd want to.

The more you build her up to the press, compare her to Sentimental Lady, the more she's worth!"

Becca's thin patience frayed. "I didn't run her as a two-year-old to avoid injuring her. As for hype about a horse, it's highly overrated. Any owner worth his salt judges an animal by the horse itself—not some press release."

"I don't understand why you're all bent out of shape about it," Dean announced as he threw the twisted empty can into a nearby trash basket.

"And I don't understand why you insist on trying to run my life!"

Dean's flushed face tensed. "Because you need me—or have you forgotten?" He paused for a moment and his face relaxed. "At least, you used to need me. Has that changed?"

"I don't know," she said. "I...I just don't like fighting with you. It seems that lately we're at opposite ends of any argument." Despite the tension in the room, she managed to smile. "But you're right about one thing," she conceded. "I did need you and you were there for me. I appreciate that, Dean, and I owe you for it."

"But," he coaxed, reading the puzzled expression on her face and knowing intuitively that she wasn't finished.

"But I don't understand why you didn't tell me about Brig and why you hid the fact that he called me several times."

Dean seemed to pale beneath his California tan. "So he told you about that, did he?"

"And Ian explained what happened."

A startled look darkened his pale eyes but swiftly disappeared. His thin lips pressed into a disgusted line. "Then you realize that I was just trying to protect you."

"From what?"

"*From Chambers!* Becca, look. You've never been able to face the fact that he used you." Becca started to interrupt, but Dean held her words at bay by raising his outstretched fingers. "It's true, damn it. That man can hurt you like nobody else. I don't know what it is about him that turns a rational woman like you into a simpering fool, but he certainly has the touch. He used you in the past, and if you give him another chance, he'll do it again. I don't think he can stop himself, it's inbred in his nature."

"You're being unfair."

"And you're hiding your head in the sand."

Becca ran her fingers through her hair, unfastening the thong which held it tied and letting it fall into loose curls to surround her face. She thought back to the warm moments of love with Brig and the happiness they had shared in the snow-capped Rockies; the passion, the tenderness, the yearning, the pain. Was it only for one short weekend in her life? Was she destined to forever love a man who couldn't return that love? Could Dean be right? Had Brig used her? "No," she whispered shakily, trying to convince herself as much as her brother. "I can't believe that Brig ever used me, or that he ever intentionally hurt me."

"Come off it, Becca!"

"That's the way I see it."

Dean's eyes were earnest, his jaw determined. "And you live with your head in the clouds when it comes to horses and men. You dream of horses that run wild and free and you try to turn men into heroes who bare their souls for the love of a woman—at least, you do in the case of Brig Chambers."

"Now you're trying to stereotype me," she accused.

"Think about it, sis." Dean gave her a knowing smile before striding toward the door.

Becca couldn't let him go until he answered one last nagging question that had been with her ever since she had spoken with Ian in the tack room. "Dean, why did Martha leave the ranch when she did?"

Dean's hand paused over the doorknob. He whirled around to face his sister, his eyes narrowed. "What do you mean?"

"I mean that she left rather suddenly, don't you think? And

it's odd that I haven't heard from her since. Not even a card at Christmas. It's always bothered me."

Dean's face froze into a well-practiced smile. "Didn't she say that she left because her daughter needed her?"

"That's what you told me."

"But you don't think that's the reason?" Dean asked, coolly avoiding her penetrating gaze. How close to the truth was she? He was unnerved, but he tried his best not to let it show. Becca was becoming suspicious—all because of Brig Chambers!

"I just wondered if it had anything to do with Brig's phone calls," Becca replied. The tension in the room made it seem stuffy.

"I doubt it, Becca. Martha's kid was sick."

"The eighteen-year-old girl?"

"Right. Uh, Martha went to live with her and that's the end of the story. Maybe she's just too busy to write."

"I don't even know where they moved, do you?"

"No." Dean's voice was brittle. "Look, I've got to run— see you later." Dean pushed open the door and hurried down the stairs. He seemed to be relieved to get out of the office and away from Becca.

An uneasy feeling of suspicion weighed heavily on Becca's mind. She worked long into the evening, but couldn't shake the annoying doubts that plagued her. Why did she have the feeling that Dean wasn't telling her everything? What could he possibly be hiding? Was it, as he so emphatically asserted, that he was interested only in protecting her? Or was there more…

BRIG SAT AT HIS DESK AND EYED THE LATEST stack of correspondence from the estate attorneys with disgust. It seemed that every day they came up with more questions for him and his staff. The accident which had taken his father's life had happened more than a month ago, and yet Brig had the disquieting feeling that the Last Will and Testament of Jason

Chambers was as far from being settled as it had ever been. He tossed the papers aside and rose from the desk.

Behind him, through the large plate-glass window the city of Denver spread until it reached the rugged backdrop of the bold Colorado Rockies. Brig hazarded a glance out the window and into the dusk, but neither the bustling city nor the cathedral peaks held any interest for him. No matter how he tried, he couldn't seem to take his mind off Rebecca Peters and that last weekend they had spent together.

The smoked-glass door to the office opened and Mona, Brig's secretary, entered. "I'm going down to the cafeteria—can I get you anything?" Brig shook his head and managed a tired smile. "How about a cup of coffee?"

"I don't think so."

Mona raised her perfect eyebrows. "It could be a long night. Emery called. He seems to think that the wildcat strike in Wyoming won't be settled for at least a week."

"Arbitration isn't working?"

"Apparently not."

"Great," Brig muttered. "Just what we need."

Mona closed the door softly behind her and leaned against it. She ran nervous fingers over her neatly styled silver hair. She was only thirty-five; the color of her hair was by choice. "Is something bothering you?" she asked, genuinely concerned.

"What do you think?"

"I think you're overworked."

Brig laughed despite himself. Mona had a way of cutting to the core of a problem. "I can't disagree with that."

"Then why don't you take some time off?" she suggested. "Or at least take a working vacation and spend some time in your father's cabin." She watched him carefully; he seemed to tense.

"I can't do that. It's impossible."

"I could route all the important calls to you."

"Out of the question," he snapped.

Mona pursed her lips, stung by his hot retort. It wasn't like him. But then, he wasn't himself lately. Not since that weekend he spent alone. Maybe the strain of his father's death affected him more deeply than he admitted. "It was just a suggestion."

"I know it was, Mona," he admitted, and his shoulders slumped. "I didn't mean to shout at you."

"Still, I do think you should consider taking some time off."

"When?"

"As soon as possible—before you really chop somebody's head off."

"Do you think you can handle this office without me?"

She winked slyly at him. "What do you think?"

"I *know* you can."

"I'll remember that the next time I ask for a raise. Now, have you reconsidered my offer—how about some coffee?"

Brig's face broke into an affable grin. "If you insist."

"Well, while I'm still batting a thousand, I really do think you should take a couple of days off. Believe me, this place won't fall apart without you."

"I suppose not," Brig conceded as the pert secretary slipped out of his office and headed for the cafeteria.

Mona had a point. Brig knew he was tense and that his temper was shorter than usual. Maybe it was because he found it nearly impossible to concentrate on his position. The glass-topped desk was littered with work that didn't interest him. Even the wildcat strike in Wyoming seemed grossly unimportant. Chambers Oil was one of the largest oil companies in the United States, with drilling rights throughout the continental U.S. and Alaska. That didn't begin to include the offshore drilling. Who the hell cared about oil in Wyoming? As far as he was concerned, Chambers Oil could write off the entire venture as a tax loss.

Brig rotated his shoulders and tried to smooth away the tension in his neck and back. Who was he kidding? It wasn't his father's estate that kept him awake at nights. Nor was it the strike in Wyoming, or any of the other nagging problems that came with the responsibility of running Chambers Oil. The problem was Rebecca Peters. It always had been, and he didn't doubt for a moment that it always would be.

Though he went through the day-to-day routine of managing his father's company, he couldn't forget the pained look in Rebecca's misty green eyes when he had accused her once again of knowing who drugged Sentimental Lady. Her violent reaction to his charge and her vicious attack against him, claiming that it was he rather than she who had been involved in the crime, was ludicrous. But it still planted a seed of doubt in his mind.

Brig tucked his hands into his back pockets and looked down the twenty-eight floors to the streets of Denver. Was it possible that Becca didn't know her horse had been drugged? Had he been wrong, blinded by evidence that was inaccurate? Even the racing board could level no blame for the crime. Ian O'Riley's reputation as a trainer might have been blemished for carelessness, but the man wasn't found guilty of the act of stimulating the horse artificially.

As he stared, unseeing, out the window he thought about Becca and her initial reaction to the race. She had been afraid and in a turmoil of anguished emotions. He could still hear her pained cries.

"It's all my fault," Becca had screamed, "all mine." Brig had dragged her away from the terror-stricken filly, holding the woman he loved in a binding grip that kept her arms immobilized. Becca had lost a shoe on the track. He hadn't bothered to pick it up.

Could he have misread her self-proclaimed guilt? Could her cries have erupted from the hysteria taking hold of her? Or was it an honest acceptance of blame, only to be denounced when she had finally calmed down and perceived the extent of the crime? He had always known that she would never intentionally hurt her horse; cruelty wasn't a part of

Rebecca's nature. But he hadn't doubted that she was covering up for the culprit. Now he wasn't so sure.

Rubbing his temples as if he could erase the painful memory, he sat down at the desk. There was a soft knock on the door and Mona entered with a steaming cup of coffee.

"Just what the doctor ordered," she chirped as she handed it to her boss.

"What did I do to deserve you?" Brig asked gratefully.

She winked slyly. "Inherited an oil fortune."

Brig took a sip from the steaming mug and smiled fondly at his father's secretary. He had inherited Mona along with the rest of the wealthy trappings of Chambers Oil. "You were right, Mona, I needed this." He held up his cup.

"Was there any doubt?" she quipped before her eyes became somber with genuine concern. She liked Brig Chambers, always had, and she could see that something was eating at him. "I'm right about the fact that you need a vacation, too," she observed.

"I'm not denying it."

"Then promise me that you'll take one."

Brig cracked a smile. "All right, you win. I promise, just as soon as I can get the estate attorneys and tax auditors off my back *and* we somehow settle the strike in Wyoming."

"Good." Mona returned Brig's grin. "I'll keep my fingers crossed," she stated as she walked out of the office.

CHAPTER NINE

THE FIRST BREAK CAME THREE WEEKS LATER. The autumn season had settled in and Brig wondered if the promise of winter had cooled the angry tempers in Wyoming. Whatever the reason, the wildcat strike had been resolved, if only temporarily, and although anger still flared on both sides of the picket line, it seemed that most of the arguments and threats of violence had been settled.

As for his father's estate, it was finally in the lengthy legal process known as probate. Brig and the rest of the staff of Chambers Oil had given the tax attorneys every scrap of information they could find concerning Jason Chambers' vast financial holdings. Brig had reluctantly included the stack of personal notes and receipts he had found in his father's locked desk drawer. Brig had to suppress a wicked grin of satisfaction as he handed the private papers to the young tax attorney and the nervous man's face frowned in disbelief at the unrecorded transactions.

The only intentional omission was the note signed by Rebecca Peters. Brig had substituted it with one of his own in the amount of fifty thousand dollars. He considered the original note to Jason as his personal business. It had nothing to do with the old man's estate. This was one matter which only involved Rebecca and himself.

It had been difficult to concentrate on running the oil company the past few weeks. The mundane tasks had been impossible as his wayward thoughts continued to revolve around Rebecca Peters. He couldn't get her out of his mind, and cursed himself as a fool for his infatuation. In the last six years he had thought himself rid of her, that he had finally expunged her from his mind and soul. One weekend in the Rockies had changed all of that, and he couldn't forget a moment of the quiet solitude at the cabin near Devil's Creek. To add insult to injury, he began picking up horse-racing magazines, hoping to see her name in print and catch a glimpse of her. He was disappointed. He found no mention of a two-year-old filly named Gypsy Wind, nor of the entrancing woman who owned her.

When the call came through that the strike was settled, Brig didn't hesitate. He was certain that his man in Wyoming could handle the tense situation in the oil fields and he knew that Mona was able to run the company with or without him for a few days. He took the secretary's advice and made hurried arrangements to fly to San Francisco. After two vain attempts to reach Becca by phone, he gave up and found some satisfaction in the fact that he would arrive on her doorstep as unexpectedly as she had on his only a few short weeks ago.

Without taking the time to consider his motives, he drove home, showered, changed, and threw a few clothes into a lightweight suitcase. After a quick glance around his apartment, he tossed his tweed sports jacket over his shoulder and called a cab to take him to the airport. He didn't want to waste any time. He was afraid his common sense might take over and he would cancel his plans. He kept in motion so as not to think about the consequences of his unannounced journey.

Ominous gray clouds darkened the sky over the buildings of Starlight Breeding Farm. It hadn't changed much since the last time Brig had visited. A quick glance at the buildings told him that only the most critically needed repairs had been completed in the last six years. All in all, the grounds were in sad shape. Brig had to grit his teeth together when he noticed the chipped paint on the two-storied farmhouse and the broken hinge on the gate. With a knowledgeable eye, he surveyed the stables. It seemed as if the whitewashed barns were in better shape than the living quarters, a tribute to Rebecca's sense of priority. A windmill supporting several broken blades groaned painfully against a sudden rush of air blowing down the valley. Brittle dry leaves danced in the wind before fluttering to rest against the weathered boards of a sagging wooden fence.

It was glaringly apparent that because of Sentimental Lady's short racing career and the fact that Rebecca hadn't owned another decent Thoroughbred, she wasn't able to make enough money to run the farm properly. That much was evidenced in the overgrown shrubbery, the rusted gutters, and the sagging roofline of the house. It would take a great deal of cash to get the buildings back into shape, money Rebecca was sadly lacking. It was no wonder she had been forced to go to Jason for a loan. No banker in his right mind would loan money to a has-been horse breeder with only a run-down breeding farm as collateral. Guilt, like a razor-sharp blade, twisted in his conscience.

Brig made his way up the uneven steps of the porch and knocked soundly on the door. His face was set in a grim mask of determination. No matter what had happened between himself and Rebecca, he couldn't allow her to live like this! No one answered his knock. He pressed the doorbell and wasn't surprised when he didn't hear the sound of a chime inside the house. After one last loud knock, he turned toward the stables. Several vehicles parked near the barns indicated that someone had to be on the property.

Rather than explore the stables, he decided to walk through the familiar maze of paddocks surrounding the barns. The first paddock had once held broodmares. Today it was empty. With the exception of a few animals, the paddocks were vacant. The last time Brig had walked through these gates, the stables had been filled to capacity with exceptional Thoroughbreds. But many of the horses were only boarded at Becca's farm, and when the scandal over Sentimental Lady had cast doubt on Becca's reputation, most of the animals were removed by conscientious owners.

Becca had never recaptured her reputation as being a responsible, successful horse breeder. A muscle in the corner of Brig's jaw worked and his eyes darkened as he wondered how much of Rebecca's misfortune was his fault. Had he truly, as she had once claimed, destroyed her reputation and her business with his unfounded accusations? How much of her burden was his?

Unconsciously he walked toward the most removed pasture, a corner paddock with the single sequoia standing guard over it. That particular field, with its lush grass and slightly raised view of the rest of the farm, had been Sentimental Lady's home when she hadn't been on the racing circuit.

As Brig neared the paddock he stopped dead in his tracks, barely believing what he saw. The first drops of rain had begun to fall from the darkened sky, but it wasn't the cool water that chilled his blood or made him curse silently to himself. Color drained from his face as he watched the coffee-colored horse lift her black tail and run the length of the far fence. She stopped at the corner, impeded in her efforts to run from the stranger. She stood as far from Brig as was possible, flattened her ebony ears against her head, and snorted disdainfully.

"Sentimental Lady," Brig whispered to himself, leaning against the top rail of the fence and watching the frightened horse intently. "I'll be damned." There was no doubt in his mind that this horse was Gypsy Wind.

He ran an appreciative eye from her shoulders to her tail. She was a near-perfect Thoroughbred, almost a carbon copy of Sentimental Lady. For a fleeting moment Brig thought the two horses were identical, but slowly, as his expert gaze traveled over the horse, he noted the differences. The most obvious was the lack of white markings on Gypsy Wind. Sentimental Lady had been marked with an offcenter star; this dark filly bore none. But that wasn't important, at least not to Brig. Coloring didn't make the horse.

The most impressive dissimilarity between the two animals was the slight variation in build and body structure. Both horses were barrel-chested, but Gypsy Wind seemed to be slightly shorter than her sister and her long legs appeared heavier. That didn't necessarily mean that Gypsy Wind's legs were stronger, but Brig hoped they were for the nervous filly's sake.

The shower increased and Brig wondered why Becca would allow her Thoroughbred to stand unattended in the autumn rain. It wasn't like Becca. She had always been meticulous in her care of Thoroughbreds, a careful breeder cautious for her horses' health. That was what had puzzled Brig and it made it difficult for him to believe that Becca was responsible for harming Sentimental Lady…unless she was protecting someone.

Slowly moving along the fence so as not to startle the horse, Brig called to her. She eyed him nervously as he approached. With the same high spirit as her sister, Gypsy Wind tossed her intelligent head and stamped her right foreleg impatiently. *Just like Lady.* The resemblance between the two horses was eerie. Brig felt his stomach knot in apprehension. He couldn't help but remember the last time he had seen Sentimental Lady alive. It was a nightmare that still set his teeth on edge. He remembered it as clearly as if it had just happened.

Sentimental Lady had virtually been lifted into her stall by Ian O'Riley and his assistants. She tried to lie down, but was forced to stay on her feet by a team of four veterinarians. A horse resting on its side for too long might develop paralysis.

Her pain was deadened with ice while the chief veterinarian managed to sedate the frantic animal. She was led to the operating room where she nearly died, but was kept alive by artificial respiration and stimulants. Brig concentrated on the slow expansion and contraction of her chest. He and Rebecca had agreed with the veterinarians. They had no choice but to operate because of the contamination in the dirt-filled wound. Though the anxious horse needed no further trauma, there were no other options to save her.

Brig watched in silent horror as the veterinarian removed the fragments of chipped bone and tried to repair the severely torn ligaments. After flushing the wound with antibiotics and saline solutions, drains were inserted in the leg. Finally an orthopedist fit a special shoe and cast onto Sentimental Lady's damaged foreleg. At that moment, the operation appeared to be successful.

The agonizing minutes ticked by as Sentimental Lady was eased out of anesthesia. When she regained control of her body she awoke in a frenzy. She struck out and knocked down the veterinarian who was with her. As her hoof kicked against the side of the stall, she broke off her specially constructed shoe. Within minutes, while Ian tried vainly to calm her, the flailing horse had torn her cast to shreds and her hemorrhaging and swelling had increased. Blood splattered against the sides of the stall.

"It's no use," Ian had told Brig. "She was too excited from the race and the pain—they'll never be able to control her again. It's her damned temperament that's killing her!" He turned back to the horse. "Slow down, Lady! Slow down." For his efforts he was rewarded with a kick in the leg.

"Get him out of there!" the veterinarian ordered, and Dean helped Ian from the stall. "I don't think there's anything we can do for her."

The options had run out. All four veterinarians agreed that Sentimental Lady couldn't withstand another operation. Even if she were stable, it would be difficult. In her current state of frenzied pain, it was impossible. An artificial limb was out of the question, as was a supportive sling: Sentimental Lady's high-strung temperament wouldn't allow her to convalesce.

Brig walked back to the waiting room where Rebecca sat with Martha. Her green eyes were shadowed in silent agony as she waited for the prognosis on her horse. Brig took one of her hands in his as he explained the options to Rebecca. Her small shoulders slumped and tears pooled in her eyes.

"But she's so beautiful," she murmured, letting the tears run down her cheeks to fall on the shoulders of her blood-stained linen suit. "It can't be…"

"This is your decision," he said quietly. Martha put a steadying arm over Becca's shoulders.

"I want to see her." Becca rose and walked hesitantly to the other room, where she could observe Lady. One look at the terrified horse and the splintered cast confirmed Brig's tragic opinion. "I can't let her suffer anymore," Becca whispered, closing her eyes against the terrible scene. She lowered her head and in a small voice that was barely audible repeated, "It's all my fault…"

Sentimental Lady's death had been the beginning of the end for Rebecca and Brig. He couldn't forget her claims that she had been responsible for the catastrophe, and hadn't fully understood what she meant until the postmortem examination had revealed that there were traces of Dexamethasone in Sentimental Lady's body. Dexamethasone was a steroid which hadn't been used in the surgery. Someone had intentionally drugged the horse and perhaps contributed to her death.

Because of Rebecca's remorse and the guilt she claimed, Brig assumed that she knew of the culprit. The thought that a woman with whom he had shared so much love could betray her horse so cruelly had ripped him apart. He tried to deny her part in the tragedy, but couldn't ignore her own admission of guilt.

The next day, when he read the newspaper reports of the event, the quote that wouldn't leave him was that of his father as Winsome had galloped home to a hollow victory. "We threw a fast pace at the bitch and she just broke down," Jason Chambers had claimed in the aftermath and shock of the accident. The cold-blooded statement cut Brig to the bone.

That had been six years ago, and with the passage of time,

Brig had sworn never to become involved with Rebecca Peters again. And yet, here he was, in the pouring rain, attempting to capture a horse whose similarities to Sentimental Lady made him shudder. He was more of a fool than he would like to admit.

"Come here, Gypsy," he summoned, extending his hand to touch the horse's wet muzzle. "Let me take you inside."

Gypsy Wind stepped backward and shook her head menacingly.

"Come on, girl. Don't you have enough sense to come in out of the rain?" He clucked gently at the nervous filly.

"Hey! What's going on here?" an angry voice called over the rising wind. *"You leave that horse alone!"*

Gypsy Wind shied from the noise and Brig whirled around to face Rebecca's brother striding meaningfully toward him. When Brig's cold gray eyes clashed with Dean's watery blue gaze, a moment's hesitation held them apart. A shadow of fear darkened Dean's eyes but quickly disappeared and was replaced with false bravado.

"You're just about the last person I expected to see," Dean announced as he climbed over the fence and reached for Gypsy Wind's halter. She rolled her eyes and paced backward, always just a few feet out of Dean's reach.

"This trip was a spur of the moment decision," Brig responded. Dean managed to catch the horse and snapped on the lead rein, giving it a vicious tug.

"Plan on staying long?" Dean asked. He led the filly into the barn and instructed a groom to take care of her.

"I haven't decided yet."

Dean shrugged as if it made no difference to him one way or the other, but his eyes remained cold. "Was Becca expecting you?" he inquired cautiously.

"No."

"Well, you may as well come up to the house and dry off. She and Ian are in town. They should be home any time."

"They left you in charge?" Brig asked pointedly.

Dean's jaw hardened and he slid a furtive glance in Brig's direction. The man had always made him uneasy. Brig Chambers was in a different league than was Dean Peters. Whereas Dean was only comfortable in faded jeans, Chambers was a man who looked at ease in jeans or a tuxedo. Even now, though he was drenched from the sudden downpour, Brig looked as if he owned the world in his tan corduroy pants, dark blue sweater, and tweed sports coat. Easy for him, Dean thought to himself, he did own the world...practically. Chambers Oil was worth a fortune! Dean didn't bother to hide the sarcasm in his voice. "Every once in a while, when Ian and Becca have to do something together, they let me run the place."

"I see," Brig stated as if he didn't and added silently to himself, *and you pay them back by leaving Rebecca's prized Thoroughbred unattended in the rain.*

DEAN WASN'T EASILY FOOLED. He could see that Brig was unhappy; it was evidenced in the dark shade of his unfriendly eyes. Dean also realized that it was a bad break having Brig find Gypsy Wind in the rain, but it couldn't have been helped. The forecast had been for sunshine and Dean had gotten wrapped up in the 49ers game on television. He had a lot of money riding on the outcome of the game. The last thing he needed was Brig Chambers nosing around here. Dean couldn't trust Chambers as far as he could throw him and Becca always went a little crazy whenever she was with Brig. *Why the hell had Brig come to the ranch now?* Dean's throat went dry as he considered the note. Maybe Chambers had changed his mind. Maybe he wanted his loan repaid on the spot! How in the world would Becca put her hands on fifty grand?

Dean stopped at the gate near the front of the farmhouse. "You know your way around, let yourself in, make yourself comfortable." He stood on one side of the broken gate, Brig was on the other. "The 49ers are playing on channel seven."

Brig's smile was polite, but it made Dean uncomfortable. There was a barely concealed trace of contempt in Brig's eyes. "I think I'll dry off and then check on the horse."

Dean raised his reddish brows. "Suit yourself," he said while pulling his jacket more tightly around him. "But take my word for it, Gypsy will be fine. Garth knows how to handle her." With his final remark, Dean turned toward the stables and headed back to the warm office over the tack room where the final quarter of the 49ers game and a welcome can of beer waited for him.

BRIG WALKED INTO THE FARMHOUSE and smiled at the familiar sight. Some of the furniture had been replaced, other pieces rearranged, but for the most part, the interior seemed the same as it was six years ago. He didn't bother with the lights, though the storm outside shadowed the rooms ominously. Mounting the worn steps slowly, he let his fingers slide along the polished surface of the railing. There was no hesitation in his stride when he reached the second floor; he moved directly toward Rebecca's room. At the open door he paused.

A torrent of long-denied memories flooded his senses. He remembered vivid images of a distant past; the smell of violets faintly scenting the air, a blue silk dress slipping noiselessly to the floor, the moonlight reflecting silver light in Rebecca's soft green eyes, and the powerful feeling of harmony he had found when he had taken her body with his. The reflection had an overpowering effect on him. He braced his shoulder against the doorjamb and plunged his fists deep into his pockets while he stared vacantly into the room. He had been a fool to let Rebecca slip away from him, a damned fool too blinded with self-righteousness to see the truth.

After letting the bittersweet memories take their toll on him, he went into the bathroom and towel-dried his hair. He tossed on his jacket and ran back to the barns, his head bent against the wind. Garth had indeed seen to the horse. Once

Brig was satisfied that Gypsy Wind was comfortable, he headed back to the house.

Headlights winding up the long drive warned him that Rebecca was returning. An ancient pickup with a trailer in tow ground to a stop against the wet gravel of the parking lot and the driver killed the rumbling engine.

Rebecca emerged from the cab of the truck, wearing a smile and a radiant gleam in her eye when she recognized Brig huddling against the wind. She couldn't hide the happiness she felt just at the sight of him.

"What are you doing in this part of the country?" she asked, linking her arm through his and leading him toward the house.

Her good mood was infectious. "Looking for you."

She winked at him and wiped a raindrop off her nose. "You always know exactly what to say to me, don't you?"

"Are you telling me that I haven't lost my touch?"

"If you had, it would make my whole life a lot easier."

"Is that right?" He took her hand in his and stuffed it into the warmth of his jacket pocket.

She hesitated just a moment as they climbed the porch stairs. "I've thought about the last time I saw you…"

He lifted his dark brows. "That makes two of us."

She was suddenly sober. "I didn't intend to argue with you. The last thing I wanted to do was fight about Gypsy Wind."

"I know."

A sad smile curved her lips as they walked through the door together. "It seems that every time we're together, we end up arguing."

They stepped into the kitchen. "It hasn't always been that way," he reminded her.

She shook her blond hair. It was loose and brushed against her shoulders. "You're wrong…even in the beginning we had fights."

"Disagreements," he insisted.

"Okay, disagreements," she responded. Without asking his

preference, she set a cup of black coffee on the table and poured one for herself. "Anyway, the point is, I made a vow to myself on the plane back from Denver."

"Sounds serious."

"It was. I told myself that I was going to get over you."

He sat back in the chair, straddling the cane backing before taking a sip of the coffee. "Well…did you?"

She made a disgusted sound in the back of her throat and shook her head. How could he sit there so calmly when she felt as if her insides were being shredded? "Not yet."

"But you intend to?"

"I thought I did…right now, I honestly don't know." She stared into the dark coffee in her cup as if she were searching for just the right words to make him understand her feelings. She lifted her eyes to meet his. "But I think it would make things simpler if you and I remained business partners—nothing more."

Brig frowned. "And you're sure that's what you want?"

"I'm not sure of anything right now," she admitted with a sigh.

"Except for Gypsy Wind."

Becca's somber expression lightened. "Have you seen her?"

"When I first got here."

"What do you think?" Becca's breath caught in her throat. How long had she waited for Brig to see the horse?

"She's a beautiful filly," he replied, keeping his tone non-committal. Looks were one thing; racing temperament and speed were entirely different matters.

"Where did you see her?"

"In Sentimental Lady's paddock."

"This afternoon?" Rebecca seemed surprised. Brig nodded. "I didn't know she was going to be let out," she thought aloud. "Ian didn't mention it to me…"

"Where is O'Riley? I thought he was with you."

"I dropped him off at his place—he lives a couple of miles down the road." She answered him correctly, but her mind was back on Gypsy Wind. "Did you talk to Dean?"

"That's how I knew you were with O'Riley."

"So Dean was with Gypsy Wind?"

"He took her inside and had...Garth, is that his name?" Becca nodded. "Garth took care of her. I double-checked her a few minutes ago. She looks fine."

"Garth is good with the horses," Becca said, still lost in thought. What was Dean thinking, leaving the Gypsy outside in the windstorm? It was difficult to understand Dean at times.

"What about your brother?" Brig asked.

A startled expression clouded Becca's sculptured features. "Dean?" She shrugged her slim shoulders. "Dean doesn't seem to have much interest in the Thoroughbreds anymore..." her voice trailed off as she thought about her brother.

"Why not?"

Becca smiled wistfully. "Who knows? Other interests, I suppose."

"Such as?"

Suddenly defensive, Becca set her mug on the table and gave Brig a look that told him it was really none of his business. "I don't know," she admitted. "People change."

"Do they?" he asked, his voice somewhat husky as he stared at her. He felt the urge to trace the pouty contour of her lips with his finger.

"Of course they do," she replied coldly. "Didn't we?"

"That was different."

"Why?"

"Because of the horse..."

"Dean was involved with Sentimental Lady, probably just as close to her as either one of us. It was hard on him."

"I didn't say it wasn't."

She ignored his remark. Angry fire crackled in her eyes. "It might have been more difficult for him than for either of us," she pointed out emphatically.

"I doubt that."

"Of course you do! That's because you weren't here, were you? You were gone, afraid to be associated with a woman whom you thought intentionally harmed her horse. Dean was the one who pulled me up by my bootstraps, Brig. He was the one who made me realize that there was more to life than one horse and one man. All the while you were afraid of ruining *your* reputation, my brother helped me repair mine!"

"I never gave a damn about my reputation!" he shot back angrily. "You know that," he added in a gentler tone.

"I wish I did," she whispered. "When I was younger, I was more confident...sure of myself...sure of you." A puzzled expression marred the clarity of her beguiling features. "And I was wrong. Now that I'm older, I'm more cautious, I guess. I realize that I can't change the world."

"Unless Gypsy Wind proved herself?"

"Not even then." She smiled sadly. "Don't misunderstand me—Gypsy Wind is important. But I feel that maybe what she represents isn't the most important thing in my life, and what might have been of greater value is gone."

His chair scraped against the floorboards. He stood behind her and let his palms rest on her shoulders as she sat in the chair. "What are you trying to say?"

"That I'm afraid it might be too late for us," she whispered.

His fingers pressed against the soft fabric of her sweater, gently caressing the skin near her collarbones. He felt cold and empty inside. Rebecca's words had vocalized his own fears. "So you think that destiny continues to pull us apart?"

She slowly swept her head from side to side. The fine golden strands of her hair brushed against his lower abdomen, adding fuel to the fires of the desire rising within him. The clean scent of her hair filled his nostrils, and he had difficulty concentrating on her words.

"I don't think destiny or fate has anything to do with it," she answered pensively. "I think it's you and me—constantly at war with each other. It's as if we won't allow ourselves the chance to be together. Our egos keep getting in the way—mine as well as yours."

The line of his jaw hardened. "Are you trying to say that you want me to leave?"

She sighed softly to herself and closed her eyes. "If only it were that simple. It's not." She shut her eyes more tightly so that deep lines furrowed her brow as she concentrated. "I'm glad you're here," she admitted in a hoarse whisper. "There's a very feminine part of me that needs to know you care."

"I always have…"

"Have you?" She reached up and covered his hand with her long fingers. "You have a funny way of showing it sometimes."

"We've both made mistakes," he admitted. The warmth from her fingers flowed into his. He lowered his head and kissed her gently on the crook of her neck. The smell of her hair still damp from a sprinkling of raindrops filled his nostrils. It was a clean, earthy scent that brought back memories of their early autumn tryst in the Rocky Mountains.

"And we're going to make more mistakes…tonight?" she asked, conscious only of the moist warmth of his lips and the dewy trail they left on her skin.

"Loving you has never been easy."

"Because you can't let yourself, Brig." With all the strength she could muster, she pulled away from his caress and stood on the opposite side of the chair, as if the small piece of furniture could stop his advances and her yearnings. "Love is impossible without trust. And you can't, not to this day, find it in your heart to trust me—"

"That's not true," he ground out, hearing the false sound of his words as they rang hollowly over the noise of the storm.

"Don't bother to lie to me…or to yourself! We're past all that, Brig, and I'm too damned old to be playing games."

There was anger in Brig's dark eyes, but also just a hint of amusement, as if he were laughing at himself. His jaw was tense, but the trace of a self-mocking smile lingered on his lips. "You are incredible, you know. And so damned beautiful…" he reached his hand toward her cheek, but she turned her head and clutched his fingers in her small fist. Her face was set in lines of earnest determination.

"I don't want to be *incredible*, Brig! And God knows there must be a thousand beautiful women who would die for a chance to hear you say just that to them—"

"But not you?"

Her green eyes flashed in defiance at the suspicious arch of his dark male brows. "I like compliments as well as the next woman. I'd be a fool if I tried to deny it. But what I want from you"—her fingers tightened around his as if to emphasize the depth of her feelings—"what I want from you is trust! I want you to be able to look me in the eyes and see a woman who loves you, who has always loved you—"

"And who put her career before my proposal of marriage."

The words stung, but she took them in stride. "I needed time."

"That's a lame excuse."

"Maybe you're right," she said.

"Would you do anything differently if you could?" he asked through clenched teeth.

"I don't know…"

"Would you?" he demanded, his face tense with disbelief.

"Yes, oh yes!"

His muscles relaxed slightly but the doubt didn't leave his face. "How would you change things, Becca?"

The question stood between them like an invisible wall, a wall that had been built with the passage of six long years. Rebecca's voice was barely audible over the sounds of the storm. "I don't think that there would have been many things I would do differently," she admitted.

"What about me?"

She fought against the tears forming in her eyes and smiled. "I've never for a minute regretted that I met you or that… I thought I was in love with you." She cleared her throat as she tried to remain calm. "But you have to know, Brig, that if I could, I would turn back the hands of time and somehow find a way to save Sentimental Lady."

The honesty in her eyes twisted his heart. "I know that, Rebecca. I've always known that you wouldn't intentionally hurt anything."

"But—"

"I just thought that you were covering up for someone whom you cared about very much."

"I had no idea who—"

He stepped toward her and folded her into his arms. "I know that now, and I'm sorry that I didn't realize it before this." As his arms tightened around her he realized that she was trembling. His lips moved softly against her hair. "It's all right now," he murmured, hoping to reassure her.

Becca tried to concentrate on the warmth of Brig's arms. She fought against the doubts crowding in her mind, but she couldn't forget his words. "I thought you were covering up for someone whom you cared for…" She had been, but it was because she had thought Brig was somehow involved. If not Brig, then who? "Someone you cared for…"

She closed her eyes and let her weight fall against Brig, trying to ignore the voice in her mind that continued to remind her that Dean, her own brother, had been acting very suspiciously the past few weeks. Dean had access to Sentimental Lady.

But *why?* What would Dean have had to gain by having the horse disqualified? *Or had he expected her to lose?*

"Becca—is something wrong?"

The familiar sound of Brig's voice brought Becca back to the present. She could feel his heartbeat pounding solidly against her chest. His breath fanned her hair. "Nothing," she lied. She was anxious to escape from her fears and wanted nothing more than the security of Brig's strong arms to support her.

"You're sure?" He was doubtful, and pulled his head away from hers so that he could look into her eyes.

"Oh, Brig—just for once, let's not let the past come between us."

"I've been waiting for an invitation like that all afternoon," he replied with a crooked smile.

With the quickness of a cat, he scooped her off the floor and cradled her gently against him before turning toward the stairs.

"You can argue with me all night long, Ms. Peters," he stated, as he strode slowly up the staircase. "But you *are* incredible, and beautiful, and enchanting, and…"

"And I wouldn't dare argue with you," she admitted with a smile. "I love every minute of this."

"Then let me show you exactly how I feel about you."

"I can't wait…"

CHAPTER TEN

BRIG WAS SILENT AS HE CARRIED BECCA into the bedroom. She was hesitant to say anything for fear it might break the gentle peace that had settled quietly between them. Instead she listened to the movement of the wind as it passed through the brittle branches of the oak trees near the house. Above the wind she could hear the reassuring sound of Brig's steady heartbeat.

Still carrying her lithely, he crossed the room and set her on her feet near the edge of the bed. His eyes never left hers as he slowly slid the top button of her blouse through the buttonhole. The collar opened. Brig gently touched the hollow of her throat with his index finger. Becca shivered at his touch while he stroked the delicate bone structure. She felt her pulse jump.

Knowing the depth of her response, he concentrated on the next button, slowly parting the blouse to expose the skin below her throat, and when the blouse finally opened, he gently pushed it off her shoulders. Her skin quivered as his finger slowly made a path from her neck to the clasp of her bra. Without moving his eyes from her face he opened the bra and slid it off her shoulders, allowing her breasts to become unbound.

Becca didn't move. She heard her shallow breathing and felt the rapid beat of her heart as she let his hands work their magic on her skin. She expected him to caress a breast; she yearned for him to take one of the aching nipples in his hands and softly massage the bittersweet agony. He didn't. She felt his hands move between her breasts to flatten against her abdomen. The tips of his fingers slid invitingly below the waistband of her jeans. Involuntarily, she sucked in her breath in order to make it easier for him to come to her.

The button was released. The zipper lowered. Her jeans were pushed over her hips to fall at her feet. She was standing nearly naked in the stormy night, with only the fragile barrier of her panties keeping her from being nude. A breeze from the partially opened window lifted her golden hair from her face and contributed to the hardening of her nipples. But it wasn't the wind that made her warm inside, nor was it the impatience of the brewing storm that electrified her nerve endings. It was the passion in the gray eyes of the man undressing her that persuaded her blood to run in heated rivulets through her body.

"Undress me," he whispered, refusing to give in to the urgent longings of his body. He felt the thrill of desire rising in him, but he fought against it, preferring to stretch the torment of unfulfilled passion to the limit.

She obeyed his command by silently moving her hands under his sweater and pushing it over his head. He had to reaffirm his resolve as he looked at her, standing before him with her arms stretched overhead as the sweater passed over his hands. Her breasts fell forward, their dark tips brushing against his abdomen. He gritted his teeth against the overpowering urge to kick off his jeans and take her in a frantic union of flesh that would be as savage as it was delicious. Rather than give in to his male urge to conquer and dominate, he waited. Every muscle tensed with his restraint, but the pain was worth the prize. He had to swallow when her fingers touched him lightly as they worked with the belt buckle and finally dropped his pants to the floor. He felt the trickle of sweat begin to run down his spine, though the room was cold. Her eyes had clouded with the same passion controlling his body.

She groaned as he kneeled and softly kissed her abdomen. Her weight fell against him and she trembled at his touch when he slipped the lacy underwear down her thighs and over her calves. His fingers ran up the inside of her leg as he raised himself to his full height and gathered her into his arms before pressing against her and forcing her onto the bed with the weight of his body.

"I want to make love to you," he whispered into her hair. "I want to make love to you and never stop."

"Then do, Brig, please make love to me." Her eyes reached for his in the darkness, promising vows she couldn't possibly keep.

He studied her face, lost in the complex beauty of a woman who was intelligent and kind, strong yet vulnerable, wise though young. How could he have ever doubted her? Why had he been such a fool as to cast away six years they could have shared together?

He lowered his head and his lips pressed against hers with all of the pain and torment warring within him. He took her face in his hands as if he had to be sure that she wouldn't disappear. Her lips parted willingly and his tongue found the delicious pleasures of her moist mouth. He groaned in surrender when her fingers dug into the solid muscles of his back.

"These last few weeks have been torturous," he confided when he finally lifted his head. "I tried to stay away—Lord knows, I tried, but I couldn't. You're just too damned mystifying and I can't seem to get enough of you."

"I hope you never can," she admitted, but before she could say anything else, his fingers caressed her breast, cupping it in his palm, feeling the soft, malleable weight before taking it gently in his mouth. She sighed with the pleasure he evoked as he stroked and suckled the nipple with his tongue and lips. The pressure of his mouth made her arch against him, hoping to fill the space between his lips with her breast. She was satisfied in the knowledge that the pleasure she was receiving was given back in kind.

She wound her fingers in his hair, cradling his face against her as if giving comfort. His hands slid lower as did his lips. Her blood pounded in her eardrums as his tongue leisurely rimmed her navel while his hands parted her legs and massaged her buttocks. "You're beautiful," he whispered against her silky skin. "I want you…"

"Then love me, Brig," she pleaded, "love me." Her needs were more than physical. Even though her body longed for all of him, it was her heart and her mind that had to have him. Her soul was crying for him to be one with her and share a lifetime together.

He moved over her, and she could feel each of his strong hard muscles against her own. Her breasts flattened with the weight of him, the coiling desire deep within her beginning to unwind in expectation. "I want you, Brig. I want you more than I ever have," she admitted roughly.

He shifted, parting her legs with his own. Her feet curled against his calves and rubbed against the hair on his legs as he became one with her. His lips claimed hers as their bodies joined and she felt the pulse of his blood when he started his unhurried movements of union. Her body responded, pushing against his in the heated tide of sexual fulfillment. Their tongues danced and joined until he pulled his head away from hers and stared into the depths of her eyes as if he were looking for her soul.

The coupling became stronger, their bodies surging together as one. She tasted the salt of his sweat on her tongue and heard the rapid beating of his heart. She groaned in contentment as the tempo increased. His eyes remained open, watching her reaction, and when he felt her quaking shudder of release and saw the glimmer of satisfaction in her velvet green eyes, he let go of the bonds he had placed upon himself and let his passion consume him in one violent burst of liquid fire. He groaned as he sagged against her, letting his weight press her into the mattress.

"Oh, God, Rebecca," he murmured. "I *do* love you." His

fingers twined in her hair and his breathing slowed. "You are incredible—whether you believe it or not."

Several minutes later, after his breathing had slowed, he rolled to her side. His arms held her tightly against him and she felt secure and warm, pressed into the hard muscles of his chest.

"Why is it that we never fight in bed?" she finally asked.

"Because we have more important things to do," he teased.

"Be serious."

"I am. Why would we fight in bed? What would be the point?" He smiled and kissed the top of her head, smelling the perfume in her tousled curls.

"What's the point when we're *not* in bed?"

He lifted his shoulders. "I don't know. Boredom?" He looked down at her and she recognized a familiar devilish twinkle lurking in his eyes.

"I doubt that…"

"So do I, Ms. Peters…so do I." He kissed her lightly on the lips before tracing their pouty curve with the tip of his finger. "Speaking of boredom," he began in a low drawl, "I've got several theories on how to avoid it."

"Do you?" She arched an elegant eyebrow as if she disbelieved him.

A wicked smile allowed just the flash of even white teeth against his dark skin. "Several," he assured her while his eyes moved lazily down the length of her naked body. He looked as if he were studying it for flaws. Satisfied that there were none, he met her gaze squarely. "Would you like a demonstration?"

"That depends."

"On what?"

Provocatively, she rimmed her lips with her tongue. "On whom you're going to test your theories on."

His finger slid down the curve of her jaw. "You'll do—if you're interested."

"What do you think?" She laughed, her green eyes dancing mischievously.

He grabbed her wrists playfully and pinned them to her sides. His face was only inches from hers in the gathering darkness. "I think, Rebecca, that you're a tease, an *incredible,* gorgeous, and wanton *tease.* And I think I know just how to handle you." Dangerous fires of renewed passion flared in his cool gray eyes.

"Idle threats," she mocked.

"We'll see about that, Becca. Before tonight is over, I'll have you begging for more," he growled theatrically.

"Save me," she taunted.

"You don't know when to give up, do you?"

"Sometimes I wish I did," she sighed, the merriment ebbing from her gaze.

"Don't ever give up, Rebecca," he chided. "It's one of the most wonderful things about you—that spirit of yours. It's as unbeaten and proud as the horses you race."

"Are you serious?"

"About you? Yes!" He released her wrists and kissed her forehead. "I was a fool to ever let you get away from me." He lowered his head and kissed the slope of her shoulder. "It won't happen again."

She felt her skin quiver with his low words of possession. When his lips claimed hers, she was ready and hungrily accepted everything he offered her. She returned his passion with renewed fervor, giving herself body and soul.

His hands moved over her skin, gently kneading her muscles and reigniting the fires of desire deep within her. His lips roved restlessly down her neck, across her shoulder, to stop in the hollow between her breasts. He pushed the soft flesh against his cheeks before he took one nipple and then the other between his lips.

Rebecca sighed and thought she would die in the ecstasy of his embrace. When he shifted his weight and parted her willing legs with his knee, she molded her body against his in an effort to get closer to him...become one with him. "That's it, Becca, let go," he encouraged by whispering against the shell of her ear. "Just love me, sweet lady," he coaxed as he entered her and began his gentle rhythmic movements.

His hands began to move in slow, sensual circles over her breasts while he slowly fanned the fires of her love until they were white hot and she groaned in frustration. When he knew that she was ready, he increased his movements against her. They found each other at the same moment, each inspiring the other to the brink of ecstasy in an explosive rush of energy that held them together until at last they were satisfied and the animal growls that came from Brig's lips were moans of contentment.

It was much later that Becca awoke from a drowsy sleep and tried to slip out of the bed unnoticed by Brig.

"Where do you think you're going?" he asked groggily, holding her against him and frustrating her attempts at escape.

"I want to check on Gypsy Wind."

"I told you she was fine." Brig ran his hand over his eyes in an effort to awaken.

"I know, I know. But that was several hours ago and the storm's gotten worse. She may be frightened."

"Is that what you're worried about?" Brig asked, propping himself on one elbow. "Or are you afraid that your brother might have let her out again?"

Becca ignored the pointed remark about Dean. It only served to reinforce her fears. "I'm worried about the horse, Brig. She's high-spirited."

"To the point that a storm would spook her?"

Becca extracted herself reluctantly from Brig's embrace. "I'm not sure...I just want to check." She slipped off the bed and began dressing in the dark.

Brig snapped on the bedside lamp and smiled lazily as he watched her struggle into her clothes. "I'll come with you."

"You don't have to."

"Sure I do." He straightened from the bed and began pulling on his pants. "That's what I came here for—to look at your wonder horse."

A stab of pain pierced Becca's heart, but she ignored it. What did she expect—words of love at every turn in the conversation? For someone who had vowed to keep Brig Chambers out of her heart, she was certainly thinking like a woman in love.

Gypsy Wind stood in the far corner of her stall, eyeing Brig suspiciously and ignoring Becca's cajoling efforts to get the filly to come forward. Not even the enticement of an apple would lure the high-spirited horse. Instead she paced nervously between one side of the stall and the other, never getting close enough for Becca to touch her.

"She's got a mind of her own," Brig stated while he watched the anxious filly.

Becca couldn't disagree. "I've noticed," she commented dryly.

"What does O'Riley have to say about her?"

"He worries a lot," Becca admitted almost to herself, as she clucked softly to the horse. "And he tries not to let on, but I'm sure he has some reservations about her."

"Because of her similarities to Sentimental Lady?"

Becca nodded. "Her temperament."

"A legitimate complaint, I'd venture."

Trying not to sound defensive, Becca replied, "Sentimental Lady's spirit wasn't all bad, Brig. She was bound to be a good horse, but her spirit made her great."

"And killed her." The words hung in the air.

"Sentimental Lady's spirit didn't kill her, Brig…*someone* did! If she hadn't been injected, she might not have misstepped, or she might not have continued to run…or she might have been able to come out of the anesthesia—"

"But she didn't!" His face had hardened as he judged Gypsy Wind on the merits of her sister. "And you and I…we let our pride get in our way. We should have figured this out long ago. We should never have let it come between us for this long."

"I don't know what we could have done to save Sentimental Lady."

"Maybe we couldn't, but the least we could have done was trusted one another enough to find the culprit."

"But—"

He turned to face her and his eyes glittered like forged steel. "I'm not blaming you—I was as much at fault as anyone. I assumed that you had something to do with it because you kept telling me that it was all your fault. I shouldn't have listened to you, should have followed my instincts instead. God, Becca, I knew you couldn't have done it, but I thought that you knew who did! That was what really got to me—that you'd protect some bum who killed your horse."

"I didn't."

"I know that now." Brig's eyebrows had pulled together as he concentrated. "We have to figure this thing out, Becca, if you really plan to race Gypsy Wind. Otherwise the same thing could happen all over again."

"I don't think anyone would want to hurt the Gypsy—"

"Just like you didn't think anyone would want to hurt Sentimental Lady," he charged.

"That was different—"

"How?"

"Different horses, different circumstances...I don't know."

"That's just the point. Until we understand the motive behind the drugging of Sentimental Lady, we'll never be certain that Gypsy Wind is safe. And we'll never be able to comprehend the motive until we find out who was behind it."

"But that might be impossible."

"Not really. Ian O'Riley should know exactly who had access to the horse and who didn't." Brig pulled pensively on his lower lip, as if he were attempting to visualize exactly what had happened to Sentimental Lady, as if by thinking deeply enough, he could reconstruct the events leading up to the tragedy.

Becca touched his arm lightly. "Brig, be reasonable—you're talking about six years ago! You can't expect Ian to remember every person who had access to the horse." Becca was incredulous and her wide green eyes reflected her feelings.

"I think you're underestimating your trainer. I'm sure he gave the California Horse Racing Board the name of every person near the horse in those last few hours before the race. The board surely has the records…"

"But that list probably includes the names of grooms who have left us. I have no idea how to reach them. And what about security guards at the track, other trainers…what could you possibly expect to find that the board overlooked?"

Brig's smile was grim, his jawline determined. "I doubt that the board overlooked anything that was reported. What I'm looking for was probably never brought to their attention."

Becca shook her head at the folly of his idea. "What can you possibly hope to find?"

"I don't know—maybe nothing. But there's a slim chance that we can dig up some shred of evidence that might shed some light on Lady's death."

"It's been too long."

Brig had started toward the door, but stopped dead in his tracks. "Don't you *want* to find out what happened?"

"Of course, but I think it's too late. All we would do is stir up the entire mess all over again. The only thing we would accomplish would be getting the press all riled up. Sentimental Lady's picture, along with yours and mine, would be thrown in front of the public again."

"That's going to happen anyway. Once the press gets wind of the fact that you've bred a sister to Sentimental Lady, they're going to be breathing down your neck so fast it will make your head swim. My investigation isn't going to change the attitude of the media."

Becca had reached up to switch off the lights, but hesitated when she felt Brig's hand on her shoulder. She turned to face him, but couldn't hide the worry in her eyes. "What is it?" he asked gently. "What makes you afraid?"

"I'm not afraid—"

"But something isn't right, Becca." His face was softened by concern for her.

"What do you mean?"

"I mean that there are a few things that just don't add up."

She drew in a deep breath and tried to mask the ever increasing dread. "Such as?"

"Such as the fact that, for the most part, you held your silence after the tragedy."

"I told you why. I thought you were involved."

"*Thought*. Past tense. You don't anymore?"

She shook her head and snapped off the lights, hoping that Brig wouldn't notice that her hands were unsteady. "No."

Becca pushed the door open with her shoulder and walked outside. She hoped that Brig would change the subject, because of the unnamed fear growing stronger within her. The wind had quieted to occasional chilly gusts that seemed to rip through Becca's light jacket and pierce her heart.

"What made you change your mind?" Brig asked after he had secured the door to the barn.

"Pardon me?"

"About my guilt—what changed your mind?"

Becca shrugged and hoped to appear indifferent. "I guess I knew it all along. It was just an easy excuse to justify your... change in attitude..."

He put his arm around her shoulder and forced her to face him. The darkness was broken only by the security lights surrounding the barns. "Rebecca, I'm sorry—God, I'm sorry. I made a horribly unjust decision about you and I've regretted it ever since. It was my mistake." He crushed her against his chest and Becca felt the burn of tears behind her eyes.

"It's all over now," she whispered, clinging to him and aware of soft drops of rain on her cheeks and hair. It felt so right, standing in the darkness, unconscious of the chill in the air, holding Brig.

"It will never be 'all over,'" he said. "But maybe we can heal the wounds by finding out what happened to Lady."

She stiffened. "I think that's impossible…"

"Nothing is. I shouldn't have to tell you that. You found a way to breed Gypsy Wind when all the cards were stacked against you."

"That was only possible because of your father."

"I know, and that's another one of the pieces of the puzzle that doesn't seem to fit."

"What do you mean?"

"I told you that things didn't add up and I mentioned your silence."

"Yes?"

"Well, another thing that won't seem to quit nagging me is the fact that you didn't race Gypsy Wind as a two-year-old."

"Ian and I thought it best, because of her legs—I told you all that, and what in the world does it have to do with your father?"

"Dad is just one other thing that doesn't make any sense."

"What do you mean?"

"I can understand him loaning you some money—but not that much. When my father gave or loaned something to a pretty young woman, he usually expected something in return."

"He did—repayment of the loan with interest."

Brig shook his head as if trying to dislodge a wayward thought. "Not good enough, Rebecca. Jason must have wanted something else."

"I think you're grasping at straws," Becca whispered, but the feeling of dread that had been with her for the past few days increased.

"Do you remember what Jason said after the race between Winsome and Sentimental Lady?"

"I know. But he was upset, we all were."

Brig raked his fingers through his hair and noticed it was wet from the rain. He ignored the cool water running under his collar. He watched Becca's reaction when he repeated his father's damning words: "'We threw a fast pace at the bitch and she just broke down.'"

Becca shuddered. "He didn't know what he was saying—"

"A handy excuse…"

Placing her palm to her forehead, Becca tried to close out the painful memories taking hold of her. "Don't, Brig…let's not dredge it all up again. What's the point?"

He took her by the shoulders and shook her until she met his eyes. "You're going to have to face everything if you really intend to race Gypsy Wind, Rebecca. You won't be able to hide here at Starlight Breeding Farm and expect the reporters to respect your privacy. All the old wounds are going to be reopened and examined with a microscope."

"You still think I had something to do with it," she accused, near hysteria. The rain, Brig's dark eyes, the haunting memories all began to unnerve her.

"No, dear one, no. But I have to know why you would go to my father for money after he said what he did."

"I had no choice. There was no other way. Dean suggested your father and I picked up on it…"

"Your brother?"

Becca hastened to explain. She had to make Brig understand. "Originally it was Dean's idea, but when I really decided to go through with it and approach Jason, Dean tried to talk me out of it. He told me I was crazy to consider the idea, that he had only been joking when he mentioned your father as a possible source of money."

"And yet he was the first to consider Jason. Interesting. I didn't think he knew Dad."

"He didn't."

"You're sure of that?" Brig's eyes narrowed as he witnessed Rebecca's face drain of its natural color.

"I...I can't be sure, but I think that if Dean had ever met your father, Jason's name would have come up in conversation at some point in time...and I don't remember that it did."

"Did they ever have the opportunity to meet?"

"Who knows?" Rebecca replied, trying to concentrate on the elusive past. "I suppose it was possible when Sentimental Lady was racing...there were a lot of parties. You remember."

"Then there was a chance that Dean met my father?"

"They could have...but so what?"

In the distant mountains a loud clap of thunder disturbed the silence. Brig chose to ignore her question. "We'd better get inside," he suggested, letting his eyes rove restlessly over her face. He kissed her cheek, catching a drop of rain with his tongue. "If you're lucky, I might consent to drying off your body..."

Rebecca managed a weak, but playful smile. "You're insufferable," she whispered, "and you've got to catch me first." She pulled out of his embrace and took off for the house at a dead run, as if the devil himself were pursuing her. When Brig caught up with her, they were both breathless and laughing. He captured her face in his hands and kissed her with all the passion he felt rising within him.

Becca closed her eyes and melted against him, conscious only of the warmth of his lips touching hers and the cool trickle of raindrops against her neck.

She was too obliviously happy to notice the menacing shadow standing in the window of the office, staring down at her with furious blue eyes.

CHAPTER ELEVEN

THE WEEK PASSED TOO QUICKLY FOR BRIG and it seemed over before it had really begun. During the days he worked with Rebecca, Ian O'Riley, and Gypsy Wind. He saw, for himself, the potential of the bay filly, but also the danger. Someone had drugged a horse such as this once before. Wouldn't they be likely to do it again? If only he knew who had been involved and what the motive had been. Seeds of suspicion had sprouted in his mind, but he kept silent about his theory until it could be proved one way or another.

Dean had made himself scarce for the duration of Brig's visit. There had always been some excuse as to Dean's whereabouts, but it only strengthened Brig's suspicions. Rebecca's brother was never around the farm, with the one exception of mealtime. Otherwise, Dean was on errands into town, or fixing a broken fence in some distant field, or just plain nowhere to be found. When Brig had questioned Becca about her brother, she had seemed unconcerned. Dean had always been his own boss and Rebecca rarely kept up on his whereabouts, as long as he carried his weight around the farm. The week that Brig had visited, Dean had done more than his share. He hadn't worked this hard in several years. Becca thought the entire situation odd, but chalked it up to the fact that Dean had never been comfortable around the wealth and power represented by Brig Chambers.

For Rebecca the week had flown by with the speed of an eagle in flight. She had felt ten years younger basking in the

happiness of working day to day with Gypsy Wind and Brig
and making love to him long into the cold autumn nights. She
found herself wishing that this precious time with Brig would
never end, that he would stay with her forever. Her love and
respect for him had grown with each passing day and she no
longer tried to fight the inevitable.

Rebecca had come to understand her love and she realized
that it would never die, nor could it be ignored. She would
have to accept the fact that she loved him, had always loved
him, and probably always would continue to love him. Though
their paths might take different courses in life, the depth of
her feelings for him would never diminish. Not with time. Not
with distance. Her love surmounted all obstacles, and if it
could never be returned with the intensity of her feelings, she
could accept that. She would take Brig on whatever terms he
offered. She was resigned to her fate of loving him, and
content in the knowledge that he cared very deeply for her.

What bothered her was the time apart from him. When
Sunday evening came, and she finally faced the fact that he
would be leaving within a few short hours, she wanted to scream
at him to stay, plead with him to content himself for a few more
days with her, beg him to love her…just one more night.

Instead, she donned what she hoped was a cheery expression and put together an unforgettable meal while he talked
to Ian O'Riley. She could watch them from the kitchen
window. A tall, dark-haired man with laughing gray eyes
hunched over the fence as he listened to the stooped form of
the grizzled old jockey. She really didn't understand why, but
the scene, set before the weathered receiving barn, brought
tears to her eyes. Hastily, she wiped them away with the back
of her hand. She had promised herself that she wouldn't give
way to the sadness she felt knowing that Brig would be gone
within a few hours, and it was a vow she intended to keep.
She didn't want to play on his emotions, or appear as just
another weepy female. Her pride wouldn't allow it.

She heard Dean's pickup before it came into view. He had been away from the farm for the afternoon and Becca hadn't expected him to return until later in the evening. Since Brig had arrived at the farm, Dean had avoided him. Dean got out of the truck, nodded curtly toward the two men who had witnessed his noisy entrance, and then headed toward the house. The back door opened to close with a thud as Dean came into the kitchen. He tossed his hat onto a hook near the door and scowled.

"I thought Chambers was leaving," he grumbled.

"He is, but he decided to take a later flight."

"Great." Dean's sarcasm was too caustic to ignore.

After seasoning the salmon with lemon butter, Becca put it into the oven and wiped her hands on her apron. "Has Brig's stay here interfered with your life, Dean?" she asked with a forced smile. "I don't see how. You've made a point of steering clear of him."

"He makes me uncomfortable."

"Why?"

"He throws his weight around too much. This is *our* farm. Why doesn't he just leave and take care of his damned oil company? You'd think he'd have more than enough to handle without coming around here and sticking his nose in where it doesn't belong."

"Brig's only trying to help."

"The hell he is," Dean cursed with an impudent snarl. "I'll tell you what he's done, Becca: He's managed to turn this entire operation around until we don't know whether we're coming or going—"

"What are you talking about?" Dean wasn't making any sense whatsoever.

"Just look at yourself, Becca! You're dancing around with a satisfied gleam in your eye, wearing aprons and smiles like some stereotyped housewife in those fifties movies!" He stared at her fresh apron and her recently curled hair in disgust. "You're a Thoroughbred-horse breeder, Becca, not some silly woman who can't think twice without asking for a man's advice!"

An embarrassed flush crept up Becca's neck and her eyes sparked dangerously. "I haven't neglected my responsibilities, if that's what you're suggesting. I've been working with Gypsy Wind every day."

"When you're not mooning over Brig."

"Brig is helping me, Dean, and I'm not going to apologize for that! Neither am I going to deny that I care for Brig."

"And you've changed, sis. You let Brig Chambers get under your skin again. I never thought you'd be so stupid!"

"You're acting like a threatened child. What is it about Brig that intimidates you?"

Dean rose to the challenge and his icy blue eyes narrowed thoughtfully. "I'm not threatened, Becca, I'm just worried— about you. I don't want to see you hurt again, that's all. I was with you the last time. Remember? I know what Brig Chambers can do to you if he wants to," Dean warned with a well-practiced frown.

"The past is gone…"

"Until you start resurrecting it by breeding a horse like Sentimental Lady and then add insult to injury by getting involved with Brig Chambers all over again. You're not asking for trouble, Becca, you're begging for it!"

Becca's small fists clenched. "I think you're wrong."

"Time will tell…"

Brig entered the room noiselessly and the conversation dissolved. If he had heard the tail end of the argument, he gave no indication of it, nor did he comment on the deadly look in Becca's green eyes and the telltale blush on her cheeks. He strode across the room to lean against a counter near Rebecca. After casting her a lazy, I'm-on-your-side wink, he crossed his arms over his chest and smiled tightly at Dean. Brig seemed relaxed and comfortable, except for the glitter of expectation in his stormy gray eyes.

Dean took a chair and shifted his weight uneasily under the power of Brig's silent stare. Becca could feel the tension electrifying the air of the small country kitchen. Ian O'Riley sauntered into the room and seemed to notice the undercurrents of strained energy. The bit of straw between his teeth moved quickly back and forth in his mouth.

"Brig asked me to stay for dinner," Ian remarked to Rebecca. "Said he wanted to talk about the horse...but if it's too much bother..."

"Nonsense. We'd love to have you," Becca replied quickly, destroying the old man's attempt at escape. Becca thought the conversation would be less strained with Ian involved.

Ian cast Becca a rueful glance before motioning toward the hallway. "I'll just give the missus a jingle. You know, check it out with the boss." His light attempt at humor did nothing to relieve the tension in the room. He shrugged his bowed shoulders and exited as quickly as he had entered, glad for his excuse to find the telephone in the hall.

"Haven't seen much of you around," Brig observed, looking pointedly at Dean.

"Been busy, I guess," Dean retorted as he half-stood and swung the chair around in order to straddle it backward. He rested his forearms on the chair back, and Becca wondered if her brother felt shielded with the tiny spokes of polished maple between himself and Brig.

Brig nodded as if he understood. "There is a lot of work around this place," he agreed complacently. Too complacently. Becca could sense the fight brewing in the air.

"I can handle it."

The affable smile on Brig's face faded. "Ian mentioned that it was your decision not to tell Rebecca that I had called her several times after Sentimental Lady's death."

Defensively, Dean managed a strained smile. "Is that what he said?"

Becca's breath caught in her throat.

"Uh-huh. And I suppose that woman…what was her name?" Brig squinted as if he were trying to remember something elusive.

"Martha?" Becca whispered.

"Right. Martha—she would confirm Ian's story, no doubt."

Dean seemed to pale slightly under his deep California tan. Becca's fingernails dug into her palms. *What was Brig doing?* It was as if he and Dean were playing some slow-motion game which they alone could understand. With a dismissive shrug of his broad shoulders, Dean answered, "I suppose she might."

"*If* I could find her," Brig added with a twisted smile. "Do you have any idea where she is?"

"Of course not!" Dean snapped angrily.

Brig's dark brows cocked in disbelief. "No one knows where she is?"

Before Becca could explain, Dean answered. "I suppose she's with her daughter somewhere. We really don't know. She doesn't work here anymore."

"But weren't you involved with that girl…Martha's daughter, Jackie?"

It was Becca's turn to be shocked. Dean had been involved with Martha's daughter? What did that mean?

"We dated a couple of times. No big deal. What's this all about, Chambers? What does Jackie have to do with anything?"

"Nothing really." Brig took an apple from the counter and began to polish it against his jeans. Dean's nerves were stretched to the breaking point. His blue eyes darted nervously around the room. "I just wanted you to admit that you told Martha not to let Becca know that I called."

"I already told you that much!" Dean's eyes flared with angry blue fire.

"I don't think we should discuss this now," Becca interjected.

"I want to get to the bottom of it!" Brig insisted.

"What's to get to the bottom of? I was just protecting my

sister, Chambers. If you can't remember what happened, I do!" Dean's lips curled in contempt and he pointed viciously at Brig. "You tried to ruin her," he accused. "You did everything in your power to see her disgraced before the entire racing establishment! Because of you Ian nearly lost his license!"

"What the devil—" Ian had returned to the kitchen and his stubbled chin frowned at the scene before him. "I thought we were through arguing about Sentimental Lady."

"We were—until Chambers came back."

Becca's anger got the better of her. "All right. That's enough! I don't want to discuss this any longer—"

"You'd better get used to it, sis. Once the word gets out that you've been seeing Chambers again, the lid is going to come off this pressure cooker and explode in your face! The press will be on you quicker than a flea on a dog!"

Brig's eyes glittered like ice. "And who's going to tell the press?"

"It's not something that's easily hidden," Dean remarked. "Especially once Gypsy Wind starts racing—that is *if* you're still around by then."

"Oh, I'll be around," Brig confirmed. It sounded more like a threat than a promise. "And by the time Gypsy Wind starts, I hope to have all the mystery surrounding Sentimental Lady's death resolved." Brig was beginning to sound obsessed. His bright gray eyes never left the strained contours of Dean's ruddy face.

Becca ran her fingers through her hair and her green eyes clouded in confusion. She stared at Brig, hoping to understand the man she loved so desperately. "I don't know how you expect to find out what the horse racing board couldn't."

The muscle in the corner of Brig's jaw worked, though he attempted a grim smile. "Maybe the board didn't have the same gut feeling that I have."

"What feeling?" Becca asked.

Dean stiffened and rose from the fragile protection of the

chair. "You've got a gut feeling—after all these years?" He laughed hollowly and the false sound echoed in the rafters. "It's been six years, man—forget it. It's not worth all the trouble and it would cost a fortune to dig up all that evidence again…" He reached for his hat, but Brig's next words made him hesitate.

"That's right, it's been six years…nearly seven. I'm not up on the statute of limitations. Are you?"

"What do you mean?" Becca asked, but Brig ignored the question.

"As for the cost of sifting through the evidence, I don't think money will be the problem. Any amount it might cost would be well worth the price to see justice served and Sentimental Lady revenged."

Dean whirled on his boot heel and leveled his angry gaze at Brig. "Money's never the problem with guys like you, is it?" he inquired as he pushed his Stetson onto his head. His words reeked of unconcealed sarcasm as he opened the door and tossed his final words to Becca. "I'm going into town… don't hold dinner!" The screen door banged loudly behind him and within a few minutes the roar of the pickup's engine filled the kitchen.

"What was that all about?" Becca asked. The strain of emotions twisted her finely sculpted face. "Why did you intentionally pick a fight with Dean?"

"I wasn't trying to argue with him," Brig responded. "I just wanted to get some answers from him, that's all."

"That isn't all," Becca refuted, her green eyes snapping. "You nearly accused him of being responsible for Sentimental Lady's death—not in so many words, maybe, but the insinuation was there."

"Now, Missy," Ian interjected kindly, "don't be jumping to conclusions."

"I'm not!" Becca retorted. "Sometimes I don't think I understand you—any of you." She tried to force her attention back to the dinner she was preparing, but found it an impossible task. Too many unanswered questions hung in the air like unwelcome ghosts from the past. It made her shudder inwardly. "What were all those questions about Martha and her daughter? Good Lord, Brig, half of the argument didn't make any sense whatsoever!" She placed a pan of rice on the stove and added under her breath, "At least not to me."

She pulled off her apron and tossed it onto the counter as she turned to face Ian. The unmasked guilt on his crowlike features added to her suspicion of collusion. It was obvious that both he and Brig knew something she didn't. "Okay, what's going on?" she demanded. "This has something to do with Dean, unless I miss my guess." She folded her arms over her chest and waited for an explanation. Fear slowly gripped her heart as the men remained silent, but she ignored the apprehension, realizing that the truth, no matter how painful it might be, was far better than the doubts which had assailed her for the past few weeks. "What is it?" she asked in a low voice that betrayed none of her anxiety.

Ian couldn't meet Becca's exacting gaze. "I shouldn't have said anything," he mumbled to himself.

"About what?" Becca asked.

"About Jackie McDonnell," Brig supplied. Ian pursed his thin lips together impatiently.

"What does Martha's daughter have to do with anything? I don't see that the fact that she dated Dean a couple of times means anything."

"It was more then a few casual dates," Brig explained.

Ian interrupted, his wise eyes anxious. "Look, Chambers, I don't think that we should say anything. We'd be out of line. It's really none of our business—"

"What are you talking about, Ian?" Becca demanded.

"He's trying to protect you, Rebecca." Brig came closer to her and she could see the worry in his dark eyes. Was it for her? He placed a steadying hand on her shoulder, but she pulled away from him in defiant anger.

"Protecting me?" she repeated incredulously. "From what? The truth?" Ian avoided her indignant gaze. "Well, I'm sick and tired of people trying to *protect* me. Just because I'm a woman doesn't mean I fall apart under the least little bit of pressure. Dean caused a major misunderstanding by lying to me and refusing to let Brig's calls get through to me, all for the sake of *protecting* me. I would think that you of all people, Ian, could trust me with the truth!"

"It's not a matter of trust, Missy."

Becca's eyes grew softer as she gazed down at the worried ex-jockey. He wore his heart on his sleeve and his face clearly reflected his concern for her. "Ian, can't you explain to me what it is that's bothering you? It's not fair for you to carry the burden all by yourself."

His silver eyebrows pinched together. "As I said, it's none of my affair."

Brig took charge of the conversation and Ian dropped his small frame gratefully into the nearest chair. The grizzled old man removed his cap and rotated it nervously in his fingers as Brig spoke.

"You thought that Martha left the farm to take care of her daughter, who was ill—right?"

Becca nodded pensively. The stern tone of Brig's voice reinforced her fears. Nervously she rubbed her thumb over her forefinger. "I wasn't here when she left," Becca whispered, her gaze locking with Brig's. "I was visiting a friend in San Francisco at the time and when I got home she had gone… without even a note of explanation."

"Didn't you think that was odd?"

"For a little while, and then Dean explained that Martha's daughter, Jackie, was seriously ill and Martha had taken Jackie to a specialist in L.A. They had relatives that lived in Diamond Bar, I think. Anyway, the only thing I considered strange was the fact that Martha never bothered to call or come back even for a short visit. What exactly are you saying here, anyway? That Dean lied? Wasn't his story the truth?" Her green eyes fixed on Ian.

"Partially," Brig allowed.

"Meaning what?"

"Meaning that Martha did leave to help her daughter."

"But?" she coaxed.

"But Jackie wasn't sick, not really." He paused for a moment and Becca's heart began to race.

"I don't understand…" Her voice was uncertain.

"The girl was pregnant."

Becca swallowed with difficulty and had to lean against the counter for support. Her voice was little more than a whisper. "And Dean was the father," she guessed. A sickening feeling of disgust rose in her stomach as Brig's dark eyes confirmed her unpleasant conjecture.

"That's right, Missy," Ian agreed in a hoarse voice. He stared at the table and coughed nervously.

"Someone should have told me…"

"Dean should have told you," Brig corrected.

"So what happened—to Jackie, and Martha and the baby?" Dean's baby. Why hadn't he confided in her? Had he ever seen his own child? What had he been thinking all these years?

Ian acted as if he didn't like talking about it, but he decided to finally let the truth come out. "Martha and Jackie moved to L.A."

"So that part wasn't a lie." It was little consolation.

"No."

"But that doesn't explain why Martha never wrote me." Becca's face was filled with genuine concern and it twisted Ian's old heart painfully.

"You have to understand, Missy, that Martha blames Dean for the pain he caused her daughter."

"Because Dean didn't marry her?"

Ian nodded. "In Martha's eyes, Dean disgraced Jackie, though heaven knows what kind of a marriage it would have been." He wiped the top of his balding head with his hand. "Jackie gave the baby up for adoption, and swore she'd never have another child. That's a pretty rough statement. Martha thought she might never have another grandchild—one she could claim as her own. She offered to adopt the baby herself, but Jackie wouldn't allow it. The girl claimed she hated the baby and wanted nothing to remind her of Dean."

"And so Martha feels the same about me."

Ian gritted his teeth. His faded blue eyes were cheerless as they held Becca's gaze. "There are too many unhappy memories here for Martha. I don't think she'll ever come back."

"Then you still hear from her?"

"Only once in a while. The missus, she sends Martha a Christmas card every year—that sort of thing."

"Does Jackie know who adopted the child?"

Ian shook his head. "Wouldn't even let the doctors tell her if it was a boy or a girl—refused to look at it when it was born. It was nearly the death of Martha. The child is better off with its adoptive parents," Ian allowed.

Becca's heart was heavy. "Didn't Dean want to know about the baby?"

Ian shook his head. "He wouldn't even talk to Jackie when she told him she was carrying his child."

"Nice guy—that brother of yours," Brig observed dryly.

When she ran her fingers over her forehead, Becca noticed that she had broken out in a sweat. She felt cold and empty inside. Why hadn't Dean confided in her? "How is Jackie now?"

Ian brightened. "She's fine, from what I understand. Married herself a young lawyer, she did."

A wistful smile curved Becca's lips. "Maybe Martha will get that grandchild yet."

"I hope so," Ian agreed.

"I'd like to call Martha or write to her. Do you have her number?"

Ian's weak smile faded. "I don't know if that would be

wise," he commented, rubbing his hand over the back of his neck. "No use in stirring up hard feelings."

"Give it time," Brig suggested.

"It's been over five years!"

"Then a few more weeks won't matter, will they?" Brig asked rhetorically.

"I'll think about it—after I talk to Dean."

Ian pinched his bottom lip with his teeth. "I don't know if I'd go bringin' it up to your brother, miss. He might not like the idea that we were talkin' behind his back."

"And I don't like the idea that he didn't level with me."

"It was hard for him…" Ian insisted.

"Dean has a lot of explaining to do."

"Just don't do anything rash," Ian said.

An uneasy silence settled upon the room as Becca finished preparing the meal. Dean didn't return, though Becca had set him a place at the table. The conversation was stilted at first as Ian explained about his plans for racing Gypsy Wind, including the proposed move to Sequoia Park. Slowly the tension in the conversation ebbed as dinner was served and then eaten. The three of them talked about the coming racing season and the stiff competition Gypsy Wind would have to face. Brig and Ian agreed that Gypsy Wind should be started as soon as the season opened, in order to establish a name for herself, since she hadn't raced as a two-year-old. They felt that the sooner she became familiar with race regimen, the better.

By the time Ian left, some of Becca's misgivings had subsided. She promised to call Grace, Ian's wife, for Martha's address and telephone number. Although Ian soundly disapproved, he patted Becca firmly on the shoulder and told her to do what she thought best.

Brig's suitcase stood by the stairs, reminding Becca that he was leaving her. She found it impossible to think of a future without him, or of the empty days when he wouldn't be by her side.

"I have to go," he admitted, checking his watch and setting aside his coffee cup.

"I know."

"I wish I could convince you to come with me."

Her green eyes were filled with sadness. "I have to stay here with Gypsy Wind."

They were sitting next to each other on the couch. His arm was draped lazily over her shoulders, his fingertips moving silently against her shoulder. "We could board Gypsy Wind at the Chambers Stables."

Becca smiled and set her cup next to Brig's. "I can't move to Kentucky. I don't fit in with the Eastern racing set…at least not anymore…" Her voice faded as she remembered a time when she felt at home anywhere—when the world was at her feet, before Sentimental Lady's tragic death.

"I would be with you," he stated softly as he moved her head to lay upon his shoulders. It felt so right.

She longed to say yes, to tell him that she would follow him to the ends of the earth if necessary, but she couldn't. There was too much yet to be done, here at The Starlight Farm. "Nothing sounds better," she admitted honestly. "But I think it would be best not to move Gypsy Wind until after the New Year when Ian plans to stable her at Sequoia."

"I'd feel better if you were closer to me."

"Then why not move the corporate offices of Chambers Oil out here?" she teased.

"Just like that?"

"Why not?"

"Be serious."

"I am."

"And I'm nearly foolish enough to take you up on your offer."

"I'd love it if you would stay with me," Becca confided, hoping beyond hope that they could find a way to be together. He kissed her gently on the forehead.

"I'll work on it, if you promise to be careful."

"I'm always careful…"

The hand over her shoulder tightened. His voice was low and threatening. "I don't trust your brother."

"You never have."

"But I wasn't convinced that he was dangerous before."

Becca laughed at the severity of Brig's features. He really believed what he was saying. "Dean might be a lot of things," she allowed. "And I admit that I've called him more than a few myself, but he's not dangerous. Irresponsible, wily, and maybe slightly underhanded, yes, but dangerous, never!"

"You're taking this too lightly."

"And you're acting paranoid. Just because my brother shirked his responsibility toward Jackie doesn't necessarily mean that he's dangerous."

"Just be careful, okay? And don't go getting him upset. Don't even mention that you know about Jackie."

"That's going to be impossible…"

"Please, Rebecca. Don't say anything until I come back."

She saw the look of concern in his eyes. "You're really worried, aren't you?"

"I just want to know what we're up against, that's all. And I don't like leaving you here alone with him."

"Brig, Dean's my brother! He would never hurt me—"

"You don't know that, Becca!" For the first time, Brig's fear infected her.

"This is more than your concern because of Jackie's baby, isn't it? You really think Dean was involved in Sentimental Lady's death."

Brig's eyes narrowed and he held her more tightly to him. "I just want to know what we're up against, and I need a couple of days to sort out a few things. Why don't you come with me, for just a few days, until I can get to the source of all this?"

"I can't leave the farm right now."

"Ian can handle it. I've already spoken with him."

"Brig, this is my home, my responsibility, my *life*. I just can't pack up and leave because you're paranoid."

Roughly, he gave her shoulders a shake. "I'm not paranoid, Becca."

"Then trust me to be able to handle myself—with my brother or anyone else."

His smile was weak. "You always were a stubborn creature," he conceded. "Do you have a gun?"

Becca paled. "*No!* And I don't need one," she asserted, her lower lip trembling.

"How can you be sure?"

"Stop it, Brig, you're scaring the hell out of me."

"Good, you should be frightened."

Her voice was as tight as her grip on the arm of the couch. "I hope this is a severe case of melodrama on your part," she whispered.

"So do I."

"Dean is my brother—"

He waved off her arguments with his open palm. "I just want you to be careful, Rebecca. You're important to me." He twined his fingers in her tawny hair and pulled her head closer to his in order to press a kiss against her lips silently promising a shared future. "Take care of yourself, lady."

Her voice caught and she had trouble forming her response. "I will," she promised.

"There's one other thing," he said as he reluctantly rose and stepped away from her. Reaching into the pocket of his corduroy slacks, he extracted a yellowed piece of paper. Becca recognized it as the note she had signed to Jason Chambers. Brig handed the small document to her. "I've taken care of this."

She took the paper, but continued to stare into his eyes, as if she was attempting to memorize their steely gray depths. "What do you mean?"

"The note doesn't exist anymore."

"I'm sorry, Brig, but I don't quite follow you."

"It's simple. As far as anyone knows, this note was never signed. You don't owe me or Chambers Oil a bloody cent."

Becca smiled sadly. "I appreciate the offer, Brig, but I can't accept it. You don't have to buy my way out for me."

"And I couldn't live with myself if I took your money. Don't you see what I'm trying to say to you—that I love you and that what I have is yours. I don't want your money, Rebecca. I want you."

"Then stay with me," she pleaded, searching his face to try to understand him. If only she could believe that he loved her with the same intensity she felt for him.

He took her hands in his. "I'll be back," he promised. "As soon as I can…"

Their last embrace was a surrender to the doubts that kept surfacing in her mind. She held him as if she were afraid he would step into the dark night and never return.

CHAPTER TWELVE

IT WAS THE SECOND DAY AFTER BRIG HAD departed that Becca's worries began to affect her work. The first night she had been anxious, but slowly her worry had developed into fear. Not only had she not heard from Brig in the last forty-eight hours, but also Dean hadn't returned, and she couldn't track him down. She had known that Dean was angry when he left the farm, but she had expected him to show up before now. This wasn't the first time he had taken off in an angry huff, but it was surprising that he hadn't come home with his tail tucked between his legs and a sheepish grin on his face after he had cooled off. This time it was different.

Ian O'Riley had shrugged off her concern with a dismissive shake of his balding head. Ian figured that Dean probably just needed to go somewhere and let off steam. He would return again, the old man assured Becca, like a bad penny. Becca wasn't so sure. In her anxiety, she had called Dean's favorite haunts in the nearby town. No one had seen him since the night he had driven into town like a madman.

She was working on the books when she heard the familiar sound of Dean's pickup rattling down the drive. A smile of relief curved her lips as the truck came to a halt near the stables. Dean was known for his theatrical entrances. She closed the general ledger and was about to head outside when she heard the clatter of his boots pounding on the stairs. He flew into the office at a dead run. Breathless from his sprint across the parking lot, wearing the same faded jeans and work shirt he had donned on Sunday, he looked tired and drawn. There was the faint smell of alcohol mingled with sour sweat on his clothes. A tender bruise blackened one of his cheeks.

Becca tried to make light of the situation, though her suspicion could not be denied. "You look like something the cat dragged in and then kicked back out again," she teased, though her green eyes reflected her concern for her brother. "But I'm glad you're back. I was really beginning to worry about you."

"I'll bet," Dean ground out caustically. It was then she noticed the look of contempt that darkened his icy blue eyes.

"Is something wrong? What happened to you? Where have you been? I called all over town, but no one knew where you were. I even thought about calling the police…" She tried to touch him on the shoulder, but he shrank away like a wounded animal.

"The police?" he echoed. "That would have been great. Jesus, Becca, you don't have to pretend any longer. I know how you feel about me."

The sarcasm in his voice made her smile disappear completely. What had gotten into him? He acted as if she intended to hurt him. "Dean, are you in some kind of trouble?"

"I'm not sure," he admitted, dropping his insolent attitude for a second. It was replaced immediately, as if he suddenly remembered that she was the enemy. "It doesn't matter," he said. "And if I am in trouble, I know who to blame."

"I'm not sure I understand what you're getting at…"

"Don't give me that line, Becca. You know as well as I do that Chambers isn't going to let up on me for a minute, is he?" He wiped the sweat from his forehead with the back of his grimy hand as if he were trying to erase a haunting memory.

"What has Brig got to do with any of this?" she asked, her voice tight, her mouth dry. Apprehension slowly began to grip her heart. Dean was in trouble—big trouble—and Brig was involved. The bloody memory of Sentimental Lady's last frantic hours kept surfacing in her mind. Dean couldn't meet her eyes.

"Ah, hell, Sis. I don't have time to sit around here and swap stories with you now. I just came back for a few of my things and a couple of bucks…"

"What are you talking about?" she demanded in a hoarse whisper filled with dread.

Dean looked at her as if he were seeing her for the first time since entering the room. He ran his hand against the corner of his mouth as he studied her. He was skeptical. "You mean you don't know?"

She shook her head, her green eyes beseeching him as she attempted to understand the brother who had once been so dear to her. He was a stranger…a frightened stranger carrying a heavy burden of guilt. She could read it in his eyes. *Good Lord, Dean must have known all along what had happened to Sentimental Lady!* The brother she had known had changed more than she had been willing to admit. Her heart froze.

"Then, I'll tell you. Chambers is responsible for this," Dean stated as he pointed angrily at his discolored cheek.

"Brig?" Becca mouthed the word. She was incredulous. It was then that she noticed the dried blood smeared on Dean's plaid shirt and the slight swelling of his lower lip.

"That's right! Your friend, Brig Chambers, champion of all that is good and right with the world," he snarled. "Defender of the little people and the big bucks. That's how you see him, isn't it? As some modern-day Prince Charming?"

"I… I see Brig as a man, a good man…"

"Ha!"

"…and I find it difficult to believe that Brig got into a fist-fight with you."

"Of course you do. Because it's not his style, right? How many times have I told you that you get crazy when you're around him? Well, you're right. Chambers didn't beat me up. He wouldn't dirty his hands. One of his goons got hold of me the other night and decided to teach me a lesson."

"Why didn't you come home?" she cried.

"Because this guy, he wouldn't let me…"

"Oh, Dean—"

"It's true!" Dean's fist pounded onto the top of the desk. Becca nearly jumped out of her skin.

She wavered for a moment, trying desperately to understand her brother, the brother she had once trusted with her life. The question faltered on her dry lips. "How…how do you know that this man…the one that hurt you…how do you know that he was connected with Brig?"

"Who else?"

"Someone who bears a grudge against you…" She was thinking as fast as she could, hoping to find someone, anyone, other than Brig who might be responsible. "…like Jackie McDonnell. Maybe she was behind it."

Dean's eyes flared dangerously. "I *know* it was Chambers, Becca." He glanced around the room nervously. "Look, I don't have much time. I need a check for a couple of grand." The checkbook was lying open on the desk. Dean picked it up.

"You need two thousand dollars?" Becca repeated. Too much was happening. She needed time to think and understand what was happening. "Why?"

"Because I'm leaving, damn it!"

"Leaving? Why?" Becca felt her entire body beginning to shake.

"I just can't sit around here any longer and watch you make a fool of yourself over Brig Chambers—"

"That's not what's bothering you."

"The hell it isn't."

Becca watched her brother through new eyes, but she gave him one last chance, praying silently that her suspicions weren't founded. "This has something to do with Jackie McDonnell and her baby, doesn't it?"

Dean laughed mirthlessly before his eyes narrowed. "Leave her out of this. And as for that kid of hers…how do I know that it was mine? Jackie had been making it with half the guys in the county. I wasn't about to raise some other man's bastard."

"Dean!"

He shook an angry finger under her nose. "I told you not to tell Brig about Gypsy Wind, but you had to, didn't you? And he had to come back here and start digging everything up all over again. This is all your fault, Becca—"

"Oh, God, no," Becca whispered. Tears pooled in her round green eyes. "Sentimental Lady—"

"Shh!" The sound of a car racing down the drive caught Dean's attention and he put a finger to his swollen lips to silence his sister. His eyes glittered dangerously when he glanced out the window and a bitter smile thinned his lips. "Damn!" A silver Mercedes was speeding on the gravel driveway. Dean recognized it as belonging to Brig Chambers. "I've got to get out of here, Becca, and now. Give me the money—"

"You can't run," she murmured, her trembling voice betraying her battered emotions.

Dean's eyes were filled with undisguised contempt. "That's where you're wrong."

"But I don't understand…"

"I just bet you don't. And you probably never will." He ripped a check out of the book and stuffed it into his pocket before grabbing the loose cash from the top desk drawer. "Just do me one last favor, will you, Becca?"

"What's that?"

"Give me a few minutes to get out of here," he requested. A small shadow of fear clouded his gaze for a split second. Becca felt her stomach begin to knot.

"What…what do you want me to do?"

He was undecided. "Hell, I don't know. Anything. Stall Brig. Do whatever you have to. Tell him you think you saw me out in the far pasture…tell him anything to get him off my back and give me a running start."

Becca's hands were shaking as she stepped toward Dean and

placed her palms against his shoulders. He stiffened while tears streamed down her cheeks. "I think I know what you're running from, Dean, and it's a mistake. You can't begin to hide—"

"You're a miserable excuse for a sister!" Dean screamed at her as he shook himself free of her grasp and knocked her to the floor. "I knew I couldn't count on you!" He ran to the window and opened it. Quickly he calculated the fall. It was only two stories, less than twenty feet. Surely he could make it. He poised on the window ledge and cast one last insolent glance of hatred at his sister. For the first time Becca noticed the shiny butt of a pistol peeking out of his pocket. He wrapped one hand around the gun, while with the other he took hold of the ledge.

"Don't!" Becca shrieked hysterically from her position on the floorboards. Her hair was tangled, her face contorted in fear, and she sobbed uncontrollably when she witnessed Dean lower himself out of the window and finally release his grip on the ledge. *"No!"* She heard him drop, the hollow sound of a body hitting unyielding earth.

Brig burst into the room. His eyes darted from the open window to Becca's ashen face and the terror reflected in her deep green eyes. The concern on his face deepened. "Are you all right?" he asked as he raced to her side and took her into the strong security of his arms. "God, Becca, are you all right?"

"I'm okay..."

"You're not hurt?" His dark eyes raked her body as if he were searching for evidence to the contrary.

"Really... I'm... I'm fine," she managed to say as she wiped her tears with the back of one hand. The other was braced behind his neck, holding him near. She needed to feel the strength of his body against hers, the comfort of his arms holding her fiercely. She had to know there was something strong in the world that she could grasp.

He held her just as desperately. For the last two hours he had feared her dead, lost to him forever, and he vowed silently that he would never again let her go, should he find her alive. He pressed his lips to the top of her head. "Dear God, Rebecca," he groaned, "I was afraid that I'd lost you." His voice was husky, his vision clouded by salty tears of relief.

The next few moments were quiet, the silence broken only by her quiet sobs, and the rapid beating of his heart. From somewhere nearby, he thought he heard a painful moan, but he ignored it, concentrating only on the warmth of the woman in his arms.

Slowly her thoughts became coherent. "Where have you been?" she asked in the faintest of whispers.

"In L.A."

"Then you didn't return to Denver?"

His smile was grim. "No. It's a long story. Your brother— where is he?"

Becca nodded feebly toward the window, afraid that Dean might be injured or worse. Reluctantly Brig released her, but before he reached the ledge the thought of Dean's hidden pistol entered Becca's weary mind. "Watch out," she called after Brig. "He's got a gun." Her heart twisted at the thought.

The sound of a pickup coughing and sparking to life caught her attention. Brig stood watching silently as the truck roared down the winding lane. "Stupid fool," he muttered through clenched teeth.

"Why did you let him go?" Once again confusion took hold of her.

"He won't get far, and I didn't come here chasing him," Brig explained. "It was you I came to see. I was worried about you." He came back to her and pulled her to her feet, wrapping his arms tightly around her waist. His eyes were filled with genuine concern. "When I heard that Dean had gotten away from Charlie—"

"Then Dean was right. It was you. You were behind it!"

Brig nodded curtly. "But, as usual, your brother used less than sound judgment. He wouldn't accept Charlie's hospitality and tried to knock him out by hitting him over the back of the head. Charlie reciprocated."

"But why did you try and hold him? I think that's called kidnapping in this state."

"No one kidnapped anyone. We just invited Dean to play poker—for forty-eight hours. I guess he didn't like the game."

"But, Brig, why?"

"Because I needed time and I had to be sure that he wouldn't hurt you while I was in L.A."

Becca shook her head, rubbing the soft golden wisps of her hair against Brig's chest. "You didn't need to worry. Dean would never hurt me."

"When it comes to you, I don't take any chances. Come on, let's go into the house and I'll pour you a drink. You look like you could use one."

"What I need is answers. I want to know what it was you were after in Los Angeles."

Becca's knees were weak and she had to lean on Brig as they walked through the gathering twilight toward the old farmhouse. Brig's arm was a steadying reinforcement on Becca's slumped shoulders. She tried to think rationally, but the headache that had begun to develop between her temples and the memory of the fear in Dean's eyes clouded her mind.

Once inside the farmhouse, Brig poured two shots of brandy. Becca accepted the drink gratefully and had to hold the small snifter in both of her hands in order not to spill any of the amber liquid. She looked small and frail as she sat on the couch cradling the glass between her fingers. Brig wondered how much of her vulnerability was the direct result of his carelessness. He silently cursed himself before draining his drink in one length swallow.

Her soft green eyes searched his. "I don't understand, Brig, why aren't you chasing Dean?"

"Because I'd rather stay with you—you need me right now." She smiled weakly despite her fears. "But I thought you wanted to capture him—oh God, will you listen to me. I'm talking about my *brother!*" She dropped her head into her palm and felt the tears beginning to rise once again in her throat.

"Shh, it's all right." He sat beside her on the couch after refilling her drink.

"How can you even think that everything's okay?"

"Because for the last six years we've all been living a lie—I'm just angry with myself for not sensing it any earlier. I let my pride get in the way of my clear thinking."

"I think we all could say that. But what about Dean?"

"He's probably already in custody."

"What?"

"I called the police and explained everything to them. They were going to pick up Dean and question him. I told them that I suspected that he would try to make a run for it after he came here."

"But how did you know that he'd be back?"

Brig's lips curved into a thoughtful frown. "Because the poker game—the one he skipped out on. It was rigged. For a while he won and big, then he started losing. By the time he took off, he didn't have a dime on him—or a credit card. He was bound to come here for some cash when he smelled that I was on to him." Brig shook his head in self-mockery. "That was a bad move on my part. He could have hurt you…"

"He would never hurt me."

"You don't know your brother anymore."

Becca's eyes were clear when she looked into Brig's stormy gray gaze. "Nothing that has happened has convinced me that Dean would intentionally harm me, at least not physically." She swirled the liquor in her glass and studied the small whirlpool. Her voice was hoarse when she spoke again. "All of this has something to do with Sentimental Lady, doesn't it?"

Brig set his empty glass on a side table. "Yes."

"And that was why you didn't go back to Denver?"

"I couldn't…not when I felt I was so close to the truth."

"But why couldn't you tell me? Why didn't you let me know what you were planning?"

Brig raked his fingers through his dark hair and his eyes closed for a moment, as if he were searching for just the right words to make her understand his motives. "Because I wanted to be sure that I was on the right track. For God's sake, Rebecca, Dean's your brother! I couldn't accuse him without the evidence backing me up."

"And now you've got it?" she asked quietly as she absently rubbed her temple. Brig's arm across her shoulder tensed and he nodded. "Oh, God," she murmured desperately. She fought against the tears threatening to spill.

"You knew, didn't you?" he asked gently.

She shook her long blond curls. "No. Not really. I…I had vague suspicions…nothing founded and I guess I really wanted to look the other way. I didn't want to believe that Dean was a part of it… I guess I hid my head in the sand." She turned away from him and her next words were barely a whisper. "It explains so much," she confided, taking a sip from the brandy. "Tell me what you found."

There was a dead quality in her voice that made him hesitate. "I should have known that Dean was involved when I found out that he had intentionally not told you about the phone calls. That didn't make much sense to me. It was as if he wanted to keep us apart. From what I could remember about him, he was always interested in Chambers Oil. He didn't object to your seeing me six years ago and I suspected he was secretly hoping that you and I would get married and he'd be that much closer to my father's wealth."

Becca felt that she should defend her brother, but Brig's assessment of the situation was so close to her own feelings, she couldn't deny his supposition. She silently nodded her agreement, trying to hold at bay the sickening feeling of betrayal taking hold of her. It was true. Before the tragedy, Dean had been more than pleased with her relationship with Brig.

"But something happened," Brig continued. "It had to have been the accident. At first, I thought like everyone else, that the reason for Dean's attitude toward me and the fact that he didn't let the phone calls through was because he blamed me for not supporting you during the investigation."

"What changed your mind?" she asked, though something inside her told her that she really didn't want to know.

"It was something you said."

"What?"

"You mentioned that Dean suggested you go to my father for the money to breed Gypsy Wind. That seemed a little out of character to me. If Dean wanted us apart, why would he risk getting the old man involved?"

"We had no choice," Becca reiterated. "There was nowhere else to turn and I really don't think Dean wanted me to contact Jason. When I decided to go, Dean objected."

"I think he was just blowing smoke…"

Becca leaned heavily against the cushions and closed her eyes. She remembered meeting with Jason Chambers in his cabin in the Rockies. He had insisted that she meet him there, away from the eyes in the office. The transaction was to be a private matter. No one would know about it except for himself and Becca. He had seemed pleased that she had come, or was it relief that had sparked in his cool brown eyes as he puffed on his pipe and let the smoke circle his head? His smile as they had shaken hands seemed vaguely triumphant and he had tucked the note away in the bottom drawer of his scarred oak desk. His response had been immediate and Becca had left the cabin feeling that if she had asked for a million dollars he would have given it to her without batting an eye. Yes, it had been strange, but she had been so elated that the oddity of the situation hadn't really taken hold of her. Until now, when Brig brought it all back to her.

"There was something else that bothered me," Brig continued. "Jason agreed to that loan...without any restrictions, right?" Becca opened her eyes and nodded her agreement. "He wasn't exactly the most philanthropic man around," Brig observed, tracing the line of her jaw with his fingertip, "especially when you consider his attitude after the match race. His remarks were so unfeeling and cruel. It just didn't make any sense that he would loan you the money to breed another horse like Sentimental Lady. The answer had to be in that final race, but I just didn't know what it was."

"So why did you decide to go to Los Angeles? I'm sorry, Brig, you've lost me."

"Because Ian O'Riley slipped up. When I asked him about Martha, he mentioned Jackie McDonnell and the child."

"So you went to L.A. to find Jackie," Becca surmised. "Did you locate her?"

Brig's expression remained grim. "Yeah. I found her and her mother..."

"Martha."

"Let me tell you, there's no love lost between Jackie and your brother."

"I know," Becca replied as she reflected on Dean's cruel statement about the girl. How had she been so blind to her own brother's deceit?

"Jackie was more than willing to tell me everything she knew about the situation, which was only that Dean had been doing a few things for my father. She couldn't, or wouldn't, admit that he had injected Sentimental Lady. Maybe she really doesn't know, or maybe she was protecting herself. If she knew about the crime, there's a chance that she could be considered an accomplice."

"So you're sure that Dean was involved," Becca whispered dryly. She held her tears at bay though they burned hotly behind her eyelids.

His fingers rubbed her shoulder. "The way I've got it

figured is that Jason paid Dean to inject Sentimental Lady within the last hour before the race, after the racing soundness examination. Dean got a bundle of money from my father and Jason Chambers' horse, Winsome, kept his flawless record intact."

"Becoming all the more valuable at stud…"

"Exactly."

Becca tried one final, futile denial. "But Dean, he never had any money…"

Brig pressed a silencing finger to her lips. "Because he spent it—"

"On what?"

"According to Jackie, your brother gambles, and I can speak from personal experience to tell you he's a lousy gambler—at least at poker."

"Then how do you know that Dean got the payoff?"

"Somehow he managed to give Jackie five thousand dollars to help with the medical costs of having the baby and to give her enough money to establish herself somewhere else, to get her off his back."

"No wonder Martha never bothered to write."

Brig's voice was soothing. "She never blamed you, but couldn't stand the sight of your brother."

Becca slumped lower on the worn couch, as if the weight of Brig's explanation were too much for her slim shoulders to bear.

"So Jackie is willing to testify against my brother and tell the police that Jason and Dean were in this together."

"I'm not sure she's that strong."

Becca's green eyes urged him to continue. "Then what?"

"I think that Dean will make a full confession when he understands that the circumstantial evidence points at him and paints a rather grim picture. He'd be smarter to play his cards right and try and keep this as quiet as possible—for everyone's sake."

"They'll be back, won't they?" Becca asked. "The reporters will be back."

"As soon as they get wind of the story."

Becca sank her teeth into her knuckles as she thought about her brother and the frightened man he had become. "Dear God," she whispered, feeling suddenly chilled to the bone. "That's why he took care of me, because of his guilt."

"And so that you wouldn't find him out."

The pain in her heart was reflected in the tortured emotions on her face. "Sentimental Lady was so beautiful...and so innocent. I can't believe that he would intentionally—"

"Dean never intended to kill the horse, Rebecca. He only wanted to disqualify her. It was the misstep and her temperament that finally killed her."

"But if he hadn't injected her—"

"We'll never know, will we?"

A shuddering sigh passed Rebecca's lips. "It doesn't matter. Sentimental Lady is dead."

"And you took the blame for that. You and Ian O'Riley."

"It's over now."

"And you can start fresh with Gypsy Wind."

"I don't even want to think about racing right now," Becca confided. "I'm so tired, and confused. I don't think I'll ever want to race again."

"You will."

"I'm not sure, Brig." She looked at him with eyes filled with agony and remorse. "If it weren't for my stubborn pride and the fact that I had to prove myself to the world as a horse breeder, none of this tragedy would have taken place...and my brother wouldn't be on the run—"

"Don't blame yourself, Becca."

She wrapped her arms about her abdomen and rocked on the couch. "Hold me, Brig," she pleaded. "Hold me until it's over..."

CHAPTER THIRTEEN

THE POLICE HAD TAKEN DEAN INTO CUSTODY that same afternoon, and when pressed with the evidence stacked against him, Dean had confessed that he had been responsible for drugging Sentimental Lady in her stall six years before.

Injecting Sentimental Lady with Dexamethasone had been Jason Chambers' idea. He had dealt with Dean in the past and knew that Becca's brother was always in debt, so he offered to pay him twenty-five thousand dollars to drug the horse. It was beneficial to both parties. Dean would be able to pay off several mounting gambling debts and an impatient loan shark. The last five thousand he would give to Jackie for the baby. The deal was sealed and Jason Chambers didn't have to worry about his horse.

According to Dean, Jason had considered Sentimental Lady strong competition and he was unsure of Winsome's ability when it came to racing against the fleet filly. To withdraw Winsome from the race was out of the question because it would be obvious that the colt was demurring to the filly. Jason couldn't take a chance on losing the race. He had to keep Winsome's racing record intact because he planned to put him out to stud and wanted to demand the highest possible fee for Winsome's services. He knew that no matter what the outcome of the race, Sentimental Lady would be disqualified when traces of the steroid were found in her test sample taken immediately after the race.

Twice Rebecca had tried to see her brother, but he had

refused, preferring not to face her or the fact that he had let her shoulder the blame for his crime. It was difficult for her, but she realized that if and when Dean wanted to see her, he would contact her. She left the police station feeling drained and exhausted and was met by a bevy of reporters who had gotten wind of the story. She was grateful for Brig's strong arms and calm sense of responsibility. After a firm "no comment" to the eager press, he had whisked her away from the throng and into his car. Within minutes they had left the inquisitive reporters on the steps of the station house.

"They're not going to leave you alone," Brig pointed out, gently smoothing her hair away from her face.

"I know," she murmured, her misty eyes darkened with pain. "But I just can't face them...not yet." She turned her head and tried to focus on the passing landscape, but she couldn't think of anything other than her brother's lies. For six years he had hidden the truth. It was ironic, she thought quietly to herself, that six years ago, when she thought Brig had betrayed her, Dean had helped her through that rough period. As it turned out, Dean had been the culprit, and now Brig was helping pull her life back together.

She felt safe once back at Starlight Breeding Farm, but her dreams were tormented with haunting images of her brother behind bars and a terrorized Sentimental Lady rearing against the pain in her bloodied foreleg. When Becca woke in the middle of the night, still trembling from the frightening images, Brig was beside her. His strong arms surrounded her and helped comfort her. "It's all right," he whispered against the tangled strands of her hair. "Everything's all right now. You're with me, darling Becca." And she believed him. In the desperate hours of the night, with the shadowed fragments of the dream still fresh, she believed him.

It was dawn which brought reality thundering back to her and forced her to rebuild her life. Two days after Dean's arrest, there was a sharp rap on the front door. As Becca raced down the stairs to answer it, she could hear a car idling in the drive. Since it was only seven in the morning, Becca knew it had to be someone with news of her brother. Her heart hammered fearfully as she conjured reasons for the unexpected visit. Had Dean decided to see her after all, or had he attempted to escape? Or was it worse? In his confused state of depression, could he have tried to harm himself?

She yanked open the door, expecting to face a grim police officer. Instead she stood face to face with a slim, attractive woman of about thirty-five, whose well-manicured appearance and practiced smile were neatly in place as her brown gaze swept over Becca's slightly disheveled appearance.

"Ms. Peters?" the woman inquired with a flash of near-perfect teeth and inviting smile.

Becca was instantly wary. She ran her fingers through her long golden hair, attempting to restore it to some kind of order. "Yes?"

"My name is Marian Gordon. I'm with the *Stateside Review*." She paused for a moment, waiting for the desired effect, and then extended her hand. Becca forced a wan smile onto her face, hoping not to appear overly alarmed. The *Stateside Review* was little more than a cheap scandal sheet which boasted a healthy nationwide circulation. The stories it covered were usually the most bizarre imaginable and Becca realized that there was probably no way to put off the inevitable. One way or the other, Marian Gordon would get her story. Becca took the slim woman's hand grudgingly, and then released it.

"What can I do for you, Ms. Gordon?" she asked coolly. Her elegant dark brows arched instinctively upward.

"Your brother is Dean Peters?" Becca drew in a long, steadying breath before nodding. "I thought so." Marian Gordon seemed pleased. Her poised smile became smug. "Mr. Peters has agreed to give me an exclusive interview concerning his arrest and alleged part in the scandal concerning Sentimental Lady's death."

"He did what?" Becca replied, stunned. Then, collecting herself, she retaliated. "Is this with or without his attorney's knowledge?"

Marian shrugged, obviously not interested in minor details. "I was hoping that I would get your cooperation, Ms. Peters. It would give the story more depth and perspective if I could hear your side of it. Don't you agree?"

"I wasn't aware there were sides."

"Obviously you haven't spoken to your brother lately."

"Obviously." Becca bit back the hot retort that hovered anxiously on the tip of her tongue. "I don't think I can comment on anything at the moment," Becca hedged with a lofty arch of her brows. It took all of her control to be polite to the sharply dressed woman.

Marian Gordon smelled a story—a big story. This could be the story that would give her career the shot in the arm it so desperately needed. Rather than be taken aback by Rebecca Peters' cool reception, she pursued that elusive big story. "Your brother claims that you've...been keeping company with Brig Chambers again. True or false?"

"It's true that I see Mr. Chambers," Becca admitted after an initial moment of hesitation. "What does that have to do with my brother or his case."

"Are you living with him?"

"Pardon me?"

Marian smiled sweetly. "I asked you if you were living with him." This was turning out better than the wily reporter had expected and she switched on her pocket tape recorder. She was right. The story was hot.

"Mr. Chambers has visited the farm," Becca replied evasively.

"Is he here now?"

Becca paused slightly. It was useless to lie. The Mercedes was visible in the driveway. No other vehicle on the farm compared to its luxury. It wouldn't take this reporter long to figure out that it belonged to Brig. "Yes. As a matter of fact, he is."

The woman's eyes lighted with unexpected pleasure. "Good. Then maybe I'll get a chance to have a word with him. This story involves him, too. You know, what with his father being involved and all." Marian couldn't believe her good fortune.

"I don't think so."

"But surely he has some thoughts about your brother and his father and why they drugged that poor horse."

Becca nodded her head and smiled. "I'm sure he does," she agreed. "And I'm sure that I can convince him to give you a call when he decides to make an official comment."

Marian was cagey. She tried another, more subtle tack. "Is there any truth to the rumor that you borrowed money from Jason Chambers in order to breed nearly a carbon-copy of Sentimental Lady? What was that horse's name—Gypsy Wind?"

Becca's suppressed temper began to flare. "I'm not sure I understand what you're insinuating."

The reporter looked appalled. *"Insinuating?"* she echoed. "Why, nothing, dear. According to your brother, you borrowed a rather large sum of money to produce a horse which would be a full sister to Sentimental Lady. Jason Chambers loaned you that money...privately of course. True?"

Forcing her fingers to unclench, Becca replied, "I bred Night Dancer to Gypsy Lady a second time. I had no idea that the offspring would be a filly, but it was. Gypsy Lady gave birth to Gypsy Wind. Now, if you'll excuse me, that's all I have to say on the subject...make that any subject."

"Well, one last thing. Can I see her?"

"What?" Becca had begun to turn, but spun back to face the tenacious reporter.

"I'd like a picture of Gypsy Wind for the paper. Surely you wouldn't mind a little free publicity for your horse. After all, she never raced as a two-year-old. The public will want to see if she's all she's cracked up to be."

Becca's thin patience shattered. "What she is, Ms. Gordon, is a fine racing Thoroughbred. She'll prove herself on the racetrack. And I don't want any photographs of her to be taken, not yet. She's very high-strung and there's no reason to upset her."

"You said she'll prove herself on the racetrack. What will she prove? That Rebecca Peters is still a qualified horse breeder?"

"That Gypsy Wind is a great filly."

"Prove it. Let me get a picture of her."

"No."

"The horse, *if* she is a champion, will have to get used to it sooner or later—"

"When the time comes. Not now." Becca's voice was stronger and filled with more determination than she had thought possible. The reporter had made her angry and she felt an impassioned need to protect Gypsy Wind.

Marian realized that she had blown whatever chance she had for a more in-depth interview, and she cast a hungry glance at Brig Chambers' car in the drive. Beyond the car were the barns. If only she could get one peek inside. Rebecca Peters was still lingering at the door and her expression was more than slightly perturbed, but Marian couldn't resist the chance for a final question. Why not? She had gotten far more than she had expected from the fiery blond woman.

"Well—no pictures. But tell me this, do you think your horse can duplicate Sentimental Lady's racing career?"

"That remains to be seen."

"Something bothers me, Ms. Peters."

"Just one thing?"

Marian let the pointed remark run off her back. "Why did you take a chance like that?"

"I'm sorry—like what?"

"Why would you borrow fifty thousand dollars to breed a horse so much like one who ended in such a tragedy? Was it for the horse—or the man? Did you really want another racing Thoroughbred, or was this one last desperate attempt to reunite with Brig Chambers?"

Becca's green eyes grew deadly. "I think that's about enough questions. Good day." Refraining from slamming the door in Marian's pleasant face, she watched the reporter step into her waiting car, make a full circle and drive down the lane. "And good riddance," Becca mumbled under her breath once she was assured that the reporter had left the farm. Becca wanted to make certain that Marian didn't try to snoop around the barns looking for Gypsy Wind.

"Bravo," a strong male voice asserted from somewhere in the house.

Becca closed the door behind her and noticed Brig leaning against the staircase, just out of Marian's range of vision from the front porch. "Have you been lurking there, listening to the entire conversation?"

Brig's grin wasn't the least big sheepish. "Most of it," he admitted.

"Then why didn't you add your two cents?"

"With that vulture? Not on your life."

"Chicken," she accused with a laugh.

He came up to her and put his hands on her waist as he looked deeply into her mocking green eyes. "You did an eloquent job," he insisted.

"And you could have helped me out."

He touched her lightly on the nose. "Not true, beautiful lady. I think my presence here would only add fuel to the rampant fires of gossip."

"I wouldn't worry too much about that. It seems as if those fires are blazing pretty well with or without you."

Brig laughed and his eyes twinkled. "It's good to see you smile again," he whispered. "You handled yourself very well and I'm proud of you. What brought about your sudden change of heart?"

"Marian Gordon's holier-than-thou attitude might have had a lot to do with it. I suddenly realized that I had to put my life back in order with or without Dean."

"Are you sure you can do that?" he asked, serious concern clouding his sharp features.

"I hope so. I can't believe that he would sell out to a cheap scandal sheet like the *Stateside Review*," she fumed.

"There were quite a few things you couldn't believe about your brother," he whispered, folding her into his arms. She sighed as she leaned against him.

"The worst is that I was so easily duped. God, what a fool I've been."

"Becca, we've all made mistakes. This whole thing about Sentimental Lady colored everyone's judgment. Besides, it's not stupid to love someone or care about them the way you did with Dean."

"Unless you become blind to their flaws."

Once again he smiled. Dear God, she thought she could die looking at the warmth of his smile. "Are you blind to mine?"

"I don't know," she whispered against his chest. "Do you have any?"

"Why don't you tell me…" His finger touched the gentle pout of her lips, forcing them apart so he could run it along the serrated edge of her lower teeth. She touched the tip of it with her tongue and the salty impression started a yearning deep within her.

He groaned and his hand lowered to the neck of her sweater. "You're the one who's perfect, lovely lady," he stated in a rough whisper. His hands gently cupped a breast through the lightly rubbed fabric of her sweater, while he softly kissed her eyelids. Feeling the weight of her breast in his palm, his throat went dry with sudden arousal. "Marry me," he pleaded. "We've run out of excuses and out of time."

His voice was as persuasive as the tips of his fingers running lightly over her nipples. He gently lifted the sweater over her head and let her naked torso crush him. "Marry me and end this torment," he coaxed.

"You're right," she agreed with an acquiescent sigh. "We have run out of time. I need you." She let her fingers twine in the coarse strands of his dark hair. His gray eyes held her bound. "We've waited much too long...let too many things come between us. I was just too stupid to understand that I have to be with you."

"The one thing you're not, Rebecca, is stupid." He cocked his head as if to study her. "Strong-willed and determined, yes. Stupid? Never!"

His lips found hers in a kiss that was savage with passion yet gentle with promise. His hands slid lightly over her body as he undressed her in the unhurried time of a patient lover. His fingers caressed her breasts as if they were new to him. They explored and demanded, creating restless yearnings that made her impatient in her hunger for him.

Warm blood ran in her veins until she could think of nothing but the quiet mastery of his hands on her body and the unyielding desire building within the most feminine depths of her being. She burned for him, ached for his touch.

His movements were slow as he gently pushed her onto the burgundy carpet and savored the sight of her white body stretched against the dark pile. His palms rubbed against her breasts until they tightened in anticipation of the warmth of his mouth covering her nipples. She was not disappointed and gasped in pleasure when she felt the gentle bite of his teeth against her supple breast.

She duplicated his movements. After removing his shirt, she traced the hard line of his muscles with the tip of her finger, past his shoulders, down his chest to stop at the waistband of his jeans. He encouraged her by moving over her and pressing his abdomen closer to her fingers. "Undress me," he commanded, the ache within him burning to be released.

Deftly she removed his pants and let her fingers and gaze

touch all of him, delighting in the feel and the sight of all of his lean, hard length. She quivered at the feel of his firm flesh against hers.

"It's your turn," he announced in a voice thickened with awakened passion. "Make love to me." Quickly he reversed their positions, pulling her over him.

A slow smile crept over her lips as she kicked off the rest of her clothes and lay the length of her body over his. She let him guide her with his hands, while slowly she pressed against him, coaxing the fires within him to burn wildly in his loins.

"I love you," he murmured, letting his impassioned gaze rove restlessly, while he watched her eyes glaze with the desire flooding her veins. He watched her stiffen over him and knew the moment she really wanted him, needed the fulfillment. Then he let go, giving in to the rising tide of passion roaring in his blood.

Brig arched up to meet Becca, while his hands pushed her tightly against him. They erupted together in a heated flow of molten lava that began in their souls and ran into each other, as their combined heartbeats echoed the thrill of spent love. Spent, they collapsed together.

Becca lay quivering in his arms, exhausted and refreshed at the same time. After a few moments of silence broken only by her shuddering sighs, Brig spoke. "I meant it, Rebecca," he reaffirmed. His grip on her tightened. "I want to marry you and I won't take no for an answer."

"I'm not foolish enough to deny you, my love," she whispered into his ear. "I think I've wanted to marry you from the first moment I met you."

He grinned at the memory. "Then let's not wait. Get up and get going." He gave her a playful slap on the buttocks to reinforce his impatience.

"Today? Right now? Are you crazy? I'm not ready—"

"Idle excuses, woman," he joked with a mock scowl. "We've waited too long to stand on ceremony. Neither one of us has any family to speak of—not close, anyway. Reno is only a few hours' drive. We could be married by this evening."

She held her hands up, palms stretched outward. "Wait. Everything's moving too fast for me. What about the farm? Your business? Gypsy Wind?"

"I've considered everything," he confirmed, tossing her the slightly wrinkled clothes. She caught them along with the satisfied twinkle in Brig's dark eyes. "The first few months will be rough. There's no denying that much. I'll have to spend some of the time in Denver. But I've already decided that I can work just as well from the San Francisco office."

She wasn't convinced. "But that's still a three-hour drive from here—"

"A lot closer than Denver. Anyway, it will have to do until we can fix this place up properly. Then I'll have an office in the house and only make the trip into the city a couple of times a week. If I'm needed in Denver—really needed—I can fly there." He jerked his jeans on and buckled the belt with authority. "Any other questions?"

Becca struggled into her clothes. "Sounds like you have it all worked out," she observed with more than a trace of awe in her voice.

"It's something I've been thinking about for a long time."

"Since when?"

"Since the night I found you on the doorstep to my father's cabin," he admitted roughly and Becca felt a wayward pull on her heart. He seemed so genuinely earnest. "I just didn't think I could convince you."

She had begun to slip into her sweater, but stopped. A wanton smile pulled at the corners of her mouth and she dropped her eyelids suggestively over misty green eyes. "Why don't you try convincing me again?" she suggested smoothly.

His dark eyes sparked at the game. "You *can* be a capricious little thing, can't you?" He crossed the room and stood over her, daring her to respond.

She rose to her full height, and then stretched to her toes in order that she could whisper into his ear. "Only with you, love. Only with you."

CHAPTER FOURTEEN

THE CEREMONY UNITING BRIG AND BECCA as husband and wife was simple and to the point. A dour-faced justice of the peace and his round sister performed the rite in Reno. Rebecca had never been happier than she was that day, holding on to Brig's strong hand and unashamedly letting the tears of joy run down her face. Although she had always envisioned a large church wedding complete with an elegant white lace dress, Becca felt resplendent in her pale pink suit and ivory silk blouse. Brig stood proudly beside her, wearing this crisp navy suit and slightly crooked smile with ease. For the first time in years, Becca knew that everything in her life had finally come together. She had even managed to push aside her lingering doubts about her brother for the time being. These few precious moments belonged to Brig alone. In the glittery town of Reno, Nevada, tucked in a valley rimmed by dusty hills, she had become Brig's wife.

Smiling contentedly to herself, she leaned against Brig's shoulder as he drove westward. A lazy sun had sunk below the horizon and twilight descended as they headed through the mountains. Aside from the soft hum of the car engine, the quiet of the oncoming night remained undisturbed. In the purple sky, shimmering stars winked in the dusk. Time seemed to have stopped and Becca was only conscious of the strong man who was now her husband. For years she had dreamed of marrying Brig, and determinedly pushed those dreams into the darkest corners of her mind. Now the marriage had become a reality and she sighed contentedly with the realization that nothing could ever drive Brig away from her.

Their time together was much too short. After spending a carefree week making love to Becca at Starlight Breeding Farm, Brig was forced to return to Denver. He couldn't put off his responsibilities as the head of Chambers Oil any longer.

Days on the farm without Brig seemed long and empty to Becca. She was restless and the pleasure she usually derived by immersing herself in work was missing. She couldn't help but wonder what Brig was doing or when he would return to her. She lived for the short telephone conversations that bound them together. Though there was more than enough work to keep her busy at the farm, she felt a deep loneliness envelop her and she impatiently counted the hours until his return.

For the most part, Brig's time was spent on airplanes between Denver and San Francisco. The challenge of moving the headquarters of a corporation the size of Chambers Oil was monumental. Though Brig had originally hoped that the transfer would take only a few weeks, he soon discovered that it would take months to accomplish his goal of resettling Chambers Oil on the West Coast. His impatience grew each day he was separated from Becca.

Becca and Ian continued to work daily with Gypsy Wind. Slowly the temperamental filly seemed to be settling into a routine of early morning workouts. When Brig was on the farm, he, too, would add his hand to trying to shape the skittish horse into the finest racing filly ever to set foot on a California racetrack. It was a slow and tedious job as Gypsy Wind had her own opinions about racing. Without Ian O'Riley's patience and love for the filly, Becca would have given up. But the feisty trainer continued to insist that Gypsy Wind was born to run in the sport of kings.

The remodeling of the buildings around the farm had started and Brig insisted that a security guard be posted round the clock to watch the barns. Becca had argued against the need for the guard, but had finally agreed when she was forced to consider Gypsy Wind's welfare. Brig convinced Becca that Gypsy Wind was a celebrity who needed all the protection available. The horse could be an easy target of a malicious attack aimed at anyone involved with Chambers Oil or Sentimental Lady. Ian O'Riley concurred with Brig, and Becca was forced to go along with his decision.

After the first few uneasy days, Becca recognized the worth of the security guard. The press had been hounding Becca day and night, and with the patient but insistent aid of the guard, Becca was able to keep the hungry reporters at bay. It was hard for Becca to retain her composure all of the time, and the press seemed adamant for a story, especially Marian Gordon. The cool reporter for the *Stateside Review* returned to Starlight Breeding Farm in search of a new angle on Gypsy Wind. The perfectly groomed Marian unnerved Becca, but she managed to hide her unease. Becca reminded herself that she was partially to blame for the furor. Not only had Dean's confession brought Sentimental Lady's tragedy back into the public eye, but the fact that Becca had married Brig Chambers had fanned the already raging fires of gossip concerning Gypsy Wind. Brig Chambers was one of the wealthiest men in the country, his father and a beautiful young model had recently perished in a traumatic plane crash, and Brig had once denounced Becca publicly—or at the very least, refused to come to her defense. Everything touching Brig Chambers was hot copy for the scandal sheets and the press was frantic for any insight, real or fabricated, into the relationship between Brig and his wife. Gypsy Wind and her famous owners were suddenly the hottest story of the year. It was no wonder that the eager reporters weren't easily discouraged. Dean had been right when he had predicted that Becca was begging for trouble by breeding Gypsy Wind.

Throughout most of the ordeal, including Dean's trial, Becca had managed to appear outwardly calm and only slightly perturbed. Though she smiled rarely in public, the security of Brig's love had given her the strength to deal with both the reporters and their insensitive questions. It was only when someone would ask too personal a question about her brother that her green eyes would darken dangerously and she would refuse to answer. Dean still refused to see her and it would take years to heal the bitter sting of his rejection.

GYPSY WIND'S FIRST RACE WAS HELD IN Sequoia Park. Brig had arranged his schedule in order to witness the running. Though the race was a little-publicized maiden, the crowd was expectant, largely due to the well-publicized fact that Gypsy Wind, a full sister to the tragic Sentimental Lady, was entered. If Brig's confidence wavered, it wasn't apparent in his casual stance or the fire of determination in his eyes. He held Becca's trembling hand in the warm strength of his palms as he watched Gypsy Wind being led to the starting gate. Gypsy Wind's moment of truth was at hand and it seemed to Becca that the entire world was watching and holding its breath. Even Ian appeared nervous. His face remained stern and lined with concentration as he shifted a match from one corner of his mouth to the other.

Gypsy Wind entered the gate without too much trouble and Becca sighed in relief when the nervous filly finally settled into the metal enclosure. Within minutes all of the stalls in the gate were filled with anxious fillies. Suddenly the gates clanged open. Gypsy Wind leaped forward and a big chestnut filly slammed into her so hard that Gypsy Wind nearly stumbled. Becca's heart dropped to her stomach as she watched her game horse adjust her stride and rally, only to be bumped at the three-eighths pole by another filly.

"Dear God," Becca murmured, squeezing Brig's hand with her clenched fingers.

Gypsy Wind was now hopelessly behind the leaders, but found it in her heart to make up some of the distance and finish a mediocre fifth in a field of seven. "Thank God it's over," Becca thought aloud, slowly releasing Brig's hand. She couldn't hide her disappointment.

Brig's smile slowly spread across his handsome features. "Well, Mrs. Peters," he announced. "I think you've got yourself a racehorse."

Becca shook her head, but the color was slowly coming back to her face. "Do you?"

Ian O'Riley cracked a pleased grin. "That you do, Missy," he replied, as if the question were directed at him. He took off his cap and rubbed his grizzled chin. "That y'do."

Ian was assured of the filly's potential, and although the press crucified the dark horse for her first run, the wily trainer was eventually proven right.

GYPSY WIND'S UNFORTUNATE EXPERIENCES during her first race affected her running style for the remainder of her career. After leaving the gate with the field, the fleet filly would drop back to avoid the heavy traffic and possibility of being bumped. With her new strategy, Gypsy Wind managed to win her next race by two lengths and the next seven starts by an ever-increasing margin over her opponents. She followed in her famous sister's footsteps and won all three jewels of the filly Triple Crown with ease. Reporters began to compare her to some of the fastest horses of the century.

Becca was ecstatic about Gypsy Wind's success. Everything seemed to be going her way. The breeding farm was being expensively remodeled, her career as a Thoroughbred horse breeder was reestablished, Gypsy Wind was winning, effortlessly, and most important, Becca was married to Brig. The only dark spot on her life was her brother, Dean. He had been found guilty of criminally tampering with Sentimental Lady and still refused to see Becca. Even during the trial, Dean had refused to look across the courtroom at Becca or even acknowledge her presence. When she had spoken with

Dean's attorney, the man had suggested that she forget about her brother until he was willing to face her again. The attorney had promised to inform Becca the minute that Dean wanted to see her.

IT WAS WHEN THE FANS AND THE PRESS BEGAN demanding a match race that Becca balked. Although she had half-expected it, the thought of a match race and reliving the nightmare of Sentimental Lady's death unnerved her. She couldn't find it in her heart to put the additional strain on herself and her horse. Already there were rumors of Gypsy Wind challenging the colts and settling the arguments concerning which horse was the finest three-year-old of the year.

In a normal racing year, one or two of the best horses prove themselves in regularly scheduled stakes races. But this year the Triple Crown races were inconclusive. Three different colts ran away with the separate events. Added to the colt dilemma was Gypsy Wind, the undisputed filly of the year. Several tracks had made offers for a match race, supposedly a race which would settle, once and for all, the arguments surrounding the favored horses.

Rebecca remained adamant. She wasn't about to race Gypsy Wind, though the other owners pressured her and the various race tracks were offering phenomenal amounts of money to field the event. The bidding by the tracks for the race was incredible, and added to that cash were offers from sponsors and television networks. With an attraction such as Gypsy Wind and the notoriety which followed her career, the sky was the limit in the bidding game, and the American public demanded the race.

Lon Jacobs, a prominent California promoter, couldn't be pushed aside. He called Becca Chambers each week, hoping to entice her into entering Gypsy Wind in a match race.

"Neither I nor Gypsy Wind have anything to gain from the

race," Becca explained to Lon Jacobs for what seemed the tenth time in as many days.

"What do you mean?" the California promoter asked incredulously. "What have you been working for all of your life, Mrs. Chambers? All those years of breeding champions certainly add up. You may well have the horse of the century on your hands, but no one's going to buy it until she stands up to the colts."

Becca closed her eyes and her fingers whitened around the receiver. "I'm just not interested."

"What about what the racing public demands? You have a certain obligation to the American people, don't you?"

Becca ran her fingers through her blond hair. "I have a responsibility to my horse and my family."

Lon Jacobs coaxed her. "I realize that the money isn't important to you. Not now. But what about the fame? With this one race you could establish yourself as one of the premier breeders in the country."

"I don't know if the race is necessary for that. The entire world knows the potential of Gypsy Wind."

"Potential, yes," he agreed smoothly. "But she hasn't really proved herself."

"I think she has."

There was an impatient edge to the promoter's voice. "Well, then think about Ian O'Riley, will you? He was the one who really bore the guilt for your brother's crime six years ago. He was the trainer who was brought before the board. His reputation was scarred irreparably when it turned out that Sentimental Lady was drugged while in his care."

Becca was silent and intuitively Lon knew he'd hit a sensitive nerve.

"Look, Mrs. Chambers, I think I can convince the owners of the other horses to agree to a race nearby. That way you wouldn't have to ship your horse all over the country. You could prove to all those people who watched Sentimental

Lady run that you knew what you were doing—that Ian O'Riley is still a damned good trainer. And Gypsy Wind would have the home-court advantage, so to speak."

"She doesn't need any advantage."

Lon laughed jovially. "Of course she doesn't. She's a winner, that filly of yours." Becca wondered if she were being conned. "So what do you say—do we have a horse race?"

"I don't know…"

"You would be doing Ian O'Riley a big favor, Mrs. Chambers. I think he's done a few for you."

Becca's decision was quick. "Okay, Mr. Jacobs. I'm willing to race Gypsy Wind one last time, against the colts, as long as it's here, at Sequoia. And after that she'll retire. I don't want to hear anything more about racing my filly."

"Wonderful," Lon cooed as he hung up the phone. Becca was left with the uncanny feeling that she might have made the worst decision of her life.

She couldn't hide her unease when Brig entered the room. "Who was on the phone?" he asked.

"It was Lon Jacobs." She managed to meet Brig's wary gaze squarely. "He wants a match race at Sequoia. I agreed."

"You did what?" Brig was astounded and an angry gleam of fire lighted his eyes. "Becca, love, why?"

"It was a weak moment," she confessed, explaining about Lon's arguments for the race.

Brig's jaw hardened in suppressed anger. "I don't think Ian O'Riley thinks you owe him any favors. You've always stood up for him, and Gypsy Wind's career added luster to his. Dean confessed to drugging Sentimental Lady. Ian was absolved of the crime."

"I suppose you're right," she said wearily.

"You know I am!" He shook his head and looked up at the ceiling as if he could find some way to understand her. When his eyes returned to hers they were as cold as stone. "Why don't you face up to the real reason you're racing Gypsy Wind?"

"The real reason?" she echoed, surprised by his sudden outburst.

"This is what you wanted all along, wasn't it? To prove that your horse could handle the colts. Six years ago, Sentimental Lady was beaten, and you've never gotten over it. You still have some goddamn burning desire to prove yourself!"

"Not true, Brig," she argued. "I told Lon Jacobs that Gypsy Wind would retire."

"Right after she races against the colts," he surmised. "What is it with you, Rebecca? Are you a glutton for punishment? Wasn't once enough?"—his eyes narrowed savagely—"or don't you give a damn about that horse of yours?"

His biting words slashed her heart. "You don't think she can do it, do you?"

"I don't care if she can win or not. I'm only concerned about you and Gypsy Wind, and I don't like the fact that you were manipulated by the likes of Lon Jacobs!" Rage blazed in his gray eyes and his jaw clenched. Before she could defend herself, he continued with his tirade. "Why take the chance, Becca? You know that match races are hard on any horse… whether she wins or loses." His anger began to ebb and he looked incredibly tired. Becca's heart turned over. "Oh, Becca, why?"

"I told you why," she whispered.

"And I told you that you're not being honest with me…or yourself."

He reached for the decanter on the bar and poured himself a stiff shot of bourbon before turning back to his den. Becca felt alone and depressed. The reconstruction of the house and the barns was finished, the grounds were once again well-tended, but there was a black void within her because she had disappointed Brig. Was he right? Did she still feel the need to purge herself of Sentimental Lady's unfortunate death, prove to the world that her filly could outdistance the colts? She felt the bitter sting of tears burn in her throat. Why had she been so foolish?

An Important Message from the Editors

Dear Reader,

Because you've chosen to read one of our fine novels, we'd like to say "thank you!" And, as a **special** way to thank you, we're offering to send you a choice of <u>two more</u> of the books you love so well **plus** two exciting Mystery Gifts — absolutely <u>FREE</u>!

Please enjoy them with our compliments...

Pam Powers

Peel off seal and place inside...

The Editor's "Thank You" Free Gifts Include:

- *2 Romance OR 2 Suspense books!*
- *2 exciting mystery gifts!*

Yes!

I have placed my Editor's "Thank You" seal in the space provided at right. Please send me 2 free books, which I have selected, and 2 fabulous mystery gifts. I understand I am under no obligation to purchase any books, as explained on the back of this card.

PLACE
FREE GIFT
SEAL
HERE

ROMANCE
193 MDL ERQS 393 MDL ERRG

SUSPENSE
192 MDL ERYS 392 MDL ERQ4

FIRST NAME	LAST NAME

ADDRESS

APT.#	CITY

STATE/PROV.	ZIP/POSTAL CODE

Thank You!

The Reader Service — Here's How It Works:

If offer card is missing write to: The Reader Service, 3010 Walden Ave., P.O. Box 1867, Buffalo, NY 14240-1867

BUSINESS REPLY MAIL
FIRST-CLASS MAIL   PERMIT NO. 717   BUFFALO, NY

POSTAGE WILL BE PAID BY ADDRESSEE

THE READER SERVICE
3010 WALDEN AVE
PO BOX 1341
BUFFALO NY 14240-8571

NO POSTAGE
NECESSARY
IF MAILED
IN THE
UNITED STATES

IN THE MONTH IT TOOK TO ARRANGE the race, Brig and Becca avoided the subject of the event. Perhaps if they chose to ignore the argument, it would disappear. Brig reluctantly agreed to go with her to the track, but he advised her in no uncertain terms how he felt about the race. He was against it from the start and considered it a monumental risk on her part. Even Ian O'Riley, the trainer who had predicted Gypsy Wind's supremacy over the colts, seemed unusually pensive and out of sorts as the day of the race drew near.

From the moment she arrived at Sequoia Park, Becca was enveloped by an eerie feeling. The doubts she had pushed into the darkest corners of her mind resurfaced. She should never have agreed to the race, or she should have insisted upon another track instead of the very same place where Sentimental Lady had run her last horrifying race. Though Gypsy Wind had raced before at Sequoia, a thousand doubts, plus Brig's fears, came to rest on Becca's slim shoulders. She attempted to tell herself that it was her imagination, that she shouldn't let the feeling of déjà vu take hold of her, but the noise of the crowd, the hype of the race, and the poised television cameras added to her overwhelming sense of unease.

Ian O'Riley was concerned. The tension in the air had affected Gypsy Wind. Though she had never been as nervous as Sentimental Lady, in the last two days Gypsy Wind had appeared distressed and was off her feed. The veterinarian hadn't found anything physically ailing the horse, and yet something wasn't right. Ian O'Riley wrestled with the decision of scratching her from the race. In the end, he decided against it. This was the filly's last chance to flaunt her speed and grace.

The day had dawned muggy, with the promise of rain clinging heavily to the air. It seemed difficult to breathe and Becca felt a light layer of perspiration begin to soak her clothes. Storm clouds threatened in the sky and the shower of light rain started just as the horses were being led to the gate. Becca prayed silently to herself. Gypsy Wind seemed to handle the adverse weather and entered the starting gage without her usual fuss. That fact alone disturbed Becca. The filly wasn't acting normally—not for her. Brig took Becca's sweaty palm in his and for a moment their worried gazes locked. *Dear God, what am I doing,* Becca wondered in silent concern.

The starting gate opened with a clang and the four horses escaped from the metal enclosure. Becca's heart leaped to her throat as she watched Gypsy Wind run gallantly, stride for stride, with the colts. Instead of hanging back as was her usual custom, the bloody-bay filly galloped with the colts, meeting the competition head-on. Determination gleamed in her proud dark eyes and her legs propelled her forward as her hooves dug into the turf.

In the back stretch, two of the colts pulled away from her, their thundering strides carrying them away from the filly and the final horse, who was sadly trailing and seemed spent. Becca's concern increased and her stomach knotted painfully, although she knew she was watching Ian O'Riley's strategy at work. The ex-jockey had decided to let the two front runners battle it out, while his horse hugged the rail. Gypsy Wind had plenty of staying power, and Ian knew that she would be able to catch them in the final quarter.

The dark filly ran easily and Becca noticed the slight movement of the jockey's hands as he urged Gypsy Wind forward. Becca's throat tightened as the courageous horse responded, her long strides eating up the turf separating her from the leaders.

As Gypsy Wind made her bid for the lead, the outside colt bumped against the black colt running close to the rail, jostling the ebony horse against the short white fence. Gypsy Wind, caught behind the two colts, stumbled as she pulled up short in order to avoid a collision.

The crowd witnessed the accident and filled the stand with noise, only to quiet as it watched a replay of the tragedy of seven years past. The jockey attempted to rein in Gypsy Wind, but she continued to race, plunging forward as she vainly attempted to catch the colts.

Becca's face drained of color. Seven years of her life rolled backward in time. "No!" she screamed, her voice lost in the noise from the stands and the address system. "Stop her, stop her," Becca begged as she pulled away from Brig's grip. A horrified expression of remorse distorted Becca's even features and tears flooded her eyes. "It can't be…it can't be!" she cried, stumbling after her horse.

One horse was disqualified, and Gypsy Wind had finished a courageous third. Becca felt Brig's strong hands on her shoulders as he guided her toward Gypsy Wind. The jockey had dismounted and Ian O'Riley was running practiced hands over the filly's forelegs. Cameras clicked and reporters threw questions toward Rebecca. She ignored the press and was thankful for Brig's strength throughout the ordeal.

Ian nodded toward Becca as she came close enough to touch the filly. "I think we might have a problem here," he admitted in a rough whisper.

"Oh, God, not again…not again," Becca prayed.

"Excuse me!" The veterinarian was at the horse's side within a minute after the race was over. Quickly he examined Gypsy Wind's leg and issued terse directives that the horse was to be taken to the nearby veterinary hospital. The horse attempted to prance away from the noise and confusion, but was finally taken away amid the shouts and oaths of racing officials, attendants, and the television crews.

Brig tried to comfort Becca, but was unable to. Guilt, like a dull knife, twisted in her heart. It was her fault that Gypsy Wind had raced. Likewise Becca was to blame for the horse's injury.

The waiting was excruciating, but didn't take long. It was quickly determined that Gypsy Wind would recover.

"It even looks like she'll be able to race again," the veterinarian admitted with a relieved smile. "She pulled a ligament in her left foreleg. It's only a slight injury and she'll be as good as new," the kindly man predicted with a sigh. "But she won't be able to race for the rest of the season."

"Or ever," Becca vowed, tears of gratitude filling her eyes. "She's retiring—for good."

"That's a shame," the veterinarian observed.

"I don't think so." She took the vet's hand and shook it fondly. "Thanks."

Brig put his arm over her shoulders. "Let's get out of here," he suggested. "Ian's staying here and there's no reason for us to stick around. If he needs us, he can call."

"Are you sure?" Becca didn't seem certain.

"Aren't you? You're the one who always had faith in Ian. He'll take care of the Gypsy."

They walked out of the hospital together and were greeted by a throng of reporters.

"Mrs. Chambers…how is Gypsy Wind?" a dark-haired man asked as he thrust a microphone in Becca's direction.

"She'll be fine," Becca replied with more conviction than she thought possible.

"But the injury?" the man persisted.

"A pulled ligament—the vet assured me it's nothing too serious."

"Then you do plan to race her again?"

Becca paused and her green eyes looked into Brig's before she turned her self-assured smile back to the reporter. "Not a chance!"

Slowly, Brig was guiding her to the car. The thick crowd of reporters followed closely in their wake, shouting questions at them. When they finally made it to the Mercedes, Brig turned on the crowd, and the irritation in his eyes was only partially hidden. "Perhaps if you asked your questions one at a time," he suggested.

It was a strong female voice that caught Becca's attention and she found herself looking into the knowing eyes of Marian Gordon.

"Mrs. Chambers," Marian greeted coldly. "How do you feel now that you know you almost killed Sentimental Lady's sister the way you killed her?"

Becca bristled, but felt Brig's strong hand on her arm.

"No one killed Sentimental Lady, Ms. Gordon. It was an unfortunate accident."

"Not an accident—your brother drugged that horse," Marian responded. "Was that with or without your knowledge?"

Brig took a step forward, but Becca held him back with the gleam of determination in her eyes. "What happened with my brother is very unfortunate, Ms. Gordon, and has nothing to do with me, or Gypsy Wind. It's also old news. I suggest that you try writing something a little more topical."

"Such as how Gypsy Wind almost went to her grave today?"

"Such as how that brave filly stood up against the colts."

Before Marian could respond, another reporter edged forward and smiled fondly at Becca. "Mrs. Chambers, do you plan on breeding a sibling to Gypsy Wind?"

"No."

"But you still will be breeding Thoroughbreds—for the future?" the young man insisted. Becca cast a speculative glance in Brig's direction. His eyes were riveted to her face.

"I'm not sure—not right now."

"How do you feel about it, Mr. Chambers?" the young reporter asked, turning his attention to Brig. A smile tugged at the corners of Brig's mouth.

"I think my wife will make her own decision. She's a very…independent woman," he observed with a twinkle in his eye. "Now, if that's all—"

The reporters realized that they had gotten as much of a story as they could and reluctantly backed away from Brig's car. Once inside the Mercedes, Becca managed a weak laugh. "So you think I'm independent?"

"Not totally, I hope."

"What's that supposed to mean?"

Brig maneuvered the car away from the racetrack and drove toward the hills surrounding Starlight Breeding Farm. "That means that I'd like to think that you depend on me—some of the time."

"You know that I do." She paused slightly. "What about you, Brig? Do you depend on me?"

His smile turned into a frown of disgust. "More than you would ever imagine," he admitted. "I don't know how I got along without you for the last six years. I must have been out of my mind."

The rest of the journey was finished in silence. Becca bathed in the warm glow of Brig's love. When they pulled through the gates guarding Starlight Breeding Farm, Becca felt her heart swell in her chest. The new buildings, freshly painted a gleaming white, stood out against the surrounding green of the hills.

Brig helped Becca out of the car and they walked to the closest paddock. Two mares were grazing peacefully, while young colts scampered nearby. The horses raised their inquiring heads at Becca and Brig, flicked their dark ears and turned their attention back to the grass. The colts ran down the length of the fence, glad for an audience. As ungainly as they appeared, there was a grace in the sweep of the colts' legs.

Becca leaned her head on the top rail of the fence. "I don't know if I can give this up," she sighed, studying the graceful lines of the colts' bodies.

"I haven't asked you to."

"But I can see it in your eyes." She turned to face him and caught the look of tenderness in his eyes. "I do love you," she admitted, throwing her arms around his neck.

"No more than I love you."

"But you want me to quit breeding horses and racing them," she accused, smiling sadly.

"Not at all, Becca. I just want you to slow down. You've proved yourself today and purged yourself of Sentimental Lady's tragedy. Go ahead and breed your horses—race them, if you want. But slow down and enjoy the rest of what life has to offer."

Slowly his words began to sink into her tired mind. She cocked her head coquettishly to the side and her shimmering honey-colored hair fell away from her face. "Just what do you have in mind?" she asked as she observed him with an interested smile.

His eyes darkened mysteriously. "I thought I might be able to convince you to forget about breeding horses long enough to consider having a child."

Her dark brows arched. "Oh you did, did you?" she returned, touching his chin lightly with her fingertips.

"We've waited too long already."

"I might agree…but tell me, just how do you propose to convince me?"

"With my incredible powers of persuasion, Mrs. Chambers—" His head lowered and his lips captured hers in a kiss filled with passion and promise. She closed her eyes and sighed as she felt her bones melt with his gentle touch.

"Persuade away, Mr. Chambers," she invited, her eyes filled with her overwhelming love. "Persuade away."

"Dear God, lady, I love you," he whispered as he scooped her into his arms, straightened, and carried her toward the house. "And I'm never going to let you get away from me again."

With his final vow, he opened the door, carried her inside, and turned the lock.

DEVIL'S GAMBIT

CHAPTER ONE

TIFFANY HEARD THE BACK DOOR CREAK OPEN and then shut with a bone-rattling thud. *It's over,* she thought and fought against the tears of despair that threatened her eyes.

Hoping to appear as calm as was possible under the circumstances, she set her pen on the letter she had been writing and placed her elbows on the desk. Cold dread slowly crept up her spine.

Mac's brisk, familiar footsteps slowed a bit as he approached the den, and involuntarily Tiffany's spine stiffened as she braced herself for the news. Mac paused in the doorway. Tonight he appeared older than his sixty-seven years. His plaid shirt was rumpled and the lines near his sharp eyes were deeper than usual.

Tiffany knew what he was going to say before Mac had a chance to deliver his somber message.

"He didn't make it, did he?" she asked as her slate-blue eyes held those of the weathered ex-jockey.

There was a terse shake of Mac's head. His lips tightened over his teeth and he removed his worn hat. "He was a good-lookin' colt, that one."

"They all were," Tiffany muttered, seemingly to herself. "Every last one of them." The suppressed rage of three sleepless nights began to pound in her veins, and for a moment she lost the tight rein on her self-control. "Damn!" Her fist crashed against the desk before the weighty sadness hit and her shoulders slumped in defeat. A numb feeling took hold of her and she wondered if what was happening was real. Once again her eyes pierced those of the trainer and he read the disbelief in her gaze.

"*Charlatan is dead,*" he said quietly, as if to settle the doubts in her mind. "It weren't nobody's fault. The vet, well, he did all he could."

"I know."

He saw the disappointment that kept her full lips drawn into a strained line. *She can't take much more of this,* he thought to himself. *This might be the straw that breaks the camel's back.* Everything that was happening to her was a shame—a damned shame.

"And don't you go blaming yourself," he admonished as if reading her thoughts. His crowlike features pinched into a scowl before he dropped his wiry frame into one of the winged side chairs positioned near the desk. Thoughtfully he scratched the rough stubble of his beard. He'd been awake for nearly three days, same as she, and he was dog-tired. At sixty-seven it wasn't getting any easier.

Tiffany tried to manage a smile and failed. What she felt was more than defeat. The pain of witnessing the last struggling breaths of two other foals had drained her. And now Charlatan, the strongest of the lot, was dead.

"It's just not fair," she whispered.

"Aye, that it's not."

She let out a ragged sigh and leaned back in the uncomfortable desk chair. Her back ached miserably and all thoughts of her letter to Dustin were forgotten. "That makes three," she remarked, the skin of her flawless forehead wrinkling into an uncomfortable frown.

"And two more mares should be dropping foals within the next couple of weeks."

Tiffany's elegant jaw tightened. "Let's just hope they're healthy."

Mac pushed his hands through his thinning red hair. His small eyes narrowed suspiciously as he looked out the window at the group of large white buildings comprising Rhodes Breeding Farm. Starkly illuminated by the bluish sheen from security lights, the buildings took on a sinister appearance in the stormy night.

"We've sure had a streak of bad luck, that we have."

"It almost seems as if someone is out to get us," Tiffany observed and Mac's sharp gaze returned to the face of his employer.

"That it does."

"But *who* and *why*…and *how?*" Nothing was making any sense. Tiffany stretched her tired arms before dropping her head forward and releasing the tight clasp holding her hair away from her face. Her long fingers massaged her scalp as she shook the soft brown tresses free of their bond and tried to release the tension in the back of her neck.

"That one I can't answer," Mac replied, watching as she moved her head and the honey-colored strands fell to her shoulders. Tiffany Rhodes was a beautiful woman who had faced more than her share of tragedy. Signs of stress had begun to age her fair complexion, and though Tiffany was still the most regally beautiful and proud woman he knew, Mac McDougal wondered just how much more she could take.

"That's just the trouble—no one can explain what's happening."

"You haven't got any enemies that I don't know about?" It was more of a statement than a question.

Tiffany's frown was pensive. A headache was beginning to nag at her. She shrugged her shoulders. "No one that would want to ruin me."

"You're sure?"

"Positive. Look, we can't blame anyone for what's happened here. Like you said, we've just had a string of bad luck."

"Starting with the loss of Devil's Gambit four years ago."

Tiffany's eyes clouded in pain. "At least we got the insurance money for him," she whispered, as if it really didn't matter. "I don't think any of the foals will be covered, not once the insurance company gets wind of the problems we're having."

"The insurance money you got for Devil's Gambit wasn't half of what he was worth," Mac grumbled, not for the first time. Why had Ellery Rhodes been so careless with the most valuable stallion on the farm? The entire incident had never set well with Mac. He shifted uncomfortably on the chair.

"Maybe not, but I'm afraid it's all water under the bridge." She pushed the letter to Dustin aside and managed a weak smile. "It really doesn't matter anyway. We lost the horse and he'll never be replaced." She shuddered as she remembered the night that had taken the life of her husband and his most treasured Thoroughbred. Images of the truck and horse trailer, twisted and charred beyond recognition, filled her mind and caused her to wrap her arms protectively over her abdomen. Sometimes the nightmare never seemed to go away.

Mac saw the sadness shadow her eyes. He could have kicked himself for bringing up the past and reminding her of the god-awful accident that had left her a widow. The last thing Tiffany needed was to be constantly reminded of her troubles. *And now there was the problem with the foals!*

The wiry ex-jockey stood and held his hat in his hands. He'd delivered his message and somehow Tiffany had managed to take the news in stride. But then she always did. There was a stoic beauty and pride in Ellery Rhodes's widow that Mac admired. No matter how deep the pain, Tiffany Rhodes always managed to pull herself together. There was proof enough of that in her marriage. Not many women could have stayed married to a bastard the likes of Ellery Rhodes.

Mac started for the door of the den and twisted the brim of his limp fedora in his gnarled hands. He didn't feel comfortable in the house—at least not since Ellery Rhodes's death—and he wanted to get back to the foaling shed. There was still unpleasant work to be done.

"I'll come with you," Tiffany offered, rising from the desk and pursing her lips together in determination.

"No reason—"

"I want to."

"He's dead, just like the others. Nothing you can do."

Except cry a few wasted tears, Tiffany thought to herself as she pulled her jacket off the wooden hook near the French doors that opened to a flagstone patio.

Bracing herself against the cold wind and rain blowing inland from the coast, Tiffany rammed her fists into the pockets of her jacket and silently followed Mac down the well-worn path toward the foaling shed. She knew that he disapproved of her insistence on being involved with all of the work at the farm. After all, Ellery had preferred to leave the work to the professionals. But Tiffany wanted to learn the business from the ground up, and despite Mac's obvious thoughts that a woman's place was in the home or, at the very least, in the office doing book work, Tiffany made herself a part of everything on the small breeding farm.

The door to the shed creaked on rusty hinges as Tiffany entered the brightly lit building. Pungent familiar odors of clean straw, warm horses, antiseptic and oiled leather greeted her. She wiped the rain off her face as her eyes adjusted to the light.

Mac followed her inside, muttering something about this being no place for a woman. Tiffany ignored Mac's obvious attempt to protect her from the tragic evidence of Charlatan's death and walked with determination toward the short man near the opposite end of the building. Her boots echoed hollowly on the concrete floor.

Vance Geddes, the veterinarian, was still in the stall, but Felicity, the mare who just two days earlier had given birth to Charlatan, had already been taken away.

Vance's expression was grim and perplexed. Weary lines creased his white skin and bracketed his mouth with worry.

He forced a weak smile when Tiffany approached him and he stepped away from the small, limp form lying in the straw.

"Nothing I could do," Vance apologized, regret and frustration sharpening his normally bland expression. "I thought with this one we had a chance."

"Why?" She glanced sadly at the dead colt and a lump formed in her throat. Everything seemed so...pointless.

"He seemed so strong at birth. Stood up and nursed right away, not like the others."

Tiffany knelt on the straw and touched the soft neck of the still-warm foal. He was a beautiful, perfectly formed colt—a rich chestnut with one white stocking and a small white star on his forehead. At birth his dark eyes had been keenly intelligent and inquisitive with that special spark that distinguished Moon Shadow's progeny. Tiffany had prayed that he would live and not fall victim to the same baffling disease that had killed the other recently born foals sired by Moon Shadow.

"You'll perform an autopsy?" she asked, her throat tight from the strain of unshed tears.

"Of course."

After patting the soft neck one last time, Tiffany straightened. She dusted her hands on her jeans, cast one final searching look at the tragic form and walked out of the stall. "What about Felicity?"

"She's back in the broodmare barn. And not very happy about it. We had a helluva time getting her away from the foal. She kicked at John, but he managed to get her out of here."

"It's not easy," Tiffany whispered, understanding the anxious mare's pain at the unexplained loss of her foal. Tiffany looked around the well-kept foaling shed. White heat lamps, imported straw, closed-circuit television, all the best equipment money could buy and still she couldn't prevent the deaths of these last three foals.

Why, she wondered to herself. *And why only the offspring of Moon Shadow?* He had stood at stud for nearly eight years and had always produced healthy, if slightly temperamental, progeny. Not one foal had died. Until now. *Why?*

With no answers to her question, and tears beginning to blur her vision, Tiffany reluctantly left the two men to attend to the dead colt.

The rain had decreased to a slight drizzle, but the wind had picked up and the branches of the sequoia trees danced wildly, at times slamming into the nearby buildings. The weather wasn't unusual for early March in Northern California, but there was something somber and ominous about the black clouds rolling over the hills surrounding the small breeding farm.

"Don't let it get to you," Tiffany muttered to herself.

She shivered as she stepped into the broodmare barn and walked without hesitation to Felicity's stall.

The smell of fresh hay and warm horses greeted her and offered some relief from the cold night. Several mares poked their dark heads out of the stalls to inspect the visitor. Tiffany gently patted each muzzle as she passed, but her eyes were trained on the last stall in the whitewashed barn.

Felicity was still agitated and appeared to be looking for the lost foal. The chestnut mare paced around the small enclosure and snorted restlessly. When Tiffany approached, Felicity's ears flattened to her head and her dark eyes gleamed maliciously.

"I know, girl," Tiffany whispered, attempting to comfort the anxious mare. "It wasn't supposed to turn out like this."

Felicity stamped angrily and ignored the piece of apple Tiffany offered.

"There will be other foals," Tiffany said, wondering if she were trying to convince the horse or herself. Rhodes Breeding Farm couldn't stand to take many more losses. Tears of frustration and anxiety slid down her cheeks and she didn't bother to brush them aside.

A soft nicker from a nearby stall reminded Tiffany that she was disturbing the other horses. Summoning up her faltering courage, Tiffany stared at Felicity for a moment before slapping the top rail of the stall and walking back to the house.

Somehow she would find the solution to the mystery of the dying foals.

THE FIRST INQUIRY CAME BY TELEPHONE two days later. Word had gotten out about the foals, and a reporter for a local newspaper in Santa Rosa was checking the story.

Tiffany took the call herself and assured the man that though she had lost two newborn colts and one filly, she and the veterinarian were positive that whatever had killed the animals was not contagious.

When the reporter, Rod Crawford, asked if he could come to the farm for an interview, Tiffany was wary, but decided the best course of action was to confront the problem head-on.

"When would it be convenient for you to drive out to the farm?" she asked graciously, her soft voice disguising her anxiety.

"What about next Wednesday? I'll have a photographer with me, if you don't mind."

"Of course not," she lied, as if she had done it all her life. "Around ten?"

"I'll be there," Rod Crawford agreed.

Tiffany replaced the receiver and said a silent prayer that the two mares who were still carrying Moon Shadow's unborn foals would successfully deliver healthy horses into the world, hopefully before next Wednesday. A sinking feeling in her heart told her not to get her hopes up.

Somehow, she had to focus Rod Crawford's attention away from the tragedy in the foaling shed and onto the one bright spot in Rhodes Breeding Farm's future: Journey's End. He was a big bay colt, whose career as a two-year-old had been less than formidable. But now, as a three-year-old, he had won his first two starts and promised to be the biggest star Rhodes Farm had put on the racetrack since Devil's Gambit.

Tiffany only hoped that she could convince the reporter that the story at Rhodes Breeding Farm was not the three dead foals, but the racing future of Journey's End.

The reputation of the breeding farm was on the line. If the Santa Rosa papers knew about the unexplained deaths of the foals, it wouldn't be long before reporters from San Francisco and Sacramento would call. And then, all hell was sure to break loose.

THE DOORBELL CHIMED AT NINE-THIRTY on Wednesday morning and Tiffany smiled grimly to herself. Though the reporter for the *Santa Rosa Clarion* was a good half an hour early, Tiffany was ready for him. In the last four years she had learned to anticipate just about anything and make the most of it, and she wouldn't allow a little time discrepancy to rattle her. She couldn't afford the bad press.

Neither of the broodmares pregnant with Moon Shadow's offspring had gone into labor and Tiffany didn't know whether to laugh or cry. Her nerves were stretched as tightly as a piano string and only with effort did her poise remain intact. Cosmetics, for the most part, had covered the shadows below her eyes, which were the result of the past week of sleepless nights.

She hurried down the curved, marble staircase and crossed the tiled foyer to the door. After nervously smoothing her wool skirt, she opened the door and managed a brave smile, which she directed at the gentleman standing on the porch.

"Ms. Rhodes?" he asked with the slightest of accents.

Tiffany found herself staring into the most seductive gray eyes she had ever seen. He wasn't what she had expected. His tanned face was angular, his features strong. Raven-black hair and fierce eyebrows contrasted with the bold, steel-colored eyes staring into hers. There was a presence about him that spoke of authority and hinted at arrogance.

"Yes...won't you please come in?" she replied, finally finding her voice. "We can talk in the den...." Her words trailed off as she remembered the photographer. Where was he? Hadn't Crawford mentioned that a photographer would be with him this morning?

It was then she noticed the stiff white collar and the expensively woven tweed business suit. A burgundy silk tie was knotted at the stranger's throat and gold cuff links flashed in the early-morning sunlight. The broad shoulders beneath his jacket were square and tense and there was no evidence of a note pad, camera or tape recorder. Stereotyping aside, this man was no reporter.

"Pardon me," she whispered, realizing her mistake. "I was expecting someone—"

"Else," he supplied with a tight, slightly off-center smile that seemed out of place on his harsh, angular face. He wasn't conventionally handsome; the boldness of his features took away any boyish charm that might have lingered from his youth. But there was something about him, something positively male and sensual that was as magnetic as it was dangerous. Tiffany recognized it in the glint of his eyes and the brackets near the corners of his mouth. She suspected that beneath the conservative business suit, there was an extremely single-minded and ruthless man.

He extended his hand and when Tiffany accepted it, she noticed that his fingers were callused—a direct contradiction of the image he was attempting to portray.

"Zane Sheridan," he announced. Again the accent.

She hesitated only slightly. His name and his face were vaguely familiar, and though he looked as if he expected her to recognize him, she couldn't remember where she'd met him…or heard of him. "Please come in, Mr. Sheridan—"

"Zane."

"Zane," she repeated, slightly uncomfortable with the familiarity of first names. For a reason she couldn't put her finger on, Tiffany thought she should be wary of this man. There was something about him that hinted at antagonism.

She led him into the den, knowing instinctively that this was not a social call.

"Can I get you something—coffee, perhaps, or tea?" Tiffany asked as she took her usual chair behind the desk and Zane settled into one of the side chairs. Placing her elbows on the polished wood surface, she clasped her hands together and smiled pleasantly, just as if he hadn't disrupted her morning.

"Nothing. Thank you." His gray eyes moved away from her face to wander about the room. They observed all the opulent surroundings: the thick pile of the carpet, the expensive leather chairs, the subdued brass reading lamps and the etchings of Thoroughbreds adorning the cherry-wood walls.

"What exactly can I do for you?" Tiffany asked, feeling as if he were searching for something.

When his eyes returned to hers, he smiled cynically. "I was an acquaintance of your husband."

Zane's expression was meant to be without emotion as he stared at the elegant but worried face of Ellery Rhodes's widow. Her reaction was just what he had expected—surprise and then, once she had digested his statement, disbelief. Her fingers anxiously toyed with the single gold chain encircling her throat.

"You knew Ellery?"

"We'd met a few times. In Europe."

Maybe that was why his face and name were so familiar, but Tiffany doubted it. A cautious instinct told her he was lying through his beautiful, straight white teeth.

She was instantly wary as she leveled her cool blue gaze at him. "I'm sorry," she apologized, "but if we've met, I've forgotten."

Zane pulled at the knot of his tie and slumped more deeply and comfortably into his chair. "I met Ellery Rhodes before he was married to you."

"Oh." Her smile was meant to be indulgent. "And you're here because…?" she prompted. Zane Sheridan unnerved her, and Tiffany knew instinctively that the sooner he stated his business and was gone, the better.

"I'm interested in buying your farm."

Her dark brows arched in elegant surprise. "You're kidding!"

"Dead serious." The glint of silver determination in his eyes emphasized his words and convinced her that he wasn't playing games.

"But it's not for sale."

"I've heard that everything has a price."

"Well in this case, Mr. Sheridan, you heard wrong. The farm isn't on the market. However, if you're interested in a yearling, I have two colts that—"

"Afraid not. It's all or nothing with me," was the clipped, succinct reply. Apparently Zane Sheridan wasn't a man to mince words.

"Then I guess it's nothing," Tiffany replied, slightly galled at his self-assured attitude. Who the hell did he think he was, waltzing into her house uninvited, and offering to buy her home—Ellery's farm?

Just because he had been a friend of Ellery's—no, he hadn't said friend, just acquaintance.

It didn't matter. It still didn't give him the right to come barging in as if he owned the place. And there was more to it. Tiffany sensed that he was here for another reason, a reason he hadn't admitted. Maybe it was the strain in the angle of his jaw, or the furrows lining his forehead. But whatever the reason, Tiffany knew that Zane Sheridan was hiding something.

Tiffany stood, as if by so doing she could end the conversation.

"Let me know if you change your mind." He rose and looked past her to the framed portrait of Devil's Gambit; the painting was mounted proudly above the gray stone fireplace.

Just so that Mr. Sheridan understood the finality of her position on the farm, she offered an explanation to which he really wasn't entitled. "If I change my mind about selling the place, I'll give Ellery's brother Dustin first option. He already owns part of the farm and I think that Rhodes Breeding Farm should stay in the family."

Zane frowned thoughtfully and rubbed his chin. "If the family wants it—"

"Of course."

Shrugging his broad shoulders as if he had no interest whatsoever in the Rhodes family's business, he continued to gaze at the portrait over the mantel.

"A shame about Devil's Gambit," he said at length.

"Yes," Tiffany whispered, repeating his words stiffly. "A shame." The same accident that had claimed the proud horse's life had also killed Ellery. Mr. Sheridan didn't offer any condolences concerning her husband, the man he'd said he had known.

The conversation was stilted and uncomfortable, and Tiffany felt as if Zane Sheridan were deliberately baiting her. But why? And who needed it? The past few weeks had been chaotic enough. The last thing Tiffany wanted was a mysterious man complicating things with his enigmatic presence and cryptic statements.

As she walked around the desk, shortening the distance between the stranger and herself, she asked, "Do you own any horses, Mr. Sheridan?" His dark brows quirked at the formal use of his surname.

"A few. In Ireland."

That explained the faint accent. "So you want to buy the farm and make your mark on American racing?"

"Something like that." For the first time, his smile seemed sincere, and there was a spark of honesty in his clear, gray eyes.

Tiffany supposed that Zane Sheridan was the singularly most attractive man she had met in a long while. Tall and whip-lean, with broad shoulders and thick, jet black hair, he stood with pride and authority as he returned her gaze. His skin was dark and smooth, and where once there might have been a dimple, there were now brackets of strain around his mouth.

He had lived a hard life, Tiffany guessed, but the expensive tweed jacket suggested that the worst years had passed.

It would be a mistake to cross a man such as this, she decided. Zane Sheridan looked as if he were capable of ruthless retribution. This was evidenced in the tense line of his square jaw, the restless movement of his fingers against his thumb and the hard glint of determination in those steel-gray eyes. Zane was a man to reckon with and not one to deceive.

The doorbell rang, and Tiffany was grateful for the intrusion.

"If you'll excuse me," she said, taking three quick steps before pausing to turn in his direction.

"We're not through here."

"Pardon me?" Tiffany was taken aback. She expected him to show some civility and leave before Rod Crawford's interview. Instinctively Tiffany knew that having Zane in the same room with the reporter would be dangerous.

"I want to talk to you—seriously—about the farm."

"There's no reason, Mr....Zane. You're wasting your time with me. I'm not about to sell."

"Indulge me," he suggested. He strode across the short distance separating them and touched her lightly on the arm. "Hear what I have to say, listen to what my offer is before you say no."

The doorbell chimed again, more impatiently this time.

"I really do have an appointment," she said, looking anxiously through the foyer to the front door. The grip on her arm tightened slightly.

"And I think you should listen to what I have to say."

"Why?"

He hesitated slightly, as if he weren't sure he could trust her and the skin tightened over his cheekbones. His rugged features displayed a new emotion. Anger and vengeful self-righteousness were displayed in the thrust of his jaw. All traces of his earlier civility had disappeared. Tiffany's heart began to pound with dread.

"Why are you here?" she asked again, her voice suddenly hoarse.

"I came to you because there is something I think that you should know."

"And that is?" Her heart was pounding frantically now, and she barely heard the doorbell chime for the third time.

"I'm not so sure that Devil's Gambit's death was an accident," he stated, gauging her reaction, watching for even the slightest trace of emotion on her elegant features. "In fact, I think there's a damned good chance that your horse is still alive."

CHAPTER TWO

THE COLOR DRAINED FROM TIFFANY'S FACE. "You...you think that Devil's Gambit might be alive?" she repeated, her voice barely a whisper. "You're not serious...."

But she could tell by Zane's expression that he was dead serious.

"Dear God," she whispered, closing her eyes. She wanted to dismiss what he was saying as idle conjecture, but he just didn't seem the type of man who would fabricate anything so bizarre. "I don't know if I can deal with this right now...." Devil's Gambit alive? But how? She'd been to the site of the accident, witnessed the gruesome truth for herself. Both the horse and the driver of the truck had been killed. Only Dustin had survived.

It was difficult to speak or to think rationally. Tiffany forced herself to look into Zane's brooding gaze and managed to clear her throat. "Look, I really do have an interview that I can't get out of. Please wait.... I...I want to talk to you. Alone." She extracted her arm from his grasp and made her way to the door. Her mind was running in crazy circles. What did he mean? Devil's Gambit couldn't possibly be alive. And Ellery—what about Ellery? Dear Lord, if what Zane was suggesting was true, there might be a chance that Ellery was still alive. But how? *Don't think like this,* she told herself. *What this man is suggesting can't possibly be true.*

Her knees were weak, and she leaned against the door for several seconds, trying to recover her lost equilibrium before the bell chimed for the fourth time. "Get hold of yourself," she murmured, but she was unable to disguise the clouds of despair in her eyes. Why now? Why did Zane Sheridan pick this time when everything at the breeding farm was in turmoil to enter her life with rash statements about the past? Forcing her worried thoughts to a dark corner of her mind, she straightened and braced herself for the interview.

With a jerk, she tugged on the brass handle and the door swung inward. Despite the storm of emotions raging within her, she forced what she hoped would appear a sincere and pleasant smile. Only the slightest trembling of her full lips hinted at her ravaged emotions.

"Mr. Crawford?" Tiffany asked the agitated young man slouching against a white pillar supporting the roof. "Please accept my apologies for the delay. My housekeeper isn't in yet and I had an unexpected visitor this morning." Her voice was surprisingly calm, her gaze direct, and she disguised the trembling in her fingers by hiding her hands in the deep pockets of her wool skirt.

The bearded, blond man eyed her skeptically, motioned to someone in the car and then handed her a card that stated that he was Rod Crawford of the *Santa Rosa Clarion*.

A petite, dark-haired woman climbed out of the car and slung a camera over one shoulder. Tiffany stepped away from the door to let the two people enter her home. In the distance she heard the familiar rumble of Louise's old Buick. The noise was reassuring. Once the housekeeper took charge of the kitchen, some of the disorder of the morning would abate. *Except that Zane Sheridan was in the den, seemingly convinced that Devil's Gambit and, therefore, Ellery were still alive.*

"Could I offer you a cup of coffee…or tea?" Tiffany asked with a weak smile.

"Coffee—black," Crawford stated curtly, withdrawing a note pad from his back pocket.

Tiffany trained her eyes on the photographer. "Anything,"

the pleasant-featured woman replied. She flashed Tiffany a friendly grin as she extended her small hand. "Jeanette Wilkes." Jeanette's interested eyes swept the opulent interior of the house and she noted the sweeping staircase, gleaming oak banister, elegant crystal chandelier and glossy imported floor tiles. "I was hoping to get a couple of pictures of the farm."

"Wonderful," Tiffany said with a smile that disguised her inner turmoil. "Please, have a seat in the living room." She opened the double doors of the formal room and silently invited them inside.

"You have a beautiful home," Jeanette stated as she looked at the period pieces and the Italian marble of the fireplace with a practiced eye. Everything about the house was first class— no outward sign of money problems.

"Thank you."

"Is this where you work?" Crawford asked skeptically.

"No…"

"If you don't mind, Jeanette would like to get some shots of the inside of the farm as well as the outbuildings. You know, give people a chance to see whatever it is you do when you're working. Don't you have an office or something?" He eyed the formal living room's expensive formal furniture with obvious distaste.

"Of course." The last thing Tiffany could afford was any bad press, so she had to accommodate the nosy reporter. She decided she would have to find a way to get rid of Zane Sheridan. His story was too farfetched to be believed; and yet there was something forceful and determined about him that made her think the Irishman wasn't bluffing.

Zane was still in the den and Tiffany wanted to keep Rod Crawford, with his probing questions, away from the visitor with the Irish accent. If the two men with their different perspectives on what was happening at Rhodes Breeding Farm got together, the results would be certain disaster. Tiffany shuddered when she envisioned the news concerning Moon

Shadow's foals and a rumor that Devil's Gambit was still alive being splashed across the front page of the *Santa Rosa Clarion*. The minute the combined reports hit the front page, she would have reporters calling her day and night.

Tiffany's mind was spinning miles a minute. What Zane had suggested was preposterous, and yet the surety of his gaze had convinced her that he wasn't playing games. But Devil's Gambit, alive? And Ellery? Her heart was beating so rapidly she could barely concentrate. She needed to talk to Zane Sheridan, that much was certain, just to find out if he were a master gambler, bluffing convincingly, or if he really did mean what he was saying and had the facts to back him up. But she had to speak to him alone, without the watchful eyes and ears of the press observing her.

Holding her back stiffly, she led Rod and Jeanette back through the foyer to the den, which was directly opposite the living room. Zane was standing by the fireplace, his eyes trained on the painting of the horse over the mantel. He had discarded his jacket and tossed it over the back of one chair, and the tight knot of his tie had been loosened. He looked as if he intended to stay. That was something she couldn't allow, and yet she was afraid to let him go. There were so many questions whirling in her mind. Who was he? What did he want? How did he know Ellery? Why did he want her to believe that Devil's Gambit might still be alive after four long years?

Without hesitation, Tiffany walked toward him. He turned to face her and his eyes were as cool and distant as the stormy, gray Pacific Ocean. If he had been lying a few moments before, he showed no trace of deceit. Yet his story couldn't possibly be true; either it was a total fabrication or he just didn't know what he was talking about.

The steadiness of his glare suggested just the opposite. Tiffany knew intuitively that Zane Sheridan rarely made mistakes. Cold dread took hold of her heart.

"Mr. Sheridan, would it be too much trouble to ask you to

wait to finish our discussion?" she asked with an unsteady smile. *What if he wouldn't leave and caused a scene in front of the reporter from the* Santa Rosa Clarion? *His story was just wild and sensational enough to capture Rod Crawford's attention.*

Zane's eyes flickered to the other two people and quickly sized them up as reporters. Obviously something was going on, and the widow Rhodes didn't want him to know about it. His thick brows drew together in speculation.

"How long?"

"I'm not sure.... Mr. Crawford?"

"Call me Rod."

Tiffany made a hasty introduction, while the bearded man came to her side and shook Zane's outstretched hand. The image of the reporter's hand linked with Zane's made her uneasy.

"I don't know," Rod was saying, rubbing his bearded chin. "I suppose it will take...what?" He eyed Jeanette for input. "An hour, maybe two. I want to ask you some questions and then we need a quick tour of the buildings."

Tiffany's throat went dry. No matter how crazy Zane's story seemed, she had to talk to him, find out what he wanted and why he thought that Devil's Gambit might still be alive.

"I have a meeting at noon," Zane stated, his calculating gaze never leaving the worried lines of her face. There was something in Tiffany Rhodes's manner that suggested it would be to his advantage to stay. But he needed to be with her alone in order to accomplish everything he had planned for six long years. He'd given her the bait, and she'd swallowed it hook, line and sinker. The satisfaction he had hoped to find was sadly lacking, and he felt a twinge of conscience at the worry in her clouded eyes.

"Look, Ms. Rhodes—can we get on with it? We've got another story to cover this afternoon," Crawford interjected.

"Of course." Tiffany returned her attention to Zane's proud face. She hoped that she didn't sound nearly as desperate as she felt. "Could you come by tomorrow, or would it be more convenient to meet you somewhere?"

"I have to catch an early flight." His angular jaw was tense, his muscles rigid, but there was the glimmer of expectancy in his eyes. *He's enjoying this,* she thought and she had to work to control her temper. She couldn't blow up now, not with Rod Crawford in the room, but there was something infuriating in Zane's arrogant manner.

Trying not to sound condescending she asked, "Then tonight?" He couldn't just waltz into her life, make outrageous statements, and then disappear as if nothing had happened. She had to know the truth, or what he was attempting to portray as the truth. She wanted to forget about him and his wild imaginings, but she couldn't dismiss him as just another publicity seeker. What did he want—*really want* from her?

Zane's gray eyes narrowed a fraction. "All right. What time?"

"How about dinner—seven-thirty?"

"I'll be here."

He picked up his jacket and flung it over his arm. Tiffany escorted him to the door and let out a long sigh of relief when he was gone. At least he had no inkling why the reporter was there, although it wouldn't be too hard to figure out, especially once the article was printed. "Maybe he'll be back in Ireland where he belongs by then," she muttered with false optimism.

Louise was serving coffee and scones when Tiffany returned to the den. After accepting a cup of black coffee, Tiffany seated herself at her desk, feeling uncomfortably close to Rod Crawford, who sat across the desk. While Jeanette snapped a few "candid" shots of Tiffany at work, Rod began the interview.

"How long have you actually managed the farm?" he asked.

"About four years."

"Ever since your husband's death?"

Tiffany felt her back tighten. "That's right. Before that I helped Ellery on the farm, but he ran it."

"I don't mean to bring up a sore subject," the wily reporter went on, "but ever since you took over, you've had quite a few bad breaks."

Tiffany smiled grimly. "That's true, but I don't like to dwell on them. Right now I'm concentrating on Journey's End."

"The three-year-old, right?"

"Yes. He has all the potential of being one of the greatest horses of the decade."

Rod Crawford laughed aloud. "I doubt if you're all that objective about your own colt."

"Obviously you've never seen him run," Tiffany replied with a slow-spreading grin. The tense air in the room dissolved, as she talked at length about Journey's End's impressive career.

"What about the recent string of deaths in the foaling shed?" Rod asked when the conversation waned. Though Tiffany had been bracing herself for the question, she found no easy answer to it.

"Three foals died shortly after birth," she admitted.

"And you don't know why?" Skepticism edged Rod's question.

Tiffany shook her head. "So far the autopsies haven't shown anything conclusive, other than that the cause of death was heart failure."

Rod settled into his chair and poised his pencil theatrically in the air. "Were the foals related?"

Here it comes, Tiffany thought. "They had different dams, of course, but both colts and the filly were sired by Moon Shadow."

"And he stands at stud here, on the farm."

"Yes, although we're not breeding him…until all this is cleared up." Tiffany's hands were beginning to shake again, and she folded them carefully over the top of the desk.

"You think he might be the cause?"

"I don't know."

"Genetic problem?"

Tiffany pursed her lips and frowned thoughtfully. "I don't think so. He's stood for almost eight years, and until now he's proved himself a good sire. Devil's Gambit and Journey's End are proof of that."

"Moon Shadow was the sire of both stallions?"

"And many more. Some not as famous, but *all* perfectly healthy and strong horses."

"So, what with Journey's End's success, you must be getting a lot of requests for Moon Shadow's services."

"That's right. But we're turning them down, at least for a while, until we can prove that whatever is happening here is not a genetic problem."

"That must be costing you—"

"I think it's worth it."

"Then you must think he's the cause."

"I don't know what's the cause. It may just be coincidence."

Rod snorted his disbelief, and Tiffany had to press her hands together to keep from losing her temper. To Rod Crawford, Moon Shadow was just another story, but to Tiffany he was a proud stallion with an admirable reputation as a race-horse and a sire. She would do anything she had to—short of lying—to protect him and the reputation of the farm.

"Have you had him tested?" Rod asked.

"Moon Shadow?" When Rod nodded, Tiffany replied, "Of course. He's been given a complete physical, and we've taken samples of his semen to be analyzed."

"And?"

"So far, nothing."

Rod twirled his pencil nervously. "What about mares that were brought to Moon Shadow and then taken home?"

Tiffany felt a headache beginning to pound. "As far as I know, only the horses on this farm have been affected. However, it's still early in the year and there are several mares who haven't yet dropped their foals."

"Have you been in contact with the owners of the mares and explained the problem to them?"

"Mr. Crawford," Tiffany stated evenly, "I'm not certain there is a problem, or exactly the nature of it. I'm not an alarmist and I'm not about to warn other owners or scare them out of their wits. What I have done is written a letter inquiring as to the condition of the foals involved. I've had seven responses, and all of them indicate that they have beautiful, healthy horses. Two owners want to rebreed their mares to Moon Shadow."

Rod frowned. "And have you?"

"Not yet."

"Because you're afraid?"

"Because I want to be certain of what is happening before I do anything that might cause any stress or trauma to the horses or the owners." Tiffany looked him squarely in the eye. "This is more than a business for me. It's a way of life, and there's more at stake than money." Rod's blank stare told Tiffany that he didn't understand anything she was saying. Perhaps no one did. Rod Crawford, or anyone else for that matter, couldn't know about the agonizing years she had spent growing up in musty tack rooms and dingy stables where the smell of ammonia had been so strong it had made her retch. No one knew that the only comfort she had found as an adolescent child was in working with the Thoroughbreds her father had been hired to train.

Before her thoughts became too vivid and painful, Tiffany spread her hands expressively over the desk and forced a frail smile at the reporter. "Look, until I know for certain what exactly it is that's happening, I'm not about to make any rash statements, and I would appreciate your cooperation—"

Rod raised a dubious blond brow. "By withholding the story?"

"By not sensationalizing the deaths and *creating* a story. I agreed to this interview because I know of the *Clarion's* reputation."

"I have to report the truth."

Tiffany smiled stiffly. "That's all I can ask for. Now, if you have any further questions about the horses involved, you can call Vance Geddes, the veterinarian who was with the mares when they delivered the foals."

"Fair enough," Rod replied.

Tiffany led the reporter and his assistant through the broodmare barn and the foaling shed, before returning outside to the brisk March air. While Rod asked questions, Jeanette took some outside shots of a field where mares grazed and spindly-legged foals ran in the shafts of late-morning sunlight.

Tiffany's face lifted with pride as she watched the dark foals run and shy behind the safety of their mothers' flanks. The newborns always held a special place in her heart. She loved to watch them stand and nurse for the first time, or run in the fields with their downy ears pricked forward and their intelligent eyes wide to the vast new world. Maybe that was why the deaths of the foals affected her so deeply.

"I'll send you a copy of the article," Rod promised just before he and Jeanette left.

"Thank you." Tiffany watched in relief as the sporty Mazda headed out the long drive. The interview hadn't been as bad as she had expected, but nonetheless, she felt drained from the ordeal.

After changing into comfortable jeans and a sweatshirt, Tiffany returned to the den and pulled out the checkbook. But before she could concentrate on the ledgers, she let her eyes wander to the portrait of Devil's Gambit, the horse that Zane Sheridan insisted was alive.

"It can't be," she murmured to herself. Devil's Gambit had been a beautifully built colt with a short, sturdy back, and powerful hind legs that could explode into a full stride of uncanny speed and grace. Jet-black, with one distinctive white stocking, Devil's Gambit had taken the racing world by storm, winning all of his two-year-old starts by ever-increasing margins. As a three-year-old his career had taken off with a flourish, and he had been compared to such greats as Secretariat and Seattle Slew.

Then, a month before the Kentucky Derby, it had all ended tragically. Devil's Gambit suffered a horrible death while being transported from Florida to Kentucky.

Tiffany had learned that Ellery had been driving and had apparently fallen asleep at the wheel. Dustin, his brother, had been a passenger in the truck. Miraculously, Dustin had survived with only minor injuries by being thrown out of the cab as the truck tumbled end over end, down an embankment, where it exploded into flames that charred beyond recognition the bodies of Ellery Rhodes and his fleet horse. Dustin's injuries had included a broken leg and minor concussion, which were treated at a local hospital. He had been out of the hospital in time to stand by Tiffany's side at Ellery's funeral.

Tiffany swallowed against the painful memory and shook her head. It had taken her several months to come to accept the death of her husband and his brave horse. And now a total stranger, a man by the name of Zane Sheridan, was trying to make her believe that it had all been a treacherous mistake.

But he didn't state that Ellery was alive, she reminded herself with a defeated smile, only Devil's Gambit. And when Zane had mentioned Ellery, it had been with a look of barely veiled contempt on his rugged black-Irish features.

What can it all mean? She slanted a glance at the portrait of Devil's Gambit and frowned. How could someone hide a horse of such renown? And who could have come up with such a scheme? And why? Certainly not for kidnapping ransom. *Get hold of yourself,* she cautioned, *you're letting your imagination run away with you, all because of some stranger's outlandish remarks.*

With a grimace she turned her attention back to the checkbook and finished paying the month-end bills. She wasn't exactly strapped for money, but each month her assets seemed to diminish. There was still a large, outstanding mortgage against the property, and several major repairs to the barns couldn't be neglected much longer.

If she regretted anything, it was allowing Ellery to build the expensive house. "You can't be a horse breeder unless you look the part," he had said with the confidence of one who understands the subtleties in life. "No one will bring their mares here if we don't *look* like we know what we're doing."

"It's not the house that counts, it's the quality of the stallions and the care of the horses," Tiffany had argued uselessly. In the end, Ellery had gotten his way. After all, it had only taken a quick signature at the bank—his signature—to get the loan to rebuild the house into a grand, Southern manor.

"This is California, not Kentucky," she had reminded him. "No one cares about this sort of thing." But her protests had fallen on deaf ears and Ellery had taken up wearing suits with patches on the sleeves and smoking a pipe filled with blended tobaccos.

The house was finished only six months before the accident. Since that time she had lived in it alone. It was beautiful and grand and mortgaged to the hilt. Ellery hadn't seen fit to purchase mortgage insurance at the time he took out the loan. "Money down the drain," he had commented with a knowing smile.

"I must have been out of my mind to have listened to him," Tiffany thought aloud as she pushed the ledgers aside and stood. How many years had she blindly trusted him, all because he had saved her life? She shuddered when she remembered the time she had seen Ellery, his face contorted in fear, as he dived in front of the oncoming car and pushed her out of its path.

Maybe it had been gratitude rather than love that she had felt for him, but nonetheless they had been married and she had depended upon him. *And now there was a chance that he was still alive.* The thought made her heart race unevenly.

After grabbing her jacket, she sank her teeth into her lower lip, walked outside and turned toward the broodmare barn. A

chilly wind was blowing from the west and she had to hold
her hair away from her face to keep it from whipping across
her eyes. Mac was leaning over the railing of one of the stalls
in the barn. His sharp eyes turned in her direction when she
approached.

"I was just about to come up to the house," he stated, a
worried expression pinching his grizzled features.

"Something wrong?"

"No…but it looks like this lady here—" he cocked his
head in the direction of the black mare restlessly pacing her
stall "—is gonna foal tonight."

Instead of the usual expectation Tiffany always felt at the
prospect of new life, she now experienced dread. The mare
in question, Ebony Wine, was carrying another of Moon
Shadow's foals.

"You're sure?" she asked, surveying the mare's wide
girth.

"Aye. She's a week overdue as it is, and look." He pointed
a bony finger at the mare's full udder. "She's waxed over and
beginning to drip."

"Has she starting sweating?"

"Not yet. It will be a while—sometime after midnight
unless I miss my guess."

"But everything else looks normal?" Tiffany asked, her
knowing gaze studying the restless horse.

"So far."

"Let me know when the time comes," Tiffany ordered,
patting the mare fondly.

"You're not going to wait up again?"

"Of course I am."

Mac took off his hat and dangled it from his fingers as he
leaned on the railing of the stall. "There's nothing you can do,
you know. What will be, will be."

"You can't talk me out of this. I'll give Vance a call and
ask him to come over." She took one last glance at the heavy-

bellied mare. "Come up to the house and get me if anything goes wrong, or if it looks like the foal will be early."

Mac nodded curtly and placed his frumpy fedora back on his head. "You're the boss," he muttered, placing his hands in the back pockets of his trousers. "I'll be in the tack room if ya need me."

"Thanks, Mac." Tiffany walked outside but didn't return to the house. Instead, she let herself through a series of gates and walked through the gently sloping paddocks away from the main buildings.

When she neared the old barn, she halted and studied the graying structure. Once the barn had been integral to the farm, but the vacant building hadn't been used for years. Ellery had insisted that the horses needed newer, more modern facilities, and rather than put money into modernizing the old barn, he had erected the new broodmare barn and foaling shed.

The weathered building with the sagging roof was little more than an eyesore, and Tiffany realized that she should have had it torn down years before. Its only function was to store excess hay and straw through the winter.

She walked toward the barn and ignored the fact that blackberry vines were beginning to ramble and cling to the east wall. The old door creaked on rusty rollers as she pushed it aside and walked into the musty interior.

It took a few minutes for her eyes to adjust to the dim light. How many years had it been since she had first seen Ellery? She had been standing near the stalls, making sure that the horses had fresh water when he had startled her.

Before that fateful day, she had seen him only from a distance. After all, she was only a trainer's daughter. A nobody. Tiffany doubted that Ellery Rhodes realized that when he hired Edward Chappel, he took on Edward's eighteen-year-old daughter, as well.

Perhaps her mistake had been to stay with her father, but Edward Chappel was the only family she had known. Her mother, Marie, had abandoned them both when Tiffany was only five. She could remember little of Marie except that she had thick, golden hair and a beautiful but weary face that very rarely smiled.

Fragments of life with her mother had come to mind over the years. Tiffany remembered that Marie insisted that her daughter's hair always be combed and that her faded clothes always be neatly starched. And there was a tune…a sad refrain that Marie would sing when she helped Tiffany get dressed in the morning. Twenty years later, Tiffany would still find herself humming that tune.

The day that her mother had walked out of her life was still etched vividly in her mind. "You must remember that Mommy loves you very much and I'll come back for you," Marie had whispered to Tiffany, with tears gathering in her round, indigo eyes. "I promise, pumpkin." Then Marie had gathered her daughter close to her breast, as if she couldn't bear to walk out the door.

Tiffany had felt the warm trickle of her mother's tears as they silently dropped onto the crown of her head.

"Mommy, don't leave me. *Please*…. Mommy, Mommy, don't go. I'll be good…Mommy, I love you, please…" Tiffany had wailed, throwing her arms around her mother's neck and then sobbing with all of her heart for hours after Marie's car had disappeared in a plume of dust.

Her father's face was stern, his shoulders bowed. "Don't blame her, Tiffy," he had whispered hoarsely, "it's all my fault, you know. I haven't been much of a husband."

Tiffany had never seen Marie Caldwell Chappel again.

At first she couldn't believe that her mother had left her, and each night she would stare out the window and pray that the tall man with the big car would bring her mother home. Later, in her early teens, Tiffany was angry that she didn't have a mother to help her understand the changes in her body and the new emotions taking hold of her. Now, as an adult, Tiffany understood that a woman who had been brought up with a taste for the finer things in life could never have been happy with Edward Chappel.

Edward had always been irresponsible, going from job to job, breeding farm to breeding farm, working with the animals he loved. But each time, just when Tiffany thought they had settled down for good and she had made one or two friends in the local school, he would lose his job and they would move on to a new town, a new school, a new set of classmates who would rather ignore than accept her. To this day, she had never made any close friends. She had learned long ago that relationships were fragile and never lasted for any length of time.

After Marie had left him, Edward had sworn off the bottle for nearly three years. Tiffany now realized that his abstinence was because of the hope that Marie would return to him rather than because of his new responsibility as a single parent.

When she was just eighteen and trying to save enough money to go to college, they'd moved to the Rhodes Farm. Edward was off the bottle again and he had promised his daughter that this time he would make good.

It was in this very barn that her life had changed. While she'd been softly talking to one of the yearlings, Ellery Rhodes had walked in on her.

"Who are you?" he'd asked imperiously, and Tiffany had frozen. When she'd turned to face him, the look on his even features was near shock.

"I'm Tiffany Chappel," she had replied, with a faltering smile.

"Ed's daughter?"

"Yes."

Ellery had been flustered. "I thought that you were just a little girl." His eyes moved from her face, down the length of her body and back again. An embarrassed flush crept up his neck. "Obviously, I was mistaken."

"Dad seems to think that I'm still about eleven," she explained with a shrug and turned back to the horses.

"How old are you?"

"Eighteen."

"Why aren't you out on your own?" It was a nosy question, but Ellery asked it with genuine concern in his gold eyes. His brows had pulled together and a thoughtful frown pulled at the corners of his mouth. For a moment Tiffany thought that he might fire her father because of her. Maybe Ellery Rhodes didn't like the idea of a girl—young woman—on his farm. Maybe one of the grooms had complained about a woman on the farm. She had already had more than her share of male advances from the stable boys.

Tiffany couldn't explain to her father's employer that she had to look after him, or that a good share of his work was done by her strong hands. Edward Chappel would be fired again. Instead she lied. "I'm only helping him out for a little while. Until I go back to college—"

Ellery's practiced eyes took in her torn sweatshirt, faded jeans and oversized boots. Tiffany knew that he saw through her lie, but he was too much of a gentleman to call her on it.

Two days later, she was called into his office. Her heart pounded with dread as she entered the old farmhouse and sat stiffly in one of the chairs near his desk.

Ellery looked up from a stack of bills he had been paying. "I've got a proposition for you, young lady," he stated, looking up at her and his gold eyes shining. "Your father has already approved."

"What do you mean?"

Ellery smiled kindly. It wasn't a warm smile, but it was caring. He explained that he had worked out a deal with her father. He liked the way she handled the horses, he claimed, and he offered to send her to school, if she promised to return to the farm and work off the amount of money her education would cost once she had graduated.

Tiffany had been ecstatic with her good fortune, and

Edward, feeling that he had finally found a way to rightfully provide for his daughter, was as pleased as anyone.

She had never forgotten Ellery's kindness to her, and she had held up her part of the bargain. When she returned to the farm two years later, she found that her father was drinking again.

"You've got to leave," he said, coughing violently. The stench of cheap whiskey filled the air in the small room he had been living in on the farm.

"I can't, Dad. I've got a debt to pay."

Edward shivered, though he was covered by several thick blankets. "You should never have come back."

"Why didn't anyone tell me you were sick—"

Edward raised a feeble hand and waved away her concerns. "It wouldn't help anything now, would it? You were so close to finishing school, I didn't want you to know."

"I think you should be in a hospital."

Edward shook his head and another fit of racking coughs took hold of him. "I want you to leave. I've got a little money. Get away from this farm, from Ellery Rhodes—"

"But he's been so good to me."

Her father's faded blue eyes closed for a second. "He's changed, Tiff…." Another fit of coughing took hold of him, and he doubled up in pain.

"I'm getting you to a hospital, right now."

Despite her father's protests, Tiffany managed to get him out of the stifling room and to the main house. When she knocked on the door, Stasia, the exotic-looking woman Ellery was living with, answered the door.

"My father needs help," Tiffany said.

Stasia's full lips pulled into a line of disgust at the sight of Tiffany and her father. Her dark eyes traveled over Tiffany, and she tossed her hair off her shoulders. "He needs to dry out—"

"He's sick."

"Humph."

Pulling herself to her full height, Tiffany looked the older woman directly in the eye. "Please. Call Ellery."

"He's not here."

"Then find someone to help me."

Edward's coughing started again. His shoulders racked from the pain. "I don't know why Ellery keeps him around," Stasia muttered, as she reached for her coat and begrudgingly offered to drive them into town.

Tiffany remained at her father's side for two days until the pneumonia that had settled in his lungs took his life.

"You stupid, lovable old fool," Tiffany had said, tears running down her face. "Why did you kill yourself—why?" she asked, as her father's body was moved from the hospital room to the morgue.

Refusing help from the hospital staff, Tiffany had run out of the building, blinded by tears of grief and guilt. If she hadn't gone away to school, if she had stayed on the farm, her father would still have been alive.

She didn't see the oncoming car as she crossed the street. She heard the blast from an angry horn, smelled the burn of rubber as tires screamed against the dry asphalt and felt a man's body push her out of the way of the station wagon.

The man who had saved her life was Ellery. He'd gathered her shaken form into his arms and muttered something about being sorry. She didn't understand why, and she didn't care. Ellery Rhodes was the only person she had ever known who had been kind to her with no ulterior motives.

Within two weeks, Stasia was gone and Ellery asked Tiffany to marry him.

Tiffany didn't hesitate. Ellery Rhodes was the first person she had met that she could depend on. He cared for her, and though he seemed distant at times, Tiffany realized that no relationship was perfect.

She wondered now if she had married him out of gratitude or grief. The love she had hoped would bloom within her had never surfaced, but she supposed that was because passionate, emotional love only existed in fairy tales.

Inexplicably, her thoughts returned to Zane Sheridan, with his knowing gray eyes and ruggedly hewn features. He was the last person she needed to complicate her life right now, and the idea that he could shed any light on what had happened to Devil's Gambit or Ellery was preposterous.

But what if there's a chance that Ellery's alive?

Without any answers to her questions, Tiffany headed back to the house to remind Louise that there would be a guest for dinner.

"YOU'RE ASKING THE IMPOSSIBLE!" John Morris stated as he eyed his client over the clear rims of his reading glasses.

"It's a simple document," Zane argued, rubbing the back of his neck and rotating his head to relieve the tension that had been building ever since he had met Tiffany Rhodes. He'd known she was beautiful; he'd seen enough pictures of her to understand that her exotic looks could be any man's undoing. But he hadn't counted on the light of intrigue and mystery in her intense gaze or the serene beauty in the curve of her neck....

"A deed of sale for a breeding farm? You've got to be joking."

Zane's eyes flashed like quicksilver. He pulled at the bothersome knot in his tie and focused his eyes on the attorney. "Just get me a paper that says that for a certain amount of money—and leave that blank—I will purchase all of the assets and the liabilities of Rhodes Breeding Farm."

The lawyer let out a weary sigh. "You're out of your mind, Zane. That is if you want anything legal—"

"I want it to be binding. No loopholes. It has to be so tight that if the buyer decides she wants out of the deal, she has no legal recourse. None whatsoever." His square jaw tightened, and the thin lines near the corners of his eyes deepened with fresh resolve. Revenge was supposed to be sweet.

So where was the satisfaction he had been savoring for nearly six years?

"You're asking the impossible. We're not talking about a used car, for God's sake."

"It can't be that difficult." Zane paced in the prestigious San Francisco lawyer's office and ran impatient fingers through his raven-black hair in disgust. "What about a quit-claim deed?"

The lawyer leaned back in his chair and held on to his pen with both hands. "I assume that you want to do this right."

"Of course."

"No legal recourse—right?"

"I already told you that."

"Then be patient. I'll draw up all the legal documents and do a title search…take care of all the loose ends. That way, once you've agreed upon a price, you can wrap it up and it *will* be binding. You can't have it both ways, not here anyway. You're not just talking about real estate, you know. There is personal property, equipment, the horses…."

"I get the picture." Zane stared out the window and frowned. The trouble was he wanted to get away from Tiffany Rhodes. Do what he had to do and then make a clean break.

There was something about the woman that got under his skin, and he didn't like the look of honesty in her slate-blue eyes. It bothered him. A lot. Whatever else he had expected of Ellery Rhodes's widow, it hadn't been integrity.

Zane shrugged as if to shake off the last twinges of guilt. "So how long will it take you?" he asked, hiding some of his impatience.

"Four weeks—maybe three, if we're lucky. I'll work out something temporary for the interim. Okay?"

"I guess it will have to be. Doesn't seem that I have much of a choice."

John drummed his fingers on the desk. "You're sure that

this woman wants to sell? I've read a little about her. She seems to be…the plucky type. Not the kind to sell out."

"She just needs a little convincing."

John scowled at the blank piece of paper in front of him. "That sounds ominous—right out of a bad B movie."

Zane smiled despite his discomfiture. It was a rare smile, but genuine, and he flashed it on his friend in a moment of self-mockery. "I guess you're right."

"Aren't I always?"

"And humble, too," Zane muttered under his breath. "Come on, counselor, I'll buy you a drink."

"On one condition—"

Zane's brows quirked expectantly.

"That you quit calling me counselor. I hear enough of that in the courtroom."

"It's a deal."

John slipped his arms into his jacket and then straightened the cuffs before bending over his desk and pressing a button on the intercom. "Sherry, I'm going out for a few minutes with Mr. Sheridan. I'll be back at—" he cocked his wrist and checked his watch "—three-thirty."

John reached for the handle of the door before pausing and turning to face his friend. "There's just one thing I'd like to know about this transaction you requested."

"And that is?"

"Why the hell do you want to buy a breeding farm? I thought you learned your lesson in Dublin a few years back."

Zane's eyes grew dark. "Maybe that's exactly why I want it." With a secretive smile he slapped his friend fondly on the back. "Now, how about that drink?"

CHAPTER THREE

TIFFANY'S FINGERS DRUMMED RESTLESSLY ON the desk as she stared at the portrait of Devil's Gambit. For so long she had believed that Ellery and his proud horse were dead. And now this man, this stranger named Zane Sheridan, insisted just the opposite. Her blue eyes were shadowed with pain as she studied the portrait of the horse. *Was it possible? Could Ellery still be alive?*

Shaking her head at the absurdity of the situation, she got up and paced restlessly, alternately staring at the clock and looking out the window toward the foaling shed. Ebony Wine would be delivering a foal tonight, Moon Shadow's foal. Would he be a normal, healthy colt or would he suffer the same cruel fate as three of his siblings?

She listened as the clock ticked off the seconds, and her stomach tightened into uneasy knots. Mac hadn't come to the house this afternoon, and Tiffany was beginning to worry. Between her anxiety for the unborn foal and worries about Zane Sheridan and his motives for visiting her, Tiffany's nerves felt raw, stretched to the breaking point.

Seven-thirty-five. Though Zane would arrive any minute, Tiffany couldn't sit idle any longer. She jerked her jacket off the wooden peg near the French doors and hurried outside, oblivious to the fact that her heels sank into the mud of the well-worn path. The darkness of the night was punctuated by the sharp wind that rattled the windowpanes and whistled through the redwoods.

Tiffany found Mac in the broodmare barn, examining the black mare. His face was grim, and Tiffany's heart nearly stopped beating.

"How's it going?" she asked, hoping that she didn't sound desperate.

Mac came to the outside of the stall and reached down to scratch Wolverine, the farm's border collie, behind the ears. Wolverine thumped his tail against the concrete floor in appreciation, but Tiffany had the impression that Mac was avoiding her gaze.

"So far so good," the ex-jockey replied, straightening and switching a piece of straw from one side of his mouth to the other. But his sharp brown eyes were troubled when they returned to Ebony Wine. The mare shifted uncomfortably in the large stall, and Tiffany noted that everything was ready for the impending birth. Six inches of clean straw covered the concrete floor, and a plastic bucket containing towels, antibiotics, scissors and other equipment necessary to help the mare give birth, had been placed near the stall.

"Might be a little earlier than I thought originally," Mac suggested. He took off his hat and straightened the crease with his fingers.

"Why?"

"This is her second foal. If I remember right, the last one came before midnight." He rammed the hat back on his head. "Could be wrong…just a feeling I've got."

"Have you called Vance?"

Mac nodded curtly. "He'll be here around eleven, earlier if we need him."

"Good."

Tiffany cast one final look toward the mare and then returned to the house. Wolverine padded along behind her, but she didn't notice. Her thoughts were filled with worry for the mare and anxiety about meeting Zane Sheridan again. He couldn't have picked a worse time to show up.

All afternoon her thoughts had been crowded with questions about him. Who was he? What did he want? How did he know Ellery? Why would he concoct such an elaborate story about Devil's Gambit being alive?

There was something about the man that was eerily familiar, and Tiffany felt that she had heard Ellery speak of him at least once. But it was long ago, before they were married, and she couldn't remember the significance, if there was any, of Ellery's remarks.

She had just returned to the house and stepped out of her muddied shoes when headlights flashed through the interior of the manor as if announcing Zane's arrival. "Here we go," she muttered to herself as she slipped on a pair of pumps and attempted to push back the tides of dread threatening to overtake her. "He's only one man," she told herself as the doorbell chimed. "One man with a wild imagination."

But when she opened the door and she saw him standing in the shadowy porch light, once again she experienced the feeling that Zane Sheridan rarely made mistakes. He was leaning casually against one of the tall pillars supporting the porch roof, and his hands were thrust into the front pockets of his corduroy slacks. Even in the relaxed pose, there was tension, strain in the way his smile tightened over his teeth, a coiled energy lying just beneath the surface in his eyes.

In the dim light, his mouth appeared more sensual than she had remembered and the rough angles of his face seemed less threatening. His jet-black hair was without a trace of gray and gleamed blue in the lamplight. Only his eyes gave away his age. Though still a sharp, intense silver, they were hard, as if they had witnessed years of bitterness. The skin near the corners of his eyes was etched with a faint webbing that suggested he had stared often into the glare of the afternoon sun.

"Sorry I'm late," he said, straightening as his bold gaze held hers.

"No problem," she returned and wondered what it was

about him that she found so attractive. She'd never been a woman drawn to handsome faces or strong physiques. But there was an intelligence in Zane's eyes, hidden beneath a thin veneer of pride, that beckoned the woman in her. It was frightening. "Please come in."

I can't be attracted to him, she thought. *He can't be trusted. God only knows what he wants from me.*

He walked with her to the den. "I'm sorry for the interruption this morning—" she began.

"My fault. I should have called." A flash of a brilliant smile gleamed against his dark skin.

Tiffany didn't bother to wave off his apology. Zane's surprise appearance on her doorstep had thrown her day into a tailspin. It had been a wonder that she could even converse intelligently with the reporter from the *Santa Rosa Clarion* considering the bombshell that this man had dropped in her lap.

"Could I get you a drink?" she inquired as she walked toward a well-stocked bar disguised in the bookcase behind her desk. Ellery had insisted on the most modern of conveniences, the bar being one of his favorites. Tiffany hadn't used it more than twice since her husband's death.

"Scotch, if you have it."

She had it all right. That and about every other liquor imaginable. "You never can guess what a man might drink," Ellery had explained with a knowing wink. "Got to be prepared... just in case. I wouldn't want to blow a potential stud fee all because I didn't have a bottle of liquor around." Ellery had laughed, as if his response to her inquiry were a joke. But he had filled the bar with over thirty bottles of the most expensive liquor money could buy. "Think of it as a tax deduction," he had joked.

"Oh, I'm sure I've got Scotch," she answered Zane. "It's just a matter of locating it." After examining a few of the unfamiliar labels, Tiffany wiped away some of the dust that had collected on the unused bottles. *What a waste.*

It didn't take long to find an opened bottle of Scotch. She splashed the amber liquor into a glass filled with ice cubes and then, with a forced smile, she handed Zane the drink. "Now," she said, her voice surprisingly calm, "why don't you tell me why you think Devil's Gambit is alive?"

After pouring herself a glass of wine, she took an experimental sip and watched Zane over the rim of her glass. "That is, if you haven't changed your mind since this morning."

A gray light of challenge flashed in his eyes and his facade of friendly charm faded slightly. "Nothing's changed."

"So you still think that the horse is alive…and you're still interested in buying the farm, right?"

"That's correct."

Tiffany let out a ragged sigh and took a chair near the desk. "Please, have a seat."

Zane was too restless to sit. He walked over to the window and stared into the black, starless night. "I didn't mean to shock you this morning." Why the hell was he apologizing? He owed this woman nothing more than a quick explanation, and even that stuck in his throat. But there was something intriguing about her—a feminine mystique that touched a black part of his soul. Damn it all, this meeting was starting off all wrong. Ellery Rhodes's widow turned his thinking around. When he was with her, he started forgetting his objectives.

"Well, you did."

"Like I said—I should have called to make sure that we would have some time to talk."

Tiffany shifted uneasily in the chair. "We have all night," she said, and when a flicker of interest sparked in his eyes she quickly amended her statement. "Or however long it takes to straighten out this mess. Why don't you explain yourself?"

"I told you, I have reason to believe that Devil's Gambit is alive."

Tiffany smiled and shook her head. "That's impossible. I…I was at the scene of the accident. The horse was killed."

Zane frowned into the night. "*A* horse was killed."

"Devil's Gambit was the only horse in the trailer. The other two horses that had been stabled in Florida were in another truck—the one that Mac was driving. They were already in Kentucky when the accident occurred." She ran trembling fingers through her hair as she remembered that black, tragic night. Once again she thought about the terror and pain that Ellery and his horse must have gone through in those last agonizing moments before death mercifully took them both. "Devil's Gambit died in the accident." Her voice was low from the strain of old emotions, and she had to fight against the tears threatening her eyes.

"Unless he was never in that truck in the first place."

Tiffany swallowed with difficulty. "What are you suggesting, Mr. Sheridan?"

"I think that Devil's Gambit was kidnapped."

"That's crazy. My husband—"

Zane's eyes flashed silver fire. "Was probably involved."

Tiffany stood on trembling legs, her hands flattened on the desk to support her. A quiet rage began to burn in her chest. "This conversation is absurd. Why would Ellery steal his own horse?"

Zane shrugged. "Money? Wasn't Devil's Gambit insured?"

"Not to his full value. After he won in Florida, we intended to increase the coverage, as he proved himself much more valuable than anyone had guessed. I had all the forms filled out, but before I could send them back to the insurance company as Ellery had suggested, I had to wait until I saw him again. Several of the documents required his signature." She shook her head at her own foolishness. "Why am I telling you all of this?" After releasing a weary sigh, she rapped her knuckles on the polished desk and clasped her hands behind her back.

"Because I'm telling you the truth."

"You think."

"I know."

Tiffany's emotions were running a savage gauntlet of anger

and fear, but she attempted to keep her voice steady. "How do you know?"

"I saw your horse."

She sucked in her breath. "You saw Devil's Gambit? That's impossible. If he were alive, someone would have told me—"

"Someone is."

There was a charged silence in the air. "It's been four years since the accident. Why now?"

"Because I wasn't sure before."

Tiffany shook her head in denial, and her honey-colored hair brushed her shoulders. "This is too crazy—where did you see the horse? And how did you know it was Devil's Gambit? And what horse was killed in the trailer—and…and…what about my husband?" she whispered. "His brother Dustin was with him. Dustin knows what happened."

"Dustin claimed to be sleeping."

Tiffany flinched. How did this man, this virtual stranger, know so much about her and what had happened that night? If only she could remember what Ellery had said about Zane Sheridan. Ellery had spent some time in Ireland—Dublin. Maybe that was the connection. Zane still spoke with a slight brogue. Ellery must have known Zane in Dublin, and that's why he was here. Something happened in Ireland, years ago. Any other reason was just a fabrication, an excuse.

"Dustin would have woken up if the truck was stopped and the horses were switched. Dear God, do you know what you're suggesting?" Tiffany took a calming swallow of her wine and began to pace in front of the desk. Her thoughts were scattered between Zane, the tragic past and the tense drama unfolding in the foaling shed. "Ellery would never have been involved in anything so underhanded."

"Didn't you ever question what happened?" Zane asked suddenly.

"Of course, but—"

"Didn't you think it was odd that Dustin had taken sleeping

pills? Wasn't he supposed to drive later in the night—switch off with Ellery so that they wouldn't have to stop?"

Tiffany was immediately defensive. "Dustin's an insomniac. He needed the rest before the Derby."

"The Derby was weeks away."

"But there was a lot of work—"

"And what about your husband? Why did he decide to drive that night? Wasn't that out of the ordinary?" Bitterness tightened Zane's features, and he clutched his drink in a death grip.

"He was excited—he wanted to be a part of it." But even to her, the words sounded false. Ellery had always believed in letting the hired help handle the horses. Before that night, he had always flown—first class—to the next racetrack.

Zane saw the doubts forming in her eyes. "Everything about that 'accident' seems phony to me."

"But there was an investigation—"

"Thorough?"

"I—I don't know…. I think so." At the time she had been drowning in her own grief and shock. She had listened to the police reports, viewed the brutal scene of the accident, visited Dustin in the hospital and flown home in a private fog of sorrow and disbelief. After the funeral, Dustin's strong arms and comforting words had helped her cope with her loss.

"Were Ellery's dental records checked?"

Tiffany's head snapped up, and her eyes were bright with righteous defiance. "Of course not. Ellery was driving. Dustin was there. There didn't need to be any further investigation." Her eyes narrowed a fraction, and her voice shook when she spoke again. "What are you suggesting, Mr. Sheridan? That my husband is still alive—hiding from me somewhere with his horse?"

Zane impaled her with his silvery stare and then ran impatient fingers through his hair. "I don't know."

A small sound of disbelief came from Tiffany's throat and she had to lean against the desk for support. "I—I don't know why I'm even listening to this," she whispered hoarsely. "It just doesn't make any sense. Devil's Gambit is worth a lot more as Devil's Gambit—in terms of dollars at the racetrack and stud fees. Anything you've suggested is absolutely beyond reason." She smiled grimly, as if at her own foolhardiness. "Look, I think maybe it would be better if you just left."

"I can't do that—not yet."

"Why not?"

"Because I intend to convince you that your horse was stolen from you."

"That's impossible."

"Maybe not." Zane extracted a small manila envelope from his breast pocket and walked back to the desk. "There are some pictures in here that might change your mind." He handed Tiffany the envelope, and she accepted it with a long sigh.

There were three photographs, all of the same horse. Tiffany scanned the color prints of a running horse closely, studying the bone structure and carriage of the animal. The similarities between the horse in the photograph and Devil's Gambit were uncanny. "Where did you get these?" she asked, her breath constricting in her throat.

"I took them. Outside of Dublin."

It made sense. The horse, if he really was Devil's Gambit, would have to be hidden out of the country to ensure that no one would recognize or identify him. Even so, Zane's story was ludicrous. "This isn't Devil's Gambit," she said, her slate-blue eyes questioning his. "This horse has no white marks... anywhere." She pointed to the portrait above the fireplace. "Devil's Gambit had a stocking, on his right foreleg."

"I think the stocking has been dyed."

"To hide his identity?"

"And to palm him off as another horse, one of considerably less caliber."

"This is ridiculous." Tiffany rolled her eyes and raised her hands theatrically in the air. "You know, you almost convinced me by coming in here and making outlandish statements that I nearly believed. Heaven knows why. Maybe it's because you seemed so sure of yourself. But I can tell you without a doubt that this is not Devil's Gambit." She shook the prints in the air before tossing them recklessly on the desk. "Nothing you've said tonight makes any sense, nor is it backed up with the tiniest shred of evidence. Therefore I have to assume that you're here for another reason, such as the sale of the farm. My position hasn't altered on that subject, either. So you see, Mr. Sheridan, any further discussion would be pointless."

Louise knocked softly on the door of the den before poking her head inside. "Dinner's ready." She eyed Tiffany expectantly.

"I don't think—"

"Good. I'm starved," Zane stated as he turned his head in the housekeeper's direction. A slow-spreading, damnably charming grin took possession of his handsome face. Gray eyes twinkled devilishly, and his brilliant smile exposed a dimple on one tanned cheek.

"Whenever you're ready," Louise replied, seemingly oblivious to the tension in the room and returning Zane's smile. "I have to be getting home," she said apologetically to Tiffany, who nodded in response. Louise slowly backed out of the room and closed the door behind her.

"I didn't think you'd want to stay," Tiffany remarked, once Louise had left them alone.

"And miss a home-cooked meal? Not on your life."

Tiffany eyed him dubiously. "Something tells me this has nothing to do with the meal."

"Maybe I'm just enjoying the company—"

"Or maybe you think you can wear me down and I'll start believing all this nonsense."

"Maybe."

"There's no point, you know."

Zane laughed aloud, and the bitterness in his gaze disappeared for a second. "Try me."

"But we have nothing more to discuss. Really. I'm not buying your story. Not any of it."

"You're not even trying."

"I have the distinct feeling that you're attempting to con me, Mr. Sheridan—"

"Zane."

"Whatever. And I'm not up to playing games. Whether you believe it or not, I'm a busy woman who has more important things to do than worry about what could have happened. I like to think I deal in reality rather than fantasy."

Zane finished his drink with a flourish and set the empty glass down on the corner of the desk. "Then you'd better start listening to me, damn it. Because I'm not here on some cock and bull story." His thick brows lifted. "I have better things to do than spend my time trying to help someone who obviously doesn't want it."

"Help?" Tiffany repeated with a laugh. "All you've done so far is offer me vague insinuations and a few photographs of a horse that definitely is *not* Devil's Gambit. You call that help?"

Zane pinched the bridge of his nose, closed his eyes and let out a long breath. "If you weren't so blind, woman," he said, his black-Irish temper starting to explode.

"Look—"

Zane held up one palm and shrugged. "Maybe you just need time to think about all of this."

"What I don't need is someone to march into my life and start spewing irrational statements."

Zane smiled, and the tension drained from his face to be replaced by genuine awe of the woman standing near the desk. In the past six years, he'd imagined coming face to face with Ellery Rhodes's widow more often than he would like to admit, but never had he thought that she would be so incredibly bewitching. His mistake. Once before Ellery Rhodes and Zane Sheridan had been attracted to the same woman, and that time Zane had come out the loser, or so he had thought at the time. Now he wasn't so sure.

"Come on," he suggested, his voice becoming dangerously familiar. "I wasn't kidding when I said I was starved."

Tiffany backed down a little. "I won't change my mind."

With a nonchalant shrug, Zane loosened the knot of his tie and unbuttoned the collar of his shirt. His chin was beginning to darken with the shadow of a day's growth of beard, and he looked as if he belonged in this house, as if he had just come home from a long, tiring day at the office to share conversation and a drink with his wife…. The unlikely turn of her thoughts spurred Tiffany into action. As a slight blush darkened the skin of her throat, she opened the door of the den. Knowing it to be an incredible mistake, she led Zane past a formal dining room to a small alcove near the kitchen.

Louise had already placed the beef stew with gravy on the small round table.

"Sit," Tiffany commanded as she pulled out a bottle of wine and uncorked it before pouring the rich Burgundy into stemmed glasses. Zane did as he was bid, but his face registered mild surprise when Tiffany took the salads out of the refrigerator and set them on the table.

After Tiffany sat down, Zane stared at her from across a small maple table. "Your housekeeper doesn't live in?"

"No."

"But she manages to keep the place up?"

Tiffany released an uneasy laugh. "I'm not that messy. I do pick up after myself, even do my own laundry and cook occasionally," she teased. What must he think of her? That she was some princess who wouldn't get her fingers dirty? Did his preconceived notions stem from his relationship—whatever that was—with Ellery? "Actually, Louise only comes in twice a week. Today I asked her to come over because of the interview with Rod Crawford. I thought I might need another pair of hands. But usually I can handle whatever comes up by myself."

"That surprises me," Zane admitted and took a sip of his wine.

Tiffany arched her elegant dark brows. "Why?"

"Because of the house, I suppose. So formal."

"And here you are stuck in the kitchen, without the benefit of seeing the crystal and silver," Tiffany said with a chuckle. "Disappointed, Mr. Sheridan?"

His gray eyes drove into hers and his voice was low when he spoke. "Only that I can't persuade you to call me by my first name."

"I don't think I know you that well—"

"Yet." He raised his glass in mock salute and his flinty eyes captured hers. "Here's to an independent woman," he announced before taking another long drink.

She was more than a little embarrassed by the intimate toast, and after a few silent moments when she alternately sipped the wine and twirled the glass in her fingers, she decided she had to level with him. Against her wishes she was warming to him, and that had to stop. "Look, *Zane*. As far as I'm concerned, you're close enough to certifiably crazy that I doubt if I'll associate with you again," she said half-seriously as she poured them each another glass of wine and then began to attack her salad. "There's no reason for first names."

"I'm not crazy, Ms. Rhodes—"

"Tiffany." Gentle laughter sparkled in her eyes. "Just concerned, right?" Her smile faded and she became instantly serious. "Why? Why are you here, now, telling me all of this?"

"It took me this long to be sure."

"Then you'll understand why I'm having trouble accepting what you're suggesting as the truth. You've had four years to think about it. I just found out this morning."

Tiffany pushed her plate aside, crossed her arms over her chest and leveled serious blue eyes in his direction. "Let's quit beating around the bush," she suggested. "So what's in this for you? You don't impress me as the kind of man who would go traipsing halfway around the world just to set the record straight and see that justice is served."

"I'm not."

"I didn't think so."

"I have an interest in what happens here."

Dread began to hammer in her heart. "Which is?"

"Personal."

"What does that mean? A grudge—revenge—vendetta— what?" She leaned on one hand and pointed at him with the other. "This morning you said you knew Ellery. I got the impression then, and now again, that you didn't much like him." Her palm rotated in the air as she collected her scattered thoughts. "If you ask me, all this interest in my horse has to do with Ellery. What's the point, Mr. Sheridan? And why in the world would you want to buy this farm? There must be a dozen of them, much more profitable than this, for sale."

Zane set aside his fork and settled back in the chair. As he pondered the situation and the intelligent woman staring beguilingly at him, he tugged on his lower lip. "The reason I want this farm is because it should have been mine to begin with. That your husband got the capital to invest in this parcel of land was a...fluke."

"Come again," she suggested, not daring to breathe. What was he saying? "Ellery's family owned this land for years."

"I don't think so. The way I understand it, he was a tenant farmer until a few years ago. The two hundred thousand dollars that your husband put into this farm as a down payment—"

"Yes?" Tiffany asked.

"He stole it from me."

"Oh, dear God," Tiffany whispered, letting her head fall forward into her waiting hands. She didn't know whether to laugh or to cry. Obviously Zane thought he was telling the truth, and he didn't seem like a dangerous psychotic, but what he was saying was absolutely ridiculous. Ellery might have been many things, but Tiffany knew in her heart he wasn't a thief.

"I think it's time for you to leave, Mr. Sheridan," she said, her voice as cold as ice. "You've been saying some pretty wild things around here—things that could be construed as slander, and—"

Footsteps on the back porch interrupted her train of thought. Panic welled in Tiffany's mind and she snapped her head upward as the familiar boot steps drew near. Within a minute, Mac was standing in the kitchen, worrying the brim of his fedora in his fingers, his dark eyes impaling hers. "You'd better come, Missy," he said, his voice uncommonly low.

"Ebony Wine?"

"Aye."

"The foal is here?"

"Will be soon, and…" His eyes shifted from Tiffany to Zane and back again. Tiffany's heart began to thud painfully in her chest. She could read the silent message in Mac's worried gaze.

"No…" she whispered, pushing the chair back so hard that it scraped against the hardwood floor. Her fearful eyes darted to Zane. "If you'll excuse me, we have an emergency on our hands." She noticed the glimmer of suspicion in Zane's eyes, but didn't bother to explain. Time was too imperative.

In seconds she was away from the table and racing toward the den. "Have you called Vance?" she called over her shoulder.

Mac pushed his hat onto his head and nodded. "He's on his way. Damn, but I should have seen this coming. I'll meet you in the shed."

Tiffany kicked off her pumps, pulled on a pair of boots and yanked her jacket off the wooden hook. Mindless of the fact that she was dressed in wool slacks, angora vest and silk blouse, she opened the French doors and raced into the dark night. She had taken only three breathless strides, when she felt the powerful hand on her arm, restraining her in its hard grasp.

"What's going on?" Zane demanded as Tiffany whirled to face the man thwarting her. Her hair tossed wildly around her face, and even in the darkness Zane could see the angry fire in her wide eyes. He hadn't been able to decipher the silent messages passing from Mac to Tiffany in the kitchen, but Zane knew that something horrible was taking place and that Tiffany felt she could do something about it.

Tiffany didn't have time to argue. She was trying to free herself. "A mare's gone into labor."

"And that upsets you?"

She jerked her arm free of his imprisoning grasp. "There might be complications. If you'll excuse me—" But he was right beside her, running the short distance from the house to the foaling shed with her, his strides long and easy.

With a sinking feeling, Tiffany realized that there was no way she could hide her secret from him any longer, and she really didn't care. The only thing that mattered was the mare in labor and the unborn colt.

CHAPTER FOUR

THE SOFT OVERHEAD LIGHTS OF THE FOALING shed were reflected in the sweat-darkened coat of Ebony Wine. As the mare paced restlessly in the stall, she alternately snorted in agitation and flattened her dark ears against her head in impatience.

Mac's arms were braced on the top rail of the gate to the foaling stall and his anxious brown eyes studied the horse. A matchstick worked convulsively in the corner of his mouth.

He spoke softly in quiet tones filled with years of understanding. "Simmer down, lady." His gravelly voice was barely audible as the distressed mare shifted under the intense pressure of an abdominal contraction.

Tiffany's heart was pounding more rapidly than her footsteps on the cold concrete floor as she walked rapidly down the length of the corridor to the foaling stall. The acrid smells of sweat and urine mingled with antiseptic in the whitewashed barn. One look at Mac's tense form told her that the birth of Ebony Wine's foal was going no better than he had expected.

Zane was at Tiffany's side, matching her short strides with his longer ones. His dark brows were drawn over his slate gray eyes. He kept his thoughts to himself as he tried to make head or tail of the tense situation. Something was very wrong here. He could feel it. Though it hadn't been stated, he had witnessed fear in Tiffany's incredible blue eyes when Mac had entered the kitchen and made the announcement that one of the mares had gone into labor. Zane had noticed something else in Tiffany's worried expression—determination and pride held her finely sculpted jaw taut, but worry creased her flawless brow. A sense of desperation seemed to have settled heavily on her small shoulders.

"Has her water broken?" Tiffany asked as she approached Mac and leaned over the railing of the stall.

Mac shook his head and ran bony fingers over the stubble on his jaw. "Not yet."

Ebony Wine was moving restlessly in the stall. Her sleek body glistened with sweat, and her ears twitched warily.

"Come on, lady," Mac whispered softly, "don't be so stupid. Lie down, will ya?"

"She didn't get off her feet the last time," Tiffany reminded the trainer.

"She'd better this time," Mac grumbled, "or we'll lose this one, sure as I'm standing here." He shifted the matchstick from one side of his mouth to the other. "Moon Shadow's colts need all the help they can get. Come on, Ebony, be a good girl. Lie down."

"Moon Shadow?" Zane asked. "He's the sire?"

Mac's troubled gaze shifted from the horse to Tiffany in unspoken apology. "That he is."

Zane's eyes narrowed as he studied the anxious mare. "Where's the vet?"

"He was at another farm—said he'd be here on the double," Mac replied.

At that moment, Ebony Wine's water broke and the amniotic fluid began cascading down her black legs.

"Looks like he might be too late," Zane observed wryly.

Without asking any further questions, he rolled up his shirt sleeves, walked to a nearby basin and scrubbed his arms and hands with antiseptic.

"What're you doing?" Tiffany demanded.

His gaze was steady as he approached her. "I'm trying to help you. I've spent most of my life with horses and seen enough foals being born to realize when a mare's in trouble.

This lady here—" he cocked his dark head in the direction of the anxious horse "—needs a hand."

Mac looked about to protest, but Tiffany shook her head to quiet him. "Let's get on with it."

Ebony Wine stiffened as Mac and Zane entered the stall. Her eyes rolled backward at the stranger. Mac went to Ebony Wine's head and talked to the horse. "Come on, Ebony, girl. Lie down, for Pete's sake."

Zane examined the horse and the bulging amniotic sac beginning to emerge below her tail. "We've got problems," he said with a dark frown. "Only a nose and one leg showing. Looks as if one leg has twisted back on itself."

"Damn!" Mac muttered. His hands never stopped their rhythmic stroking of Ebony Wine's head.

Tiffany felt her heart leap to her throat. Moon Shadow's foals were having enough trouble surviving, without the added problems of a complicated birth. Against the defeat slumping her shoulders, Tiffany forced her head upward to meet the cruel challenge fate had dealt the mare. Her vibrant blue eyes locked with Zane's. "What do you want me to do?"

"Help with supplies." He pointed in the direction of the clean pails, scissors and bottles of antiseptic. "We've got to get that foal out of there, and my guess is that this lady isn't going to want our help."

The sound of the door to the foaling shed creaking open caught her attention and brought Tiffany's head around. Vance Geddes, his round face a study in frustration, let the door swing shut and hurried down the corridor to Ebony Wine's stall.

He took one look at the horse and turned toward the basin. "How long has she been at it?" he asked, quickly washing his hands.

"Over half an hour," Mac replied.

"And she won't lie down?"

"Not this one. Stubborn, she is."

"Aren't they all?" Vance's gaze clashed with the stranger

attending to Ebony Wine. Zane responded to the unspoken question. "Zane Sheridan."

"'Evening," Vance said.

"I was here on other business, but I thought I'd help out. I've worked with Thoroughbreds all my life, and I think we've got problems here. One leg's twisted back. The foal's stuck."

"Great," Vance muttered sarcastically, entering the stall as quietly as possible. "Just what we need tonight." His eyes traveled over the mare. "How're ya, gal? Hurtin' a little?" he asked as he studied the glistening horse.

"How can I help?" Tiffany asked, forcing her voice to remain steady as she noticed the tightening of Vance's jaw.

"Be ready to hand me anything I might need," Vance replied and then positioned himself behind the mare to confirm what Zane had told him. "Damn." He shook his blond head and frowned. "All right, let's get him out of there."

Ebony Wine moaned as her womb contracted, and the foal remained stuck in the birth canal.

"This is gonna be touchy," Vance whispered, as warning to the tall man standing next to him.

Zane's body tensed and he nodded curtly, before he helped Vance carefully push the foal back into the mare so that there was less danger of breaking the umbilical cord and to give more room to coax the bent leg forward. Time was crucial, and both men worked quickly but gently, intent on saving the mare and her offspring.

Tiffany assisted with the towels and antiseptic, silently praying for the life of the unborn horse. Her throat was hot and tight with the tension in the confining stall. Sweat began to bead on Zane's forehead, and his intent eyes never left the mare. The muscles in his bronze forearms flexed as he worked on righting the foal. Tiffany's heart was hammering so loudly, it seemed to pound in her ears.

Ebony Wine pushed down hard with all the muscles of her abdomen. As the mare pushed, Vance and Zane stood behind her and pulled down steadily toward her hocks in rhythm with the birth contractions.

With the first push, the tiny hooves and the head of the foal emerged. On the second contraction, the mare gave a soft moan, and the men were able to pull the shoulders, the broadest part of a foal's body, through Ebony Wine's pelvis. Once the shoulders emerged, the rest of the foal followed.

The umbilical cord broke.

Zane dropped to the floor and, mindless of the fluid pooling at his knees, he ripped open the tough amniotic sac. Vance was beside him and worked on the colt's nose, so that it could breathe its first breaths of air.

Tiffany brought towels and held them near the foal so that Vance could take them as he needed them. Her eyes watched the little black colt's sides as she prayed for the tiny ribs to move. *Dear Lord, don't let him die. Please don't take this one, too.*

Because the colt had to be pulled out of the mare, the umbilical cord had broken early, and he was shortchanged of the extra blood in the placenta that should have passed into his veins. Both men worked feverishly over the small, perfect body.

The foal's lips and eyelids looked blue as it lay wet and motionless in the straw.

"Oh, God, no," Tiffany whispered, as she realized that it had been far too long already since the birth. She dropped the towels and her small hands curled into impotent fists. "Not this one, too."

Ebony Wine nickered, ready to claim her foal. Mac gently held the frustrated mare as she tried to step closer to the unmoving black body lying on the floor of the stall.

Zane held his hands near the colt's nose to feel for breath. There was none. "He's not breathing," he whispered, looking up for a second at Tiffany before bending over the colt and pressing his lips to the nostrils, forcing air into the still lungs.

Vance knelt beside Zane, checking the colt for vital signs, while Zane fruitlessly tried to revive the colt.

"It's no use," Vance said at last, restraining Zane by placing a hand on his shoulder. "This one didn't have a prayer going in."

"No!" Tiffany said, her voice trembling and tears building in her eyes. "He's got to live. He's got to!"

"Tiff…" Vance said wearily. The vet's voice trailed off. There were no adequate words of condolence. For a moment the only sounds in the building were the soft rain beating against the roof and the restless shifting of the mare's hooves in the straw.

Mindless of the blood and amniotic fluid ruining her clothes, Tiffany fell into the straw beside the inert body of the beautifully formed black colt. Her throat was swollen with despair, her eyes blurred with fresh tears. "You have to live, little one," she whispered in a voice filled with anguished desperation. She touched the foal's warm, matted coat. "Please… live."

Her fingers touched the small ears and the sightless eyes. "Don't die…."

"Tiffany." Zane's voice was rough but comforting as he reached forward and grabbed her shoulders. He felt the quiet sobs she was trying to control. "He was dead before he was born—"

Tiffany jerked herself free. "No!" Her hands were shaking as she raised them in the air. "He was alive and healthy and…"

"Stillborn."

That single word, issued softly from Zane's lips, seemed to echo against the rafters.

A single tear wove a solitary path down her cheek. Tiffany let her arms fall to her sides. "Oh, God," she whispered, pulling herself to her full height and shaking her head. Blood discolored her silk blouse, and straw stuck in her angora vest as well as her hair. "Not another one." Her small fist clenched and she pounded it on the rough boards of the stall. "Why? Why is this happening?" she demanded, hopelessly battling an enemy she couldn't see…didn't understand.

Ebony Wine snorted, and Tiffany realized she was disturbing the already distraught mare. She let her head drop into her palm, leaned against the wall and closed her eyes against the truth. *Why the foals? Why all of Moon Shadow's foals?*

"Come on, let's go back to the house," Zane suggested, placing his strong arms gently over her shoulders.

"I should stay," she whispered as cold reality began to settle in her mind. She felt a raw ache in her heart as she faced the tragic fact that another of Moon Shadow's foals was dead before it had a chance to live. It just wasn't fair; not to the mare, not to the farm, and not to the poor lifeless little colt.

"We'll take care of things," Mac assured her, giving Zane a look that said more clearly than words, "Get her out of here." Mac was holding the lead rope to Ebony Wine's halter, and the anxious horse was nickering to the dead foal.

"I'll make some coffee...up at the house," Tiffany murmured, trying to pull herself together. She was shaking from the ordeal but managed to wipe the tears from her eyes.

"Don't bother for me," Vance said, working with the afterbirth. "I'll stay with the mare until Mac can watch her and then I'll call it a night."

"Same goes for me." Mac's kind eyes rested on Tiffany. "You just take care of yourself, Missy. We'll handle the horses."

"But—"

"Shh, could be three, maybe four hours till I'm finished with this old gal here," Mac said, cocking his head sadly in the black mare's direction. "After that, I think I'll hit the hay. I'm not as young as I used to be, ya know, and the missus, she'll be looking for me." He winked at Tiffany, but the smile he tried to give her failed miserably.

Numbly, leaning against Zane's strong body, Tiffany slowly walked out of the foaling shed and into the night. The rain was still falling from the darkened sky. It splashed against the sodden ground, and the large drops ran through her hair and down her neck.

She felt cold all over, dead inside. Another of Moon Shadow's foals. Dead. Why? Her weary mind wouldn't quit screaming the question that had plagued her for nearly two weeks. She shuddered against the cold night and the chill of dread in her heart. Zane pulled her closer to the protective warmth of his body.

Hard male muscles surrounded her, shielded her from the rain as well as the storm of emotions raging in her mind. Lean and masculine, Zane's body molded perfectly over hers, offering the strength and security she needed on this dark night. For the first time in several years, Tiffany accepted the quiet strength of a man. She was tired of making decisions, weary from fighting the invisible demons that stole the life-blood from innocent newborns.

The house was still ablaze with the lights she had neglected to turn off. Zane led her into the den and watched as she slumped wearily into the chair near the fireplace. The sparkle in her blue eyes seemed to have died with Ebony Wine's foal. Her arms were wrapped protectively over her breasts, and she stared sightlessly into the smoldering embers of the fire.

"I'll get you a drink," he offered, walking to the bookcase that housed the liquor.

"Don't want one."

He picked up a bottle of brandy before looking over his shoulder and pinning her with his intense gray gaze. "Tiffany, what happened?" he asked quietly. She continued to gaze dully at the charred logs in the stone fireplace. He repeated his question, hoping to break her mournful silence. "Just what the hell happened out there tonight?"

"We lost a colt," she whispered, tears resurfacing in her eyes.

"Sometimes that happens," he offered, waiting patiently for the rest of the story as he poured two small glasses of the amber liquor.

She lifted her gaze to meet his and for a moment he thought she was about to confide in him, but instead she shrugged her slim shoulders. "Sometimes," she agreed hoarsely as she watched his reaction.

How much could she trust this stranger? True, he had tried to help her with the unborn colt and in a moment of weakness she felt as if she could trust her life to him. But still she hesitated. She couldn't forget that he was here on a mission. Not only did he want to buy the farm, but he was filled with some insane theory about Devil's Gambit being alive.

Zane's stormy eyes glanced over her huddled form. Her soft honey-brown curls were tangled with straw and framed her elegantly featured face. Her tanned skin was pale from the ordeal. Dark, curling eyelashes couldn't hide the pain in her wide, innocent eyes.

She's seen more than her share of pain, Zane guessed as he walked over to her and offered the drink that she had declined.

"I don't want—"

"Drink it."

She frowned a little. "Just who do you think you are, coming in here and giving me orders?"

He smiled sternly. "A friend."

Tiffany found it difficult to meet the concern in his eyes. She remained rigid and ignored the glass in his outstretched hand.

With an audible sigh, Zane relented. Dealing with this beautiful woman always seemed to prove difficult. "All right, lady. Drink it. *Please.*"

Tiffany took the glass from his hand and managed an obligatory sip. The calming liquor slid easily down her throat, and as she sipped the brandy she began to warm a little. *Who was this man and why did he care?*

Zane walked over to the fireplace and stretched the tension out of his shoulders, before stoking the dying fire and finally taking a seat on the hearth. He propped his elbows on his knees and cradled his drink in his large hands.

She didn't follow his actions but kicked off her shoes, ignoring the mud that dirtied the imported carpet. Then she drew her knees under her chin as if hugging herself for warmth against an inner chill.

Zane's eyes never left her face. As he watched her he felt a traitorous rush of desire flooding his bloodstream and firing his loins. As unlikely as it seemed, he suddenly wanted Ellery Rhodes's beautiful widow and wanted her badly. The urge to claim her as his own was blinding. In a betraying vision, he saw himself kissing away the pain on her regal features, lifting the sweater vest over her head, slipping each button of her blouse through the buttonholes.

Zane's throat tightened as he imagined her lying beneath him, her glorious, dark-tipped breasts supple and straining in the moonlight....

"Stop it," he muttered to himself, and Tiffany looked upward from the flames to stare at him.

"Stop what?" she whispered, her eyes searching his.

Zane's desire was thundering in his ears, and he felt the unwelcome swelling in his loins. "Nothing," he muttered gruffly as he stood, walked across the room and poured himself another drink. He downed the warm liquor in one long swallow as if the brandy itself could quell the unfortunate urges of his body.

For God's sake, he hadn't reacted to a woman this way since Stasia. At the thought of his sultry Gypsylike ex-wife, Zane's blood went ice-cold, and the effect was an instant relief. The ache in his loins subsided.

He set his glass down with a thud, jarring Tiffany out of her distant reverie. "Do you want to talk?" he asked softly, walking back across the close room to face her. He placed himself squarely before her, effectively blocking her view of the fire.

She shook her head and ran trembling fingers through her hair. "Not now..."

His smile was sad, but genuine. "Then I think you should get cleaned up and rest. It's after midnight—"

"Oh." For the first time that night, Tiffany was aware of her appearance. She looked down at her vest and saw the blood-stains discoloring the delicate gray wool. The sleeves of her pink blouse were rolled over her arms and stained with sweat and blood. She felt the urge to cry all over again when she looked up from her disheveled clothing and noticed the concern in Zane's gentle gray eyes.

Instead of falling victim to her emotions, she raised her head proudly and managed a stiff smile. "I'll be fine in the morning. This night has been a shock."

"Obviously."

"If you'll excuse me…"

When she rose from the chair, her knees felt unsteady, but she managed to stand with a modicum of dignity despite her disheveled appearance.

Zane picked up her barely touched glass. "I don't think you should be alone."

Involuntarily she stiffened. Ellery's words from long ago, just after her father had died, echoed in her mind. "You shouldn't be alone, Tiffany," Ellery had insisted. "You need a man to care for you." In her grief, Tiffany had been fool enough to believe him.

She lifted her chin fractionally. "I'll be fine, Mr. Sheridan," she assured him with a calm smile. "I've been alone for over four years. I think I can manage one more night."

He noticed the slight trembling of her fingers, the doubt in her clear blue eyes, and realized that she was the most damnably intriguing woman he had ever met.

"I'll stay with you."

"That won't be necessary."

"The mare's not out of the woods yet."

Tiffany hesitated only slightly. Zane's presence did lend a certain security. She remembered his quick, sure movements as he tried to revive Ebony Wine's dead colt. With a shake of her head, she tried to convince herself that she didn't need him. "Mac can take care of Ebony Wine."

"And it wouldn't hurt to have an extra pair of hands."

She was about to protest. She raised her hand automatically and then dropped it. "Don't get me wrong, Zane," she said softly, her tongue nearly tripping on the familiarity of his first name. "It's not that I don't appreciate what you've done tonight. I do. But the foal is dead." She shuddered and hugged her arms around her abdomen. "And Mac will attend to Ebony Wine." She shook her head at the vision of the dead little colt lying on the thick bed of straw. "I…I think it would be best if you would just leave for now. I know that we still have things to discuss, but certainly they'll wait until morning."

"I suppose." Zane glanced at the portrait of Devil's Gambit hanging proudly over the mantel. He had the eerie feeling that somehow the tense drama he had witnessed earlier in the foaling shed was linked to the disappearance of the proud stallion. *Impossible.* And yet he had a gut feeling that the two tragic events were connected.

As if Tiffany had read his thoughts, she shuddered. Zane was across the room in an instant. Tiffany wanted to protest when his strong arms enfolded her against him, but she couldn't. The warmth of his body and the protection of his embrace felt as natural as the gentle rain beating softly against the windowpanes. He plucked a piece of straw from her hair and tenderly let his lips press a soft kiss against her forehead. The gesture was so filled with kindness and empathy that Tiffany felt her knees buckle and her eyes fill with tears.

"I…I think you should go," she whispered hoarsely, afraid of her response to his masculinity. *Damn him!* She wanted to lean on him. What kind of a fool was she? Hadn't she learned her lessons about men long ago from Ellery?

"Shh." He ignored her protests and led her gently out of the den, through the foyer and up the stairs. "Come on, lady," he whispered into her hair. "Give yourself a break and let me take care of you."

She felt herself melt inside. "I don't think, I mean I don't need—"

"What you need is to soak in a hot tub, wrap yourself in one of those god-awful flannel nightgowns and fall into bed with a glass of brandy."

It sounded like heaven, but Tiffany couldn't forget that the tenderness of the man touching her so intimately might be nothing more than a ploy to extract information from her. At this moment she was too tired to really give a damn, but she couldn't forget her earlier instincts about him. He was engaged in a vendetta of sorts; she could feel it in her bones. Try as she would, Tiffany couldn't shake the uneasy feeling that Zane Sheridan, whoever the hell he was, would prove to be the enemy.

Zane left Tiffany in the master bedroom. Once she was certain he had gone downstairs, she peeled off her soiled clothes, threw them in a hamper and walked into the adjacent bathroom.

As she settled into the hot water of the marble tub, her mind continued to revolve around the events of the past few weeks. If the first foal's death had been a shock, the second had been terrifying. Now two more foals by Moon Shadow had died mysteriously. Each foal had been only a few hours old, with the exception of Charlatan, who had survived for a few hope-filled days.

Just wait until Rod Crawford gets hold of this story, she thought as she absently lathered her body. The wire services would print it in a minute and she'd have more reporters crawling all over the place than she could imagine. If that wasn't enough, Zane Sheridan's theories about Devil's Gambit's fate would stir up the press and get them interested all over again in what was happening at Rhodes Breeding Farm. *And the scandal. Lord, think of the scandal!*

Tiffany sank deeper into the tub, and didn't notice that her hair was getting wet.

What about Zane Sheridan? Was he here as friend or foe? She sighed as she considered the roguish man who had helped her upstairs. One minute he seemed intent on some vague, undisclosed revenge, and the next his concern for her and the farm seemed genuine. *Don't trust him, Tiffany*, the rational side of her nature insisted.

"Men," she muttered ungraciously. "I'll never understand them." Her frown trembled a little as she thought about Ellery, the husband she had tried to love. Marrying him had probably been the biggest mistake of her life. The moment she had become Mrs. Ellery Rhodes, he seemed to have changed and his interest in her had faded with each passing day. "Dad warned you," she chided herself. "You were just too bullheaded to listen."

The distance between her and her husband had become an almost physical barrier, and Tiffany had foolishly thought that if she could bear Ellery a child, things might be different. He might learn to love her.

What a fool! Hadn't she already known from her own agonizing experience with her mother that relationships between people who loved each other were often fragile and detached? In her own naive heart, she had hoped that she would someday be able to reach Ellery. Now, if what Zane Sheridan was saying were true, Ellery might still be alive.

"Oh, God," she moaned, closing her eyes and trying to conjure Ellery's face in her mind. But try as she would, she was unable to visualize the man she had married. Instead, the image on her mind had the forceful features on a virtual stranger from Ireland. "You bastard," she whispered and wondered if she were speaking to Zane or Ellery.

Her tense muscles began to relax as she rinsed the soap from her body and then turned on the shower spray to wash her hair.

Once she felt that all of the grime had been scrubbed from her skin, she turned off the shower, stepped out of the tub and wrapped herself in a bath sheet. After buffing her skin dry, she grabbed the only nightgown in the room, an impractical silver-colored gown of thin satin and lace.

Just what I need, she thought sarcastically as she slipped it over her head and straightened it over her breasts. She smiled to herself, grabbed her red corduroy robe and cinched the belt tightly around her waist. She was still towel-drying her hair when she stepped into the bedroom.

As she did, her gaze clashed with that of Zane Sheridan.

"What are you doing here?" she asked, lowering the towel and staring at him with incredulous slate-blue eyes.

"I wanted to make sure that you didn't fall asleep in the tub."

She arched an elegant brow suspiciously. "Didn't you hear the shower running?" When a slow-spreading smile grew from one side of his face to the other, Tiffany's temper snapped. "I don't need a keeper, you know. I'm a grown woman."

His eyes slid over her body and rested on the gap in her overlapping lapels. "So I noticed."

Angrily, she tugged on the tie of her robe. "You're insufferable!" she spit out. "I could have walked in here stark naked."

"Can't blame a guy for hoping—"

"I'm in no mood for this, Zane," she warned.

He sobered instantly and studied the lines of worry on her beautiful face. "I know. I just thought I could get you to lighten up."

"A little difficult under the circumstances."

"You lost a foal. It happens."

Her lips twisted wryly. "That it does, Mr. Sheridan. That it does." She sat on the corner of the bed and supported herself with one straight arm while pushing the wet tendrils of hair out of her face with her free hand. "It's been a long day."

"I suppose it has." He strode across the room, threw back the covers of the bed and reached for a drink he had placed on the nightstand. "I checked on Ebony Wine."

Tiffany watched his actions warily. Why was he still here and why was she secretly pleased? She raised her head in challenge and ignored her rapidly pounding heart. "And?"

"You were right. Mac took care of her. She's a little confused about everything that went on tonight, still calling to the foal. But she's healthy. The afterbirth detached without any problem and Mac had already cleaned her up. He thinks she'll be ready to breed when she shows signs of foal heat, which should be the middle of next week. The veterinarian will be back to check her tomorrow and again before she goes into heat."

Tiffany nodded and accepted the drink he offered. "It's a little too much for me to think about right now," she admitted, swirling the brandy in her glass before taking a sip.

"It's the business you're in."

Tiffany stared into the amber liquor in her glass and moved her head from side to side. "And sometimes it seems like a rotten way of life."

Zane ran his hand around the back of his neck. "It's never easy to lose one, but it's the chance you take as a breeder."

"And the living make up for the dead?"

Zane frowned and shrugged. "Something like that. If it bothers you so much, maybe you should get out of the business," he suggested.

"By selling the farm to you?" Her eyes lifted and became a frigid shade of blue.

"I didn't think we would get into that tonight."

"You brought it up."

"I just voiced your concerns."

"Oh, God," she whispered, setting her unfinished drink aside. "Look, I'm really very tired and I can't think about all this tonight."

"Don't. Just try and get some sleep."

She managed a wan smile and walked around to her side of the bed. "I guess I owe you an apology and a very big thank-you. I…really appreciate all the help you gave in the foaling shed."

Zane frowned. "For all the good it did."

Tiffany raised sad eyes to meet his questioning gaze. "I don't think there was anything anyone could have done."

"Preordained?"

She sighed audibly and shook her head. The wet hair swept across her shoulders. "Who knows?" She sat on the edge of the bed, her fingers toying with the belt holding her robe together. "Goodbye, Zane. If you call me in the morning, we can find another time to get together and talk about your hypothesis concerning Devil's Gambit and my husband."

"I'll be here in the morning," he stated, dropping into a chair facing the bed and cradling his drink in his hands.

"Pardon me?" she asked, understanding perfectly well what he meant.

"I'm staying—"

"You can't! Not here—"

"I just want to check with Mac once more, and then I'll sleep downstairs on the couch."

Visions of him spending the night in her house made her throat dry. She couldn't deny that he had been a help, but the thought of him there, in the same house with her, only a staircase away, made her uneasy. Her fingers trembled when she pushed them wearily through her hair. "I don't know," she whispered, but she could feel herself relenting.

"Come on, Tiff. It's after two. I'm not about to drive back to San Francisco now, just to turn around and come back here in six hours."

Tiffany managed a smile. "I don't suppose that makes a whole lot of sense." Her blue eyes touched his. "You don't have to sleep in the den. There's a guest room down the hall, the first door to the left of the stairs."

He returned her hint of a smile and stood. For a moment she thought he was about to bend over the bed and kiss her. She swallowed with difficulty as their eyes locked.

Zane hesitated, and the brackets near the corners of his mouth deepened. "I'll see you in the morning," he said, his eyes darkening to a smoky gray before he turned out the lamp near the bed and walked out of the room.

Tiffany expelled a rush of air. "Oh, God," she whispered, her heart thudding painfully in her chest. "I should have made him leave." He was too close, his rugged masculinity too inviting.

Maybe he would come back to her room, or maybe he would sift through the papers in the den looking for something, anything, to prove his crazy theories. But all the important documents, the computer data disks and the checkbook were locked in the safe; even if Zane rummaged through the den, he would find nothing of value.

That's not why you're concerned, her tired mind teased. *What scares you is your response to him.* She rolled over and pushed the nagging thoughts aside. Despite all of her doubts, she was comforted that Zane was still with her. Somehow it made the tragedy of losing the foal easier to bear.

ZANE HIKED HIS QUICKLY DONNED JACKET around his neck and felt the welcome relief of raindrops slide under his collar. He needed time to cool off. Being around Tiffany, wanting to comfort her, feeling a need to make love to her until the fragile lines of worry around her eyes were gone, unnerved him. The last thing he had expected when he had driven to Rhodes Breeding Farm was that he would get involved with Ellery Rhodes's widow.

He heard the roar of an engine as he started to cross the parking lot. Turning in the direction of the sound, Zane walked toward Mac's battered truck. Mac rolled down the window as Zane approached. Twin beams from the headlights pierced the darkness, and the wipers noisily slapped the accumulation of rain from the windshield.

"Everything okay?"

"Aye," Mac replied cautiously. "The mare's fine."

"Good." Zane rammed his fists into the jacket of his coat. "What about the colt?"

"Vance will handle that." The wiry trainer frowned in the darkness. "He'll give us a report in a couple of days."

"Good." Zane stepped away from the truck and watched as Mac put the ancient Dodge pickup into gear before it rumbled down the driveway.

Wondering at the sanity of his actions, Zane unlocked his car and withdrew the canvas bag of extra clothes from the backseat. He always traveled with a change of clothes, his briefcase and his camera. He slung the bag over his shoulder and considered the briefcase. In the leather case were the papers his attorney had toiled over. According to John Morris, every document needed to purchase Rhodes Breeding Farm was now in Zane's possession. So why didn't owning the farm seem as important as it once had?

Zane cursed angrily and locked the briefcase in the car. Knowing that he was making a grave error, he walked back into the house, locked the doors and mounted the stairs. After throwing his bag on the guest bed, he took off his shoes and turned down the covers.

Then, on impulse, he went back to her room. He paused at the door and then strode boldly inside. His blood was thundering in his eardrums as he lowered himself into the chair near the bed. It took all of his restraint not to go to her.

Zane watched the rounded swell of her hips beneath the bedclothes, and the smoldering lust in his veins began to throb unmercifully. *You're more of a fool than you thought,* Zane chastised himself silently.

He noticed the regular rhythm of her breathing and realized that she had fallen asleep. The urge to strip off his clothes and lie with her burned in his mind. He fantasized about her response, the feel of her warm, sleepy body fitted to his, the agonizing glory of her silken fingers as they traced an invisible path down his abdomen....

A hard tightening in his loins warned him that his thoughts were dangerous; still he couldn't help but think of slowly peeling off her bedclothes and letting the shimmery night-gown peeking from the edges of her robe fall silently to the floor. He wanted to touch all of her, run his tongue over the gentle feminine curves of her body, drink in the smell of her perfume as he touched her swollen breasts....

Quietly he placed his drink on the table and walked over to the bed.

Tiffany moaned in her sleep and turned onto her back. In the dim light from the security lamps, with the rain softly pelting against the windows, Zane looked down at her. How incredibly soft and alluring she appeared in slumber. All traces of anxiety had left the perfect oval of her face. Her still-damp hair curled in golden-brown tangles around her shoulders and neck.

The scarlet robe had gaped open to display the silvery fabric of a gossamer gown and the soft texture of her breasts beneath. Tiffany shifted slightly and the hint of a dark nipple shadowed the silvery lace covering it.

Zane clenched his teeth in self-restraint. Never had he wanted a woman more, and he told himself that she was there for the taking. Hadn't he seen her vulnerability? Hadn't he witnessed the way she stared at him? Deep within her, there was a need to be taken by him; he could sense it.

He closed his eyes against the pain throbbing in his loins and dropped to his knees by the bed. "What have you done to me?" he whispered as he lovingly brushed a strand of hair from her eyes.

This woman was once the wife of Ellery Rhodes, a person he had intended to destroy. Zane couldn't help but wonder, as he stared into the sleep-softened face of Ellery Rhodes's widow, if just the opposite were true.

Would he be able to carry forth his plans of retribution, or would Ellery Rhodes's wife reap her sweet vengeance on him?

CHAPTER FIVE

WHEN TIFFANY OPENED HER EYES she noticed that the first purple light of dawn had begun to filter into the room. With a muted groan, she stretched between the cool sheets and rolled over, intent on returning to sleep.

Her cloudy vision rested on the chair near the bed and her breath got lost somewhere in her throat.

Zane was in the room. The realization was like an electric current pulsing through her body, bringing her instantly awake. What was he doing here?

He was slumped back in the chair, his head cocked at an uncomfortable angle, his stocking feet propped against the foot of the bed. He had thrown a spare blanket over himself, but it had slipped to the floor. His unfinished drink sat neglected on the bedside table.

"You wonderful bastard," she whispered quietly, before a silent rage began to take hold of her. Why hadn't he left as he had promised? Why had he decided to stay here—in her bedroom? Conflicting emotions battled within her. On the one hand, she was pleased to see him. It was comforting to watch his beard-darkened face relaxed in quiet slumber. There was something slightly chivalrous in the fact that he had stayed with her on the pretense of caring for her. She supposed that in all honesty she should consider his actions a compliment, an indication that he cared for her—if only a little.

On the other hand, she was quietly furious that he would force himself so boldly into her life. Whatever it was that he wanted at Rhodes Breeding Farm, he obviously wanted very badly. Badly enough to pretend interest in Tiffany and her horses.

The smile that had touched the corners of her mouth began to fade. Zane stirred in the chair, and Tiffany knew that he would soon be awake. No better time than the present to take the bull by the horns! She slipped out of the bed and cinched her robe tightly under her breasts before planting herself in front of his chair.

"Liar!" she whispered loudly enough to disturb him.

The muscles in Zane's broad shoulders stiffened slightly. He grumbled something indistinguishable and his feet dropped to the floor as he tried to roll over.

"What the hell?" he mumbled, before opening his eyes. He awoke to find himself staring up at Tiffany's indignant blue gaze. Stretching in the uncomfortable chair, he tried to rub the stiffness from his neck and cramped shoulders. "What're you going on about?" he asked.

"You said you'd sleep downstairs or in the guest room."

A devilish grin stole across his features. "So I did."

Her blue eyes narrowed. "Don't you have any shame?"

"None." He pulled himself out of the chair and stretched his aching muscles. God, he hurt all over. It had been years since he'd slept sitting up; and never in his thirty-six years had he kept vigil on a beautiful woman, a woman who obviously didn't appreciate his efforts.

"I should have known."

"Known what?" He rubbed his hands over the stubble of his beard and then threw his head back and rotated his neck to relieve the tension at the base of his skull. "Don't you have any coffee around here?" he asked once he'd stretched.

Tiffany crossed her arms self-righteously over her breasts and glared up at her unwelcome visitor. She was still wearing her robe, Zane noticed, though the gap of the lapels had been pulled together when she had tied the belt around her small waist. "Known you'd end up here."

"It's too early in the morning for this outraged virgin routine, Tiff," he said, rubbing the stubble on his chin. "We're both adults."

Her lips pressed together in anger. "Virginity isn't the issue."

He raised a brow in overt disbelief. "Then what is? Morality?"

"Sanity," she shot back. "Your being in here borders on the insane. I don't know who you are, what you want, where you live, why you're here in the first place…. God, Zane, for all I know you could be married with a dozen kids."

His dark glare silenced her. "I'm not married," he said gruffly.

"Good. Because I certainly wouldn't want some outraged wife calling me and demanding to talk to her husband." He looked as if she had slapped him.

"I came in here to check on you last night and you're acting as if I'm some kind of criminal, for God's sake."

She let out a ragged breath and her hands dropped to her sides. "It's just that I don't really know you," she said softly.

"Sure you do," he cajoled, his slate-colored eyes warming slightly when he noticed the flush of indignation on her cheeks.

Tiffany attempted to remain angry, but it was nearly impossible as she stared into Zane's incredible gray eyes. They were a reflection of the man himself, sometimes dark with anger, other times filled with a compelling intimacy that touched her heart and caused her pulse to jump. Slowly, by calculated inches, this man was working his way into her heart. She felt more vulnerable and naked than she had in years. The emotions beginning to blossom within her had to be pushed aside. She couldn't chance an involvement with him; it was far too dangerous.

Zane rubbed his eyes and stretched before smiling lazily. "Has anyone ever told you you're beautiful when you're angry?"

"Dozens," she returned sarcastically.

"Or that you're gorgeous when you wake up?"

Tiffany swallowed back a lump in her throat. "Not quite as many." She ran her long fingers through her knotted hair and slowly expelled a sigh. Arguing with him would get her nowhere. "I guess I haven't been very hospitable this morning," she conceded, lowering herself to a corner of the bed.

"Some people wake up in a bad mood."

"Especially if they find a stranger in their room?"

His gray eyes touched hers and his voice lowered to an intimate whisper. "We're not strangers."

Her elegant brows arched skeptically. "No?"

"No." He shook his head and frowned decisively.

"Then tell me," she suggested as one long, nervous finger began tracing the line of delicate stitching on the hand-pieced quilt. "Just how would you describe our relationship?"

A mischievous light gleamed in his eyes and his voice lowered suggestively. "How about two strong-willed people thrown mercilessly together by the cruel tides of fate?"

Tiffany couldn't help but laugh. "Seriously—"

"Seriously?" He sobered instantly. "Why don't we start as friends?"

She nodded silently to herself as if agreeing with an earlier-drawn conclusion. "Ah. Friends." Looking up, she found Zane staring intensely at her. "Friendship isn't formed in one night. Not when one of the 'friends' doesn't know anything about the other."

"Or suspects that he's holding out on her?"

She stiffened slightly. "Right." Folding her hands in her lap, she forced her eyes to meet the stormy gray of his. "You came here yesterday and announced that you intended to buy this farm. You also insisted that Devil's Gambit was alive. These aren't the usual kinds of statements to kick off an amiable relationship."

Before he could respond, she pointed an accusing finger up at him and continued, "And there's more to it than you've told me. I get the distinct impression you're here for other reasons, that you were probably involved with Ellery in the past and you're holding a grudge against him...or what used to be his before he died...."

Zane didn't deny it, but the mention of Ellery's name caused his face to harden. An unspoken challenge flashed from his eyes.

"My husband is dead—"

"You think." He rammed his fists into his pockets and walked over to one of the tall, paned windows. Leaning one shoulder against the window frame, he surveyed the farm. From his vantage point he could look past the white buildings near the house to the gently rolling hills in the distance. It was barely dawn. A gentle drizzle was falling, and wisps of fog had settled in the pockets between the hills to color the lush green meadows a hazy shade of blue.

Standing apart from the main buildings, its shape barely visible in the clinging fog, was the sagging skeleton of an old weather-beaten barn, the one structure on the farm that was in sharp contrast to the rest of the modern facilities. The old relic was out of sync with the times. Why had Ellery kept it?

Tiffany watched Zane with new fear taking hold of her heart. What was he saying? Did he really believe that Ellery could still be alive after all these years?

Her voice was suddenly hoarse and she was forced to clear her throat. "Look…"

He continued to stare at the rain-washed countryside.

"If you think that Ellery is alive, I want to know about it and I want to know now. This minute. No more stalls."

Zane lifted his hands dismissively. "I don't really know. The only thing I'm certain about is the horse."

"But you said—"

He whirled to face her, his burning hatred resurfacing in his eyes. "What I said was that I don't know what happened to your husband, but I wouldn't rule out the possibility that he could very well be alive and hiding out somewhere."

Tiffany's dark brows drew together, and she shook her head as if she could physically deny the doubts and fears beginning to plague her. "That doesn't make any sense!"

Zane's scathing eyes slowly traveled up her body to rest on her troubled face. He shook his head as if he couldn't begin to understand what was happening between himself and Ellery Rhodes's wife. "If your husband did leave you, then he's not only a crooked bastard, he's crazy to boot."

"You didn't much like him, did you?"

"I didn't like him at all." Zane uttered the words without any trace of emotion, as if he were simply stating a fact. He noticed the worry clouding her gaze, the weariness in the slump of her shoulders, and he silently wondered how such a beautiful woman could have linked up with the likes of Ellery Rhodes. Stasia's passion for money was understandable, but Tiffany? The bitter thought of Stasia heightened his curiosity and got the better of him. "Tell me, what kind of a marriage did you have?"

"Pardon me?"

"How was your relationship with Ellery?"

Searching gray eyes probed hers and seemed to pierce her soul. Just how much did this man want from her? "I don't think this is the time or the place—"

"Cut the bull, Tiffany."

"It's really none of your business—"

"Like hell! I just spent the night with you, lady, and I think that counts for something." His skin tightened over his cheekbones and his jaw hardened. An unspoken challenge flared in his intense gaze.

"Wait a minute. You didn't 'spend the night' with me. You merely sat in a chair in my room."

"Tell that to the rest of the people on the farm."

"I really don't give a rip what anyone else thinks, Zane," she replied, coloring only slightly. "What I do with my life is my own business."

He quirked a disbelieving brow.

"By the same token, I expect that you wouldn't go around to the workers and brag that you slept in the boss lady's room." Her heart was pounding wildly, but she managed to keep her voice steady.

Zane rammed fingers through his dark hair. "But I did."

"No reason to brag about it, especially since nothing happened."

"Not for any lack of wanting on my part," he admitted with a sigh of frustration. His eyes had darkened, and a tiny muscle worked furiously in the corner of his jaw. The tension that sleep had drained from his body resurfaced, and Tiffany realized for the first time just how badly this man wanted her. Her pulse jumped, and she had to force herself to stand and face him. Things were moving too rapidly, and she couldn't begin to deal with the bold desire written on Zane's rugged features.

"This conversation isn't getting us anywhere," she whispered, her voice becoming thick as her eyes lingered in the smoky depths of his. "I...I'm going to clean up and get dressed and then I'll fix you that cup of coffee. It's the least I can do since you helped out here last night...and were such a gentleman in the bargain." She motioned with a suddenly heavy hand toward the door of the room. "There's a bath down the hall, if you'd like to shave or change...."

He noticed her hesitation. "I brought a change of clothes."

"You did? Why?" Tiffany demanded. Had he intended to spend the night? Was he using her? If so, then why hadn't he tried to force himself upon her last night? Surely he had sensed her attraction to him. Zane Sheridan was a very fascinating man, and it had been a long time since she had been with a man...so very long.

"I thought I was going straight to the airport from here," he replied, abruptly bringing her back to the present.

She flushed from her wanton thoughts and smiled. "I see. Then I'll meet you downstairs later."

Without any further protests, Zane left the room. Tiffany waited until she heard him on the stairs, then she slowly closed the door to the bedroom and locked it.

A few minutes later she heard water running in the guest bathroom at the other end of the hall, and she smiled. "You're a fool," she whispered to herself as she stripped off the vibrant red robe, flung it carelessly on the foot of the bed and walked into her private bathroom. "A stranger just spent the night in your room, and if you had your way, he would be back here in a minute making furious, passion-filled love to you."

After turning on the shower, she shook her head and smiled at her unfamiliar and traitorous thoughts. "Tiffany, my friend," she warned her reflection in the steamy mirror, "this fascination with Zane Sheridan can only spell trouble."

Dropping her silvery nightgown on the floor, she stepped into the hot spray of water.

AFTER BRAIDING HER HAIR INTO A SINGLE PLAIT, applying just a little makeup and dressing in her favorite pair of faded jeans and a loose sweater, Tiffany headed downstairs to the kitchen. The airy room was bright with copper pots and pans suspended over the stove, plants arranged strategically on the gleaming tile counters, and oversized windows offering a view of the pasture near the broodmare barn.

The coffee was perking, muffins were baking in the oven and the previous night's dishes had been placed in the dishwasher before she heard Zane on the stairs. The inviting aromas of baking bread, coffee and cured ham wafted through the large kitchen.

"Efficient, aren't you?" he stated, offering her a lazy grin.

"I try to be." She glanced over her shoulder and felt her heart begin to pound irregularly as her eyes were caught in the silvery web of his gaze. Zane's black hair was still wet from his shower, his shadow of a beard had been shaved off to reveal the hard angle of his jaw and he was dressed casually in tan cords and a teal-blue sweater. Without his formal attire, he appeared more rakishly handsome than ever. Looking at him caused an uneasy fluttering in Tiffany's stomach.

He leaned against the counter, seemingly content to watch her work. Turning back to the coffee, she poured a cup and tried to hide the fact that her hands were unsteady.

"Cream or sugar?"

"Black is fine." He took an experimental sip, all the while observing Tiffany over the rim of the stoneware mug. "What happened to your cook?"

"She doesn't come in every day—remember? Only a couple of days a week to keep the house up, and on special occasions."

Zane observed her sure movements. God, she wasn't what he'd expected in Ellery Rhodes's wife. "You're a bit of a mystery," he thought aloud as his eyes wandered from her braid, past her slim waist to the inviting swell of her jean-clad hips.

"Ha. And what about you? Appearing on my doorstep with an offer on the farm and a wild tale about Devil's Gambit being kidnapped by Ellery…." She let her voice trail off. She couldn't think that Ellery was alive, couldn't deal with it now. Ellery wouldn't have left. He couldn't have. Not when he knew that she would think he was dead! Though their marriage had been less than ideal, certainly Ellery cared for her in his own, distant way. He wouldn't have put her through the pain of the funeral, the adjustment to widowhood, the problems of running the farm alone….

"Not to mention dead husbands," he offered, as if reading her thoughts.

Tiffany's shoulders flexed, and she held back the hot retort forming on her tongue. It wouldn't be wise to anger him, not yet. She had to find out what he wanted, what kind of game he was playing with her. With an effort, she turned her attention to the boiling water on the stove. Carefully she cracked and added the eggs.

"My husband isn't alive," Tiffany whispered, as if to convince herself.

"You're sure?"

She didn't answer him right away. She removed the muffins from the oven, and, when they were cooked, spooned the poached eggs from the pan. Only then did she say, "Ellery wouldn't let me think he was dead—he wouldn't put me through that kind of pain," she insisted, her quiet dignity steadfastly in place.

"Ellery Rhodes was a bastard." Zane's words were soft, but they seemed to thunder in the small kitchen.

"Your opinion."

"Granted, but correct nonetheless."

"And one I think you should keep to yourself!"

His bitter smile grew slowly from one side of his arrogant face to the other. He took a long swig of his coffee and noticed that Tiffany had paled. "Did you love him so much?"

"I don't understand," she began, but under his direct gaze, she changed the course of her thoughts. "Of course I loved him."

"Enough to cover up for him?"

Her simmering anger ignited, and pride took control of her tongue. "Wait a minute, Sheridan. You're way out of line."

He studied the honesty in her deep blue eyes and frowned into his mug. "My apologies," he muttered, before downing the rest of his coffee.

"If I had any brains at all, I'd throw you and your outlandish stories out of this place—"

"But you can't."

"Why not?"

He settled into the cane-backed chair he had occupied at the table the night before and flashed her a devastating smile that seemed to touch the darkest corners of her soul. "Because you believe me—" She raised her hands as if to protest and he silenced her with a knowing glare. "At least you believe a little."

Tiffany's chest was incredibly tight. She found it difficult to breathe. "I think, Mr. Sheridan, the only reasons I haven't asked you to leave are, one, because we didn't finish our discussion last night—a discussion that I have to admit piqued my curiosity about you—and two, because you helped out here last night when I was desperate." *And because I find you the most incredibly interesting man I've ever met,* she added silently to herself as she put the muffins in a basket and set them on the table next to the platter of ham and eggs. The attraction she felt to him was as crazy as the stories he spun about Devil's Gambit, and yet she couldn't fight it.

They ate in silence, neither breaking the unspoken truce while they consumed the hearty breakfast Tiffany had prepared.

After the table had been cleared, Tiffany heard Mac's footsteps on the back porch. Automatically she reached for the pot of coffee and poured a large mug of the dark liquid before adding both sugar and cream to the cup.

"Mornin'," Mac grumbled as he accepted the mug Tiffany offered. He took off his hat and placed it on top of the refrigerator. His eyes swept the interior of the kitchen and rested on Zane. The frown that began on Mac's crowlike features was quickly disguised as he took a long swallow of coffee.

So Sheridan had spent the night, Mac thought. He didn't much like the idea, didn't trust the Irishman. But Tiffany did what suited her, and if Zane Sheridan suited her, then it was none of Mac's business what went on between them. Tiffany had been alone too long as it was, and if he was uncomfortable in the Irishman's presence, Mac silently told himself it was his own problem.

"It's late for you to be getting in," Tiffany teased the ex-jockey with a warm grin.

"Not after a night that ended at three this morning."

Winking fondly at Mac, Tiffany moved toward the stove. "How about some breakfast?"

"Thanks much, but no." Mac eyed the leftover blueberry muffins but shook his head. "The missus, she made me eat before I left." He patted his lean stomach. "Couldn't hold anything else." He propped an elbow against the pantry door, finished his coffee and fidgeted. "I checked Ebony Wine this morning."

"I was about to go out there myself."

"No need. She's fine." Mac stared out the window toward the foaling shed and scowled. "She wasn't much of a mother the last time she foaled, so I don't reckon she'll miss this one much...." He shifted his weight from one foot to the other and set his empty cup on the blue tiles. "She should go into foal heat soon—next week, maybe. You plan on breeding her when she does?"

"If Vance says she's all right," Tiffany replied.

"To Moon Shadow?" Mac asked, and at the look on Tiffany's face he knew he'd made a monumental mistake saying anything in front of Zane Sheridan. He could have kicked himself for his lack of tact, but then he'd supposed that Sheridan knew what was going on. Apparently Tiffany hadn't confided in Sheridan, and Mac had let the cat out of the bag. Damn it all to hell anyway. Moving his slim shoulders in a gesture of indifference, Mac tried to undo the damage he'd caused before it was too late. "No reason to worry about it now, we've got a few days."

"I...I think I'll look in on Ebony Wine," Tiffany stated, wiping her hands on a towel hanging near the stove and steering the conversation toward safer ground. "She had a rough night."

"Didn't we all?" Mac frowned but a good-natured twinkle lighted his faded eyes. In his opinion, Tiffany Rhodes was as smart as she was pretty. "I've got to go into town—check with a guy about some alfalfa. Need anything else?"

"Just a few groceries, but I can get them later."

"Suit yourself." He nodded in Zane's direction, forced his rumpled fedora back onto his head and walked out the door.

Zane's silvery eyes rested on Tiffany's face. The near-perfect features were slightly disturbed. Obviously something the old man said bothered her. It was as if she was hiding something from him. Zane had experienced that same sensation yesterday morning when the reporter was at the house, and again last night while attending to the still-

born colt. Something was bothering Tiffany Rhodes, and
Zane suspected that it was more than his remarks about
Devil's Gambit.

"Are you coming with me?" Tiffany asked as she walked
down the short hallway to the den, slipped on her boots and
pulled a worn suede jacket from the wooden hook near the
French doors.

"Nothing better to do," Zane admitted, striding with her.

"Good." She scooped some envelopes from the top drawer
of the desk, stuffed them into her pocket and headed outside.
"I just want to drop these in the mail and pick up the paper
before I go back to the foaling shed." She unlocked the French
doors and stepped outside into the brisk morning air.

The world smelled fresh and new from the morning rain.
Birds twittered in the trees, and the fog had begun to lift.
Though the drizzle had let up, raindrops still clung tenaciously
to the branches of the maple trees lining the drive. Shallow
pools of water rested on the uneven surface of the asphalt.

Despite the problems with the foals and Zane's outlandish
remarks about Devil's Gambit, Tiffany felt refreshed, as if the
gentle morning rain had washed away the fears of the night.
She noticed the dewy, crystallike web of a spider in the rhodo-
dendrons, and the woodsy scent of the earth beginning to
warm from the first rays of a partially hidden sun.

It seemed the most natural thing in the world when Zane's
fingers linked with hers, warming her hand. When he pulled
on her hand, forcing her to stop near a thicket of oaks close
to the end of the drive, she turned to face him and offered a
smile. "What?"

"You don't know that you're driving me crazy, do you?"
he asked gently, his gray gaze probing the vibrant blue depths
of her eyes.

"And all the while I thought your wild stories and insane
ideas about Devil's Gambit were genetic. Now it's my fault."
Her blue eyes sparkled in the morning sunlight.

"Be serious," he suggested, his voice low and raspy. "I've wanted you from the first moment I laid eyes on you."

Tiffany laughed softly. "Now it's time for you to be serious."

"I am."

"You don't even know me—"

"I know you well enough to realize that we're good together."

"In what way?"

"All ways."

"Just because you helped Ebony Wine and you…saw to it that I fell asleep last night, it isn't enough to—"

"Shh." He tugged on her arm, forcing her closer. As he looked down upon her she felt as if he were stripping her of the barriers she had so carefully placed around herself, around her heart. She smelled the clean, masculine scent of him, felt the warmth of his body, knew in a minute that he intended to kiss her and that she wouldn't do a damn thing about it.

When his lips touched hers, she closed her eyes and couldn't withhold the moan that came from her throat. Both of his hands reached upward to cup her face. Strong fingers held her cheeks while his lips moved slowly, provocatively over her mouth. He touched the underside of her jaw, gently stroking the delicate pulse in her neck. When he lifted his head, his eyes had grown dark with unspoken passion.

Tiffany swallowed with difficulty, and her blood began to throb wildly in her veins. Feminine urges, long dormant, began to heat and swirl within her, captivating her mind as well as her body.

"Tiffany," he whispered hoarsely against the shell of her ear as his hand slowly found and removed the band at the end of her braid of hair. His fingers worked the shimmery golden-brown strands until her hair tumbled free of its bond to frame her face in soft brown curls.

Her arms wound around his waist as his mouth dipped once again to the invitation of her parted lips. This time the kiss deepened, and Tiffany felt the thrill of his tongue as it sought out and mated with hers.

Liquid fire seemed to engulf her as desire flooded her veins and throbbed in her ears. *I can't want this man,* she reasoned with herself, but logic seemed to slip away. *He's using me....* But she found that she didn't care.

Beneath the still-naked branches of the towering oaks, she returned his passionate kiss and sighed in contentment when he pressed up against her and the evidence of his desire strained against the fabric of his cords.

Dear God, I don't want to love you, she thought as his arms encircled her and held her tightly to him. *I can't let myself fall for you.... I don't even know who you are or what you want from me. Is this moment just a diversion, an intricate part of your plan, or are your feelings real?*

Logic began to cool her blood, and he felt her withdrawing from him. "Let me love you," he whispered, refusing to let her go, his powerful arms holding her a willing captive.

She shook her head and tried to deny the traitorous feelings burning in her breast. "I can't...I just...can't."

"Because you still love your husband." His voice was low and damning. Dark fire smoldered in his eyes.

Her clear eyes clouded and her teeth sunk into her lower lip. When she shook her head, sunlight caught in the honeyed strands of her hair. "Because I don't know you well enough," she countered.

"You never will, unless you take a chance."

"I am. Right here. Right now. With you. Please...try to understand."

His arms dropped. "Understand what? That you don't know me?" He stepped away from her, granting a small distance between their bodies. "Or is it that you're suspicious of my motives?" His dark eyes searched her face. "Or maybe it's because you think I might be just slightly off my rocker."

She laughed despite the tension in the crisp morning air.

"That just about says it all," Tiffany admitted, tossing her tangled hair away from her face. "Except that I think things are moving a little too fast for me," she said, her breathing still irregular. "Yesterday we were strangers, earlier this morning, 'friends,' and now you're suggesting that we become lovers. I'm not ready for all of this—not yet."

"Don't play games with me."

"It takes two to play," she reminded him, holding her head high, her gaze steady.

"You're a mature woman, Tiffany, not some seventeen-year-old girl. You've been married—"

"And I don't have casual affairs."

"There's nothing casual about what I feel for you." His arms encircled her waist, his warm hands splaying naturally against the small of her back.

"Give it time, Zane," she pleaded in a raspy whisper. He was so near she could feel the warmth of his breath in her hair, sense the desire heating his veins, witness the burning passion in his eyes. Her expression clouded with the indecision tormenting her mind. *How easy it would be to lie naked with him in the morning sun....*

With a sound of frustration he released her and leaned against the scaly trunk of one of the larger oaks in the thicket. Lethargic raindrops fell from the branches of the tree and glistened in his dark hair. He cocked his head to the side and forced a ragged but devastating smile. "Okay—so why not give me a chance to prove myself?"

"I am. You're still here, aren't you?"

She turned on her heel, walked the short distance to the road, extracted the envelopes from her pocket and placed them in the mailbox. Then, almost as an afterthought, she retrieved the morning paper from the yellow cylinder nailed to the fence post.

Rather than consider the implications of her mixed emotions toward Zane, she opened the paper and stared down at the headlines. Her breath froze in her throat. "Oh, dear God," she whispered as her eyes scanned the front page.

The bold headline seemed to scream its message to her in powerful black and white:

LOCAL BREEDER PLAGUED BY MYSTERIOUS DEATHS.

CHAPTER SIX

TIFFANY FELT AS IF THE WET EARTH WERE BUCKLING beneath her feet. She stared at the two pictures on the front page of the *Clarion*. One photograph had been taken yesterday. It was a large print of Tiffany sitting at her desk. The other, slightly smaller picture was of Moon Shadow after his loss in the Kentucky Derby.

Tiffany read the scandalous article, which centered on the mysterious deaths of the foals. Not only did Rod Crawford imply that there was something genetically wrong with Moon Shadow, who had sired all of the colts, but he also suggested that Tiffany, in an effort to save her reputation as a horse breeder, had hidden the deaths from the public and the racing commission. Crawford went on to say that any horse bred to Moon Shadow was likely to produce foals with genetic heart defects.

The article reported that since Tiffany had assumed control of Rhodes Breeding Farm, she had encountered more problems than she could handle. From the time her husband and the legendary Devil's Gambit had died, and Tiffany had been in charge of the farm, she had experienced nothing but trouble. It appeared that either Tiffany Rhodes was the victim of fate or her own gross incompetence.

"No!" Tiffany whispered, forcing the hot tears of indignation backward. She crumpled the damning newspaper in her fist. No mention had been made of Journey's End or any other of Moon Shadow's living, healthy progeny. Rod Crawford had twisted and butchered her words in a piece of cheap sensational journalism. Nausea began to roil in her stomach. "Damn it, nothing is wrong with him! Nothing!"

Her words sounded fragile into the late morning air, as if she were trying to convince herself.

Zane had watched as Tiffany read the article. She had paled slightly before anger settled on her elegant features. Now she was clenching the newspaper in her small fist and trembling with rage.

"What happened?" he demanded.

"Rod Crawford wrote his article," Tiffany explained.

"The reporter who was here just yesterday?"

Tiffany let out a furious sigh and looked upward to the interlaced branches of the oak and fir trees. Shafts of sunlight passed through the lacy barrier to dapple the wet ground. "I didn't think the article would be printed this soon," she replied, somehow stilling her seething rage, "but I guess in the case of a scandal, even the *Clarion* holds the presses."

She expelled an angry breath and coiled her fist. "Damn it all, anyway!" She had trusted Rod Crawford and the *Clarion*'s reputation, and her trust had backfired in her face. The slant of the article was vicious, a personal attack intended to maim Tiffany's reputation. It was the last thing she had expected from a paper with the reputation of the *Santa Rosa Clarion*.

Zane touched her lightly on the shoulder in an attempt to calm her. "What are you talking about?"

"This." Her breasts rose and fell with the effort as she handed him the newspaper.

As Zane quickly scanned the article, his dark brows drew together in a savage scowl and his skin tightened over his cheekbones. A small muscle worked furiously in the corner of his jaw, and his lips thinned dangerously.

After reading the story and looking over the photographs, he smoothed the rumpled paper and tucked it under his arm. Every muscle had tensed in his whip-lean body. He was like a coiled snake, ready to strike. "Is there any truth in the article?"

"Enough to make it appear genuine."

"Great." He frowned and pinched the bridge of his nose with his thumb and forefinger, as if attempting to ward off a threatening headache. "Why didn't you tell me about this?"

Tiffany clenched her impotent fists. "I had enough to worry about with you and your crazy theories about Devil's Gambit. I didn't want to cloud the issue with the problem with Moon Shadow's foals."

"Even after last night, when I was with Ebony Wine?"

"There wasn't time." Even to her own ears, the excuse sounded feeble.

"And that's why you didn't want me near Rod Crawford. You were afraid I'd tell him what I knew about Devil's Gambit, he would report it and something like this—" he held up the newspaper and waved it in her face angrily "—might happen."

"Only it would be much worse."

He shook his head in disbelief. "I wouldn't have, you know." He could read the doubts still lingering in her eyes and silently damned himself for caring about her.

As if physically restraining his anger at her lack of trust in him, he handed the paper back to Tiffany. "I guess I can't blame you—I did come storming in here yesterday." He managed a stiff smile and pushed his hands into the back pockets of his cords. After taking a few steps, as if to increase the distance between them, he turned and faced her. Thoughtful lines etched his brow, but the intense anger seemed to dissolve. "So tell me—the colt that was born last night—he was sired by Moon Shadow. Right?"

"Yes."

Zane raked frustrated fingers through his hair. "Then the death last night will only support the allegations in Crawford's newspaper column."

Tiffany felt as if everything she had worked for was slowly slipping through her fingers. "I suppose so," she admitted with a heavy sigh. Dear God, what was happening to her life?

Suddenly everything seemed to be turning upside down. Zane Sheridan, a man whom she barely knew, whom she desired as a man but knew to be an enemy, was clouding her usually clear thinking at a time when she desperately needed all of her senses to prove true. He was voicing her worst fears, and she had trouble keeping the worried tears at bay.

"You should have told me."

"I couldn't."

"Because you didn't trust me and you thought that I might use the information on Moon Shadow against you," he said flatly, as if reading her thoughts.

So close to the truth! Was she so transparent to this man she had met only yesterday? Or was it because he knew more about her than he was willing to admit? "Something like that," she allowed, raising one suddenly heavy shoulder. "It really doesn't matter now."

"Look, woman," he said, barely able to contain his simmering anger. "You'd better start trusting me, because it looks like you're going to need all the friends you can get."

Her eyes took on a suspicious light. "But that's the problem, isn't it? I'm not quite sure whether you're on my side or not—friend or foe."

"Wait a minute—" He looked at her incredulously, as if she'd lost her mind. "Didn't I just tell you that I'm attracted to you? Wasn't I the man trying to make love to you just a few minutes ago?"

Tiffany elevated her chin fractionally. Now was the time to see exactly where Zane stood. Her dark brows arched suspiciously. "Sleeping with the enemy isn't something new, you know. It's been documented throughout history."

"Oh, give me a break!" he spit, his palms lifting upwards as if he were begging divine interference. "Did Ellery scar you so badly that you can't trust any man?"

"Ellery has nothing to do with this."

"The hell he hasn't!" Zane thundered, shaking his head in

disbelief. His arms fell to his sides in useless defeat. "You're not an easy woman to like sometimes," he said softly as he approached her. He was close enough to touch. He was offering his strength, his comfort, if only she were brave enough to trust him.

"I haven't asked you to like me—"

He reached out and grabbed her arm. "Oh, yes, you have. Every time you look at me with those wide, soul-searching eyes, you beg me to like you. Every time you smile at me, you're inviting me to care about you. Every time you touch me, you're pleading with me to love you."

Tiffany listened in astonishment, her heart beginning to pound furiously at his suggestive words. She closed her eyes in embarrassment. How close to the truth he was! His fingers wrapped more tightly over her upper arms, leaving warm impressions on her flesh.

"Look at me, dammit," he insisted, giving her a shake. When she obeyed, Zane's flinty eyes drilled into hers. "Now, lady, it looks as if you've got one hell of a problem on your hands. There's a good chance that I won't be able to help you at all, but I don't think you're in much of a position to pick and choose your friends."

She tossed her hair away from her face and proudly returned his intense stare. "Maybe not."

"So let's try to figure out why those foals are dying, right now."

"How?"

"First I want to take a look at Moon Shadow."

Tiffany hesitated only slightly. Zane was right. She needed all the allies she could find. She checked her watch and discovered that it was nearly noon. No doubt the telephone was already ringing off the hook because of the article in the morning paper. There was no time to waste. Straightening her shoulders, Tiffany cocked her head in the direction of the stallion barns.

"Mac usually takes him outside about this time. He's probably getting some exercise right now."

MOON SHADOW WAS IN A FAR CORNER of the field. His sleek black coat shimmered in the noonday sun and he tossed his arrogant ebony head upward, shaking his glossy mane and stamping one forefoot warily.

Zane studied the nervous stallion. As a three-year-old, Moon Shadow had been impressive. He boasted a short, strong back, powerful hindquarters and long legs that could propel him forward in an explosion of speed at the starting gate that had been unmatched by any of his peers. He'd won a good percentage of his starts including two jewels of the Triple Crown. His most poignant loss was the Kentucky Derby, in which he had been jostled and boxed in near the starting gate and hadn't been able to run "his race," which had always been to start in front, set the pace and stay in the lead.

Zane blamed Moon Shadow's Derby disaster on several factors, the most obvious being that of a bad jockey. Moon Shadow's regular rider had been injured the day of the race, and his replacement, Bill Wade, was a green, uncaring man who had later lost his license to ride.

Mac was leaning over the fence, a piece of straw tucked into a corner of his mouth. Suddenly the black horse snorted, flattened his ears to his head, lifted his tail and ran the length of the long paddock. His smooth strides made the short dash appear effortless.

"He knows he's got an audience," Mac said as Tiffany approached. Wolverine was resting at the trainer's feet. At the sight of Tiffany, he thumped his tail on the moist ground. She reached down and scratched the collie's ears before propping her foot on the lowest board of the fence and resting her arms over the top rail.

"He's going to have more," Tiffany said with a sigh.

Mac's eyes narrowed. "More what?"

"More of an audience."

"What d'ya mean?" Instantly Mac was concerned. He read the worry in Tiffany's eyes.

"I'm afraid Moon Shadow is going to get more than his share of attention in the next couple of weeks. Take a look at page one." Tiffany handed Mac the paper before shading her eyes with her hand.

"Son of a bitch," Mac cursed after reading the article. He pushed his hat back to the crown of his head. "A pack of lies— nothing but a goddamn pack of lies." His eyes flickered from Zane to Tiffany before returning to Moon Shadow. "Damn reporters never have learned to sort fact from fiction." After smoothing the thin red hair over his scalp, he forced the frumpy fedora back onto his head. "A good thing you and Vance already told the Jockey Club about the dead colts."

"Yeah, right," Tiffany agreed without much enthusiasm. "But wait until the owners who have broodmares pregnant with Moon Shadow's foals get wind of this."

Mac frowned and rubbed the toe of his boot in the mud. "You'll just have to set them straight, Missy. Moon Shadow's a good stud. He's got the colts to prove it. Why the hell didn't that bastard of a reporter write about Journey's End or Devil's Gambit?"

Tiffany's eyes moved from Mac to Zane and finally back to the stallion in question. "I don't know," she answered. "Probably because he needed a story to sell papers." And he'd get one, too, if Zane decided to publicize his conjectures about Ellery and Devil's Gambit.

"How many foals were affected?" Zane asked.

"Three—no, Ebony Wine's colt makes four," Tiffany replied softly. "Three colts and a filly. Two died shortly after birth, the colt last night was stillborn and Charlatan…well, he lived longer, a couple of days, but…" Her voice faded on the soft afternoon breeze.

The silence of the afternoon was interrupted only by the

wind rustling through the fir needles and the sound of Moon Shadow's impatient snorts.

"And they all died from heart failure?" Zane asked, staring at the proud stallion as if he hoped to see the reasons for the tragic deaths in the shining black horse.

Tiffany nodded, and Mac shifted the piece of straw from one corner of his mouth to the other.

"Seems that way," Mac muttered.

"Unless Vance discovers something different in the autopsy of the colt born last night," Tiffany added and then shook her head. "But I doubt that he'll find anything else."

"What about other horses bred to Moon Shadow?"

"Fortunately, none of the foals of mares from other owners have been affected—at least not yet. I've corresponded with all of the owners. So far, each mare has delivered a strong, healthy foal."

"Thank God for small favors," Mac mumbled ungraciously.

"Some owners even want to rebreed to Moon Shadow," Tiffany said, almost as an afterthought.

"But you're not breeding him?"

"Not until we find out what's going on."

"I don't blame you." Zane's gaze returned to the imperious stallion, who was tossing his head menacingly toward the spectators.

"He knows we're talkin' about him," Mac said fondly. "Always did like a show, that one." He rubbed the back of his weathered neck. "Should've won the Triple Crown, ya know. My fault for letting that son of a bitch ride him."

"Mac's been blaming himself ever since."

"I should've known the boy was no good."

"Quit second-guessing yourself. Ellery thought Bill was a decent jockey. Moon Shadow didn't win and that's that."

Mac frowned as he stared at the horse. "The closest I've come to a Triple Crown. Moon Shadow and Devil's Gambit were the finest horses I've ever seen race."

Tiffany stiffened at the mention of Devil's Gambit. "Mac's prejudiced, of course. The owners of Secretariat, Seattle Slew and a few others would have different opinions. But Moon Shadow sure used to be a crowd-pleaser," Tiffany remarked thoughtfully as she stared at the fiery black stallion.

"Aye. That he was," the old trainer agreed sadly as he rubbed the stubble on his chin. "That he was."

Tiffany spent the rest of the day showing Zane the farm. As Mac had stated, Ebony Wine seemed none the worse from her trauma the night before, and if Vance Geddes gave his okay, Tiffany wanted to breed her as soon as the mare was in heat.

As much as it broke her heart, Tiffany decided that Moon Shadow couldn't be allowed to sire any more foals until it was proved beyond a doubt that the cause of his foals' deaths wasn't genetic.

By the time she and Zane headed back to the house, it was late afternoon. The March sun was warm against Tiffany's back. As they walked toward the back porch, she slung her jacket over her shoulder. Zane had been with her all day, and it seemed natural that he was on the farm, helping with the chores, offering her his keen advice and flashing his devastating smile.

"So you've already had him tested," Zane remarked as he held open the screen door to the broad back porch.

"Yes. And so far the semen samples have shown nothing out of the ordinary. I've asked for additional tests, but Vance Geddes seems to think that nothing will be discovered."

"What about the mares?"

She frowned and sighed. "Each horse has been examined by several vets. Blood samples, urine samples...every test available. The mares seem perfectly healthy.

"So all of the evidence points to Moon Shadow."

Tiffany nodded as she wedged the toe of one boot behind the heel of the other and kicked it off. She placed the scarred boots in the corner of the porch near the kitchen door. "It looks that way," she admitted.

"But you don't believe it."

"A good stud just doesn't go bad overnight." She pursed her lips together and ran weary fingers through her unruly hair. "Something has to have happened to him—I just don't know what."

"All the mares were bred to him around the same time?"

"Within a few weeks—I think. However, there are still mares who haven't dropped their foals."

"And you think they may have problems?"

Her blue eyes clouded with worry. "I hope to God they don't," she whispered as she started toward the door to the house. Zane's hand on her arm restrained her.

"I need to ask you something," he said quietly. The tone of his voice sent a prickle of fear down her spine.

"What?"

"Do you have any enemies, anyone who would want to hurt you?" His eyes had darkened as they searched her face.

"None that I can think of."

"What about this Crawford, the guy who wrote the article? Why would he want to distort the truth?"

"I couldn't begin to hazard a guess." She looked at the paper Zane was still carrying under his arm. "I guess the *Clarion* is into sensationalism these days."

"No personal reasons?"

"No."

His eyes drove into hers. "How about someone else who might want to see you exposed as incompetent?"

Tiffany stiffened, and cold dread settled between her shoulder blades. "Like whom?"

"I don't know—a competitor maybe?" When she shook her head in disbelief, her hair tumbled over her shoulders. He tightened his fingers around her arms. "A spurned lover?"

"Of course not!"

His grip relaxed a little. "You can't think of anyone who would want to hurt you? Someone with a big enough grudge against you or this farm to want to see your dirty laundry in black and white?" He was staring at her boldly, daring her to reply. "It would have to be someone with inside information."

Tiffany's eyes grew cold, and she felt a painful constricting of her heart. "The only person who remotely fits that description is you."

Zane stiffened. Tiffany saw the anger flash in his eyes, but he didn't bother to refute her accusation. His lips thinned until they showed white near the corners. "You know there was no love lost between myself and your husband. If Ellery were alive today, I'd probably do what I could to ruin him." He looked away from her and for a moment, pain was evident in the rugged planes of his face. "I despised the man, Tiffany, but you have to believe that I would never intentionally hurt you."

"Even if Ellery is still alive?" she whispered.

He closed his eyes against the possibility. The craving for vengeance that had festered in his blood still poisoned him, but as he gazed down upon Tiffany's face, Zane knew that he was lost to her. His hatred for Ellery couldn't begin to match the intensity of his feelings for this proud, beautiful woman. "If Ellery Rhodes walked through the door tonight, I would still detest him. But—" he reached out and gently stroked her chin "—because of you, I would leave."

Tiffany swallowed the uncomfortable lump forming in her throat and ignored the hot sting of tears against her eyelids. How desperately she longed to believe him. "Even if I asked you to stay?"

"What are you saying, Tiffany?" he asked, his face close to hers. "If Ellery is alive, would you leave him for me?"

"I…I don't know," she admitted, confused at the emotions warring within her. She ached to say yes and fall into Zane's arms, never to look back. If only she could love him for now, this moment, and cast away any thought to the future, or the past.

Slowly he pulled her to him, and Tiffany felt his larger body press urgently against hers. She leaned on him, and he kissed her forehead. "I can't make things different between us," he said, gently smoothing her hair away from her face.

"Would you, if you could?"

"Yes," he replied quickly as he had a vision of her lying naked in Ellery Rhodes's bed. "I wish I'd known you long ago."

In the privacy of the screened porch, with the fragrance of cherry blossoms scenting the air, nothing seemed to matter. It was a private world filled with only this one strong, passionate man. Tears pooled in Tiffany's eyes and clung to her lashes. "I think that it's better not to dwell on the past…or wish for things that could never be."

He tilted her face upward with his hands, and his lips claimed hers in a kiss that was filled with the desperation of the moment, and the need to purge all thoughts of her husband from her mind.

Her lips parted willingly for him, and his tongue touched the edges of her teeth before slipping into her mouth and plundering the moist cavern she so willingly offered.

A raw groan of frustrated longing escaped from his lips as he molded his hungry body to hers. She wound her arms around him, held him close, clinging to him as if afraid he would leave her empty and bereft.

"Tiffany," he whispered into her hair and let out a ragged breath. "Oh, Tiffany, what am I going to do with you?"

Whatever you want, she thought, returning his kiss with a bursting passion that had no earthly bounds.

His hands found the hem of her sweater and slipped underneath the soft fabric to press against the silken texture of her skin. Her breath constricted in her throat, and when his fingers cupped the underside of her breast she felt as if she were melting into him. A soft moan came from her throat as his fingers softly traced the lacy edge of her bra. She felt the bud of her nipple blossom willingly to his touch as his fingers slid slowly upward.

Zane's breathing became labored, a sweet rush of air

against her ear that caused tantalizing sparks of yearning to fire her blood. "Let me love you, sweet lady," he pleaded, fanning her hair with his breath.

If only I could! Her desire throbbed in her ears, burned in her soul, but the doubts of the night filtered into her passion-drugged mind, and before she lost all sense of reason, she pulled away from him, regret evidenced in her slumberous blue eyes. "I…I think it would be best if we went inside," she said raggedly, hoping to quell the raging storm of passion in her blood.

The tense lines along the edge of his mouth deepened. "You want me," he said, holding her close, pressing the muscles of her body to his. "Admit it."

Her heart was an imprisoned bird throwing itself mercilessly against her rib cage. She lost her sense of time and reason. "I want you more than I've ever wanted a man," she whispered, trying to pull free of his protective embrace. "But wanting isn't enough."

"What is?"

Love, her mind screamed, but the word wouldn't form on her lips. How often before had she felt love only to see it wither and die? The love of Tiffany's mother had been so fragile that Marie had left her only daughter in the care of a drunken father. Edward's love hadn't been strong enough to conquer the drink that eventually killed him, and Ellery… Ellery probably didn't know the meaning of the word.

"I…I'm not sure," she admitted, her voice quavering unexpectedly.

"Oh, hell," Zane swore in disgust, releasing her. "Neither am I." He looked thoroughly disgusted with himself, and he rammed his hands into his pockets, trying to quiet the fury of desire straining within him. The heat in his loins seemed to sear his mind. Never had he wanted a woman so painfully. He felt as if his every nerve were raw, charged with lust.

Tiffany stared at Zane until her breathing had silenced and her racing pulse had slowed to a more normal rate. She entered the house, and the smells of roast and cinnamon filled her nostrils. "Louise?" she called as she went into the kitchen. The plump woman with graying hair and a ready smile was extracting a deep-dish apple pie from one of the ovens. "I thought you were going out of town for the weekend."

"Not until tomorrow." Louise set the hot pie on the tile counter and turned to face Tiffany. "I thought maybe you could use a little help around here today."

"You read the article in the *Clarion*."

Louise's full mouth pursed into an angry pout. "Yep. I read it this morning and canceled my subscription before noon. That was the trashiest piece of journalism I've ever read. Rod Crawford should be strung up by his—" her eyes moved from Tiffany to Zane "—hamstrings."

Tiffany smiled at the angry housekeeper. "You shouldn't have canceled your subscription."

"Humph. What I should have done was write a letter to the editor, but I suppose that would only make the situation worse, what with the publicity and all."

At that moment the phone rang, and Tiffany reached to answer it.

"It's been ringing off the hook all afternoon." When Tiffany hesitated, Louise continued. "Reporters mostly. A couple of other breeders, too. The messages are on your desk."

"I'll take the call in the den," Tiffany decided, straightening her shoulders.

"Vultures," Louise muttered as she opened the oven and checked the roast.

Tiffany answered the phone in the den on the sixth ring.

"Tiffany, is that you?" an agitated male voice inquired.

"Yes."

"This is Hal Reece." Tiffany's heart sank. Reece had bred one of his mares to Moon Shadow. Was he calling to tell her that the foal was dead? Her palms began to sweat and her pulse jumped nervously.

"What can I do for you, Mr. Reece?"

The stuffy sixty-year-old paused before getting to the point. "I read an article about your farm in the *Clarion*. No one told me there was any genetic problem with Moon Shadow."

"There isn't."

"But the article stated—"

"What the article stated was only half the story." Tiffany's eyes clashed with Zane's as he entered the den.

"Then you're saying that those foals didn't die?" he questioned, relief audible in his voice.

"No," Tiffany replied, bracing herself by leaning on the desk. "It's true we've lost a few foals—"

"Moon Shadow's foals," he clarified.

"Yes. But there is no reason to think that the problem is genetic. I've had Moon Shadow tested by several veterinarians. You're familiar with Vance Geddes, aren't you?"

"Why, yes. Good man, Geddes."

"He's been involved with the problem from day one. He's concluded that there's no evidence that the deaths were genetically related."

"But certainly they were linked."

"It appears that way."

"And the natural assumption is that it was the sire, as all the foals were his."

Tiffany heard the hopeful note in Hal's voice. She hated to discourage him. Forcing herself to remain calmly professional, she held her voice steady as she clutched the receiver in a deathlike grip. "Moon Shadow has proved himself a good stud. Journey's End and Devil's Gambit are proof enough of that. Most of the foals that he sired this year had no problems."

"No other owner has complained?" Reece asked, sounding dubious.

"None, and I've been in contact with each of them. So far, Moon Shadow has sired twenty-three perfectly healthy foals—something Mr. Crawford neglected to print."

"But three have died."

There was no use in hiding the truth from Reece or any of the other owners who had bred their expensive mares to Moon Shadow. It would only look worse later. Tiffany gritted her teeth and closed her eyes. "Four. We lost another colt last night."

"Oh, God!" His voice sounded weak.

Zane was standing near the fireplace, one shoeless stockinged foot propped against the stone hearth.

"When is your mare due to foal?" Tiffany asked.

"Any day now."

"I'm sure you'll find that you have a healthy Thoroughbred on your hands."

"I'd better, Tiffany," Hal said softly. "I'm not a rich man, I can't afford a loss like this. I'm sure the insurance company wouldn't cover the cost of my stud fee—"

"Mr. Reece, if you do happen to lose the colt and we discover that the problem stemmed from breeding your mare to Moon Shadow, I'll refund the stud fee."

"And then what? My mare's lost nearly a year of prime breeding time."

Tiffany's face became rigid. "I won't be able to do anything about that, Mr. Reece. It's the chance we take as breeders." She heard herself repeating Zane's advice of the night before. "When your mare does foal, I'd appreciate a call from you."

"You can count on it. Good day," he replied frostily, and Tiffany replaced the receiver. As soon as she set it down the phone rang again.

"Don't answer it," Zane advised, seeing the way she had paled during her lengthy conversation.

"I have to."

"The calls can wait."

"I don't think so. I have ten or twelve owners who are probably in a state of panic."

The phone rang again.

"It could be the press," Zane argued.

"Then I'll have to deal with them as well. I can't just hide my head in the sand. This was bound to happen sooner or later." She reached for the phone and answered it. A male voice demanded to speak to Tiffany Rhodes.

"This is she," Tiffany replied. The man identified himself as a reporter for a San Francisco paper. The telephone call was a short interview, and by the time it was over, Tiffany felt drained.

Zane sat on the edge of the desk, his worried gaze studying her as she turned around, clicked on a small computer in the bookcase and started typing onto the keyboard when luminous green letters appeared on the screen.

"What're you doing?"

"Getting a printout of all the owners who still have broodmares pregnant with Moon Shadow's foals. I think it would be best if I called them, rather than having them read a story like the one in the *Santa Rosa Clarion*."

"This can wait until morning."

Tiffany shook her head and refused to be deterred. "I'd just as soon get it over with. The sooner the better." The printer began rattling out the list of owners as Tiffany checked the phone messages Louise had stacked on her desk. "Great," she mumbled. She held up one of the messages and handed it to him. "A reporter for a television station in San Francisco wants an interview." She smiled grimly. "What do you bet that it's not to talk about Journey's End's career?"

Zane frowned. "No wager from me, lady. I learned a long time ago not to bet money unless it was a sure thing—and then only when the man you're betting against is honest." His voice was low, and edged in anger. From the look on Zane's face, she knew that he was somehow referring to Ellery.

The printer stopped spewing out information, and the silence in the small room seemed deafening.

At that moment, Louise appeared, balancing a tray in her plump hands. "I thought you two could use a cup of coffee," she explained. Noticing the tension in the room and the silent challenge in Tiffany's eyes, Louise pursed her lips together thoughtfully and amended her offer. "Or I could get you something stronger—"

"Coffee's fine," Zane replied, turning to watch her and sending a charming grin in her direction.

"Yes, thank you," Tiffany said, once Zane's gaze had released her.

"Dinner will be in about an hour."

Tiffany managed a frail smile. "Louise, you're a lifesaver."

The large woman chuckled. "I'm afraid you'll need more than a hot meal before the evening's done."

"Don't be so optimistic," Tiffany remarked cynically.

"Just my nature," Louise replied before leaving the room.

"What else have you got on that computer?" Zane asked, studying the list of owners.

"Everything."

"Like what?"

"Health records on the horses, the price of feed, the stud fees we charged, equipment. Everything."

"Including a profile of your Thoroughbreds?"

"Every horse that's been a part of the farm."

"Can you get me a printout on Moon Shadow?"

She managed a tight smile. "Sure."

"How about the mares he was bred to, especially the four that lost their foals?"

Tiffany sat down at the keyboard. "This has already been done, you know."

"Humor me. I need something to do while you're tied up with the phone. I may as well be doing something constructive since I canceled my flight."

"Can't argue with that." Tiffany requested the information from the computer, and when the printer started spewing out profiles of the horses in question, Tiffany started with the first of what promised to be several uncomfortable telephone calls to the owners of mares bred to Moon Shadow.

CHAPTER SEVEN

"HERE, DRINK SOME OF THIS," ZANE SUGGESTED. He handed Tiffany a glass of white wine. "Maybe it will improve your appetite."

"And my disposition?" She accepted the glass and took a sip of the white Burgundy. The cool liquid slid easily down her throat, and she eyed her plate of forgotten food with a sigh.

"They really got to you, didn't they?" Zane asked as he leaned back in his chair and frowned into his glass. He had finished Louise's dinner of roast beef, parslied potatoes and steamed broccoli before noticing Tiffany's neglected plate.

"Let's just say I'm glad it's over," she replied and then amended her statement, "or I hope to God it is."

What if any of the unborn foals were to die shortly after birth? What would happen to her and the farm? The telephone conversations with the owners who had mares bred to Moon Shadow hadn't gone well at all. By the time she had contacted or left messages with all the owners, Tiffany had felt as if every nerve in her body had been stretched as tightly as a piano wire. During two of the more difficult calls, she had been threatened with lawsuits, should the foals be born with life-threatening heart problems.

She couldn't begin to do justice to Louise's delicious meal. With a weary shake of her head, she pushed her plate aside, leaned back in the chair and ran tense fingers through her hair.

Zane offered her a sad, understanding smile. "Come on, the

dishes will wait. Let's finish this—" he held up the opened bottle of wine "—and relax in the study."

"I don't think that's possible."

"Come on, buck up." He got up from the table and placed a comforting hand on her shoulder. "Things are bound to get better."

"That's a strange statement, coming from you," she stated. He shrugged his broad shoulders and his smile faded. "But I guess you're right," she continued, slapping the table with new resolve. "Things can't get much worse." *Unless another foal dies.*

The den seemed warm and intimate. The glowing embers of the fire and the muted illumination from a single brass lamp with an emerald-colored shade softened the corners of the room and reflected on the finish of the cherry-wood walls. The thick Oriental carpet in hues of green and ivory, the etchings of sleek horses adorning the walls and the massive stone fireplace offered a sense of privacy to the room.

Zane stoked the smoldering coals in the fireplace. *As if he'd done it a hundred times. Here. In her home.* His actions seemed so natural, as if he were an integral part of the farm. As he knelt before the fire, he lifted a chunk of oak from the large basket sitting on the warm stones of the hearth. "This should do it," he mumbled to himself as he placed the mossy log on the scarlet embers. Eager flames began to lick the new fuel and reflect in golden shadows on Zane's angular face. His shirt was stretched over his back, and Tiffany watched his fluid movements as he worked. When the fire was to his satisfaction, he dusted his hands together and studied the ravenous flames.

As she sipped her wine and observed him, Tiffany felt the long dormant stirring of feminine desire. Urges that were better denied began to burn in her mind. *I won't let myself fall for him,* she promised but knew that her efforts would prove futile. He was already an integral part of her life. Ever since last night, when he had bent over the lifeless foal and tried to force air into the still lungs, Zane Sheridan had become a part of Rhodes Breeding Arm. Whether she liked it or not.

She dragged her eyes away from his strong physique and concentrated on the clear liquid in her wineglass. "Don't you have some place you have to be?" she asked.

The lean frame stiffened. He hesitated for just a moment before turning to face her. "Later."

"Tonight?" she asked in attempted nonchalance. Her tongue caught on the solitary word.

He nodded curtly. "I've got some early appointments in San Francisco tomorrow." He noticed the slight tensing in her shoulders. *Damn her, that strong will and pride will be her downfall...or mine.* "Things I can't put off any longer." He finished his wine and stared at her. "Is that a hint?"

"No...I mean, I just think it's strange that you've been here—" she made a big show of checking her watch "—over twenty-four hours and still haven't gotten down to the reason you came."

"The time of reckoning—right?" His eyes met her gaze boldly before glancing at the portrait of the horse.

She took a seat on the edge of the gray corduroy couch. "Close enough. But first I want to thank you for helping last night. I really appreciate everything you did...."

"You're sure about that?"

She remembered waking up and finding him sleeping in the uncomfortable chair with his feet propped on her bed. "Yes," she whispered. "For everything."

"And now you want to know about Devil's Gambit," Zane thought aloud as he stood and stretched his arms over his head. It was an unconscious and erotic gesture. His sweater rose, displaying all too clearly his lean abdomen. His belted cords were slung low over his hips and Tiffany glimpsed the rock-hard muscles near his navel. She imagined the ripple of the corded muscles of his chest, his muscular thighs and lean flanks…. She had to look away from him and force her mind from the sexual fantasy she was envisioning. What was wrong with her? She'd never reacted this way to a man, not even Ellery. Until Zane Sheridan had walked into her life, she had considered herself nearly uninterested in the opposite sex.

One look from Zane's steely gray eyes had drastically altered her entire perception of her own sexuality. Her new feelings were at once exciting and frightening. Zane was the one man she couldn't begin to trust…not with her body or her soul. He had already admitted that he was waging a vendetta of sorts, and she didn't doubt for a minute that he was the kind of man who would use and destroy her because of his hatred of Ellery.

Zane took a final sip of his wine and then set the empty goblet on the mantel. "I meant to tell you about Devil's Gambit last night," he explained, "but Ebony Wine had other things on her mind."

Tiffany nodded and clutched the stem of her crystal glass more tightly as she remembered the agonizing scene in the foaling shed and the innocent stillborn colt. Had it been only last night? So many things had changed, including her respect and feelings for Zane. "So what about now?"

Zane angled his head to the side and studied the wariness in her eyes. She was sitting on the edge of the gray cushions, waiting for him to explain his reasons for being there. "No time like the present, I suppose." He walked over to the bar and splashed three fingers of Scotch into an empty glass. "I think your horse—"

"You mean Devil's Gambit?"

"Right. I think he's in Ireland, using an alias."

"Now I know you're crazy." What did he mean about Devil's Gambit being in Ireland? His story was getting more far-fetched by the minute.

If she had any guts at all, she would tell him to get out of her house…her life, take his wild stories and shove them.

Instead she twirled the stem of the wineglass in her fingers and stared up at him.

"Just hear me out. Have you ever heard of a horse named King's Ransom?"

"Yes," she admitted, recalling the Irish Thoroughbred. "But I really don't keep up on the European horses, not as much as I should, I suppose. There just isn't enough time. Dustin handles that end of the business."

"I'm not surprised," Zane replied with obvious distaste.

"What does that mean?"

"Only that sometimes it's hard to tell Ellery and Dustin apart." He paced across the room before sitting on the warm stones of the hearth.

"So you know Dustin?" That knowledge came as a shock to her and she felt a new wariness steal over her heart. *Hadn't Dustin mentioned King's Ransom to her—something about the horse's fame as a stud?* Tiffany couldn't recall the conversation....

"We've met." Zane leaned his elbows on his knees and cradled his drink with both of his hands.

"And you don't like him any more than you liked Ellery."

"As I said, they're too much alike to suit my taste."

Tiffany was stunned. Dustin had his faults, of course, but she'd come to rely on her brother-in-law and his savvy for horses. It seemed as if Zane were determined to destroy anything and anyone who was solid in her life.

"Not much does, does it?" she countered.

"What?"

"Suit your taste."

He hesitated. His eyes darkened and for a moment she imagined that he might suggest that she suited him. Instead he lifted an appreciative dark brow. "You're right—not much."

Tiffany's throat constricted, and she sipped her wine to clear the tight lump that made it difficult to breathe.

If he noticed her discomfort, Zane chose to ignore it and get to the point. "Anyway, this horse, King's Ransom, was a disappointment when he raced. He had all the qualities to perform on the track—great bloodlines, perfect conformation and a long, easy stride. He had the look of a winner about him, but he just didn't seem to have the grit…or heart to be a champion. He never finished better than fifth, and consequently he was retired about seven years ago and put out to stud.

"The first of his offspring began running about four years ago, and even though they inherited all his physical characteristics, none of the colts and fillies were anything to write home about. It seemed as if they all ended up with his lack of drive."

"So what does this have to do with Devil's Gambit?" Tiffany asked. Her blue eyes mirrored her worry. Despite her arguments to the contrary, she was beginning to understand what Zane was hinting at.

"I'm getting to that. All of a sudden, less than two years ago, when that year's two-year-olds and three-year-olds hit the track, look out! Overnight, King's Ransom was producing some of the fastest horses in Europe."

"That's not impossible," Tiffany said uneasily. She felt a sudden chill and shivered before getting up and walking closer to the fire…to Zane.

"But highly improbable. It's the same principle as what's happening here with Moon Shadow, in reverse. Just as a good stud won't go bad overnight, the reverse is true. A mediocre stallion doesn't become the greatest stud in Ireland by a fluke." Zane was looking up at her with his magnetic gray eyes. He knew that he had Tiffany's full attention. Her glass of wine was nearly untouched, her troubled blue eyes reached into the blackest corners of his soul. *God, she was beautiful.* He swirled his drink and stared into the amber liquor, trying to still the male urges overcoming him.

"I own a mare that I bred about five years ago to King's Ransom," Zane continued. "The colt that was born from that union was just what I expected—a solid horse, a plodder, but nothing that would compare to his recent foals. I rebred that same mare to King's Ransom three years ago, and the resulting filly has already won two races and come in second in another. This horse is a full sister to the first."

Tiffany's dark honey-colored brows drew together pensively as she tried to remember what it was about King's Ransom... Vaguely she recalled a conversation with Dustin. Dustin had been going on and on about King's Ransom and his ability as a sire. At the time, it hadn't seemed all that important. Dustin was always raving about one horse or another—comparing his current favorite to the horses he and Tiffany owned.

"It might be worth it to breed one of the mares, say Felicity, to King's Ransom," Dustin had insisted.

"But the cost of shipping her would be prohibitive," Tiffany had replied. "The insurance alone—"

"I tell you, that stud's got what it takes!" Dustin had been adamant. "He could sire the next Devil's Gambit!"

Now, as Dustin's words came back to her, Tiffany paled. If what Zane was suggesting was true, then Dustin must have been involved! "I...I don't believe it," Tiffany said, taking a sip of her wine and trying to ignore the chilling implications running through her mind.

This was absurd. Ludicrous. Her relationship with Dustin had always been solid, and after Ellery's accident it had been Dustin who had helped her over the rough spots, given her his ear, offered a strong shoulder to cry on.

"Believe it. Devil's Gambit is siring foals and King's Ransom is getting all the credit. Your horse is being used, Tiffany!"

She squared her shoulders and trained disbelieving eyes on Zane. "I don't know why you came here," she said. "If it was to trick me into selling the farm, then you may as well leave now. All of this—" she moved both arms in a sweeping gesture meant to encompass everything that had transpired between them "—has been a very entertaining show, but I don't believe any of it. You're wasting your breath."

Zane pursed his lips together in frustration. With a frown he got up, crossed the room and picked up his briefcase.

"God, Tiffany, you don't make it easy," he muttered as he set the leather case on the wooden desk and silently wondered why it bothered him so much that he had to prove himself to this woman. He could hardly expect that she would believe his story without proof. After snapping the case open and extracting a white envelope, he handed the slim packet to her.

With trembling fingers Tiffany opened the envelope and extracted a faded photograph of a black stallion.

"This," he said angrily while pointing at the horse in the photo, "is a picture of King's Ransom. He looks a lot like Devil's Gambit, don't you think?"

The resemblance was eerie. Tiffany couldn't deny what was patently obvious. Even though the photograph was old and faded it was glaringly evident that the stallion's size and conformation were incredibly like that of the dead horse.

Zane reached inside his briefcase again. This time he took out the manila envelope he had given her the night before. It still contained the photographs he had insisted were those of Devil's Gambit. Tiffany might have believed him last night except for the fact that the white stocking on the horse's foreleg was missing.

"Are those two horses the same?" he demanded. His jaw was rigid, his gaze blistering as he searched her face.

She studied the photographs closely. A cold chill of dread skittered down her spine. The horses were nearly identical, but definitely not one and the same. Only by placing the photographs side by side was Tiffany able to discern the subtle differences between the two horses. The slope of the withers was different, as was the shape of the forehead. Only a professional would notice the small dissimilarities.

Tiffany closed her eyes against Zane's damning truth.

"Are they the same horse?" he repeated, his voice low.

Slowly, she shook her head.

Zane set the pictures on the desk and expelled a heavy sigh. Finally, he had gotten through to her! He poked a long finger at the more recent photograph. "This," he said, "is the stallion that's supposed to be King's Ransom. I say he's Devil's Gambit."

Tiffany swallowed against the dryness settling in her throat. Here was the proof that her husband had lied to her, that her proud stallion was still alive, that everything she had believed for four years was nothing more than an illusion created by her husband. *Devil's Gambit and Ellery were alive!* "How did you know?" she finally asked in a forced whisper.

He rubbed his hand over his chin and closed his eyes. "I didn't really know, not for a long time. I guess I became suspicious when the second foal, the filly, exhibited such a different temperament from her brother.

"When she started racing as a two-year-old, I was certain she was the fastest horse on the farm, though her bloodlines weren't nearly as good as several other horses."

He walked over to the fire and looked into the golden flames, as if searching for easy answers to his life. "I didn't think too much about it until I got to talking to several other owners who had noticed the same phenomenon on their farms: all of King's Ransom's latest offspring were markedly different from his first foals." Zane smiled to himself, amused by a private irony. "No one was really asking questions—all the owners were thrilled with their luck, and of course, King's Ransom's stud fees have become astronomical since the latest colts and fillies have begun racing."

Tiffany lifted her hands and shook her head in silent protest. "It still could be a coincidence," she whispered. Her suggestion was a desperate attempt to right her crazily spinning world, to hold on to what she had believed to be true for four long years, and both she and Zane knew it.

"Look at the pictures, Tiffany," Zane quietly insisted.

"You're knowledgeable enough to realize those two stallions are different. Something isn't right at Emerald Enterprises."

"Pardon?"

"Emerald Enterprises owns the farm."

"And therefore King's Ransom."

"If that's what you want to call him."

Still the connection to her horse wasn't completely clear. "And you think Devil's Gambit is somehow involved?"

"I know he is."

"Because…someone switched horses, planned the accident, thereby killing the replacement horse and Ellery? Then what about Dustin? How did he manage to escape with his life?"

"Maybe he planned it."

The words settled like lead in the room. Only the occasional crackle and hiss of the fire disturbed the thick, condemning silence. "Dustin wouldn't…" she said, violently shaking her head. "He couldn't kill Ellery…they were brothers…very close…."

"Maybe it wasn't intentional. I told you I think Ellery was in on the swindle."

Her frigid blue eyes held Zane's gaze. "That doesn't make a hell of a lot of sense, you know," she rasped, her body beginning to shake from the ordeal of the past two days. "Ellery owned the horse. Devil's Gambit was worth a lot more alive than he was dead!" She raised a trembling hand in the air to add emphasis to her words, but Zane reached for her wrist and clutched it in a deathlike grip.

"Just hear me out. Then you can draw your own conclusions."

"I already—"

He broke off her protests by tightening his fingers over her arm. "Please listen." His grip relaxed but his stormy eyes continued to hold her prisoner.

"All right, Zane. I'll listen. But in the end, if I don't believe you, you'll have to accept that."

"Fair enough." He released her and took a seat on the

corner of the desk. His stormy eyes never left the tense contours of her elegant face. "When I requested a third breeding to King's Ransom, at the high stud fee, I was granted it. But because of the stallion's 'temperamental state' I wasn't allowed to witness my horse being bred."

"And you didn't buy that excuse?" Tiffany guessed.

"It sounded like bull to me. It just didn't make a lot of sense. I'd witnessed the first breeding but was out of the country when the second foal was conceived."

"So what happened?"

"I began asking a lot of questions. Too many to suit the manager of the farm. All of a sudden I was told that King's Ransom's services were, after all, unavailable. He was booked to cover far too many mares as it was, and I was asked to pick up my mare and leave."

"Before she was bred?"

"Right."

Tiffany began to get a glimmer of the truth, and it was as cold as a winter midnight.

Zane walked over to the hearth. As he sat on the warm stones he studied the amber liquor in his glass. "I picked up the mare, and the manager didn't bother to hide his relief to be rid of me. As I was leaving I saw a horse I recognized as King's Ransom running in a distant field. I thought it odd, since the manager had told me not five minutes before that King's Ransom was supposedly in the breeding shed."

"So you took these pictures!" she said breathlessly, the scenario becoming vivid in her confused mind.

"I'm a camera buff and happened to have my camera and telephoto lens with me. I grabbed what I needed from the glove box and photographed the horse. I took several shots and noticed that the stallion was running with a slight misstep. I hadn't heard about any injury to King's Ransom, and that's when I began to suspect that there might be two horses using the same name."

Tiffany's eyes were wide and questioning. "And from that you just deduced that one of the horses was Devil's Gambit?"

"It wasn't that difficult, really," Zane stated, his silvery eyes delving into hers. "Black Thoroughbreds are fairly uncommon, much rarer than bay or chestnut."

Tiffany nodded, her heart freezing with the fear that he was telling the truth. Dear God, what had Ellery done?

"Because of King's Ransom's age and coloring, it was relatively easy to discover what horse was being used in place of him to cover his mares. I did some research, and once I saw the pictures of Devil's Gambit again, I knew that he was the sire responsible for the faster offspring in the past few years."

"This is all still conjecture, you know," she said, trying to find any way possible to refute what he was saying. Even as she did so, she knew that she was grasping at straws.

"You're right. Except for one fact."

Tiffany steeled herself. "Which is?"

"That six years ago the ownership of the breeding farm where King's Ransom is standing at stud changed hands. A corporation now owns the farm. It took a lot of digging, but I finally found out that the primary stockholder in Emerald Enterprises is none other than your brother-in-law."

"Dustin?" Tiffany gasped, hoping with all her heart that Zane would come up with another name, any other name.

"One and the same."

Tiffany felt weak but outraged. Her knees buckled and she leaned against the desk for support. Even if everything Zane told her was the truth, she had to settle it herself with Dustin and Ellery...*if* Ellery was alive. *If* she could. Two very big "ifs." For a moment her voice failed her. When at last she could speak, all she could manage was a hoarse whisper. "I think, Mr. Sheridan," she suggested, "that you'd better leave."

"Are you so afraid of the truth?"

Tiffany closed her eyes, and her finely arched brows

drew together. *Yes, Zane,* she thought, *I am afraid. I'm afraid that what you're telling me is reality. I'm afraid the man I trusted as a brother-in-law lied to me, I'm afraid that my husband has betrayed me and I'm afraid, so afraid of you—and what you do to me!*

She reached for her wineglass with shaking fingers. Her voice was husky. "You seem to have done your homework," she admitted. "But just because Dustin owns part of the farm in Ireland—"

"Did you know about it?" he demanded.

She managed to shake her head, and the golden light from the fire caught in the soft brown silk of her hair. Zane fought against the sudden tightness in his chest.

"Don't you think that's odd—since you're still business partners here in the States?"

Odd as hell, she thought to herself as she pushed the hair from her face and stared at the ceiling. Her brother-in-law had been the one solid thing in her life when her world had shattered in pain and desperation on the night that Ellery and Devil's Gambit were killed. Becoming a widow had been a new and frightening experience, and the scandal about Ellery and his tragic horse had only made facing widowhood worse. Reporters hadn't left her alone for over two weeks. If it hadn't been for Dustin and his strength… "I don't know everything about Dustin's business. He's just my brother-in-law, not my…"

"Husband?"

Her throat was parched, and the words forming in her mind were difficult to say. "Have you…did you…see any evidence to indicate that Ellery might still be alive?" she asked, her fingers tightening over the edge of the desk fiercely enough that her knuckles showed white.

"No."

A lump formed in her throat. "But you can't be sure?" she insisted in a breathless whisper.

Zane frowned darkly. "Oh, lady, I wish I could answer that one for you," he said fervently.

She felt the sting of tears and forced them back. "If Ellery was alive, he wouldn't have let me believe that he was dead," she said as much to convince herself as Zane. Her small hands balled into fists, and she pounded them against the varnished surface of the desk she had used for four years…Ellery's desk. "You know that you're destroying everything I've worked for, don't you? In two days, everything I've believed in is slowly being torn apart…and I don't understand why."

"Don't you want to know if your husband is alive?"

"Yes!"

"And if he is?"

"Oh, God." She clasped her hand over her mouth before she managed to steady herself. "I…I don't know."

"Would you divorce him?"

She shook her head and pressed back the tears threatening her eyes. "No. Not until I heard his side of the story."

"And when you did?" Zane asked, his features becoming harsh.

Tiffany let out a ragged breath. "I don't know. It's all so unbelievable—I don't have all the answers."

Zane's eyes bored into her as if searching for her soul. *Damn Ellery Rhodes and what he had done to his beautiful wife!* Despite the desire for revenge seeping through his blood, Zane knew as he watched Tiffany battle against tears that he could never hurt her. It would be easy to make love to Rhodes's wife, but Zane knew instinctively that she would never forgive him if he took advantage of her vulnerable state and she later found out that her husband was alive.

She managed to slowly get hold of herself. "Why does all this matter to you, and why on earth would you want to buy this farm?" she questioned, her voice a whisper. "You have your choice of every breeding farm on the market—so why this one?"

"I'm not interested in just any farm. I already have one in Ireland."

"And that's what you do—breed horses, when you're not bothering widows?"

His lips thinned in disgust. Against his better judgment, Zane crossed the room and stood near the desk, near the attractive woman leaning against the polished surface. Her head was thrown back, her white throat exposed, her silken hair falling in a reckless tumble of honey-brown that touched the desk.

"Have I bothered you so much?"

"More than you'll ever guess," she admitted, straightening. She rubbed her arms, hoping to warm the inner chill of dread settling between her shoulders. After glancing up at the portrait of Devil's Gambit, she turned cold, suspicious eyes on Zane.

"You really believe everything you've told me, don't you?"

"It's the truth."

"And is that why you want the farm? Do you want to buy me out, and then blow this whole thing wide open about Devil's Gambit? That way there would be an investigation and you would have a chance, as owner of Rhodes Breeding Farm, of recovering him?"

"I don't think it would work that way," Zane said stiffly. "You would still own the horse. That's not the reason I want this farm."

"Then what is, Zane? Why did you come here in the first place?" He was much too close, but she didn't give in an inch. Proudly she faced him, her soft lips pressed into a frown, her skin stretched tightly over the gentle curve of her cheek.

Zane's dark eyes drove into her very soul. "Ellery Rhodes stole from me."

"What are you talking about?"

Deciding to distance himself from her, Zane walked over to the bar and splashed another drink into his glass. *How much could he confide to Ellery Rhodes's widow without blowing everything?* "It's not a subject I like to discuss," Zane admitted after taking a long swallow of the warm Scotch. "But about six years ago Ellery won a large amount of cash from me."

"And you hate him for that?" Tiffany was incredulous. What kind of a man was Zane?

"Not until I found out that the game was rigged. Oh, by the way, your brother-in-law, Dustin, was in on it, too."

"I don't believe it."

"Believe it. Your husband was little more than a thief."

Tiffany was numb from the tattered state of her emotions. "And you've waited all this time, just to get even with him," she guessed, her voice without inflection. "It didn't matter that he was dead—you just had to do something, *anything* to get even."

Zane saw the disbelief and silent accusations in Tiffany's eyes. He wanted to purge himself, tell all of the story, but couldn't. Stasia's betrayal had been long ago, but it was still an open wound that continued to bleed. He'd accused himself of still loving his ex-wife, even after she'd run off with Ellery Rhodes. But Zane knew better. He doubted if he had ever loved Stasia, but his battered pride was still raw from her deceit.

"I want this farm," he said as thoughts about Stasia gave him renewed conviction. The look on his face was intense, slightly threatening.

"I'm sorry, Zane. I told you yesterday that if I ever decided to sell, the first option would be Dustin's."

"Even when you know that he deliberately lied to you?"

"If he did, you mean. I can't believe—"

Zane cut her off by slicing the air with his hand. He strode over to the desk, reached inside his briefcase and handed her a thick packet of legal documents.

"What are these?" she asked, slowly scanning the complicated pages.

"Corporate documents, ownership papers."

"How did you get them?"

"It doesn't matter. Just read." He hated to put the damning

evidence in front of her, but she'd been so bullheaded about Ellery and Dustin, he'd had no choice. Tiffany didn't strike him as the kind of woman who would live in a fantasy world, but maybe when a woman loved a man as passionately as Tiffany loved Rhodes... He frowned darkly and finished his drink in one swallow. His inner vision of Tiffany entwined in Ellery Rhodes's arms turned his thoughts back, and a senseless anger took hold of his mind.

Tiffany sifted through the documents, and as she did her heart contracted painfully. Dustin's signature was scrawled all over the legal papers concerning Emerald Enterprises and the purchase of the farm in question. Without a doubt, some of Zane's story was true. Just how much, she would have to determine on her own, when issues such as the dead foals and her feelings for Zane didn't clutter her mind. Pursing her lips together she handed the papers back to Zane.

"They're yours," he said.

"I don't want them."

"I have extra copies, and I think you might want to go over these more carefully while I'm gone."

"You're leaving?" *Oh, God, not now. Not when I need your arms to protect me...*

"Have to," he admitted with obvious reluctance.

"I see," she replied, stunned. How long did she expect him to stay? He'd already mentioned that he had business back in San Francisco. It was only a matter of time until they went their separate ways.

She stared sightlessly down at the documents she still held in her hands. Since Zane had been with her, she had avoided thinking about the time he would leave. *This is crazy, let him go, before you do something you'll regret later....*

His hands molded over her upper arms. The warmth of his touch made her knees weaken, and she had to fight the urge to fall against him for support.

"While I'm gone, I want you to consider selling the farm

to me," he said sharply, his gentle fingers in stark contrast to his harsh words.

He was a man of contradictions, ruthless one moment, kind the next; sensitive to her desires as a woman, yet insensitive to her needs as a person. She told herself she couldn't possibly fall in love with him and yet she knew that fate had already cast the die. She was falling desperately and hopelessly in love with the stranger from Ireland.

"It's just not that easy, Zane. Dustin still owns twenty-five percent—I can't make a decision without him."

"Then consider selling out your portion. I'll deal with Dustin later." The tone of his voice was harsh, his jaw hard.

"It's just not possible."

"Anything's possible, Tiffany. Don't you know that?"

As possible as falling in love with you? Dear Lord, what has happened to my common sense?

As if reading her unspoken question, Zane smiled gently. The tense line of his jaw relaxed as slumberous eyes embraced hers. One long finger traced the elegant curve of her neck. "I'll be back in a few days," he promised.

Her lips trembled beguilingly. "There's no need. You know my position on selling the farm—"

"And what about Devil's Gambit?"

She frowned and pushed an errant lock of golden hair over her shoulder. "I...I don't know," she admitted, eyeing the portrait of the proud stallion. She needed time alone, time to think and sort out everything Zane had stated. How much of his story was fact and how much was pure fiction?

"You'll need a contact in Ireland."

The thought that Zane might be leaving the country shocked her. For this short time she'd had with him, she felt as if they'd grown incredibly close.

"I'll have to think about that—"

"Tiffany?"

"Yes?" She looked up and found him staring at her. For

most of the evening he had forced himself to stay away from her physically. But standing next to her with the warmth of the fire against his back, smelling the scent of her perfume, seeing the honest regret in her blue eyes, was too much to bear. The restraint he had placed upon himself began to dissolve into the shadowy room.

He touched the seductive contour of her jaw, and she closed her eyes. His hands were gentle as they lingered near her throat. "Come with me to San Francisco," he suggested impulsively as his blood began to heat and he forgot his earlier promise to himself. He wanted Tiffany Rhodes as he'd never wanted a woman.

"Oh, Zane, I can't."

"Why not?" His fingers had wrapped around her nape, under the curtain of her hair. She had trouble thinking clearly as his hands drew her near to him, and his lips touched her eyelids.

"I have…too many things to do…too much to think about…."

"Think about me—"

"That, I can assure you, I will," she promised fervently, her words the barest of whispers.

When his lips touched hers, he tasted more than the flavor of rich Burgundy. His tongue skimmed the soft surface of her mouth, gently prying her lips apart. Tiffany had no desire to stop him. She felt reckless, daring. Her raw emotions had pushed rational thought aside. Though she barely knew him, her body trembled at his touch, thrilled at his gentle caress.

His fingers slid down her arms to wrap securely over her waist, pulling her willing body to his. He moaned when he felt her hands, which had been gently touching his shoulders, grip the corded muscles more tightly. She was warm, pliable, yielding….

Silently cursing the doubts in his mind, he crushed her body to his. He felt the heat in her blood, tasted her need when her mouth opened willingly to him, smelled the heady scent of perfume mingling with burning pitch. The ache in

his loins began to pound with the need of this woman—
Ellery Rhodes's wife.

Tiffany let her arms hold him close. She knew he would
be leaving soon, and she had to savor each sweet second she
had with him. When she felt the weight of his body gently
push her to the floor, she didn't resist. Her hands linked behind
his head, and she let herself fall until the soft cushion of the
carpet broke her fall and was pressed against her back.

"I want you," he whispered, his face taut with desire. "God
forgive me, but I want you."

Her blue eyes reflected the golden flames of the fire, and
her hair was splayed in tangled curls on the deep, green carpet.
Passion darkened her gaze and lingered in her eyes. "There's
no need for forgiveness," she murmured, her fingers stroking
the back of his neck, his tensed shoulder muscles.

Her blood was pulsing violently through her veins, heating
the most intimate parts of her. Her heart felt as if it would burst
with need, want. It continued to beat an irregular rhythm in
her ears, making her oblivious to anything but the desire of
this man…this stranger. As she gazed into his silvery eyes, she
wondered if what she was feeling was love or lust and found
she didn't care.

"Tiffany," he whispered against her hair. He was lying over
her, his chest crushing her breasts as if he were afraid she
would escape, his long legs entangled with hers. "I didn't want
this to happen." His ragged breathing was filled with reluctance.

"I know," she whispered.

He kissed the curve of her neck and tingling sensations
raced wildly down her body. Dear Lord, she couldn't think
when he was touching her, couldn't reason…. Before she could
try to explain her feelings, his rugged face loomed over hers.
He gazed down upon her and passion darkened his eyes. *Think
of Ellery,* she told herself, *there is a slim chance that he might
be alive. Though he betrayed you, he is still your husband.*

Zane's lips captured hers, and despite the arguments in her mind she wrapped her arms around his neck and let her fingers wander in his thick, obsidian hair. His touch was electric, and all the nerves in her body screamed to be soothed by him.

I can't do this, she thought wildly, when his hands rimmed the boat neck of the sweater and teased the delicate skin near her collarbone. He lowered his head and pressed his moist tongue to the hollow of her throat, extracting a sweet torment that forced her pulse to quiver.

He kissed her again, more savagely this time, and she responded with a throaty moan. When he lifted his head, he gazed into her eyes, then pulled the sweater over her head, baring her breasts to the intimate room. A primitive groan slid past his lips as he looked down at her. The lacy bra, the sheerest of barriers to him, displayed the ripeness of her breasts and their pink tips. Already the nipples were rigid, thrusting proudly against the silky fabric and offering the comfort to soothe him if he would only suckle from them. "God, you're beautiful," he said, running first his eyes and then his tongue over the delicious mounds of white and feeling the silken texture of her skin beneath the sheer lace. She trembled with the want of him.

The wet impression of his tongue left a dewy path from one rose-tipped peak to the next. Tiffany struggled beneath him, arching up from the carpet and pulling him to her with anxious fingers digging into the thick muscles of his shoulders.

In a swift movement he removed his sweater and tossed it beside Tiffany's on the floor. She stared at him with love-drugged eyes. His chest was lean and firm; dark skin was covered when she lifted a hand to stroke him, and his nipples grew taut as she stared at him.

He lowered himself over her and covered her mouth with his. His tongue tasted of her, dipping seductively into her mouth only to withdraw again. The heat within her began to ache for all of him. She wanted him to touch her, fill her, make long, passionate love to her until the first shafts of morning light filtered through the windows.

When his mouth moved slowly down her neck to pause at the shadowy valley between her breasts, she cried out his name. "Zane, please," she whispered, begging for his touch. Thoughts of a distant past with Ellery infiltrated her mind. *I couldn't feel this way with Zane if Ellery were still alive.... I couldn't!*

In response to her plea, he unclasped the bra and removed it from her, staring at the blushing beauty of her breasts.

"What do you want, sweet Tiffany?" he asked, his slumberous gray eyes searching hers.

Her throat tightened and she closed her eyes. Her dark lashes swept invitingly downward. "I want you—all of you."

He dipped his head and ran his tongue over one proud nipple. "Do you want me to love you?"

"Please...Zane...yes!" *Didn't he know? Couldn't he see the love in her eyes as she opened them to search his face?*

"All of you?" He kissed the other nipple, but his eyes locked with hers for an electrifying instant. His teeth gently teased the dark point, and she quivered from the deepest reaches of her soul.

"All of me," she replied and groaned when he began to suckle hungrily at one delicious peak. His large hands held her close, pressing against her naked back and warming her exposed skin. Tiffany felt waves of heat move over her as he kissed her, caressed her, stroked her with his tongue. She cradled his head, holding him close, afraid he would leave her bereft and longing. As his mouth and tongue tasted her, drew out the love she felt, the hot void within her began to throb with desire.

"Make love to me, Zane," she whispered when the exquisite torment was more than she could bear. "Make love to me and never let me go...."

It was the desperate cry of a woman in the throes of passion. Zane knew that Tiffany had unwittingly let her control slip. He positioned himself above her and his fingers toyed with the waistband of her jeans, slipping deliciously on her warm abdomen. She contracted her muscles, offering more of herself, wanting his touch. Her body arched upward eagerly, her physical desire overcoming rational thought.

Her fingers strayed to the button on his cords and he felt it slide easily through the buttonhole. Her hands did delightful things to him as she slid the zipper lower. He squeezed his eyes shut against his rising passion. His need of her was all-consuming, his desire throbbing wildly against his cords. His fingers dipped lower to feel the smooth skin over her buttocks, and he had to grit his teeth when she began to touch him.

"Tiffany," he whispered raggedly, forcing himself to think straight. He remembered all too vividly that Ellery Rhodes could very well be alive. If Zane took her now, and Ellery was alive, Tiffany would never forgive him. "Wait." His voice was hoarse. With gentle hands he restrained her fingers. She stared up at him with hungry, disappointed blue eyes.

God, what he wouldn't give to forget all his earlier vows to himself. If he made love to her now, before the mystery surrounding Devil's Gambit was resolved, before he had purchased the farm, she would end up hating him.

"I…had no intention…" *Of what? Making love to Ellery Rhodes's woman? As just revenge for what he did to you?* "…of letting things get so out of hand."

She read the doubts on his face and closed her eyes. "Forgive me if I don't believe you," she murmured, trying to roll away from him. "But I seem to recall a man who, this very morning, matter-of-factly insisted that we become lovers." Tears of embarrassment flooded her eyes.

"It's not for lack of any wanting on my part," he replied.

That much she didn't doubt. She'd felt the intensity of his desire, witnessed the passion in his eyes, felt the doubts that had tormented him. "Then what?" she asked, reaching for her sweater. "Are you teasing me, trying to find a way to convince me to sell the farm to you?" she accused.

He flinched as if she had physically struck him, and his entire body tensed. "You know better than that."

"I don't think I know you at all. I think I let my feelings get in the way of my thinking."

His fist balled impotently at his side and his face hardened. "Would you feel better about it, if we resumed what we started and I took you right here...even though Ellery might still be alive?"

"Of course not," she gasped. Her blood had cooled and reason returned.

He reached out and tenderly pushed her hair from her eyes. "Then wait for me," he asked, his voice low. "I just want to make sure that you won't regret anything that might happen."

"Are you sure you're concerned for my feelings, or your own?"

"Oh, lady," he whispered, forcing a sad smile. His fingers trembled slightly when he brushed a solitary tear from her eye. "Maybe a little of both." He reached for her and his fingers wrapped possessively around her neck. Closing his eyes against the passion lingering in his blood, he kissed her sensuously on the lips. "I'll be back...."

CHAPTER EIGHT

"This isn't the smartest thing you've ever done, Missy," Mac warned as he finished his coffee and pushed his hat onto his head. He scraped his chair back from the table and placed the empty cup on the tile counter, not far from the area where Louise was rolling dough.

"The least you could do is show a little support," Tiffany teased. She smoothed the hem of her cream-colored linen suit and smiled at Mac's obvious concern.

"After that newspaper article in the *Clarion,* I'd think you'd have more sense than agree to another interview."

"Can't argue with that," Louise chimed in as she placed a batch of cinnamon rolls in the oven.

"Okay, so the interview with Rod Crawford was a mistake. This one will be different." Tiffany leaned against the counter and attempted to look confident.

"How's that?" Mac's reddish brows rose skeptically on his weathered face.

"The reporter from the *Times* is Nancy Emerson, a roommate of mine from college."

"Humph." Louise was busily making the second batch of rolls and didn't look up as she spread the cinnamon and sugar over the dough. "How do you know she won't do the same thing that Crawford did? In my book a reporter's a reporter. Period."

"Nancy's a professional."

"So was Crawford."

"I talked about the interview. I told her I would only do it if it didn't turn out to be a hatchet job."

"I bet she liked that," Louise remarked sarcastically as she began furiously rolling the dough into a long cylinder. "It's none of my business, mind you, but didn't you bank on the reputation of the *Clarion?*"

"Yes," Tiffany said with a sigh.

Mac noted Tiffany's distress. "Well, if you think you can trust her—"

"I just know that she won't print lies," Tiffany insisted. "She's been with the *Times* for over six years and written dozens of articles on horse racing in America and abroad. She's extremely knowledgeable and I figured she'd give an unbiased, honest report." Tiffany lifted her palms in her own defense. "Look, I had to grant an interview with someone. I've had over a dozen calls from reporters in the past three days."

"I can vouch for that," Louise agreed as she sliced the rolls and arranged them in a pan.

Louise had insisted on working at the farm every day since Zane had left and Tiffany was grateful for the housekeeper's support. Life on the farm had been hectic in the past few— had it only been four?—days. It seemed like a lifetime since she'd been with Zane.

"Well, I guess you had no choice," Mac allowed.

"None. The longer I stall, the more it seems as if we're hiding something here."

"Aye. I suppose it does," Mac mumbled as he sauntered to the back door. "I'll be in the broodmare barn if you need me." He paused as his fingers gripped the doorknob, glanced back at Tiffany and shifted uncomfortably from one foot to the other. "It looks like Alexander's Lady's time has come."

Tiffany felt her heart fall to the floor. Alexander's Lady was pregnant with Moon Shadow's foal. Tiffany closed her eyes and gripped the edge of the table. Louise stopped working at the counter.

"Oh, Lord," the large cook muttered, quickly making a sign of the cross over her ample bosom. Then, with a knowing eye in Tiffany's direction, she smiled kindly. "This one will be all right, honey...I feel it in my bones."

"I hope to God you're right," Tiffany whispered.

"It's in His hands now, you know. Not much you can do 'bout it," Mac advised with a scowl. "Worryin' ain't gonna help."

Tiffany studied Mac's wrinkled brow. "Then maybe you should take your own advice."

"Naw—I'm too old and set in my ways to stop now. Anyway, worryin's what I do best." The trainer raised his hand in the air as a salute of goodbye and opened the door to the back porch, just as the doorbell chimed. Mac's frown deepened. "Looks like your friend is here."

Tiffany managed a thin smile. "Good. We may as well get this over with."

"Good luck," Louise muttered, once again hastily making the sign of the cross with her flour-dusted hands as Tiffany walked out of the kitchen.

"Tiffany! You look great," Nancy said with heartfelt enthusiasm as Tiffany opened the door.

The slim, dark-haired woman with the bright hazel eyes appeared no different than she had six years ago. Dressed in navy-blue slacks and a crisp red blouse and white jacket, Nancy looked the picture of efficiency. Short dark-brown curls framed a pixielike face filled with freckles and smiles.

"It's good to see you, Nance. Come in." Tiffany's grin was genuine as she hugged her friend. It had been years since she'd seen Nancy. Too many years. The two women had parted ways right after college. Tiffany's father had died, and Nancy had moved to Oregon to marry her high school boyfriend.

"And what a beautiful house," Nancy continued, her expressive hazel eyes roving over the sweeping green hills surrounding the white-clapboard and brick home. "This is something right out of *Gone with the Wind!*"

"Not quite, I don't think."

"All you need is a couple of mint juleps, a porch swing and—"

"Rhett Butler."

Nancy laughed. "I suppose you're right. But, God, Tiff, this is *fabulous!*"

"The house was Ellery's idea," Tiffany admitted as Nancy's eager eyes traveled up the polished oak banister and marble stairs to linger on the crystal chandelier. "He thought the farm would appear more genuine if it had a Southern atmosphere."

"This is beyond atmosphere, Tiffany, this is flair!"

Tiffany blushed a little under Nancy's heartfelt praise. She'd forgotten what it was like to be around the exuberant woman. Though Nancy had to be thirty, she didn't look a day over twenty-five, and part of her youthful appearance was due to her enthusiasm for life.

Tiffany showed Nancy the house and grounds of the farm. "This is heaven," Nancy insisted as she leaned against a redwood tree and watched the foals romp in the late-morning sun.

"I like it."

"Who wouldn't? Let me tell you, I'd give an arm and a leg to live in a place like this."

Tiffany laughed. "And what would you do? You're a city girl by nature, Nance."

Nancy nodded in agreement. "I suppose you're right."

"You'd miss San Francisco within the week.'

"Maybe so, but sometimes sharing a two-bedroom apartment with two kids and a cat can drive me up the wall. The girls are five and four, and you wouldn't believe how much energy they have."

"They probably get it from their mother. Genetics, you know."

"Right. Genetics. The reason I'm here."

Tiffany ignored the comment for now. "So why don't you bring the kids out here for a weekend sometime?"

Nancy's bright eyes softened. "You mean it?"

"Of course."

"They're a handful," the sprightly reporter warned.

"But they'd love it here, and I adore kids."

Nancy was thoughtful as she stared at the horses frolicking in the lush grass of the paddock. "So why didn't you have any?"

Tiffany shrugged. "Too busy, I guess. Ellery wasn't all that keen on being a father."

"And you?"

"It takes two."

Nancy sighed and lit a cigarette. A small puff of blue smoke filtered toward the cloudless sky. "Boy, does it. Raising the kids alone is no picnic. Ralph has them every other weekend, of course, but sometimes… Oh, well. Look, I'm here for an interview, right? Tell me what you've been doing since you took over the farm."

Nancy took a tape recorder from her purse and switched it on. For the next hour and a half Tiffany answered Nancy's questions about the farm—the problems and the joys.

"So what's all this ruckus over Moon Shadow?" Nancy asked, her hazel eyes questioning.

"Hype."

"What's that supposed to mean?"

"Come on, I'll show you." Tiffany led Nancy to the stallion barn and Moon Shadow's stall. Moon Shadow poked his ebony head out of the stall, held it regally high and flattened his ears backward at the sight of the stranger. "Here he is, in the flesh, the stallion who's been getting a lot of bad press."

"What you referred to as 'hype'?"

"Yes. He's fathered over a hundred Thoroughbreds in the past eight years, several who have become champions."

"Like Devil's Gambit?"

Tiffany's heart seemed to miss a beat. She didn't want to discuss Devil's Gambit with anyone, including Nancy. "Yes, as well as Journey's End."

"Rhodes Breeding Farm's latest contender. He promises to be the next Devil's Gambit," Nancy observed.

"We hope so."

Moon Shadow's large brown eyes wandered from Tiffany to the reporter and back again. Tiffany reached into the pocket of her skirt and withdrew a piece of carrot. The proud stallion nickered softly and took the carrot from Tiffany's hand.

"He's been a good stud," Tiffany emphasized while rubbing the velvet-soft black muzzle.

Tiffany continued to talk about Moon Shadow's qualities and the unfortunate incidents with the dead foals. Whenever Nancy posed a particularly pointed question, Tiffany was able to defend herself and her stallion by pointing to his winning sons and daughters.

Nancy had snapped off her tape recorder and stayed through lunch. Tiffany felt more relaxed than she had in days when she and Nancy reminisced about college.

"So what happened between you and Ralph?" Tiffany asked, as they drank a cup of coffee after the meal.

Nancy shrugged. "I don't really know—it just seemed that we grew in different directions. I thought that the kids would make a difference, but I was wrong." When she saw the horrified look in Tiffany's eyes, she held up her hand. "Oh, don't get me wrong, Tiff. It wasn't that Ralph wasn't a good father—" she shrugged her shoulders slightly "—he just wasn't comfortable in the role of breadwinner. Too much responsibility, I suppose. Anyway, it's worked out for the best. He's remarried, and I'm dating a wonderful man."

"And the girls?"

Nancy sighed and lit a cigarette. "It was rough on them at first, but they seem to be handling it okay now."

"I'm glad to hear it."

"It's hard to explain," Nancy said softly. "It just seemed that the longer we lived together, the less we knew each other or cared...."

"That happens," Tiffany said. Hadn't she felt the same doubts when Ellery was alive? Hadn't there always been a distance she was unable to bridge?

"Yeah, well..." Nancy stubbed out her cigarette. "As I said, I think it's for the best. Oh, God, look at the time! I've got to get out of here."

Tiffany watched as Nancy gathered her things, and then she walked her friend to the car. "I was serious when I told you to bring the kids out for a weekend. Just give me a call."

"You don't know what you're asking for."

Tiffany laughed. "Sure I do. It'll be fun. Come on, Nance, those girls could use a little fresh country air, and they'd love being around the horses."

Nancy eyed the rolling hills of the farm wistfully. "Be careful, Tiff, or I just might take you up on your offer."

"I'm counting on it."

Nancy's car was parked in the shade of a tall maple tree near the back of the house. When they reached the car, Nancy turned and faced Tiffany. "This has been great," she said. "The best interview I've done in years."

"Do you do many stories about Thoroughbreds?" Tiffany asked.

"Some—mainly from the woman's angle," Nancy replied. "Most of the time I write human interest stories—again, from the woman's perspective. The reason I got this assignment is that I read the article in the *Clarion* and stormed into my editor's office, insisting that since I knew you, I would be the logical person to write a more in-depth article for the *Times*. He really couldn't argue too much, since I used to cover all the local and national races." Her hazel eyes saddened a little. "I think you, and not your horse, were the victim of bad press, my friend."

Tiffany shrugged, but smiled. "Maybe." A question formed in her mind, and she had to ask. "When you were working on the races, did you ever hear of a stallion named King's Ransom?"

"Sure. But he wasn't much of a champion, not until recently. From what I understand his services as a stud are the most sought-after in Ireland."

"Who owns him?"

Nancy smiled. "That's the interesting part. It's kind of a mystery. He's syndicated of course, but the largest percentage of the stallion is owned by Emerald Enterprises." Tiffany's heart felt as if it had turned to stone. *Zane had been telling the truth!*

"Which is?"

"A holding company of sorts," Nancy replied.

"I see," Tiffany said, her heartbeat quickening. "What about a man by the name of Zane Sheridan?" she asked.

Nancy was about to get into the car but paused. "Now there's an interesting man."

"Oh?" Tiffany cocked her head to the side and the smile on her lips slowly faded. "Do you think he's somehow involved with Emerald Enterprises?"

"I don't really know, but I doubt it. He owns a farm near the one owned by Emerald Enterprises. Why are you so interested?"

"I'm not…not really." Tiffany lied in ineffectual nonchalance. "He was here a couple of days ago, looking at some horses."

"He's a bit of a mystery," Nancy said. She leaned against the car door and stared up at the blue sky as she tried to remember everything she could about the breeder from Ireland. "He's a tough guy, from what I hear. Ruthless in business. He grew up on the streets of Dublin. Had several scrapes with the law and ended up working as a stable boy at an Irish Thoroughbred farm in the country. The owner of that particular farm took a liking to him, sent him to school, and once educated, Sheridan made a small fortune breeding horses." She sighed as she tried to remember the fuzzy details of a scandal that had occurred in the past.

"And then, well, it's kind of foggy, but from what I remember, he was in some sort of trouble again. A scandal, and he lost his fortune and his wife. I can't remember all the details right now."

The news hit Tiffany like a bolt of lighting. Though stunned, she managed somehow to ask, "His wife is dead?"

"No—she ran off with this guy named…God, what was it? Rivers, I think. Ethan Rivers, an American…. Like I said, it's kind of a mystery. No one really knows what happened to this Rivers character or Sheridan's wife."

The thought of Zane being married did strange things to Tiffany. "How long ago was this?" she asked.

"Geez, what was it? Five years, maybe more like seven, I'm really not sure." She pursed her lips as she thought and then, when she checked her watch, nearly jumped out of her skin. "Look, I've got to go. Deadlines, you know. I'll call you soon."

"Good. I'd like that."

Nancy got into her car and settled behind the wheel. The engine started, and Nancy rolled down the window. "The article on the farm should be in the paper no later than Thursday. I'll send you a copy." With a brilliant smile, she fingered a wave at Tiffany and forced the little car into gear.

Tiffany watched the car disappear down the tree-lined drive, but her mind was miles away. Nancy's visit had only increased her restlessness. Where was Zane and why hadn't he called?

HOURS LATER, TIFFANY WAS WALKING back from the half-mile track near the old barn when she heard a familiar voice.

"Tiffany!"

A tall man wearing a Stetson was running toward her. Tiffany shielded her eyes from the ever-lowering sun and smiled when she recognized her brother-in-law.

"Dustin!" She hadn't expected him back for another week.

"Hello, stranger," he said as he reached her and gathered her into his arms to twirl her off the ground. How had she ever doubted him? "What's this I hear about you getting some bad press, little lady?"

"Some?" Tiffany repeated with a shake of her head. "How about truckloads of it."

"You can't be serious." He flashed her a brilliant smile.

"Four of Moon Shadow's foals have died—all from heart failure."

Dustin lifted his hat, pushed a lock of brown hair out of his eyes and squinted into the setting sun toward the exercise track, where Mac was still working with a yearling. "So I read."

"You and the rest of the world." Tiffany pushed her hands into the pockets of her jeans. Her conversation with Zane came hauntingly back to her, and she wondered just how much she could confide in Dustin. He did own twenty-five percent of the farm and was entitled to know everything that was going on…well, almost everything. "I have owners who are threatening me with lawsuits if the mares they bred to Moon Shadow drop foals that die."

"How many mares are involved?" Dustin's hand reached out and took hold of her arm. They had been walking toward the old barn where Tiffany had been headed. Near the building, Dustin stopped her.

"About twelve," she said. "Some of them took the news fairly well. The others, well…they weren't so understanding."

"In other words they're ready to rip your throat out."

"Close enough."

"Damn!" Dustin let out an angry blast. "This is the last thing we need right now. Okay, so what about the mares that have already foaled?"

"The foals that eventually died were from our mares. So far, every mare bred to Moon Shadow from another farm has dropped a healthy colt or filly."

"So much for small favors."

"I guess we should consider ourselves lucky that this isn't a contagious virus," she said.

"You're sure?" Dustin didn't sound convinced.

"Um-hm. Vance checked everything carefully. At first he thought it might be sleepy foal disease, but fortunately it wasn't."

"Yeah, fortunately," Dustin muttered sarcastically.

Tiffany pushed open the door to the old barn and checked the supply of grain stacked in sacks in the bins. The interior was musty and dark, the only light filtering through the small window on the south side of the building and the open door. Dustin leaned against a post supporting the hayloft and watched her make notes in a small notebook.

Once she had finished counting and was satisfied that the inventory of feed was about what it should be, she started back toward the door.

Dustin's hand on her arm stopped her. His topaz-colored eyes pierced into hers. "So what happened to those foals?"

Tiffany shook her head and her honey-brown tresses glowed in the shadowy light from the windows. "Your guess is as good as mine."

"What does Vance say?"

"Nothing good, at least not yet."

He leaned against the post, shoved the hat back on his head so he could see her more clearly and drew Tiffany into the circle of his arms. His voice was low with concern, his gold eyes trained on her lips. The intimate embrace made Tiffany uncomfortable. All Zane's accusations concerning Dustin began to haunt her. Maybe she should ask him flat out about the circumstances surrounding Devil's Gambit's death, but she hesitated. There was just enough of the truth woven into Zane's story to give her pause.

Dustin read the worry on her features. "Do you think there's a possibility that Moon Shadow's to blame for the deaths?"

Tiffany frowned and tried to pull away from him. "No."

"But all the evidence—"

"Is circumstantial."

"I see." Dustin released her reluctantly and cleared his throat. "So what are you doing with him?"

"Nothing. I can't breed him. Not until I know for certain that the problem isn't genetic."

"Then you do have reservations?"

Tiffany bristled slightly. "None, but what I don't have is proof. Unfortunately, Moon Shadow has already been tried and convicted by the press. He's as good as guilty until proved innocent."

"Bitter words…"

"You haven't been here trying to talk some sense into the reporters, the owners, the television people."

"No," he conceded with obvious regret. "But I bet you handled them."

Tiffany lifted a shoulder. "As well as I could. I had an interview with Nancy Emerson from the *Times* this morning."

Dustin smiled. "Your old roommate?"

"Uh-huh."

He breathed deeply. "Good. It never hurts to know someone in the press."

Tiffany decided to set her brother-in-law straight. "I didn't buy her off, you know."

"I know, I know, but at least she's on our side. She should be objective. Thank God for small favors."

Something in Dustin's attitude made Tiffany uneasy. *You're overreacting,* she told herself, all because of Zane Sheridan and his wild accusations.

Dustin smoothed back his wavy hair. "I've got to hand it to you, Tiff. You've come a long way," he said appreciatively. "There was a time when I didn't think you would be able to pull yourself together."

"I have you to thank for getting me back on my feet," she replied, uncomfortable with the personal tone of the conversation. She was reminded of Zane and the accusations he had made about Dustin. Today, in the fading sunlight, those allegations seemed positively absurd. Dustin was her brother-in-law, her friend, her partner. The man who had pulled her out of the depths of despair when Ellery and Devil's Gambit had been killed.

Then what about the farm in Ireland, the one owned by Emerald Enterprises? What about Dustin's signature on the ownership papers? What about King's Ransom?

She decided to broach the difficult subjects later, once she had learned the reason for Dustin's unexpected visit. Was it possible that he knew Zane had been here? Had someone tipped Dustin off, possibly Zane himself?

Tiffany felt a growing resentment and anger at Zane. Single-handedly he had destroyed her trust in the only family she had ever known.

"Come on," she suggested, pushing her worrisome thoughts aside as she walked through the open door of the barn. "I'm starved. Louise made some cinnamon rolls this morning, and I bet we can con her out of a couple."

Dustin looked as if he had something he wanted to say but held his tongue. Instead he walked with Tiffany to the house and waited patiently while she kicked off her boots and placed them on the back porch.

"Are you staying long?" she asked, once they were in the kitchen and seated at the table.

Dustin hedged slightly. "Just a couple of days."

"And then?"

"Back to Florida."

"To check on Journey's End?"

"Right." He took a long swallow of his coffee, and his golden eyes impaled her. "You think you could spare the time to come with me?" he asked, his voice uncommonly low.

Tiffany ignored the hidden innuendoes in his tone. They'd covered this territory before, and Dustin obviously hadn't taken the hint. The scene in the old barn emphasized the fact. Dustin had never hidden the fact that he would like to pursue a more intimate relationship with her, but Tiffany just wasn't inter-ested. Dustin seemed to assume that her lack of interest was due in part to loyalty to Ellery, and Tiffany didn't argue the point. He just couldn't seem to get it through his thick skull that she wasn't interested in a relationship with a man—any man.

Except Zane Sheridan, her mind taunted. Would she ever be able to get him out of her mind? In four days, he hadn't phoned or stopped by the farm. All of his concern for her while he was here must have been an act, a very convincing act. Still, she couldn't forget him.

"Tiff!"

"Pardon?"

Dustin was frowning at her. He'd finished his coffee, and the cup was sitting on the table. His empty plate showed only a few crumbs and a pool of melted butter where his cinnamon rolls had sat. "You haven't heard a word I said," he accused.

"You're right."

"So where were you?"

"What?"

"You looked as if you were a million miles away."

"Oh, I guess I was thinking about Moon Shadow," she lied easily, too easily. "Mac thinks another one of his foals will be born tonight."

Dustin leaned back in his chair and let out a low whistle. "No wonder you're worried. If this one dies, the press will be crawling all over this farm again. Maybe I'd better stay a few extra days."

Waving off his offer, she shook her head. "No reason. You know you're welcome to stay as long as you like, but if you have things to do, go ahead and do them. I can handle everything here."

He walked around the table, stood behind her and placed his hands on her shoulders. "You're sure?"

Tiffany tensed. "Of course I am."

As if receiving her unspoken message, he dropped his hands to his sides. "You know that's one of the qualities I admire about you, Tiff, your strength."

"I guess I should be flattered."

Dustin stepped away from her and rested his hips against the counter. All the while his eyes rested on her worried face. "Is something else bothering you?" he asked.

"Isn't that enough?"

"I suppose so." He shrugged his broad shoulders and folded his arms over his chest. Silent reproach lingered in his eyes. The air in the kitchen became thick with tension.

Tiffany heard the screen door bang shut. Within minutes Mac was in the kitchen.

"Don't tell me, you smelled the coffee," Tiffany guessed, reaching for a cup and feeling relieved that the inquisition with Dustin was over for the moment.

"Aye, that I did."

"Well, pull up a chair, sit yourself down and help yourself to a roll, while I get you a mug."

Mac's faded eyes rested on Dustin. Not bothering to hide a frown, he cocked his head toward the younger man. "'Evenin', Dustin. Didn't expect you back for a while."

Tiffany handed Mac the cup.

Dustin managed a tight grin as he offered the older man his hand. "I read an article about the foals dying and thought I should come back—" his gold eyes moved to Tiffany "—since no one bothered to tell me what was going on."

"I thought I'd wait until Vance had something concrete to go on," Tiffany stated.

"And how long would you have waited?"

"Not much longer."

"It was a hell of a way to find out, you know," Dustin said, his anger surfacing, "by reading about it in the paper." He rammed his fingers through his hair in frustration. For a moment he appeared haunted.

"You're right. I should have called, but I didn't because there wasn't a damned thing you or I or anyone else could do."

"I suppose you're right about that," Dustin conceded with

a frown and then turned his attention to Mac. "I was just trying to convince Tiffany here that she ought to come to Florida and see for herself how Journey's End is doing."

"Not a bad idea," Mac agreed, though there were reservations in his eyes. He removed his hat and took a chair at the table. "That way she could check up on Bob Prescott, see that he's doing a good job of training the colt."

Prescott was a young trainer who traveled with the horses while they were racing. He was a damned good man around a horse, but there was something shifty about him that Mac didn't like. The missus called it jealousy. Mac wasn't so sure, but he couldn't put his finger on the problem, and Bob Prescott had molded Journey's End into a fine racing machine.

Dustin's smile froze. "See, Tiffany, even Mac agrees that you could use a vacation. A little Florida sun might do you a world of good."

Tiffany managed a thin smile for both men and finished her coffee. "It'll have to wait until we're over this crisis." She leaned back in the chair and held up a finger. "However, you can bet I'll be at the Derby this year."

"You think Journey's End will make a good show of it?" Dustin asked as he placed his empty cup in the sink and wiped an accumulation of sweat from his brow.

"Not a show nor a place, but a win," the crusty old trainer predicted.

"High praise coming from you," Dustin observed.

"Journey's End is a fine colt. He's got the heart, the look of eagles if you will, but his temperament's got to be controlled...guided." He lifted his wise old eyes to Dustin's face. "I just hope that Bob Prescott knows what he's doing."

"He does."

"Then Journey's End should win the Derby," Mac stated without qualification. "He's the best horse I've seen since Devil's Gambit or Moon Shadow."

Dustin nearly choked on his final swallow of coffee and

turned the subject away from Devil's Gambit. "We all know why Moon Shadow lost the Derby, don't we?" Dustin asked pointedly.

Mac's faded eyes narrowed. "Aye, that we do. I haven't made any excuses about it, either. I should never have let that jockey ride him."

"He was Ellery's choice," Tiffany intervened, sensing an argument brewing between the two men.

"And I shouldn't have allowed it." Mac straightened his wiry frame from the chair, and his fedora dangled from his fingers as he turned to Tiffany. "I called Vance. I'm sure we'll have another foal before morning."

Tiffany took in a ragged breath. "Let me know when the time comes."

"Aye. That I will." With his final remarks, Mac walked out of the room and the screen door banged behind him.

Tiffany whirled on Dustin. "That was uncalled for, you know," she spit out.

"What?"

"Those remarks about Moon Shadow and the Derby."

"Serves the old man right. I never have figured why you keep that old relic around, anyway."

Tiffany was furious and shaking with rage. "Mac's not old, nor a relic, and he's the best damned horseman in this state, maybe the country. He knows more about Thoroughbreds than you or I could hope to know in a lifetime. Let's just hope, brother-in-law, that he doesn't take your remarks to heart and quit on us. We'll be in a world of hurt, then, let me tell you!"

Dustin had visibly paled but scoffed at Tiffany's remarks. "You're giving him too much credit," he said with a shrug as he stared out the window. "You're genuinely fond of the old goat, aren't you?"

"Mac's been good to me, good to this farm, good to Ellery and good to you. Why you continue to ridicule him is beyond me. Unless you'd secretly like to see him leave."

"It wouldn't affect me one way or the other."

"Like hell, Dustin. We had an agreement, remember?" she reminded him. "I run the operations of the farm, you handle the PR. Right now, because of all the adverse publicity with Moon Shadow's foals, it seems to me that you've got more than your share of work cut out for you!"

With her final remark Tiffany stormed out of the kitchen, tugged on her boots and went off to make amends with Mac. Why did Dustin have to provoke the trainer now when she needed Mac's expertise the most?

MAC WAS ALREADY AT HIS PICKUP WHEN Tiffany caught up with him. "I'm sorry," she apologized. She was out of breath from her sprint across the back lawn and parking lot.

"No need for that, Missy," Mac said with a kindly smile as he reached for the door handle on the old Dodge. "What Dustin said was the truth."

"No, it wasn't. Even with his regular jockey, there was no assurance that Moon Shadow would win."

"He was the odds-on favorite."

"And we all know how many long shots have won when it counted. Besides, it's all water under the bridge now," she assured him. "We'll just pin our hopes on Journey's End. And maybe this time, we'll win the Derby."

"I hope so," Mac said, pursing his lips together thoughtfully as he studied the lush Northern California countryside that made up the pastures of Rhodes Breeding Farm. "It's time you got a break." He opened the door to the truck. "I'll be back after dinner to check on Alexander's Lady. My guess is she'll foal around midnight."

"See you then." Tiffany stepped away from the old truck and Mac started the engine before shoving it into gear. Tiffany felt her teeth sink into her lower lip as she watched the battered old pickup rumble down the long driveway.

THREE HOURS LATER TIFFANY WAS IN the foaling shed, watching, praying while the glistening chestnut mare labored. The air was heavy with the smell of sweat mingled with ammonia and antiseptic.

Vance and Mac were inside the stall with the horse while Tiffany and Dustin stood on the other side of the gate. Alexander's Lady was lying on her side in the thick mat of straw, her swollen sides heaving with her efforts.

"Here we go," Vance said as the mare's abdomen contracted and the foal's head and shoulders emerged. A few minutes later, the rest of the tiny body was lying beside the mare.

Vance worked quickly over the newborn, clearing the foal's nose. As Tiffany watched she noticed the small ribs begin to move.

Tiffany reached for the switch that turned on the white heat lamps to keep the precious animal from catching cold.

"Let's leave the lamps on for two or three days," Vance suggested, his round face filled with relief as the filly tested her new legs and attempted to stand. "I don't want to take any chances."

"Neither do I," Tiffany agreed, her heart warming at the sight of the struggling filly. She was a perfect dark bay, with only the hint of a white star on her forehead.

Tiffany slipped into the stall and began to rub the wet filly with a thick towel, to promote the filly's circulation. At that moment, the mare snorted.

"I think it's time for Mom to take over," Vance suggested, as he carefully moved the foal to the mare's head. Alexander's Lady, while still lying on the straw, began to nuzzle and lick her new offspring.

"Atta girl," Mac said with the hint of a smile. "'Bout time you showed some interest in the young-un." He stepped out of the stall to let mother and daughter get acquainted.

Vance stayed in the stall, watching the foal with concerned eyes. He leaned against the wall, removed his glasses and began cleaning them with the tail of his coat, but his thoughtful gaze remained on the horses, and deep furrows lined his brow.

"Is she all right?" Tiffany asked, her heart beating irregularly. Such a beautiful filly. She couldn't die!

"So far so good." But his lips remained pressed together in an uneasy scowl as he attended to the mare. Alexander's Lady groaned and stood up. She nickered softly to the filly.

As if on cue, the little newborn horse opened her eyes and tried futilely to stand.

"Come on, girl. You can do it," Tiffany whispered in encouragement. The filly managed to stand on her spindly, unsteady legs before she fell back into the straw. "Come on…"

"Good lookin' filly," Mac decided as the little horse finally forced herself upright and managed the few steps to the mare's side. "Nice straight front legs…good bone, like her dad." Mac rubbed his hand over the stubble on his chin.

Tiffany's heart swelled with pride.

"She looks fine," Vance agreed as he watched the filly nuzzle the mare's flanks and search for her first meal.

"So did Charlatan," Tiffany reminded him, trying her best not to get her hopes up. The filly looked strong, but so had Felicity's colt. And he had died. A lump formed in Tiffany's throat. She couldn't imagine that the beautiful little filly might not live through the night.

"Keep watch on her," Vance stated, his lips thinning.

"Round the clock," Tiffany agreed. "We're not going to lose this one," she vowed, oblivious to the worried glances being exchanged between the veterinarian and the trainer.

"What have you decided to name her?" Dustin asked, seemingly entranced by the healthy young horse.

"How about Survivor?" Tiffany replied. "Better yet, how about Shadow's Survivor?"

"As in Moon Shadow?" Dustin inquired.

"Yes." Tiffany glanced at the suckling baby horse. The fluffy stub of a tail twitched happily. "I like it."

"Isn't it a little premature for a name like that?"

"I hope not," Tiffany whispered. "I hope to God, it's not."

"Missy," Mac said gently, touching her sleeve.

"Don't say it, Mac," Tiffany said, holding up her hand. "This little filly is going to make it. She's got to!" Tiffany's lips pressed together in determination, as if she could will her strength into the little horse.

"I just don't want you to be too disappointed."

"I won't be." Tiffany's jaw tensed, and her blue eyes took on the hue of newly forged steel. "This horse is going to live."

"I'll stay overnight in the sitting-up room, watching the monitor. If anything goes wrong, I'll call," Mac volunteered.

"Good." Vance washed his hands and removed his bloodied white jacket. "I want this filly babied. I want her to stay inside for a full three days, under the lamps. We're not out of the woods yet, not by a long shot. And as for the mare, make sure she gets bran mash for three days."

"You got it," Mac agreed, casting one last worried glance at the filly. "Now, Missy, why don't you go up to the house and get some sleep? You can take over in the morning."

Tiffany glanced at the two horses. "Gladly," she whispered.

As she walked out of the foaling shed and into the windy night, Tiffany felt the sting of grateful tears in her eyes. Large crystalline drops began to run down her cheeks and catch the moon glow. *Everything would be perfect,* she thought to herself as she shoved her hands into the pockets of her jacket and started walking on the path to the house, *if only Zane were here to see for himself the strong little daughter of Moon Shadow.*

CHAPTER NINE

Zane cradled his drink in his hands as he stared at the two other men in the office. His attorney, John Morris, sat behind the oiled teak desk. The other fellow, a great bear of a man, had been introduced by John as Walt Griffith. He was staring out the window at the black San Francisco night.

Walt Griffith wasn't what Zane had expected. When Zane had asked John to hire the best private investigator in California, he'd expected to meet a slick L.A. detective, a man who was street smart as well as college educated. Instead, John had come up with Griffith, a semiretired investigator nearly seventy years old, with thick, gray hair, rotund waistline, clean-shaven jowls and an eye-catching diamond ring on his right hand.

Griffith made Zane slightly uneasy, but he managed to hide his restlessness by quietly sipping his bourbon and water.

"So you want to locate your ex-wife," Griffith said at last while frowning at the city lights illuminating that particular section of Jackson Square.

"That's right." Zane shifted uncomfortably in his chair, and his lips tightened at the corners.

"Maybe she doesn't want you to know where she is."

"She probably doesn't." Zane cocked his head and studied the large man. What was he getting at?

Griffith clasped his hands behind his back. "I wouldn't do this for anyone, you know, but John and I—" he looked at the worried attorney "—we go way back. He says you're straight."

"Straight?" Zane repeated, turning his eyes to the attorney. John took off his reading glasses and frowned.

"I assume that John knows you well enough," Griffith continued. "He told me you weren't a wife-beater or some other kind of psycho."

Zane cocked a dubious dark brow at his friend. "Thanks," he said with a trace of sarcasm.

Griffith turned and leaned against a bookcase filled with leather-bound law books. He withdrew an imported cigar from the inside pocket of his suit coat and studied the tip. "Let me tell you, boy," he said, pointing the cigar in Zane's direction. "I've seen it all, and I'm not about to do anything that smacks of brutality." His small, brown eyes glittered from deep in their sockets, and Zane had the distinct impression that Griffith had gotten himself into trouble more than once from something "smacking of brutality." "If I didn't owe John a favor, I wouldn't have bothered to take your case at all. You seem to have somewhat of a checkered past yourself."

Zane forced a severe smile and his gray eyes met Griffith's intense stare. "I wouldn't physically abuse a woman, any woman. Including Stasia."

"Abuse doesn't have to be physical."

Zane's anger got the better of him, and his fingers tightened around his drink. "There's no love lost between Stasia and me," he admitted, his eyes sparking furiously. "But I have no intention of hurting her. Actually, the less I have to do with her, the better. The only reason I want to locate her is because I think she'll be able to help me with some answers I need." Zane smiled at the irony of it all. "Believe me, Griffith, if there was another way to deal with this problem, I'd be glad to hear it. I don't relish the thought of confronting my ex-wife any more than you want this assignment."

Griffith struck a match and lit his cigar. As he puffed, a thick cloud of pungent smoke rose to the ceiling. "Answers?"

he asked, rolling Zane's words over in his mind. "About the other woman?"

Zane nodded.

Griffith's thick gray brows rose questioningly as he became interested in the Irishman's case. "Does she know you're checking up on her?"

Zane was cautious. He had to be with this man. "Tiffany?"

"Right."

Zane shook his head and scowled into his drink. "No."

"Humph." Griffith drew in on the cigar until the tip glowed red. "This other woman—this Rhodes lady, what's she to you?" he demanded.

"A friend."

Griffith shook his great head, and his eyes moved from Zane to John. "I thought you said he'd put all his cards on the table."

"He will." John glared severely at Zane. "You wanted the man." He motioned to indicate the investigator. "So help him."

At that moment, Zane realized he'd run out of options. He hesitated only slightly, and the smile that curved his lips appeared more dangerous than friendly. "All right, counselor, I'll level with Griffith, *if* he promises that everything I tell him will be kept in the strictest confidence."

"Goes without saying," Griffith grumbled, lowering himself into the chair next to Zane and folding his hands over his round abdomen. "Now, Mr. Sheridan, kindly explain why you're so interested in these two women, your wife and your... 'friend.'"

As SHE CAME DOWNSTAIRS THE MORNING after Alexander's Lady had foaled, Tiffany felt as if a great weight had been lifted from her shoulders. She had slept soundly, and only once, at about four, had she woken up. After turning on the monitor in the den and assuring herself that both the mare and the filly were alive and resting as well as could be expected, she trudged back up the stairs and fell into her bed. She had gone to sleep again instantly and had awakened refreshed.

"Good morning," Tiffany said with a cheery smile as Louise entered the kitchen and placed her purse on the table.

Louise's eyes sparkled. "It must be, from the looks of you," she decided. "Don't tell me—that Sheridan fella is back again."

"No," Tiffany quickly replied. She avoided the housekeeper's stare by pulling a thermos out of the cupboard near the pantry, and managed to hide the disappointment she felt whenever she thought about Zane. "Alexander's Lady is now the mother of a healthy filly," Tiffany stated, forcing a smile.

"Thank God!" Louise removed her coat and hung it in the closet. "This calls for a celebration!"

"Champagne brunch maybe?" Tiffany suggested.

Louise thought for a moment and then nodded. "Why not? It's about time we had some good news around here." She pulled her favorite apron out of the closet, tied it loosely around her waist and began rummaging through the drawers looking for the utensils she needed. After grabbing a wooden spoon, she tapped it thoughtfully against her chin and said, "I can fix something for when? Say around noon?"

"That would be perfect," Tiffany agreed. "Vance should be back by then and maybe we can persuade him to stay."

At that moment the telephone rang, and without thinking Tiffany reached for the receiver and settled it against her ear. "Hello?" she said into the phone, hoping for a fleeting second that the caller would be Zane.

"Tiffany? Hal Reece, here."

Tiffany's heart fell to the floor, and her stomach tightened painfully. Obviously his mare had foaled. Her fingers tightened around the receiver. "Yes?"

"I just wanted to report that Mile High delivered."

Tiffany braced herself for the worst. She was already imagining how she would deal with the press, the lawsuit, the other owners.... "When?"

"Three nights ago."

"And?" Tiffany's heart was thudding so loudly she was sure Hal could hear it.

Louise stopped rattling in the cupboards; the serious tone of Tiffany's voice warned her of impending doom. Usually she wouldn't eavesdrop, but this time, under the circumstances, the kindly housekeeper couldn't hide her interest in the strained conversation.

"And, I'm glad to say, we have three-day-old colts—healthy ones," Hal announced.

"Colts? Plural?"

"That's right, Tiffany," Hal said, his voice nearly bursting with pride. "Can you believe it? After everything we worried about, I end up with twins—and beauties at that."

"Wonderful," Tiffany replied as she sagged against the pantry doors and tried desperately to keep her voice professional. Louise's worried face broke into a wide grin.

"I knew it all along, you know," the proud owner went on, "but we did have a few tense moments during the labor. From the look on the trainer's face while Mile High was delivering, I thought the colt was stillborn, but that wasn't his concern at all! He just hadn't expected number two." Hal went on to describe in minute detail all the physical characteristics of each of his new horses and ended by saying, "Look, Tiffany, I would have called you a couple of days ago, but, well, I wanted to be sure that...you know, we didn't have any problems."

"I understand," Tiffany replied, remembering Charlatan's short life. "I'm just pleased that it turned out so well."

"Yes, yes. And, uh, look, I'm sorry about the things I said the other night. I was...well, there's just no excuse for my behavior."

"It's okay," Tiffany said with a sigh.

"Have you heard from any of the other owners?" Hal asked.

"You're the first."

"Well, good luck. And mind you, if anyone tries to give you any trouble, let me know. Maybe I'll be able to help."

"Thank you."

He was about to ring off, but changed his mind. "One other thing, Tiffany."

"Yes?"

"As soon as all this...ballyhoo over Moon Shadow passes, I'd like to breed a couple of mares to him again."

Tiffany smiled. Hal Reece's words were the final olive branch offered to bridge the rift between them. "Thank you," she said gratefully, "I'll be in touch."

Tiffany hung up the phone and grinned at Louise.

"Good news?" Louise guessed with a knowing smile.

"The best. Hal Reece's mare gave birth to twins. *Healthy* twin colts. Three nights ago. They've been examined by a vet, given a clean bill of health and even insured by the insurance company."

"That does it," Louise said with a toss of her head. "We'll have that celebration brunch after all."

"Hal is only one owner," Tiffany murmured as if to herself, "but at least it's a start." After pouring herself a hot cup of coffee, she filled the thermos, pushed open the door with her shoulder and started down the steps of the back porch. Wolverine, who had been lying beneath a favorite juniper bush near the brick stairs, trotted over to greet her.

"How's it going, boy?" Tiffany asked, checking to see that he had food and fresh water in the appropriate dishes. The collie tilted his head to the side, and his tail wagged slowly as she spoke. Tiffany set the thermos on the top step, took a sip from her coffee and scratched the old dog behind the ears. "Haven't you been getting enough attention lately?" she asked in an understanding voice. "All those horses are kind of stealing the show right now, aren't they?"

Wolverine whined and placed a furry paw on her bent knee.

Tiffany laughed and shook her head. "You're still the boss, though, aren't you?" As she picked up her things and turned toward the foaling shed, Wolverine trotted behind her, content with the little bit of attention he'd received.

The hinges on the door creaked as Tiffany entered the whitewashed building. Mac was standing at Alexander's Lady's stall and writing on a white card that Tiffany recognized as the foaling record.

"Good morning, Missy," the trainer said, without bothering to look up. When his job was finished, he placed the foaling record back on the post near the stall. Once the card was complete, Tiffany would enter the appropriate information into the farm's computer.

"That it is," she said, mimicking Mac's speech pattern.

Mac's brown eyes twinkled. "What's got you in such good spirits?" Forcing a tired smile, he leaned over the railing of the foaling box. "Could it be this little lady, here?"

"She's got a lot to do with it," Tiffany admitted. The little filly hid behind the protection of her mother's flank. At the filly's skittish behavior, Alexander's Lady's ears flattened to her reddish head, and she positioned herself between the intruders and her foal.

"Mama's takin' her job seriously," Mac decided.

"Good."

The newborn poked her inquisitive nose around the mare's body and stared at the strangers through intelligent brown eyes.

"I told you she'd make it," Tiffany said. The precocious little bay looked so healthy. *The filly couldn't die. Not now.*

Mac's knowing eyes traveled over the mare and foal, but he didn't offer his thoughts to Tiffany. She read the hesitation in his gaze. It's still too early to tell, he was saying without uttering a word.

As Tiffany watched the two horses, she realized that the stall had already been cleaned. The smell of fresh straw and warm horses filled the small rooms attached to the broodmare barn which were used for the express purpose of foaling.

"You didn't have to stay in the sitting-up room," Tiffany remarked, knowing that she was wasting her breath. Mac was from the old school of horse training. "There's a monitor in the den."

"Aye, and what good does it do ya?"

"I used it last night."

Mac laughed. "As if you don't trust me." She was about to protest, but he stilled her with a wave of his arm. "I like to be close, especially since we've had so much trouble. If anything goes wrong, I'm right next door." He cocked his head in the direction of the sitting-up room positioned between the two foaling boxes. "It's what I'm used to."

Tiffany didn't argue. Mac had been around horses long before the introduction of video cameras and closed-circuit television. "There's fresh coffee up at the house, and Louise is in the process of whipping up a special brunch, if you can stick around."

"The missus—"

"Is invited, too."

Mac rubbed a hand over the stubble on his chin and cracked a wide smile. "She might like that, ya know. She's always grumblin' 'bout cookin' for me," he teased.

"I'll bet." Tiffany laughed in reply. Emma McDougal positively doted on her husband of over forty years, but Mac was none the worse for his wife's spoiling. "Why don't you grab a cup of coffee, or take this thermos and then go home for a while? Bring Emma back with you around eleven."

"And what about you?"

"I'll stay here until Vance arrives." Tiffany checked her watch. "And then, if Vance approves, we'll let John watch the horses."

"If you think you can trust him—"

Tiffany waved Mac off. "John's only nineteen, I grant you, but he's been around horses all his life, and he's the best stable boy since—"

"You?" Mac asked, his eyes saddening.

Tiffany pushed aside the unpleasant memories. When she had been a stable boy to her father, Mac had been with the horses on the racing circuit, but he had learned of her duties through Ellery. "Maybe," she acknowledged. "Now, go on, get out of here."

Mac took his cue and left Tiffany to watch over the new mother and filly. The little bay foal scampered around her mother on legs that had grown stronger with the passing of the night. "You're going to make it, aren't you?" Tiffany asked, before glancing at the foaling record and noting that everything had been recorded perfectly. The time that the mare's water broke, when the foal was born, when it stood, and when it first suckled were duly noted along with the foal's sex and color. Everything looked normal.

Tiffany looked at the impish bay horse and let out a long sigh. "Let her live," she prayed in a soft whisper that seemed to echo through the rafters in the high ceiling.

She was just straightening up the sitting-up room when she heard the door to the foaling shed creak open.

"Tiffany?" Dustin called softly.

"In here." She peeked around the corner and was surprised to find Dustin dressed in a business suit. "What's going on?" she asked, pointing a moving finger at his neatly pressed clothes.

"I'm going back to Florida."

"Today?" She stepped back into the corridor to meet him. His face was set in hard determination, and a small frown pulled at the corners of his mouth.

"Have to."

Tiffany held her palms up in the air. "Wait a minute! You just got here yesterday."

Dustin's gold eyes held hers. "Do you want me to stay?" he asked, his voice much too familiar in the well-lit building. The only other sound was the whisper of hay being moved by the horses' feet.

"Yes…no…" She shook her head in bewilderment. "If you want to. What's the rush?"

He looked genuinely disappointed and refused to smile. "I

only came back to make sure that you were all right," he admitted, his frown deepening. "And from the looks of it, you're fine." His eyes slid down her slim form. She was clad only in worn jeans and a pink pullover, but with her hair wound over her head and the sparkle back in her intense blue eyes, she appeared both elegant and dignified, a no-nonsense lady who had her act together.

"Did you expect to find me in a crumpled heap—falling apart at the seams?"

Dustin shook his head but didn't smile at her attempt to lighten the mood. "I guess not. But it happened once before," he reminded her.

"That was different. Ellery was killed." She watched the smooth skin over Dustin's even features but saw no trace of any emotion that would betray his inner thoughts. Dustin acted as if he believed his brother dead.

"Right," he agreed.

"As well as Devil's Gambit."

Dustin looked up sharply, and in that split second Tiffany knew that he was lying to her. For the past four years, Dustin had been lying through his even white teeth. Without considering the consequences of her actions, she turned toward the stall and forced herself to appear calm, though her heart was pounding irregularly in her chest. It was time to find out how much of Zane's story was fact and how much was fiction, and she had to do it now, before Dustin left.

"I was thinking," she remarked, sliding a furtive glance in Dustin's direction.

"About?"

"Well, I still don't want to use Moon Shadow as a stud. Not until I understand what happened to those four foals, and I hear from the other owners."

Dustin nodded. Tiffany saw the movement from the corner of her eye. She propped her elbows on the rail and continued to watch the filly.

"So I was hoping to send some of our mares to other stallions, if it's not too late to nominate them."

"Sounds good to me." Dustin checked his watch and shifted from one foot to the other.

"You have any ideas on whom I should call?" she asked, her throat dry with dread.

"What?"

She shrugged. "Well, you're always high on one horse or the other. You know, a few years ago you thought we should breed Felicity to King's Ransom."

Dustin stiffened. The movement was slight, nearly imperceptible, but Tiffany caught it. "He's a good sire. Proof enough of that on the European tracks recently."

"Do you still think it's a good idea to send Felicity to him?"

"An impossible one, I'd say. King's Ransom's got to be booked solid."

Tiffany lifted one shoulder. "I just thought that maybe you knew the owner—could pull a few strings."

Dustin's eyes narrowed in suspicion. He came over to the stall and stood next to her. "You want favors? That's not like you, Tiff. You're the one who always plays by the rules."

"This is an unusual case—"

Dustin's arms reached for her, drew her close. "What is it with you?" he whispered against her hair. "What's going on here?" His finger traced the line of her jaw before lingering on the pout of her lips.

Her mind racing fast, Tiffany slid out of the circle of his arms and clasped her arms behind her back. She cocked her head upward to meet his gaze. "I just feel pushed against a wall sometimes," she said, knowing she was treading on thin ice with the turn in the conversation. She forced her hands into the pockets of her jeans and hoped to God that she wasn't betraying her inner feelings.

"And how would breeding one of our horses to King's Ransom change that?"

"It wouldn't, I suppose. There are plenty of good studs, here in the States." Lord, she hoped that she was a better actress than she had ever given herself credit for. "But we need a winner—a real winner."

"We've got Journey's End," he volunteered, intrigued with the change in her. His brother's widow was a mystifying creature; wild one minute, sedate the next. Intelligent, proud and sexy as hell. Dustin decided then and there that he would gladly give half his fortune for the chance to tame her fiery spirit.

"I know," Tiffany replied. "But what we really need is another horse like Devil's Gambit."

Dustin paled slightly, his hands dropped to his sides, but for the most part, he managed to keep his composure intact. "He's gone, Tiff. So is Ellery. You've got to face it. You're never going to have another horse just like Devil's Gambit, and you've got to forget this unreasonable loyalty to a dead man."

He captured her arm with his fingers and tugged her gently to him. "You need to live again, Tiffany. Without the ghosts of the past surrounding you. Ellery is gone…. Think about letting another man into your life." He paused dramatically, and his gilded eyes darkened with passion.

Tiffany wanted to recoil from him and shout that another man was already in her life, that she had committed her heart to a man she barely knew, and she was dying inside without him. Instead, she pulled away before the embrace became more heated.

"Think about me," he suggested, his eyes raking over her in lusty appraisal.

"I…I have too much on my mind to think about starting new relationships," she said, knowing the excuse was as feeble as it sounded. If she wasn't careful, Dustin would see through her act. "The foals—" she angled her head in the direction of the newborn filly "—Journey's End's career…a lot of things."

Dustin tugged at his stiff collar, but his golden eyes never left her face. "You said you felt pushed against the wall."

"I do." She lifted her shoulders in a nonchalant gesture and gambled with what she hoped was her trump card. "Someone's offered to buy me out."

Dustin froze. "What?"

It was too late to back down now. "A man was here last week."

"*What* man?"

"An Irishman. Zane Sheridan."

Dustin looked as if he would sink right through the floor. All of his well-practiced composure seemed to slide through the concrete.

"Ever heard of him?"

"Yeah. I know him." Dustin shook his head. "What does he want with this farm? He already breeds horses in Europe."

"Maybe he wants to break into the American market," Tiffany suggested, her fingers tightening over the railing of the stall. God, she was a terrible liar.

Dustin began to pace the length of the short corridor. "Maybe," he said as if he didn't believe a word of it. His mouth tightened and he ran a hand over his brow to catch the droplets of cold sweat that had begun to bead on his forehead. "I suppose he told you all sorts of wild stories."

"Like?" Tiffany coaxed.

"Like—hell, I don't know." He held up a hand in exasperation and looked up at the cross beams of the shed. "I may as well be honest with you, Tiff."

Here it comes. Dustin is about to confess, Tiffany thought, suddenly cold with dread.

"There wasn't much love lost between Sheridan and Ellery," Dustin announced. His topaz eyes softened, as if he wished he could save her some of the pain he was about to inflict. For the first time Tiffany realized that Dustin did, in his own way, truly love her. "They were involved in a poker game—for high stakes. Sheridan lost. I don't think the man likes to lose, and he took it none too well, let me tell you. He even went so far as to claim that Ellery had been cheating.

God, I was there. I don't know how Ellery could have cheated. From where I sat, Ellery won fair and square."

"How—how much money was involved?"

"Somewhere around two hundred thousand dollars, I think. Supposedly it wiped Sheridan out. But apparently he's back on his feet again."

Tiffany's mouth was dry with tension. "You haven't seen him since?"

"No, but I know he breeds horses in Ireland. I've seen a few of them race. He's got a two-year-old filly who's ripping up the tracks."

"The filly sired by King's Ransom?"

Dustin cast her a worried glance and nodded curtly. "I wouldn't trust that man, Tiffany. He's got a reputation in Europe for being ruthless." Dustin began stalking back and forth in front of the stall. "I don't understand why he wants to buy you out. What did you say to his offer?"

"That I wasn't interested, and if I ever did want to sell out my part of the operation, you had first option."

Some of the tension in his shoulders dissipated. "Good." He raked his fingers through his hair. "Did he say anything else?"

"Not much," Tiffany lied with a twinge of regret. "But I think he'll be back with a concrete offer."

"Great," Dustin muttered, his gold eyes impaling her. "Whatever you do, Tiff, don't sell out to that bastard."

"Are you still interested in owning all the farm?" she asked. Several years before, Dustin had offered to buy her out, but she had steadfastly refused.

"Of course I am. I just never thought you'd want to sell."

"I'm not sure that I do."

"Then you will give me first option?"

"When the time comes...."

Dustin appeared relieved, but there was something else that he was hiding from her; she could read it in the shadows of his eyes.

"Dustin." She touched his sleeve lightly. "Is there something you're not telling me?"

Dustin walked away from her and pushed his hands into the back pockets of his slacks. His shoulders slumped in defeat. "Well, maybe I shouldn't be telling you this," he grumbled, condemning himself. "It's all water under the bridge now."

Tiffany's heart nearly stopped. Was Dustin going to admit that Devil's Gambit was alive and siring foals as part of an incredible charade that would rock the Thoroughbred racing world on two continents? She felt almost physically ill with dread.

"Ellery was involved with a woman back then."

"Oh, God," she whispered, rocked to the very core of her soul as she began to understand what Dustin was saying. She felt cold all over; her heart was heavy in her chest. "A woman that Zane was in love with?" she guessed, praying that she had misunderstood her brother-in-law.

Dustin's brows quirked at Tiffany's familiar use of Sheridan's name. He let out an angry oath. "More than that, I'm afraid. She was Zane Sheridan's *wife, Stasia.*"

Tiffany sucked in her breath and her throat began to ache painfully. Truth and fiction began to entangle in her confused thoughts. What was Dustin saying? "Wait a minute…" Dustin was giving her too much information and it made her head swim. She had thought he was going to confess about Devil's Gambit, but instead he had brought up Zane's ex-wife…and *Ellery.* Dear God, was that why Zane had come to the farm, his gray eyes filled with revenge? Had he pretended interest in her only to throw her off guard? "Nancy Emerson said something about Zane's wife running out on him, but not with Ellery. The man's name was—"

"Ethan Rivers."

Tiffany swallowed against the dread flowing in her blood. "No." She had to deny what Dustin was suggesting and her shoulders slumped.

"Tiffany, listen!"

She shook her head and fought against hot tears. "Are you trying to tell me that Ellery used an alias?" She clamped her fingers over the top rail of the stall for support.

"Sometimes."

Pained blue eyes delved into Dustin's murky gaze. "But why?" Alexander's Lady sensed the tension and snorted.

Dustin waved off Tiffany's question as if it were insignificant. "Sometimes it was just easier…if people didn't know we, Ellery and I, were brothers."

"I don't understand." *And I don't think I want to. It would be easier not to think that Ellery used me in the past and that Zane is using me still….*

"You don't have to," Dustin said harshly and then softened a little when he saw her stricken face. "Tiffany, it really doesn't matter, not now. When Ellery and I were first getting started, we had to do a lot of…maneuvering to get established. Sometimes, when we were in Europe trying to sell some of our stock, it was just easier for Ellery to pose as a rival bidder to drive up the price of one of our own horses. Once in a while it backfired and no one bought the horse in question, but other times, well, we came out of it a few dollars richer. We didn't really hurt anyone by it."

Tiffany's eyes grew round with horror. "Oh, no?" she rasped as anger replaced despair. She leaned against a post for support, but her blue eyes blazed with rage. "You can justify it any way you want, even give it such fancy terms as 'maneuvering to get established,' Dustin, but I think what you and Ellery did was manipulate people and the system to pad your wallet." Tiffany felt sick inside, empty. "That's illegal—"

"Probably not," Dustin denied. "Immoral, maybe, and probably unethical—"

"And crooked." She saw the fury spark in his eyes and she forced control on her own anger. "Oh, Dustin. Why didn't Ellery tell me?" she asked in a broken whisper. Her knees threatened to give way. She had been married to Ellery, loved him in her own way, and he had betrayed her trust.

"Hey, don't get down on Ellery," Dustin said as if reading her thoughts. "This all happened before he knew you, and he did a hell of a lot for you and your bum of a father. Where would you have been if Ellery hadn't supported you, paid your way through college and then married you?"

"I don't know," she admitted. "But the lies—"

He touched her chin and lifted it, forcing her to look into his eyes. He felt her tremble with rage. "Look, it's over and done with," Dustin said, his eyes searching hers. "Ellery's dead…." He lowered his head and would have kissed her if it hadn't been for the question she had to ask.

"Is he, Dustin?" she demanded, pulling away from him and wrapping her arms protectively over her breasts.

Dustin was visibly stunned. "What kind of a question is that?"

"A legitimate worry, wouldn't you say?"

"Tiffany, listen to what you're saying!"

"How do I know that he isn't alive and using that alias…Ethan Rivers…or another one for that matter, in Europe somewhere?" Her hands were shaking at her sides. "For all I know, he could be living in France or England or Ireland, racing horses, married to someone else." She was rambling and she knew it, and she had to get hold of herself before she tipped her hand and gave her act away.

"I was there, Tiffany, at the accident. I saw Ellery…." His face went ashen and in that single moment of honesty, Tiffany believed her brother-in-law. "As hard as it is for you to accept, Ellery's gone."

Tiffany managed to square her shoulders, but tears pooled in her eyes before trickling down her face in a broken silvery path. "I didn't really doubt it," she admitted, brushing the unwanted tears aside. "But you've just told me some things that are a little hard to accept."

Dustin glanced at his watch again and cursed. "Damn! I've

got to go if I'm going to catch that plane." He looked at her longingly once again, silently offering himself.

Tiffany shook her head and lifted it with renewed determination. Her eyes, when they met Dustin's direct gaze, were cold.

"If you need me—"

"No. Journey's End needs you," she said. "The Florida Derby is next week."

"You could come down," he suggested without much hope.

"Not until I make sure that this little one—" Tiffany cocked her head in the direction of the inquisitive filly "—and her brothers and sisters are okay."

With a reluctant sigh, he turned away. "I'll call," Dustin promised, wondering why the hell he cared. He had lots of women who would do anything he wanted, so why was he hung up on his brother's wife?

"Good."

With only a moment's indecision, Dustin walked crisply out of the foaling shed, and Tiffany slumped against the wall in relief. *Ellery* was Ethan Rivers? *Ellery* had run off with Zane's wife, Stasia? The woman who had been Ellery's mistress when Tiffany was in college?

Tiffany's head was throbbing with unanswered questions. "Oh, Zane," she whispered brokenly. "What are you involved in?"

She was still going over the conversation with Dustin in her mind when Vance Geddes arrived to check the mare and foal. His brow knitted with worry as he started the examination, but the furrows slowly eased as he studied the frisky filly.

"It looks like she's going to make it," he said, relief audible in his voice. "By the time Charlatan was this old, there were already signs of distress."

"Thank God," Tiffany murmured, her mind only half on the conversation. Where was Zane? Why did he want the farm? Why hadn't he explained about Stasia and Ellery?

"Tiffany?" Vance asked for the second time.

"Oh, what?"

Vance shook his head and offered a small smile. "I said it looks as if we can take her out in a few days. I think you've got yourself a racehorse here."

"Wonderful." Tiffany eyed the little filly fondly. "Now we really do have a reason to celebrate."

"Pardon?"

"I was hoping that you could join the rest of us for lunch…brunch—" she lifted her shoulders "—whatever you want to call it."

"I'd be glad to. Just let me get cleaned up."

"I'll meet you at the house," she said, leaving the foaling shed and instructing the stable boy to look after the mare and filly. She headed toward the house and didn't notice the warm spring sunshine, the gentle breeze lifting the branches of the fir trees near the drive or the crocuses sprouting purple, gold, and white near the back porch.

All of her thoughts were centered on Zane and what, if anything, he wanted from her.

By the time Tiffany got back to the house, Louise was working furiously. The smell of honey-glazed ham, home-made apple muffins, black coffee and steamed vegetables filled the room. Louise was humming as she carefully arranged a rainbow of fresh fruit in a crystal bowl.

"It smells great in here," Tiffany said as she walked into the kitchen and tried to shake off the feeling of impending dread that had settled on her shoulders during her discussion with Dustin. "What can I do to help?"

Louise smiled. "Nothing. All the work's about done. Just go change your clothes. We're eating on the sun porch."

"Ummm. Fancy."

"It's a celebration, isn't it?"

"That it is. Let me set the table—"

"Already done."

"You are efficient, aren't you?"

"I don't get much of a chance to show off anymore. It feels good," Louise admitted, holding up the clear bowl of fruit for Tiffany's inspection. The cut crystal sparkled in the late morning light.

"Beautiful," she murmured, and the housekeeper beamed. "If you're sure there's nothing I can do…"

"Scat! Will ya?" Louise instructed with a severe frown that broke down completely as she laughed.

Tiffany chuckled. "All right. I'll be down in about twenty minutes."

She walked toward the stairs and remembered the times she and Ellery had entertained. It had been often and grand. Louise had always enjoyed "putting out a spread" as she had called it. Ellery had insisted that entertaining potential buyers was all part of the business, and he had been at his best when dressed in a black tuxedo and contrasting burgundy cummerbund while balancing a glass of champagne between his long, well-manicured fingers.

It seemed like aeons ago. And all that time, while Tiffany was married to Ellery, he was probably leading a double life as a stranger named Ethan Rivers, and having an affair with Zane Sheridan's ex-wife, Stasia.

Tiffany's heart twisted painfully and she balled small fists in frustration. How could she have been so blind?

It would be easy to blame it on youth or naiveté, but the truth of the matter was that she had been so anxious to love someone and have him love her in return, she had closed her eyes to the possibility that her husband had been anything but what she had wanted to see.

Stop punishing yourself, she warned, as she slipped out of her clothes, rewound her hair onto her head and stepped into the shower. *It's over and done!*

Or was it? Was Dustin telling the truth when he said that Ellery was dead, or was it just part of a complex cover-up to hide the fact that Devil's Gambit was alive and that another

horse and *another man* died in the fire? Oh, dear God, would
Ellery have been involved in anything so vile as murder? The
thought turned her blood to ice water and she had to steady
herself against the wet tiles. A cold wave of nausea flooded over
her, and Tiffany felt for a minute as if she were going to vomit.

"Oh, God," she cried softly, forcing herself to stand.

No matter what else, she couldn't—wouldn't—believe that
Ellery would take part in the death of another human being.

She turned off the shower and wrapped herself in a bath
sheet without really thinking about what she was doing. With
trembling fingers, while her head was still pounding with the
cold truth of the past, she dressed in a bright dress of indigo
polished silk, and pinned her hair in a tousled chignon. After
touching up her makeup and forcing her morbid thoughts to
a dark corner of her mind where she could examine them
later, she started down the stairs. As she did, the doorbell
chimed loudly.

"I'll get it," she called to Louise and hurred down the remaining three steps to the foyer and walked to the door, her
heels echoing sharply against the imported tile.

Squaring her shoulders, she opened the door, expecting to
find Mac's wife, Emma McDougal. Instead, her eyes met the
silvery gaze of the only man who had ever touched her soul.

"Zane," Tiffany whispered, and felt the need to lean against
the door for support. It had been more than a week since she had
seen him, and in that time so many truths had been uncovered.

Now, as she looked at the man she loved, Tiffany felt as if
she were staring into the eyes of a total stranger.

CHAPTER TEN

ZANE LEANED AGAINST ONE OF THE WHITE columns supporting the roof of the porch and stared at Tiffany. His hands were thrust into the pockets of his jeans, and his slumped posture was meant to be casual, but his shoulder muscles were tight, so tense they ached.

God, she was beautiful, more beautiful than he remembered. Dressed in shimmering blue silk, with her golden brown hair pinned loosely to her crown, Tiffany looked almost regal. A single strand of gold encircled her throat, and thin layers of silk brushed against her knees.

After what seemed like a lifetime, Zane finally spoke. "Are you going out?" he asked, his gray eyes delving into hers. One look at Ellery Rhodes's widow had destroyed all of Zane's earlier promises to himself. After the meeting with Griffith just three days ago, he had silently vowed that he would stay away from Ellery Rhodes's widow. Now, as he gazed into her intriguing blue eyes, he knew that keeping away from her would be impossible. Despite all the excuses he'd made to himself to the contrary, seeing Tiffany again was the single reason he had returned to Rhodes Breeding Farm.

Tiffany, recovering from the shock of seeing him again, managed to square her shoulders and proudly hold his gaze. Though her heartbeat had quickened at the sight of him, she forced herself to remember Dustin's condemning words. *Sheridan's got a reputation for being ruthless.... Ellery was involved with Zane Sheridan's wife.*

"No," she finally replied, "I'm not going out…. We're having a special lunch, sort of a celebration."

Zane detected new doubts in her exotic blue eyes, doubts that hadn't clouded her gaze when he had last seen her. The small hairs on the back of his neck prickled in warning. Something was wrong here, and he intended to find out what it was. Silently he cursed himself for staying away so long. In the course of the past week, someone had destroyed all the trust Tiffany had previously felt for him. It didn't take long to figure out who was to blame, and his fists balled at the thought of Dustin Rhodes.

Zane straightened and walked closer to her. "Tiffany, what's wrong?" he asked, gently placing his fingers on her shoulders and pulling her close.

"Don't," she whispered, knowing that her battle was already lost. She wanted to melt into him. Just seeing him again had been enough to make her heartbeat race in anticipation. Maybe Dustin had been wrong about Zane, maybe he had lied.

She leaned heavily on Zane, letting his strong arms wrap around her. Her face was pressed to his chest, and she could feel the warmth of his breath on her hair, hear the even rhythm of his pounding heart.

Don't fall under his spell again, a small voice inside her cautioned. *Remember what Dustin said about Ellery and Zane's wife. He's probably here just to get information about Stasia. He's been using you all along.*

"Tiffany?" Zane urged, his voice low, husky. She closed her eyes and let his earthy scent fill her nostrils. It felt so right to have his arms around her. Without examining her motives, she clung to him as if she expected him to vanish as quickly as he had appeared.

"I…I didn't think you were coming back," she whispered, ignoring the doubts filling her mind. He was here, now, with her. Nothing else mattered.

"I said I would."

"But it's been—"

"Too long." The corded arms tightened around her, and his warm hands splayed against the small of her back, pressing her body to his and heating her skin through the thin material of her dress. "I should have called," he admitted, feeling his body beginning to respond to the soft, yielding contour of hers, "but I've been in and out of airports for the better part of a week."

She lifted her head and studied the weariness in his face. Wherever he'd been, the trip had taken its toll on him. The brackets near the corners of his mouth had deepened, and there was a general look of fatigue in his eyes. His clothes, a pair of jeans and a plaid shirt, were clean but slightly rumpled, and his chin was just beginning to darken from the day's growth of beard.

"Have you been out of the country?" she asked.

"Part of the time."

Because of Devil's Gambit, or your wife?

Tiffany knew that she should pull away from him, now, before she was lost to him forever. She shouldn't let him into her house or her life. Not again. Too many events in his past were entangled with Ellery's life and left unexplained. There were too many questions that demanded answers....

For a passing moment she considered confronting him with what she had learned from Dustin, just to gauge his reaction, but she couldn't. The sight of his drawn face, wind-blown black hair and slightly wrinkled clothing did strange things to her heart. Despite all of Dustin's accusations, despite the lies, she still loved this rugged man from Ireland with every fiber of her soul.

"Come inside," she invited, managing, despite her doubts, the trace of a smile. "Louise is making a special brunch."

"Why?" Zane's dark brows cocked expressively. He was getting mixed signals from Tiffany; one moment she seemed to have a wonderful secret she wanted to share with him, and her indigo eyes sparkled; the next second her smile would fade and her lips would compress into a determined line of defiance.

"Alexander's Lady had a filly—a healthy filly," Tiffany said, pushing her dark thoughts aside.

Zane relaxed a little, and he gently touched her cheek. She had to concentrate to keep her mind on the conversation. "I assume from your expression that she had been bred to Moon Shadow."

"Yes." Tiffany attempted to extract herself from his embrace, to put some mind-clearing distance between his body and hers, but his strong arms refused to release her.

"When was the filly born?"

"Just last night."

"Isn't the celebration a little premature?" he asked softly, remembering the other colt, the one that had lived a day or so before collapsing from heart failure and dying.

"Maybe, but I doubt it. Vance thinks the filly will live," Tiffany said with conviction. She recognized the unspoken question in Zane's eyes and knew that he was thinking about Charlatan's short life. "Vance wasn't so sure last night," she admitted, "but this morning the filly's been scampering around her stall like a champion. Even Vance has taken her off the critical list."

Zane hazarded a charming half-smile that touched Tiffany's heart. "That is good news." He kissed her lightly on the forehead, and Tiffany's heart seemed to miss a beat. *How could she react this way, love this man, when he had lied to her?*

"And there's more," she managed to say. "Hal Reece called and told me that his mare, Mile High, gave birth to twin colts—healthy colts, about three days ago. He's even been able to insure them."

Zane's grin spread slowly over his rugged features. He squeezed her for a minute and laughed. God, when was the last time he'd laughed? It had to have been years ago.... It was so easy with Tiffany, so natural. "You're right, you should celebrate."

Tiffany's eyes warmed. "Louise would love it if you joined us."

"Us?"

"Mac and his wife Emma, Vance, Louise and myself." She read the hesitation in his gaze and realized that he felt like an outsider. Her elegant features sobered. "It's not a private party, Zane," she said softly with a seductive smile, "and you're very much a part of it. After all, you were here the night Ebony Wine delivered. Besides, Louise would skin me alive if she knew you were here and wouldn't have brunch with us after all the work she's gone to."

"Then how can I refuse?"

"You can't."

She pulled away from him, but his fingers caught her wrist. "Tiffany?"

"What?"

When she turned to face him, he tugged on her arm again and pulled her close against his body. "Just one more thing."

"Which is?" she asked breathlessly.

In answer, he lowered his head and his lips brushed seductively over hers. His breath was warm and inviting, his silvery eyes dark with sudden passion. "I missed you," he whispered against her mouth, then his lips claimed hers in a kiss that was as savage as it was gentle. The warmth of his lips coupled with the feel of his slightly beard-roughened face made her warm with desire.

Tiffany moaned and leaned against him, letting her body feel the hard texture of his. His tongue gently parted her lips and flickered erotically against hers. Heat began to coil within her before he pulled his head away and gazed at her through stormy gray eyes.

"God, I missed you," he repeated, shaking his head as if in wonder at the conflicting emotions warring within his soul.

Tiffany had to clear her throat. "Come on. Louise will have my head if her meal gets cold." Still holding his hand, she led him toward the back of the house and tried to forget that Zane had once been married to Ellery's mistress.

"I HAVEN'T EATEN LIKE THIS SINCE THE last time I was here," Zane remarked to Louise, who colored slightly under the compliment. Everyone was seated at the oval table in the sun room, which was really an extension of the back porch. The corner of the porch nearest the kitchen had been glassed in, affording a view of the broodmare barn and the pasture surrounding the foaling shed. Green plants, suspended from the ceiling in wicker baskets or sitting on the floor in large brass pots, surrounded the oak table, and a slow-moving paddle fan circulated the warm air.

"We should do this more often," Tiffany decided as she finished her meal and took a sip of the champagne.

"Used to be," Mac mused while buttering a hot muffin, "that we'd have parties all the time. But that was a long time ago, when Ellery was still alive."

Tiffany felt her back stiffen slightly at the mention of Ellery's name. When she looked away from Mac she found Zane's gray eyes boring into hers. An uncomfortable silence followed.

"Hasn't been any reason to celebrate until now," Louise said, as much to diffuse the tension settling in the room as to make conversation. Her worried eyes moved from Tiffany to Zane and back again.

"What about Journey's End's career?" Vance volunteered, while declining champagne. He shook his head at Mac, who was tipping a bottle over his glass. "I've got two more farms to visit today." When Mac poured the remainder of the champagne into his own glass, Vance continued with his line of thinking. "If you ask me, Journey's End is reason enough to celebrate."

"Maybe we'd better wait on that," Tiffany thought aloud. "Let's see how he does in the Florida Derby."

"That race shouldn't be too much of a problem if Prescott handles him right," Mac said.

"What then?" Zane asked the trainer.

"Up to Kentucky for the Lexington Stakes."

"And then the Kentucky Derby?"

"That's the game plan," Mac said, finishing his drink and placing his napkin on the table. He rubbed one thumb over his forefinger nervously before extending his lower lip and shrugging. "I just hope Prescott can pull it off."

"He's a good trainer," Emma McDougal stated. She was a petite woman of sixty with beautiful gray hair and a warm smile. She patted her husband affectionately on the knee in an effort to smooth what she saw as Mac's ruffled feathers. She knew that as much as he might argue the point, Mac missed the excitement of the racetrack.

"When he keeps his mind on his horses," Mac grumbled.

"Don't you think he will?" Zane asked.

Mac's faded eyes narrowed thoughtfully. "He'd better," he said with a frown. "We've come too close to the Derby before to let this one slip through our fingers."

Tiffany pushed her plate aside. "Delicious," she said to Louise before turning her attention back to the trainer. "Would you like to work with Journey's End in Lexington? You could help Bob Prescott get him ready."

"Oh, there's no doubt I'd like to, Missy," Mac replied, ignoring the reproachful look from his wife. "But it wouldn't do a lick of good. Journey's End, he's used to Prescott. We can't be throwin' him any loops, not now. Me going to Kentucky would probably do more harm than good."

"So the die is cast?" Tiffany asked, feeling a cold premonition of doom as she looked through the windows and noticed the thick bank of clouds rolling over the mountains from the west.

"Aye, Missy. That it is…that it is."

TIFFANY SPENT THE REST OF THE AFTERNOON with Zane, and for the first time in more than a week she began to relax. She had planned to drive into town in the afternoon but decided that she'd rather spend the time on the farm.

In the early evening, she took Zane into the foaling shed and proudly displayed Shadow's Survivor. Within the confines of the large stall, the inquisitive filly cavorted beneath the warm heat lamps.

"Vance says she'd be able to go outside in a couple of days," Tiffany said.

"I'll bet you're relieved." Zane's eyes moved from the mare and foal to Tiffany.

"I'll be more relieved when I hear from the rest of the owners," she responded as she led Zane out of the foaling shed. "Until I know that no more foals will die, I can't really relax."

Dusk was just beginning to settle on the hills surrounding the farm. Lavender shadows lengthened as the hazy sun settled behind the ridge of sloping mountains to the west. Clouds began to fill the darkened sky. "This is my favorite time of day," she admitted, watching as the stable boys rounded up the horses for the evening. The soft nickering of mares to their foals was interspersed with the distant whistle of a lonely stallion. Tiffany chuckled. "That's Moon Shadow," she explained. "He always objects to being locked up for the night."

"Do you blame him?" Zane asked.

"Oh, no. That's what makes him a winner, I suppose."

"His defiance?"

She frowned into the gathering darkness and linked her arm through his. A cool breeze pushed her dress against her legs as they walked. "I prefer to think of it as his fire, his lack of docility. He's always had to have his way, even as a foal. He was the boss, had to be in the lead."

"The heart of a champion."

Tiffany pursed her lips thoughtfully and her elegant brows drew together. "That's why I hate what's been happening to him—all this conjecture that there's something wrong with him."

"Have you found an answer to what happened to the dead foals?"

After expelling a ragged sigh, Tiffany shook her head. "Nothing so far. Vance has gone to independent laboratories, asked for help from the Jockey Club and the racing commission, and still can't get any answers."

"Not even enough information to clear Moon Shadow's name?"

"No." She placed a restraining hand on her hair as the wind began to loosen her chignon. "The new foals—the healthy ones—should prove that the problem isn't genetic."

"Unless another one dies."

She shuddered inside at the thought.

Zane noticed the pain in her eyes and placed a comforting arm over her shoulders. "You really love it here, don't you?"

"What?"

He rotated the palm of his free hand and moved his arm in a sweeping gesture meant to include the cluster of buildings near the center of the farm, the sweeping green pastures enclosed by painted white fences, the horses grazing in the field and the gentle green hills guarding the valley. "All of it."

She couldn't deny the attachment she felt for this farm. It was the only home she'd known. She felt as much a part of it as if it had been in her family for generations. It was, and would always be, the only thing she could call her heritage. "Yes," she answered. "I love it. I love the horses, the land, the excitement, the boredom, *everything*."

"And is that what I felt when I came back here this morning?"

"What do you mean?"

"When I arrived here, you looked at me as if I were a thief trying to steal it all away from you."

"Did I?"

He didn't answer, but she saw the determination in the angle of his jaw. He wouldn't let up until he found out what

was bothering her. She had no recourse but to lie or to confront
him with what she'd learned from Dustin.

The day with Zane had been so wonderful, and she knew
that it was about to end. "It had nothing to do with selling the
farm to you, Zane. You, or anyone else, can't force me to sell."

The arm around her tightened. She felt the unleashed
tension coiling his body. "Then what?"

"While you were gone, a few things happened," she
admitted. They had been walking down a wide, well-worn
path, past the old barn and through a thicket of maple trees
surrounding a small pond. The water in the small lake had
taken on an inky hue, reflecting the turbulent purple of the sky.

"What things?"

"Dustin came home."

All of the muscles in Zane's body tightened. The thought
of Dustin Rhodes, here, alone with Tiffany, made his stomach
knot with dread. It was insane to feel this...jealousy. Dustin
owned part of the farm; he could come and go as he pleased.
Zane's jaw hardened, and his back teeth ground together in
frustration.

"You weren't expecting him?"

"No."

"Then why did he return?"

"He said it was because of all the bad press surrounding
Moon Shadow. He wanted to make sure that I was all right."

"He could have called."

"I suppose," she admitted, taking a seat on a boulder near
the pond. "But I think he wanted to see me face to face."

"Why?" Zane demanded, his eyes glittering in the dark night.

"Dustin helped me pick up the pieces when Ellery was
killed," she whispered. "I was pretty shook up."

"Because you loved your husband so much?" he asked,
reaching for a flat stone and thrusting it toward the water. He
watched as it skipped across the pond creating ever-widening
ripples on the water's smooth surface.

"Because my whole world was turned upside down." The wind picked up and clouds shadowed the moon.

"And if he walked back into your life right now?" Zane asked, bracing himself against the truth.

"It would be upside down all over again."

"And who would you lean on?"

Tiffany breathed deeply. "I hope that I'm strong enough to stand by myself—no matter what happens," she said softly.

The air was thick was the promise of rain, and the clouds covering the moon became more dense. High above, the branches of the fir trees danced with the naked maples.

Zane turned to face her and his broad shoulders slumped in resignation. Gray eyes drove into hers. "You know that I'm falling in love with you, don't you?"

Tiffany's heart nearly stopped. *If only I could believe you, Zane. If only you hadn't lied to me. If only I could tell what was true and what was false.*

She wrapped her arms around her knees and shook her head. "I don't think love can enter into our relationship," she said, staring at the dark water and refusing to face him.

"It's nothing I wanted," he admitted and pushed his hands into his back pockets. "But it happened."

"Zane—" her protest was cut short when he strode purposely over to the rock and scooped her into his arms. "Please don't…" she breathed, but it was the cry of a woman lost. When his lips crushed against hers, she responded willingly, eagerly to him, mindless of the wind billowing her dress or the heavy scent of rain in the air.

He gently laid her on the grass near a stand of firs, and his fingers caught in the golden strands of her hair. Slowly he withdrew the pins and twined his fingers in the silken braid as he pulled it loose. The golden hair fell to her shoulders, framing her face in tangled honey-brown curls.

"I've wanted to make love to you from the first moment I saw you," he whispered. His body was levered over hers, and his silvery eyes caught the reflection of the shadowy moon. She trembled when his hands lingered on her exposed throat to gently stroke the sensitive skin near her shoulders.

"That's not the same as loving someone," she replied, her voice breathless as his hand slowly, enticingly, slid down the silky fabric of her dress and softly caressed her breast.

A spasm of desire shot through her. "Oh, my God," she whispered while he looked at her, touching her with only one hand. Her breathing became rapid and shallow as slowly he caressed the silk-encased peak, rubbing the sheer fabric against her. Tiffany began to ache for the feel of his hands against her skin.

The fingers slid lower, down her thigh, to the hem of her dress. She felt the warm impression of his fingertips as they stroked her leg through her sheer stocking.

I shouldn't be doing this, she thought wildly. *I don't even really understand what he wants of me....*

"Tell me you want me to make love to you," he rasped against her hair. His tongue traced the gentle shell of her ear, and his breath fanned seductively against her skin.

"Oh, Zane…I…" Her blood was pounding in her temples. She trembled with desire.

"Tell me!"

"Oh, God, yes." She closed her eyes against the truth and felt the hot tears moisten her lashes. *I don't want to love you,* she thought for a fleeting moment. *Dear Lord, I don't want to love you.* He lowered his head and kissed her eyelids, first one and then the other, tasting the salt of her tears and knowing that he couldn't deny himself any longer.

"I love you, Tiffany," he whispered, while his fingers strayed to the pearl buttons holding the bodice of her dress together, and his lips touched her neck, moving over the smooth skin and the rope of gold. His tongue pressed against the flickering pulse in the hollow of her throat.

"No." *If only she could trust him.*

"I've loved every minute I've spent with you…."

Each solitary button was slowly unbound, and the shimmery blue fabric of her dress parted in the night. Her straining breasts, covered only by a lacy, cream-colored camisole and the golden curtain of her hair, pressed upward. The dark points seductively invited him to conquer her, and Zane felt hot desire swelling uncomfortably in his loins at the dark impressions on the silky fabric.

He groaned at the sight of her. He slowly lowered his head to taste one of the ripe buds encased in silk. His tongue toyed with the favored nipple until Tiffany's heart was pounding so loudly it seemed to echo in the darkness. His hands caressed her, fired her blood, promised that their joining would be one of souls as well as flesh.

Somewhere in the distance, over the sound of Zane's labored breathing, she heard the sound of lapping water and the cry of a night bird, but everything she felt was because of Zane. Liquid fire ignited from deep within her and swirled upward through her pulsing veins.

His warm tongue moistened the lace and left it wet, to dry in the chill breeze. She shuddered, more from the want of him than the cold. When his hands lifted the dress over her head, she didn't protest.

Tenderly at first, and then more wildly, he stroked her breasts until she writhed beneath him, trying to get closer to the source of her exquisite torment. He removed the camisole slowly and then let his lips and teeth toy with one sweet, aching breast. Tiffany moaned throatily, from somewhere deep in her soul.

His tongue moistened the dark nipple until it hardened beautifully, and then he began to suckle ravenously, all the while touching the other breast softly, making it ready. Just when Tiffany thought she could stand no more of the sweet torment, he turned to the neglected breast and he feasted again.

"Oh, Zane," Tiffany cried, her fever for his love making

demands upon her. She was empty, void, and only he could make her whole again.

His hands continued to stroke her while he slowly removed the remaining scanty pieces of her clothing. She felt her lace panties slide over her hips. Warm fingers traced the ridge of her spine and lingered at the swell of her hips.

He touched all of her, making her ready, while she slowly undressed him and ran her fingers hungrily over his naked chest. His muscles rippled beneath her touch, and she was in awe at the power her touch commanded.

He kicked off his jeans almost angrily and was only satisfied when he was finally lying atop her; hard male muscles pressed heatedly against their softer feminine counterparts.

The need in him was evident; his eyes were dark with desire, his breathing labored, his heartbeat thudding savaging against her flattened breasts. A thin sheen of sweat glistened over his supple muscles. His lips pressed hungrily, eagerly over hers.

"Let me love you, sweet lady," he coaxed, rubbing against her seductively, setting her skin aflame with his touch.

Her blood pulsed wildly in her veins. All thoughts of denial had fled long ago. The ache within her, burning with the need for fulfillment, throbbed with the want of him.

"Please," she whispered, closing her eyes against the glorious torment of his fingers kneading her buttocks.

Her fingers stroked him, and he cried out her name. He could withhold himself no longer.

With only a fleeting thought that this woman was the widow of Ellery Rhodes, he gently parted her legs and delved into the warmth of the woman he loved. His body joined with hers and he became one with the wife of the man he had vowed to destroy. He whispered her name, over and over again, as if his secret incantation could purge her from his soul.

He watched in fascination as she threw back her head and exposed the white column of her throat. Her fingernails dug into the muscles of his back before she shuddered in complete surrender. His explosion within her sent a series of shock waves through his body until he collapsed over her.

"I love you, Tiffany," he whispered, his breathing as raspy as the furious wind. He twined his fingers in her hair and let his head fall to the inviting hollow between her breasts. *Oh, but to die with this beautiful woman.*

Tiffany's entire body began to relax. The warmth within her seemed to spread into the night. Zane touched her chin with one long finger and kissed her lips.

Lying naked in the dark grass, with only the sounds of the night and the gentle whisper of Zane's breath, she felt whole. Large drops of rain began to fall from the black sky, but Tiffany didn't notice. She was only aware of Zane and his incredible touch. His fingers traced the curve of her cheek. "I meant it, you know," he whispered, smiling down at her.

"What?"

"That I love you."

Tiffany released a tormented sigh and pulled herself into a sitting position. "You don't have to say—"

His fingers wrapped possessively around her wrist and his eyes bored into hers. "I only say what I mean."

"Do you, Zane?" she asked, her face contorted in pain as the doubts of the morning and her conversation with Dustin invaded her mind. God, how desperately she wanted to believe him.

"What is it, Tiffany?" he asked, suddenly releasing her. "Ever since I arrived, I've gotten the feeling that something isn't right. What happened?"

Tiffany decided there was no better time for the truth than now. Before she became more hopelessly in love with him, she had to settle the past. She reached for her dress, but Zane restrained her. "I want answers, Tiffany."

"Not nearly as badly as I do." She pulled away from him and grabbed her clothes. As she quickly dressed, she began to talk. "I told Dustin that you had been here and expressed interest in buying the farm." The rain began in earnest, running down her face and neck in cold rivulets.

Zane's expression grew grim. "He wasn't too pleased about it, I'd guess."

"That's putting it mildly. He nearly fell through the floor."

"And what did he suggest?"

"That I shouldn't even consider selling to you. In fact, he seemed to think that I shouldn't have anything to do with you."

"He's afraid, Tiffany."

She began working on the buttons of her dress while Zane slipped on his jeans. "That's what I thought, too. At one point I was certain that Dustin was going to confess about switching horses and admit that Devil's Gambit is alive."

Zane was reaching for his shirt but stopped. "Did he?"

"No."

He slipped his arms through the sleeves but didn't bother with the buttons. His shirttails fluttered in the wind. "Then what, Tiffany? Just what the hell did he tell you that upset you so?"

Tiffany wrapped her arms around her breasts and stared at Zane. The wind caught her hair and lifted it off her face which was glistening with raindrops. "Dustin said that not only did you lose most of your money to Ellery in an honest poker game—"

"Honest my ass!"

"—but that Ellery also ran off with your wife."

Zane gritted his teeth together and rose. "Damn!" he spit out as he stood and stared at the pond, legs spread apart, hands planted on his hips.

Tiffany's heart ached as she watched him. *Deny it, Zane,* she thought. *Tell me Dustin lied...anything...tell me again that you love me.*

"He told you only part of the story," Zane said. He walked over to the boulder and propped one foot on it as he stared across the small lake. "It's true, Stasia ran off with Ellery, and at the time I felt like killing them both."

He still loves her, Tiffany realized, and fresh tears slid down her cheek to mingle with the drops of rain.

"So did you come here looking for her?" she asked, her voice thick and raw.

"No."

"Then why?"

"I can't lie to you, Tiffany."

"You already have."

"No—"

"I asked you if you were married," she whispered.

"And I'm not."

"You just conveniently forgot that you had been?" She looked up at the cloudy sky. "You never even mentioned her."

"She's not something I like to think about," he confessed.

"But your feelings were strong enough to bring you here. You can't expect me to believe that you're not looking for her."

He walked over to the grassy knoll on which she was sitting, knelt down and placed his fingers over her shoulders. She quivered betrayingly at his familiar touch. "I knew she wouldn't be here, but yes, I need to find her."

Tiffany closed her eyes against the truth. "Why?"

"Because she's the only one who can clear up what happened to Devil's Gambit...and Ellery."

"Ellery is dead," Tiffany murmured, hugging her knees to her and setting her chin on them.

"How do you know?"

"I asked Dustin."

"He wouldn't tell you the truth—"

"Dustin cares about me, Zane. He admitted some pretty horrible things, such as conning other owners at the yearling sales in Europe. He said that Ellery would pose as another person, someone named Ethan Rivers."

"Did he explain about Devil's Gambit?"

"No."

"But?" he coaxed.

"From his reaction, I'd have to guess that your assumption about Devil's Gambit is correct. He wouldn't admit that Devil's Gambit was alive, but it was fairly obvious when I mentioned King's Ransom and Devil's Gambit in the same breath that something wasn't right."

"You should be more careful around him," Zane warned. "He's dangerous, and he has a lot to lose if he's uncovered."

"I'm not sure that he's the man in charge."

"What do you mean?"

"I don't know, just a feeling I got that there was someone else pulling his strings."

"I don't know who it would be."

"Neither do I."

"That's why I have to find Stasia," Zane said. "She might be able to help us."

"I doubt it."

Zane lifted his head and his sharp eyes bored into Tiffany. "You knew her?" he guessed incredulously.

Tiffany nodded, remembering Stasia's long, dark hair, even features and seductive dark eyes. Stasia's sultry beauty was enough to capture any man, including Zane. "She was here on the farm with Ellery when I was in college. Later, once I had returned, my father died and Ellery asked me to marry him."

"What happened to Stasia?"

"I don't know. Ellery wouldn't talk about it. The day after he asked me to marry him, she moved out. I never saw her again, but I'm sure that she despises me."

"Probably," he said with a snort. "Stasia knows how to carry a grudge." He saw the unasked questions in Tiffany's wide eyes and began to explain about a time in his life he would rather have forgotten.

"When I met Stasia, she was barely eighteen. She was beautiful and anxious to get out of a bad home situation. I thought at the time that I was in love with her, and we got married. I was just starting then, trying to set up a successful farm of my own. Fortunately, I had a few decent breaks. I was lucky and after a few years, I…we, Stasia and I, owned a small farm about thirty miles from Dublin. It was a beautiful place," he said, smiling slightly at the fond memories, "thick green grass, stone fences twined with bracken, the rolling Irish countryside…a perfect place for breeding Thoroughbreds. That's when I started breeding successfully. And how I met Ethan Rivers."

"Ellery," Tiffany whispered.

Zane's smile had left his face and his rugged features pulled into a dark scowl. "One and the same. It happened about six years ago. Ethan was looking for some yearlings and came out to the farm. Later that night we began drinking and playing poker with another man from America who was supposedly interested in some of my horses."

"Dustin," Tiffany guessed, not daring to breathe.

"Right again. Anyway, on that night, Dustin folded early, claimed the stakes were too high for him. But I kept on drinking and playing, urged on by my lovely wife."

"Oh, no—"

"That's right. Stasia was already involved with Ethan Rivers, and when I lost it cost me two hundred thousand dollars. I had to sell the farm to pay Rivers off."

"But if you thought the game was crooked—"

"I didn't. Not then. Only much later, when I went back to that pub and got to talking to one of the regulars, I learned that the old man, who was named O'Brien, had watched the game and thought it might be rigged. A few days later, he'd overheard Dustin and his brother talking—about the game and Stasia."

"Why didn't he talk to you sooner?" she asked. "There must have been plenty of time before you sold the farm."

"O'Brien was caught eavesdropping by Ellery. Ellery was furious that he might be found out, and he threatened the old man with his life. O'Brien didn't doubt for a minute that Ellery would make good his threats to kill both him and his wife. By the time his conscience got the better of him and he found me, I'd managed to sell the farm."

"Who would buy it so quickly?"

Zane's jaw became rigid and his eyes turned deadly. "A corporation."

Tiffany finally understood, and her throat went dry with dread. "Emerald Enterprises."

"That's right. The farm I used to own now belongs to Dustin and Ellery, if he's still alive."

"Oh, God, Zane," she murmured, covering her face with her hands. *Had she been so young and foolish that she had never seen Ellery for what he really was?* She lifted her eyes and felt her hands curl into fists of frustration. "I don't understand. Knowing how you must feel about him, why would Dustin allow you to breed any of your mares to King's Ransom?"

"First of all, I didn't know that Emerald Enterprises was Dustin Rhodes. The original sale of the farm was handled through a broker, and neither Dustin's name nor Ellery's ever appeared on any of the documents. As for Dustin, either he's just gotten cocky and doesn't think he'll be discovered, or maybe he thinks I've buried the hatchet. After all, I have been able to put myself back on my feet. It took several years, mind you, but I was able to start again. I didn't lose everything when I sold the farm, and I managed to keep two good mares and a stallion."

"And from those three horses, you started again?"

"Yes. Fortunately I'd already established myself as a breeder. The three good horses and my reputation gave me a decent start."

"And...and your wife?"

"She left me immediately. I suspected that she'd followed Ethan—who I later found out was Ellery—to America. When Stasia filed for divorce, I didn't fight her.

"I spent the next several years working to reestablish myself."

"And you never forgot taking your revenge on Ellery," Tiffany whispered as thunder rumbled in the distant hills.

"No. That's the reason I came here. When I heard that Ellery had married, I assumed that it was to Stasia." Zane walked back to the lake and stared across the black water, watching as the raindrops beat a staccato rhythm on the clear surface. "Of course later I learned that he had married a woman by the name of Tiffany Chappel."

"And you wondered what had become of your ex-wife." Tiffany felt a sudden chill as she finally understood Zane's motives. He had come looking for Stasia....

"Yeah, I wondered, but I found that I really didn't give a damn." He shrugged his broad shoulders. "The next thing I heard about Ellery Rhodes was that he, along with his famous horse, had been killed. My fever for revenge had cooled, and I decided to put the past behind me."

"Until you found the horse you think is Devil's Gambit."

"The horse I *know* is Devil's Gambit."

Zane hazarded a glance at the threatening sky before looking back at Tiffany and noticing that she was shivering.

"Come on," he suggested softly. "We'd better get inside before we're both soaked to the skin."

Tiffany refused to be deterred when she was so close to the truth. Her emotions were as raw as the wind blowing over the mountains. Everything Zane was suggesting was too farfetched, and yet parts of his story were true. Even Dustin had backed him up. She ran shaky fingers through her hair and watched his silhouetted form as he advanced on her and stared down at her with bold gray eyes.

"When I figured out the scam that Ellery and his brother had pulled, I knew he had to be stopped. Using one stud in place of another, and falsifying the death of Devil's Gambit is a scandal of international proportions."

"Then you think that Ellery is still alive?" she murmured, feeling lost and alone.

"That, I'm not sure of."

"Dear God," she whispered, sagging against him. Had she

just made love to a man while still married to another? Guilt and fear darkened her heart. "I don't think he's alive," she murmured.

"Because Dustin says so?" he asked cynically.

"Yes. And because I don't believe that Dustin or Ellery would have let another man die in that trailer." The image of the truck carrying Devil's Gambit, as well as Ellery, charred and twisted beyond recognition, filled her mind and she shuddered.

Zane placed comforting arms over her shoulders and kissed her rain-sodden hair before urging her forward, toward the path that led to the house. "You have to face the fact that your husband might still be alive," he whispered.

"I...I don't—"

"Shh!" Zane whispered, cutting off her thought. He cocked his head to one side and listened.

"What?" Tiffany heard the faint sound rumbling in the distance, barely audible over the rising wind. With a sickening feeling, she recognized the noise. "Oh, no!" The sound became louder and more clear. Thundering hooves pounded the wet earth, charging through the pastures with lightning speed. "One of the horses is loose," she said, turning toward the direction of the sound and trying to break free of Zane's arms.

"Wait." Zane restrained her just as the black horse broke through the trees and bolted toward the lake. He raced to the edge of the pond with his ebony tail hoisted and his long legs stretching with boundless energy.

"Moon Shadow," Tiffany whispered, her heart pounding with dread as she watched the magnificent creature rear and whirl on his hind legs when he reached the water's edge.

Tiffany started toward him, all her thoughts centered on the horse and how he could injure himself by slipping on the wet grass. Zane's fingers tightened over her arm. "I'll go after the horse, you call the police."

"The police?" Tiffany's mind was racing with the stallion.

"If he gets out and onto the road, it could get dangerous. Not only for him, but for motorists as well."

"Oh, God. I don't think he can get out," she said, trying to convince herself. Shielding her eyes against the rain, she squinted into the darkness, searching the black night, trying to recall the boundaries of the farm. The horse splashed in the water and started off at a dead run to the opposite side of the pond.

"What's on the other side of the lake?" Zane pointed in the direction in which Moon Shadow disappeared.

"Nothing...some trees, it's all fenced."

"No gate?" He started to follow the stallion, his long legs accelerating with each of his strides.

"Yes, but it should be closed."

"Good. With any luck, I'll be able to catch him." Zane chased after the horse while Tiffany turned toward the buildings near the house.

Her heart was pounding as she ran through the open field, stumbling twice when her heels caught in the mud. Once, when she fell, she heard her dress rip, but didn't bother to see how bad the damage was. All her thoughts centered on Moon Shadow. *Who had let him out? Was it carelessness on the part of the stable boy or...what?* At the sinister turn of her thoughts, she raced more quickly. *No one would let the prized stallion out on purpose!*

Once she made it to the stallion barn, her heart hammering, her lungs burning for air, she noticed that the door to Moon Shadow's stall was swinging outward. It caught in the wind and banged loudly against the building. Other stallions within the building stamped nervously and snorted at the strange sounds.

Tiffany hurried inside and with numb fingers, flipped on the lights, flooding the building with illumination. The horses moved restlessly in their stalls.

As quickly as her trembling fingers could punch out the number, she called Mac. Rain peppered the roof of the barn as she counted the rings...three, four, five..."Come on," she urged. Finally the trainer answered.

"'Lo," Mac called into the phone.

"Moon Shadow's out," Tiffany explained breathlessly to the trainer. "His stall was unlatched and he bolted."

Mac swore loudly. "Where is he?"

"I don't know," she replied, trying to remain calm. Her chest was heaving, her words broken, her heart thudding with fear. "He took off past the old barn and the pond."

"God in heaven," Mac whispered. "We've been workin' on that fence on the other edge of the lake."

Tiffany swallowed hard against the dread creeping up her throat. "Is it down?" she whispered, her fingers clenched around the receiver.

"I don't think so…." He didn't sound too sure.

"What about the gate?"

"It should be closed."

"But you're not certain?"

Mac swore roundly and then sighed. "I'll be right over. Is anyone else around?"

"Just Zane. Everyone went home for the night."

"I'll call John and a few of the other stable hands that live close. We'll be at the house in ten minutes."

"I'll meet you there."

She hung up and then dialed the number of the local police. Within minutes she was explaining her situation to the officer on the other end of the line.

When she had finished with the phone call, Tiffany hurried outside and listened to the sounds of the night. The rain was beginning to sheet and run on the pavement. It gurgled in the gutters and downspouts. In the distance, faint to her ears, she heard the sound of running hoofbeats…on asphalt.

"Oh God," she swore in desperation. *Moon Shadow was on the road!*

Tiffany began running down the long driveway toward the county road that bordered the farm. She heard the truck before she saw it, the loud engine reverberating through the night.

"No," she cried, spurred even faster. Her legs were numb, her lungs burning. Headlights flashed between the trees bordering the farm, and the roar of the truck's engine filled the night.

She heard the squeal of locked brakes, and the sound of the truck's dull horn as it slid out of control on the wet pavement.

"Moon Shadow!" Tiffany shrieked over the deafening noise.

A stallion squealed, the truck tore through the trees, crashing against the solid wood until finally there was nothing but silence and the sound of the pouring rain.

"Oh, God, no," Tiffany whispered as she raced to the end of the drive. Tears blurred her vision and her voice seemed distant when she screamed. *"Zane..."*

CHAPTER ELEVEN

TIFFANY RACED DOWN THE SLICK PAVEMENT of the county road, mindless of the rain running down her back. The smell of burning rubber filled the night and the truck's headlights angled awkwardly up through the broken branches of the giant oaks, like a pair of macabre searchlights, announcing the place of the accident.

As she approached, all she could hear was her own ragged breath and running footsteps. "Zane, dear God, where are you?" she screamed, listening for a sound, any sound indicating there was life in the wreckage. Her mind filled with a dozen bloody scenarios involving Zane and Moon Shadow, but she pushed her horrible thoughts aside and dashed toward the jackknifed truck.

"Goddam it, man, what the hell was that horse doing loose?" a gravelly voice demanded. The truck driver was crawling out of the cab and swearing profusely. Rain poured down upon him, and the broken branches of the trees snapped as he stepped onto the road.

Zane must be alive! Who else would be absorbing the angry trucker's wrath?

Tiffany made it to the wrecked truck. Her heart was thudding wildly in her chest, and she had to gasp for air. The truck was lying on its side, the cab at an awkward angle. It looked like some great downed beast with a broken neck. In her mind's eye Tiffany saw another truck, the rig that had taken Ellery and Devil's Gambit from Florida to Kentucky, the one that had rolled over and burst into flame, killing both horse and driver. Her stomach turned over at the painful memory.

From inside the cab the sound of a CB's static pierced the darkness and brought her thoughts crashing to the present.

"Zane?" she cried, looking into the darkness, searching for any sign of the man and the horse.

"Hey, lady! Over here!" The large truck driver commanded her attention by calling out in his gravelly voice. "What're you doin' out here? Jesus, God, you're soaked to the skin!"

"Zane… My horse—"

"That black son of a bitch? He's your goddamn horse?" His agitated swearing continued. "Christ, woman, can't you see what that horse of yours did? He ran right up the road here—" the trucker pointed a burly arm toward the bend in the road "—like some demon. Scared the hell out of me, let me tell you."

"He got out…. I'm sorry…." She looked around frantically, dread still taking a stranglehold of her throat. "Where is he…? Where is Zane?"

"Who the hell is Zane? The horse?"

"No!"

"Tiffany," Zane shouted from somewhere in the thick stand of oak and fir trees near the road. Tiffany's head snapped in the direction of the familiar sound, her heart nearly skipped a beat and relief washed over her in soothing rivulets.

Without another glance at the truck driver, who was busy clearing debris from the road and placing warning flares near his truck, Tiffany hurried toward the familiar welcome of Zane's voice.

Then she saw him. Wet, bedraggled, mud-streaked and walking toward her. He was leading a lathered Moon Shadow, who skittered and danced at all the commotion he had inadvertently caused. "Oh, God, Zane," she cried, "you're alive."

Without further thought, she ran to him and threw her arms around his neck. "I thought…Oh, God, I heard the horse and the truck. I was sure that…" Tears began running freely down her face, and she sobbed brokenly, clinging to him.

"Shh." He wrapped one strong arm around her and kissed her forehead, smearing mud on her face. "I'm all right, and I think Moon Shadow will be, too. But you'd better have the vet look at him. He's limping a little."

"What happened?" she asked, refusing to let go of the man she loved, letting her body feel his, confirming that he was here, alive and unhurt. Rain glistened in his ebony hair, sweat trickled down his jutted chin and a scarlet streak of dried blood cut across his hollowed cheek. Still he was the most ruggedly handsome man she had ever known.

"The fence was down. I followed Moon Shadow through it and called to him, but he wouldn't listen."

"Of course," Tiffany replied, patting the horse's sweaty neck fondly. "He never does."

"He just took off down the road. Bolted as if he were jumping out of the starting gate. I heard the truck coming and tried to stop him by cutting across a field. That's when I got this." He pointed to the ugly slash on his face. "When I realized I didn't have a prayer of catching him in time, I called to the horse and yelled at the truck driver, waving my arms, hoping to catch his eye. Even though I was farther down the road, I thought the driver might see my shirt before the black horse. Anyway, Moon Shadow jumped over the ditch and ran into the trees just as the truck hit the brakes."

"Hey, you think I could get some help over here?" the furious trucker shouted.

Zane went to help the driver just as Mac's old Dodge rumbled down the road. After parking the pickup some distance from the mangled truck and trailer, Mac scrambled out of the Dodge. "Holy Mother of God," he whispered as he eyed the wrecked truck. He expelled a long whistle and grabbed the lead rope from the front seat of his pickup. "What the devil happened?"

Then he saw Moon Shadow. Knowing that Zane and the

trucker were doing everything that could be done with the truck, Mac walked over to Tiffany and snapped a lead rope onto Moon Shadow's wet halter. "Well, Missy," he said, eyeing the wrecked truck. "It looks as if you've had yourself quite a night." His eyes narrowed as he surveyed the anxious stallion.

"One I wouldn't want to repeat," she admitted. "Zane says Moon Shadow's walking with a misstep," she said. "Left hind leg."

"Let's take a look at him." Mack talked to the horse while he ran his fingers down his back and along each leg. "Yep, it's a little tender," Mac decided. "But I don't think anything's broken, probably bruised himself, maybe a pulled tendon. I'll take him back to the barn, cool him down and check for any other injuries." He tugged on the rope, and Moon Shadow tossed his great black head. "I always said *you* should have been the one named Devil's something or other," Mac grumbled affectionately to the nervous stallion.

The sound of a siren pierced the night and increased in volume. Bright, flashing lights announced the arrival of the state police. A young officer parked his car, leaving the lights flashing in warning, and walked stiffly toward the crumpled truck. "What happened here?" he demanded.

"One of the horses got out," Zane replied, tossing a broken branch off the road.

"And I damned near hit him," the trucker added with a shake of his head. "Just lucky that I didn't."

The officer's suspicious eyes moved from Zane to Tiffany. "Are you the lady who called?"

"Yes."

"*Before* the accident?"

"That's right. I was afraid something like this might happen."

The officer studied the wreckage and whistled. "Where's the horse?"

"Over here." Mac led Moon Shadow to the officer. The black stallion shied away from the flashing lights of the police car, and reared on his back legs. The lead rope tightened in Mac's hands, but he began to talk to the horse and gently led him away from the crowd.

"Blends in with the night," Officer Sparks remarked, watching the nervous black stallion shy away from the crumpled vehicle. The policeman turned his hard eyes back on Tiffany. "How'd he get out?"

"Someone left the stall door unlatched, and he found a hole in a fence we're repairing."

"Wait a minute, let's start at the beginning." He walked back to his car, reached for a note pad on the dash and began writing quickly.

"Why don't we do this inside," Zane suggested, "where it's warmer and drier?"

The young officer pursed his lips together and nodded. "Fine. Just let me take a few measurements and report what happened on the radio. Then we'll call a tow company and see if we can get this rig moved."

Three hours later the ordeal was nearly over. After two cups of coffee and what seemed to be a thousand questions, the police officer was satisfied that he could accurately report what had happened. The trucker had taken the name of Tiffany's insurance company and had left with the towtruck driver, who had driven up with a truck similar in size to the wrecked rig. Moon Shadow was back in his stall and Mac had attended to his injury, which turned out to be a strained tendon. With Zane's help, Mac had applied a pressure bandage and called Vance, who had promised to stop by in the morning and examine the horse.

"You're sure Moon Shadow's all right?" Tiffany asked the trainer. She was just coming back into the kitchen. After the police officer and the trucker had left, she had gone upstairs, showered and changed into her bathrobe. Her hair was still wet, but at least she was clean and warm.

"He'll be fine," Mac assured her. He was sitting at the table and finishing his last cup of coffee.

"Where's Zane?"

Mac scowled at the mention of the Irishman. "He went to clean up. Same as you." He looked as if he were about to say something and changed his mind. "He knows horses, that one."

"Who? Zane?"

"Aye."

"I think he's worked with them all his life." Tiffany poured herself a cup of the strong coffee and took a sip as she leaned against the counter. "Mac, is something bothering you?" Tiffany asked, her brows drawing together in concern. "Is Moon Shadow all right?"

Mac was quick to put her fears to rest. "Oh, I imagine he'll have a few stiff muscles tomorrow, and it won't hurt to have Vance take a look at him. But I think he'll be fine."

"Great," Tiffany said with a relieved sigh.

Just then, Zane strode into the kitchen, wearing only a clean pair of jeans and a T-shirt that stretched across his chest and didn't hide the ripple of his muscles as he moved. He had washed his face and the scratch there was only minor.

"Another cup?" Tiffany asked, handing Zane a mug filled with the steaming brew.

"Thanks."

Mac rotated his mug between both of his hands and stared into the murky liquid. He pressed his thin lips together and then lifted his head, eyeing both Tiffany and Zane.

"Now, Missy," he said, "who do ya suppose let Moon Shadow out?"

Tiffany was surprised by the question. She lifted her shoulders slightly. "I don't know. I think it was probably just an oversight by one of the stable hands."

"Do ya, now?"

"Why? You think someone let him out on purpose?" Tiffany's smile faded and a deep weariness stole over her. So much had happened in one day and she was bone tired.

Mac reached for his hat and placed the slightly damp

fedora on his head. "I checked the stallion barn myself earlier. Moon Shadow was locked in his stall."

Tiffany dropped her head into her hand. "I don't want to think about this," she whispered quietly, "not now."

"I think you have to, Missy," Mac said. "Someone deliberately let the stallion out."

"Buy why?"

"That one I can't answer." His gaze moved to Zane. "You wouldn't know anything about it, would you?"

Zane's gray eyes turned to steel. "Of course not."

"Just askin'," Mac explained. "You were here when it happened." He rubbed his hand over his chin. "And the way I understand it, you had a grudge against Ellery Rhodes."

"That was a long time ago," Zane replied.

"Aye. And now you're here. Pokin' around hopin' to buy the place." He shot a warning glance to Tiffany.

"Mac," she said, horrified that he would consider Zane a suspect. "Zane caught Moon Shadow tonight. If it hadn't been for him, the horse might be dead."

Mac rubbed the tired muscles in the back of his neck and frowned. "I know you're a fine horse breeder," he said to Zane. "You have the reputation to back you up, but sometimes, when revenge or a woman's involved, well...a man's head can get all turned around."

"I would never do anything to jeopardize a horse," Zane stated calmly. "And I care too much for Tiffany to do anything that might harm her." His voice was low and deadly. His indignant eyes impaled the old trainer.

Mac managed to crack a smile. "All right, Sheridan. I believe you. Now, can you tell me what you think is going on around here? It seems to me that someone is trying to sabotage the operation. Who would do that? Maybe a man interested in buying a farm and gathering a little revenge to boot?" With his final remark, Mac pushed his chair away from the table. The legs scraped against the wooden floor. After straightening his tired muscles, he turned toward the back porch. He paused at the door, his hand poised on the knob, and glanced over his shoulder at Tiffany. "And just for the record I'll be sleeping in the stallion barn tonight. Wouldn't want to have another 'accident,' would we?"

"You don't have to—"

"I'm sleeping in the barn, Missy," Mac insisted. "That's all right with you, isn't it?"

"Of course, but really, there's no need…."

Mac tugged on the brim of the fedora over his eyes before stepping outside. Tiffany heard his footsteps fade as he walked down the back steps.

"Mac's grasping at straws," Tiffany said, feeling the need to explain and apologize to Zane. She lifted her palms and managed a frail smile. "He…he's just trying to find an explanation."

"And I'm the logical choice."

"Everyone else has been with the farm for years, and, well, Mac's a little suspicious when it comes to strangers."

Zane set his empty cup on the counter and rammed his hands into this pockets. His eyes narrowed, and his lower jaw jutted forward. "And what do you think, Tiffany?"

She lifted trusting eyes to his. "I *know* you didn't let Moon Shadow out."

"So who did?"

"God, I don't know. I'm not really sure I want to. I'm just so damned tired…" She felt her shoulders slump and forced her back to stiffen. "If I had to guess I'd say that it was probably just some kids who broke into the place and thought they'd get their kicks by letting the horse out."

"Not just any horse," he reminded her. "Moon Shadow."

"He's been getting a lot of attention lately."

"How would the kids know where to find Moon Shadow?"

"His picture's been in the paper."

"And at night, to an untrained eye, Moon Shadow looks like any other black horse."

"But—"

"What about your security system?" Zane demanded.

"You said yourself that the fence was down."

"Wouldn't that dog of yours bark his head off if a stranger started poking around the place?" he demanded, daring her to ignore the logic of his thinking.

"I...I guess so."

"You see," he surmised, "there are too many unanswered questions. I don't blame Mac for thinking I was involved." He raked his fingers through his hair and let out an exasperated sigh.

"He's just worried...about me."

"So am I." Zane's arms circled her waist and he leaned his forehead against hers. "Someone's trying to ruin you and I think I know who."

Tiffany squeezed her eyes shut and shook her head, denying his suggestion before he had a chance to speak. "Dustin," she thought aloud, "you think he's behind all this?"

"No question about it."

"But he's in Florida—"

"Is he?"

Tiffany hesitated. She hadn't actually seen Dustin get on a plane. "Journey's End races the day after tomorrow."

"And Dustin was here this morning." His strong, protective arms drew her close. "If you do have a saboteur, sweet lady, I'm willing to bet on your brother-in-law."

"Just because one horse got out—"

"And four foals died."

"No!" Tiffany tried to jerk away but couldn't. His powerful arms flexed and imprisoned her to him.

"And the story was leaked to the press."

"It wasn't leaked—we never tried to hide what was happening with the foals." She sprang instantly to Dustin's defense. No matter what else had happened, Dustin was the man who had helped her when Ellery had died. "Dustin himself was concerned about the story in the papers. That's why he came back."

"So he claimed."

"You're just trying to find someone, anyone, to blame all this on!"

"No, Tiffany, no," he whispered, his breath fanning her damp hair. "I'm trying to make you understand the only logical explanation. If you think Dustin's so innocent, what about Devil's Gambit and King's Ransom?"

"I…I can't explain that."

"What about the fact that Ellery may still be alive?"

"But he's not—"

"We're not sure about that," Zane said slowly, making no attempt to release her. She sagged wearily against him. "But we both know that Dustin posed as a rival bidder, interested in Ethan Rivers's horses, when in fact Ethan was Ellery and Dustin was his brother. Dustin admitted to bidding on his own horses, just to drive the prices up."

Tiffany's throat went dry. "But I just can't believe that Dustin would try and ruin our operation. It doesn't make any sense. He owns part of the farm."

Zane's voice was firm. "Has it ever occurred to you that Dustin might want to own it all? Hasn't he already offered to buy you out?"

"Only because he thought it was too much for me," she whispered, but the seeds of distrust had been planted, and she hated the new feelings of doubt that were growing in her mind. Three weeks ago she would have trusted Dustin with her life. Now, because of Zane's accusations, she was beginning to doubt the only person she could call family. She shuddered, and Zane gathered her still closer, pressing her face against his chest.

"I'm not saying that Dustin doesn't care for you," he said, gently stroking her hair.

"Just that he's using me."

"He's the kind of man who would do just about anything to get what he wants."

She shook her head and stared out the window. Raindrops ran down the paned glass. "Funny, that's just what he said about you."

Gently Zane lifted her chin with his finger, silently forcing her to look into his eyes. "I've done a few things in my life that I'm not proud of," he admitted. "But I've never cheated or lied to anyone."

"Except me?" Tears began to scald her eyes.

"I didn't lie about Stasia."

"You omitted the facts, Zane. In order to deceive me. Call it what you will. In my book, it's lying."

A small muscle worked in the corner of his jaw, and he had to fight the urge to shake her, make her see what was so blindingly clear to him. He couldn't. He'd wounded her enough as it was. Tiffany seemed to stare right through him. "I've never wanted anyone the way I want you, Tiffany," he whispered. "I wouldn't do anything that would ever make you doubt me."

Her throat tightened painfully, and she squeezed her eyes against the hot tears forming behind her eyelids. "I want to trust you, Zane. God, I want to trust you," she admitted. "It's just that you've come here when everything seems to be falling apart…"

"And you blame me?"

"No!"

"Then look at me, damn it!" he insisted. Her eyes opened and caught in his silvery stare. "I love you, Tiffany Rhodes, and I'll do everything in my power to prove it."

She held up a protesting palm before he could say anything else. She felt so open and raw. Though he was saying the words she longed to hear, she couldn't believe him.

He took her trembling hand and covered it with his. "You're going to listen to me, lady," he swore. "Ever since I met you that first morning when Rod Crawford was here, you've doubted me. I can't say that I blame you because I came here with the express purpose of taking your farm from you…by any means possible."

Her eyes widened at his admission.

"But all that changed," he conceded, "when I met you and began to fall in love with you."

"I...I wish I could believe you," Tiffany whispered. "More than *anything* I want to believe you." Her voice was raspy and thick with emotion. She felt as if her heart were bursting, and she knew that she was admitting far more than she should.

His fingers tightened over her shoulders. *"Believe."*

"Oh, Zane..."

"Tiffany, please. Listen. I want you to marry me."

The words settled in the kitchen and echoed in Tiffany's mind. Her knees gave way and she fell against him. "I want you to be my wife, bear my children, stand at my side...." He kissed the top of her head. "I want you to be with me forever."

She felt the tears stream down her face, and she wondered if they were from joy or sadness. "I can't," she choked. "I can't until I know for certain that Ellery is dead."

Zane's back stiffened. "I thought you were convinced."

"I am." Her voice trembled. "But what if there's a chance that he's *alive*?"

His arms wrapped around her in desperation, and he buried his head into the hollow of her shoulder. "I'll find out," he swore, one fist clenching in determination. "Once and for all, I'll find out just what happened to your husband."

"And if he's alive?" she whispered.

"He'll wish he were dead for the hell he's put you through."

She shook her head and pushed herself out of his possessive embrace. "No, Zane. If Ellery's alive, he's still my husband."

"A husband who used and betrayed you." Anger stormed in his eyes, and his muscles tensed at the thought of Ellery Rhodes claiming Tiffany as his wife after all these years. *The man couldn't possibly be alive!*

"But my husband nonetheless."

"You're still in love with him," he charged.

"No," she admitted, closing her eyes against the traitorous truth. "The only man I've ever loved is you."

Zane relaxed a bit and gently kissed her eyelids. "Trust me, Tiffany. Trust me to take care of you, no matter what happens in the future." He reached for her and savagely pressed her body to his, lowering his head and letting his lips capture hers.

Willingly, her arms encircled his neck, and she let her body fit against his. The warmth of him seemed to seep through her clothes and generate a new heat in her blood.

When his tongue rimmed her lips, she shuddered. "I love you, Zane," she murmured as her breath mingled and caught with his. "And I want to be with you."

He leaned over and placed an arm under the crook of her knees before lifting her off the floor and carrying her out of the kitchen. She let her head rest against his shoulder and wondered at the sanity of loving such a passionate man. Zane's emotions, whether love or hate, ran deep.

Carefully he mounted the stairs and carried her to her bedroom. Rain slid down the windows and the room was illuminated only by the shadowy light from the security lamps near the barns. "I never wanted to fall in love with you," he admitted as he stood her near the bed and his fingers found the knot to the belt of her robe. Slowly the ties loosened, and he pushed the robe over her shoulders to expose the satiny texture of her skin.

She was naked except for a silky pair of panties. Zane kissed her lips, the hollow of her throat, the dark stiffening tips of each gorgeous breast as he lowered himself to his knees.

She wanted to fall to the floor with him, but his hands held her upright as slowly he removed the one scanty piece of cloth keeping her from him. His fingers lingered on her skin and rubbed her calves and thighs as he kissed her abdomen, moistening the soft skin with his tongue. His eyes closed, and Tiffany felt his eyelashes brush her navel. Tingling sensations climbed upward through her body, heating her blood as it raced through her veins.

The heat within her began to turn liquid as his tongue circled her navel. Tiffany's knees felt weak, and if it hadn't been for the strong arms supporting her, she would have slid to the floor and entwined herself with him.

Zane's hands reached upward and touched the pointed tip of one swollen breast. It hardened expectantly against the soft pressure of his fingers and Tiffany closed her eyes against the urge to lie with him. Zane groaned against her abdomen, and his hot breath warmed her skin.

"Zane," she pleaded, the sound coming from deep in her throat as her fingers caught in his black hair. "Love me."

"I do, sweet lady," he murmured against her skin, his warm hands pressing against the small of her back, pushing her closer to him.

As if in slow motion, he forced her backward, and she fell onto the bed. Her hair splayed against the comforter in tangled disarray. Her cheeks were flushed, as were her proud breasts with their alluring dark peaks.

As she watched him, Zane quickly removed and discarded his clothes. When completely naked, he came to her. Lying beside her elegant nude body, he caught his fingers in the silken tresses of her hair and rolled atop her. Corded male muscles strained against hers as he captured one blossoming nipple in his mouth. His tongue slid enticingly over the soft mound, and she cradled his head against her, moaning in contentment as he suckled. Her breasts, swollen with desire, ached for his soothing touch, yearned for the tenderness of his lips and tongue.

"Tiffany, I love you," he vowed as his hands roved over her skin, exploring the exquisite feel of her. His lips murmured words of love against her ear, forcing the heat within her to expand until she could stand the torment no longer.

"Please," she whispered into his ear, her fingers running over the smooth skin of his upper arms and back, feeling the ripple of solid muscles as he positioned himself above her. "Now!"

The ache in his loins throbbed for release, and he took her eagerly, becoming one with her in the heated splendor of his love. His lovemaking was violent, explosive, as he claimed her for his own and purged from her body forever any thoughts of the one man who had betrayed them both.

Tiffany soared to the heavens, her soul melding with Zane's as the clouds of passion burst open and showered her in hot bursts of satiation. She shuddered against his hard male frame; her love for him was complete and infinite. Tiffany knew that no matter what the future held, she would never stop loving him.

"I love you," she heard him vow again and again. Listening to the wonderful sound, she smiled and curled her body close to his to fall into a deep, exhausted sleep.

IT WAS BARELY DAWN WHEN TIFFANY awakened. She reached for Zane, but he was gone. The bed sheets were cold. Thoughts of the night before began swimming in her sleepy mind; then she heard him walk back into the room.

"Zane?" she murmured, groggily trying to focus her eyes.

He came to the bed and sat on the edge near her. "I didn't mean to wake you."

He was completely dressed, as if he were leaving. "What's going on?" she asked, glancing at the clock. It was only five-thirty. Even Mac didn't start work until after six.

"I have to go."

"Where?"

"Back to San Francisco."

She looked into his eyes and saw the sadness lingering in the gray depths. "Why?" she asked, forcing herself into a sitting position. She tugged at the comforter to cover her naked breasts and then leaned forward so that her face was near his. Something was wrong. She could feel it. In the course of a few short hours, Zane's feelings toward her had changed. Her heart, filled with love of the last few hours, twisted painfully.

"I have things I have to do," he said. "You'll just have to trust me."

"Does this have anything to do with Dustin?" she asked, shivering from the cold morning air.

"I don't know." He placed a warm hand on her shoulder. "Just trust me, okay?"

She nodded and forced a frail smile. "You'll be back?"

He laughed and broke the tension in the room. "As soon as I can. If I'm not back in a couple of days, I'll call."

"Promises, promises," she quipped, trying to sound light-hearted. He was leaving. Her heart seemed to wither inside her.

"I left the phone number of my hotel on the note pad in the kitchen. If you get lonely—"

"I already am." Lovingly she touched the red scratch on his face. "My hero," she whispered with a seductive smile.

"Hardly."

She curled her hand around his neck and pulled his face next to hers.

"Look, lady, if you don't cut this out, I'll never get out of here," he growled, but a pleased grin stole over his angular features to charmingly display the hint of straight white teeth against his dark skin.

"That's the idea."

Zane let out an exasperated sigh. "Oh, Tiffany, what am I going to do with you?"

"I don't know," she murmured against his ear as her fingers began working at the buttons of his shirt. "Use your imagination."

An hour later he was gone, and Tiffany felt more alone than she ever had in her life. She was more alone than she had been on the morning her mother had abandoned her, for then she had still had Edward, and when her father had died, she had married Ellery. When Ellery was suddenly killed, Tiffany had relied on Dustin.

Now, as she cinched the belt of her robe more tightly

around her waist and stared out the window at the rain-washed countryside, Tiffany was completely alone. She had no one to rely upon but herself. She shivered more from dread than from the morning air, and she watched as Zane's car roar to life and disappeared through the trees.

CHAPTER TWELVE

AFTER ZANE HAD GONE, TIFFANY FOUND IT impossible to return to bed. Instead she dressed and walked outside, stopping only to scratch Wolverine behind the ears. The dog responded by wagging his tail enthusiastically.

"Some hero you are," Tiffany reprimanded fondly. "Where were you last night when I needed you?"

She refilled Wolverine's bowls and walked to the stallion barn. The rain had become no more than a drizzle, but the ground was still wet, and when she ventured off the pavement, her boots sank into the soaked earth.

Mac was already up and checking on Moon Shadow's injury.

"So how is he?" Tiffany asked, patting the black stallion's neck and forcing a smile at the grizzled old trainer. Mac had slept in his clothes and it was obvious from the way he was walking that his arthritis was bothering him.

"Moon Shadow?" He pointed a thumb in the direction of the horse's head. "He's fine."

"And you?"

"Getting too old for all this excitement."

"Why don't you take a day off?" Tiffany asked. "You deserve it."

"Not now, Missy," he said, shaking his head. "What would I do while the missus knits and watches those soap operas? Nope. I'm better off here. 'Sides, I want to see what Vance has to say after he looks this old boy over." Mac gently slapped

Moon Shadow's rump, and the stallion snorted and tossed his head in the air.

"I thought I'd check on Shadow's Survivor next," Tiffany said.

"Good idea."

Mac walked with her and Wolverine trotted along behind. The rain had stopped and the clouds were beginning to break apart, promising a warm spring day. Tiffany realized for the first time that the flowering trees were beginning to bloom. Pink and white blossoms colored the leafless trees with the promise of spring.

"Say, Missy," Mac said as they approached the foaling shed.

"Yes?"

"I noticed that Sheridan's car is gone."

"He left early this morning."

"Because of what I said last night?"

"No." Tiffany shook her head and smiled sadly.

"I was out of line."

"You were concerned. We all were…are." She ran her fingers through her hair and squared her shoulders. "Something's got to give, doesn't it? We can't go on this way much longer."

Mac frowned and reached for the handle of the door. "You're right—it's time our luck changed, for the better."

They walked inside the foaling shed and heard the soft nickering of Alexander's Lady. A tiny nose attempted to push through the rails of the stall. "Here's our good news," Tiffany said with a smile as she tried to reach out and touch the skittish filly. "Maybe I should change her name to that. How does Good News strike you?"

"Better'n Shadow's Survivor or whatever the hell you came up with before," the old man chuckled.

"I don't know…."

"She's your horse, Missy. You name her whatever you like." Mac grinned at the sprightly little filly. "Just wait, little one," he said to the inquisitive young horse. "As soon as we get the okay from the vet, you'll get your first look at the world."

THE REST OF THE DAY WAS FILLED WITH more good news. Two owners called to say that their mares had delivered healthy foals sired by Moon Shadow, and Vance Geddes checked Moon Shadow's leg injury and gave the stallion a clean bill of health.

"As soon as that tendon heals, he'll be good as new," Vance predicted after examining the stallion.

"He sure knows how to get into trouble," Tiffany complained with a fond look at the horse in question.

"Maybe it's not the horse," Vance suggested.

"What do you mean?"

"Seems to me, he had a little help getting out of the stall last night."

"I suppose."

"Got any ideas who unlatched his stall door?" Vance asked, placing all his veterinary supplies back in his case and walking out of the stallion barn.

"No. I thought it might be vandals, but Zane seems to think it was an inside job, so to speak."

"Somebody with a grudge?"

Tiffany lifted her shoulders. "I couldn't guess who."

"You got any trouble with employees?"

"Not that I know of."

"Haven't fired anyone, a stable boy...or maybe done business with someone else, made a competitor angry?"

"No." She sighed wearily and spotted Louise's car rumbling down the long drive. "I've thought and thought about it. I'm sure I've made a few enemies, but no one that would want to hurt me or my horses.... At least I don't think so."

Vance put his bag into the truck and grimaced. He turned his kindly bespectacled eyes on Tiffany. "Just be careful, okay? Anyone who would let Moon Shadow out would do just about anything to get what he wants."

"If only I knew what that was," she said anxiously. "Any news on the foals' deaths?"

"Not yet," Vance said, sliding into his pickup, "but I've got a couple of new ideas. They're long shots…probably end up in dead ends, but maybe…"

"Keep me posted."

"Will do." Vance had just pushed his key into the lock and was about to start the engine, but Louise shouted at him. "Hey, wait!" the housekeeper called as she bustled up to Vance's truck. She was waving a newspaper in the air. "Look, here, on page one." She proudly handed Tiffany the sports section from the *Times*. In the lower left-hand corner was a picture of Journey's End along with the article written by Nancy Emerson.

Tiffany's eyes skimmed the columns of fine print and her face broke into a smile. Then, slowly, she reread Nancy's report, which did bring up the subject of the dead colts but also concentrated on Moon Shadow's career as well as his two strongest progeny, Devil's Gambit and Journey's End. The article ended on an upbeat note, suggesting that Moon Shadow's victories on the racetrack and as a proved sire overshadowed the unfortunate deaths of the four foals.

"Wonderful," Tiffany said, feeling a little relief. "At least we got a chance for rebuttal."

"Now," Vance stated, "if we can just come up with the reason those foals died."

"You think you're on to something?"

"I'm not sure," Vance replied. "I'll let you know in a couple of days. Like I said—it could be another dead end."

"Let's hope not," Tiffany prayed fervently.

"Come on, you two," Louise reprimanded. "Things are turning around, just you wait and see."

"I don't know about that," Tiffany replied.

"Why? What happened?"

"Moon Shadow got out last night. It looks as if someone did it deliberately."

"What!" Louise was more than shocked.

As the two women walked toward the back porch, Tiffany

explained the events of the evening before and Louise clucked her tongue in disbelief.

"But who would do such a thing?" Louise wondered once they were in the kitchen.

"That's the mystery."

"You got any ideas?"

"No…but Zane seems to."

Louise's eyes sparkled. "That one, he'll figure it out. Just you wait and see."

When the telephone rang, Tiffany expected the caller to be Zane, but she was disappointed.

"Hello, Tiff?" Dustin asked through the fuzzy long-distance connection.

"Dustin? Where are you?"

"In Florida and, well, brace yourself for some bad news."

Tiffany slumped against the pantry, the receiver pressed against her ear. Her fingers curled over the handle until her knuckles showed white. "What happened?" she asked, dread steadily mounting up her spine.

"It's Journey's End," Dustin said.

Tiffany's heart pounded erratically, and she felt as if her whole world were falling apart, piece by piece. "What about him?"

"He was injured. Just yesterday, while working out. From everything we can tell, he's got a bone chip in his knee."

"Oh, God," Tiffany said, letting out her breath in a long sigh. When would it end? She ran shaking fingers through her hair and wished that Zane were with her now.

"It looks bad, Tiff. I think his career is over—"

"Before it really began."

"We can retire him to stud."

"I guess that's about the only thing we can do," she reluctantly agreed, her shoulders slumping. "Other than the knee, how is he?"

"The vet says he'll be okay, but we'd better not count on

him racing anymore. It wouldn't hurt to have Vance look at him when he gets home."

"How is Bob Prescott taking the news?"

There was a long silence on the other end of the line. "That's a little bit of a sore point, Tiff. I think Prescott ran him knowing that something was wrong."

"No!"

"I can't prove it."

Tiffany felt sick inside. "Let me talk to him," Tiffany demanded, rage thundering through her blood. The last thing she would stand for was anyone on her staff mistreating a horse.

"Too late."

"What?"

"I fired him."

"On suspicion?" Tiffany was incredulous.

"He's been involved in a couple of shady things," Dustin said. "I just didn't want to take any more chances."

"But who will replace him?"

"I'm talking to a couple of guys now. Big-name trainers…I'll call you after I meet with them."

"I don't know—"

"Look, I've got to go. I'll make all the arrangements to send Journey's End home."

"Wait. Before you hang up."

"What?" Dustin demanded impatiently.

"Last night someone let Moon Shadow out of his stall."

There was silence on the other end of the line. "What do you mean 'someone let him out'?" Dustin asked, his voice cold.

Tiffany gave a brief account of the events of the evening and Dustin's voice shook with rage. "Zane Sheridan was there again? What does he want this time? Don't tell me he's still pressuring you into selling to him."

"No, Dustin, he's not," Tiffany replied.

"Then why the hell is he hanging around?"

"Maybe he enjoys my company—"

"I'll bet. If you ask me, he's the culprit who let Moon Shadow out. He's probably trying to make it tough on you so you'll sell him the farm." Dustin swore descriptively.

"I don't think so."

"That's the problem, isn't it—sometimes you just don't think. Period."

With his final words, Dustin slammed down the phone, and Tiffany knew in her heart that everything Zane had said about her brother-in-law was true. A deep sadness stole over her, and she spent the rest of the day locked in the den, going over the books, hoping to block out the bitter truth about Dustin and what he had done.

Dustin would be back on the farm with Journey's End by the end of the week. When he arrived, Tiffany planned to confront him with the truth.

FOUR DAYS LATER, SHE STILL HADN'T HEARD from Zane. Things had settled into the usual routine on the farm, and she had spent her time working with Mac and the yearlings.

The fence had been repaired, and there had been no other disturbances on the farm. Moon Shadow was healing well, and Mac had prepared a neighboring stall in the stallion barn for Journey's End. "A shame about that one," the old trainer had remarked when he learned about the accident. "Sometimes fate seems to deal out all the bad cards at once."

Later that night, Tiffany was seated in the den going over the books. The house was dark except for the single desk lamp and the shifting flames of the fire burning noisily against dry oak. Tiffany felt cold and alone. The portrait of Devil's Gambit seemed to stare down from its position over the mantel and mock her. Where was Zane? Why hadn't he called?

She tried to force her attention back to the books and the red ink that was beginning to flow in the pages of the general ledger. The farm was losing money. Without Moon Shadow's stud fees or any income from Journey's End's racing career, Tiffany had little alternative but to sell several of the best yearlings.

The rap on the French doors surprised her, but she knew in an instant that it had to be Zane. She saw his haggard face through the glass, she opened the doors with trembling fingers and flung herself into his arms.

He stepped in with a rush of cold air that chilled the room and fanned the glowing embers of the fire and billowed the sheer draperies. "Thank God you're here," she whispered against his neck before lifting her head and studying the intensity of his gaze.

The look on his face was murderous. Dark shadows circled his gray eyes, and a weariness stole over his features making the angular planes seem more rugged and foreboding. He looked as if he hadn't slept in weeks.

"Zane?" she whispered as his dark eyes devoured her.

"It's just about over," he said as he closed the door and walked over to the fire to warm himself.

"What is?"

"Everything you've been going through." He reached for her and drew her close to him. "I wish I could make it easier for you—"

"Easier?"

"Shh." He brushed his lips over hers, and his hands locked behind her back, gently urging her body forward until her supple curves pressed against him and he groaned, as if in despair. She felt her body respond to his and heard the uneven beat of her own heart when he kissed her hungrily and his tongue touched hers. Her fingers lingered at his neck, and she felt the coiled tension within him, saw the strain on his face.

"What happened?" she asked, when at last he drew his head back.

"It's a long story."

"I've got the rest of my life to listen," she murmured.

Zane managed a wan smile. "Oh, lady, I've been waiting

for four days to hear you say just those words," he whispered, his arms tightening around her. "God, I've missed you." He kissed the curve of her neck, his lips lingering near her earlobe, before he gently released her.

"So tell me."

He rammed his fingers through his black, windblown hair and poured them each a drink. "I found Stasia," he admitted roughly, Tiffany's heart nearly missed a beat. "It wasn't all that easy, and if she'd had her way, I never would have located her."

He walked over to Tiffany and handed her a snifter of brandy, before taking a long swallow of the warm liquor and sitting on the hearth, hoping that the golden flames would warm his back.

"How did you find her?"

"A private investigator by the name of Walt Griffith."

His gray eyes searched hers. "I had him do some checking on you, too—"

"What!"

He smiled devilishly and his eyes twinkled. "I didn't figure you'd like it any more than Stasia did. But it was necessary. To find Ellery."

Tiffany nearly dropped her drink. Her hands began to shake as she lifted the glass to her lips.

"I'm getting ahead of myself," Zane said. "Walt found Stasia living with some artist-type in Carmel. When I approached her she was shocked, but managed to fall right back into character—she agreed to tell her side of the Ellery Rhodes story for a substantial fee."

"You paid her?" Tiffany was outraged.

Zane's eyes rested on her flushed face and he smiled. "Believe me, it was worth it."

Tiffany wasn't so sure. "What did you find out?"

"About the accident that supposedly killed Devil's Gambit."

Tiffany's heart was pounding so loudly it seemed to echo against the cherry-wood walls. "Wait a minute," she insisted as the cold truth swept over her in a tidal wave of awareness. "What you're saying is that—"

"Stasia was Ellery's mistress. Even when he was married to you, he was having an affair with my ex-wife. Seems that they were hooked on the excitement of carrying on when there was the danger of being discovered."

"I…" Tiffany was about to say that she didn't want to believe it, but she knew it was the truth. She'd come to the same conclusion herself once she had talked to Dustin. The affair explained so much about Ellery that she had never understood.

"So Ellery?" she asked breathlessly.

"Was killed in the accident," Zane assured her.

"I…never wished him dead," Tiffany whispered, walking across the room and sitting next to Zane on the hearth.

"I know. You just had to know the truth." Zane looked into her eyes and smiled. "It's going to be all right, you know."

"God, I hope so."

"We'll be together."

Tiffany's eyes filled with tears of happiness. "Then you're right—everything will work out."

"Stasia admitted that the horses were switched," he said, continuing with his story. "Ellery had thought that the insurance forms had already been processed—"

"The ones that were waiting for his signature?"

"Yes. No one but Ellery, Dustin and Bob Prescott knew that Devil's Gambit had pulled a ligament after his last race."

"Not even Mac?"

"No."

"When?"

"While exercising a few days after his last race. It looked as if Devil's Gambit, the favored horse, wouldn't be able to race in any of the Triple Crown races. If Ellery could make it look as if Devil's Gambit had died in an accident, when in fact it was really another, considerably less valuable horse who was killed, he could breed Devil's Gambit under an alias in another country, collect stud fees and get the insurance money to boot. It was better odds than just putting him out for stud before he'd really proved himself."

"Oh, God," Tiffany said with a long sigh. Nervously she ran her fingers through her hair.

"It wasn't a foolproof plan by any means and it was extremely risky. But Ellery enjoyed taking risks—remember the stunts he and Dustin would pull in Europe when he posed as Ethan Rivers?"

Tiffany nodded, her stomach turning over convulsively. What kind of a man had she married? How had she been so blind?

"There was always the chance that Devil's Gambit would be recognized because of the Jockey Club identification number tattooed on the inside of his lip. And of course there was the remote possibility of something going wrong with Ellery's plans."

Tiffany had broken out in a cold sweat. She wrapped her arms around herself as she relived the horrible night when she was told that Ellery and Devil's Gambit were killed.

"Everything backfired when Ellery was trapped in the truck and killed along with the switched horse, which, by the way, Bob Prescott supplied. It seems that the trainer was involved in the scam with Ellery and Dustin."

"And all this time I've let him work with our horses.... God, how could I have been so stupid?"

"There's no shame in trusting your husband, Tiffany," Zane said softly and kissed the top of her head before smiling. "In fact, your next one will insist upon it."

She felt his warm arm slide around her waist. "And Dustin—what about him?" she asked.

"He decided to gamble and carry out Ellery's plan."

"With Bob Prescott?"

"Right. Stasia claims he was absolutely furious that the insurance forms hadn't been signed, and that you, not he, as the new forms indicated, would get the settlement." Zane shrugged and finished his drink in one swallow. "But by that time it was too late."

"So what are we going to do?"

His arm tightened possessively around her, and his fingers toyed with the lapels of her robe. "For now, go to bed. Tomorrow we'll deal with Dustin."

"How?"

"I have it on good authority that he'll be here with Journey's End. Come on." He pulled her gently to her feet and walked her to the stairs. "I haven't slept in days—" he slid an appreciative glance down her body "—and somehow I get the feeling that I'll have trouble again tonight."

They mounted the stairs entwined in an embrace. Once in her bedroom, he let his hand slip inside her bathrobe and felt the shimmery fabric of her nightgown. "I've been waiting for so long to be with you again," he whispered into her ear as he untied the belt of the robe, pushed it gently over her shoulders and let it drop unheeded to the floor.

TRUE TO ZANE'S PREDICTION, DUSTIN arrived around nine. He marched into the kitchen and stopped abruptly. The last person he had expected to see was Zane Sheridan. Dustin's composure slipped slightly and his broad shoulders stiffened. His jeans and shirt were rumpled from the long, cross-country drive, and three days' growth of beard darkened his chin. In contrast, Zane was clean-shaven and dressed in fresh corduroy pants and a crisp shirt. His hair was neatly combed, and the satisfied smile on his face made Dustin's hair stand on end.

The differences in the two men were striking.

Dustin cast a worried glance in Tiffany's direction before placing his Stetson on a hook near the door.

"'Morning, Dustin," Zane drawled. He was leaning against the counter sipping coffee while Tiffany made breakfast.

Dustin managed a thin smile. "What're you doing here?"

"Visiting." Zane took another long drink.

The meaning of Zane's words settled like lead on Dustin's shoulders. "Oh, no, Tiffany," he said. "You're not getting involved with this bastard, are you?" He hooked a thumb in Zane's direction.

Zane just smiled wickedly, but Tiffany stiffened. "I don't see that it's any of your business, Dustin. Is Journey's End in the stallion barn?"

"Yes."

"With Mac?"

"He was there and that veterinarian, Geddes."

"Good."

Dustin became uneasy. "What's going on?"

Zane propped a booted foot on a chair near the table. "That's what we'd like to know." Zane's gray eyes glittered ominously, and Dustin was reminded of a great cat about to spring on unsuspecting quarry. His throat went dry.

"Tiffany?" Dustin asked.

She turned to face her brother-in-law and he saw the disappointment in her eyes. *She knows. She knows everything!* Dustin's palms began to sweat, and he tugged at the collar of his shirt.

"I think you need to answer a few questions, Dustin. Did you let Moon Shadow out the other night?" she charged.

Dustin's gold eyes narrowed treacherously, but he refused to fall into any of Sheridan's traps. "Of course not. I...I was in Florida."

"It's over, Rhodes," Zane cut in. "I checked the flights. You were booked on a red-eye."

"No—I mean, I had business in town...."

Tiffany's shoulders slumped, but she forced her gaze to bore into Dustin's. "Zane says that Devil's Gambit is alive in Ireland, that he's siring foals while King's Ransom is taking all the credit." Dustin whitened. "Is it true?" Tiffany demanded, her entire body shaking with rage and disappointment.

"I don't know anything about—"

"Knock it off," Zane warned, straightening to his full height. "You're the primary owner of Emerald Enterprises, which happens to own a farm where King's Ransom stands. I saw Devil's Gambit and I've got the pictures to prove it." His face grew deadly. "And if that isn't enough proof to lock you up for the rest of your life, Stasia is willing to talk, for the right price."

"None of this is happening." Dustin turned his gold eyes on her. "Tiff, you can't believe all this. Sheridan's just out for revenge, like I told you…. Oh, my God," he said as he recognized the truth. "You're in love with the bastard, aren't you? What's he promised to do, marry you?" He saw the silent confirmation in her eyes. "Damn it, Tiffany, don't be a fool. Of course he proposed to you. He'd do anything to steal this farm from you."

"The only time I was a fool, Dustin," Tiffany stated, her voice trembling with rage, "was when I trusted you."

"I helped you—when your world was falling to pieces, I helped you, damn it."

"And you lied. About Devil's Gambit and about Moon Shadow." Her eyes blazed a furious shade of blue. "You let me think that Moon Shadow was the cause of the dead foals and you leaked the story to Rod Crawford."

"What are you saying?" Dustin demanded.

"That the jig is up. Vance Geddes has discovered that the only unhealthy foals sired by Moon Shadow were all conceived during one week—a week you were on the farm," Zane said, barely able to control his temper. "He hasn't discovered what you injected the mares with yet, but it's only a matter of time before he knows just what happened."

"That doesn't mean—"

"Give it up, Rhodes!"

Dustin turned furious eyes on Tiffany. "You've got it all figured out, haven't you? You and your lover! Well, I'm not going to bother to explain myself. It looks as if I'm going to need an attorney—"

"I'd say so," Zane stated. "The police are on their way. They've already rounded up Bob Prescott, and I'm willing to bet that he sold you out."

Dustin visibly paled. He lunged for Tiffany; his only chance of escape was to take Tiffany hostage.

Zane anticipated the move and as Dustin grabbed for Tiffany, Zane landed a right cross to Dustin's cheek that set him on his heels.

"Don't even think about it," Zane warned as Dustin attempted to get up. In the distance, the sounds of a police siren became audible. "I'd be thinking very seriously about an attorney myself, if I were you," he said.

When the police arrived, they read Dustin his rights and took him in for questioning. As he left he was still rubbing his jaw and glaring angrily at Zane.

"I've waited a long time for that," Zane admitted. He stepped onto the back porch and watched while the police cars raced out the drive with Dustin in custody.

"I just can't believe it's over," Tiffany murmured, her eyes looking over the rolling hills that she'd grown to love. "And to think that Dustin was behind it all...."

Zane tilted her chin upward and looked into her worried eyes. "Like you said, it's over." He kissed her tenderly on the eyelids and tasted the salt of her tears, before leading her back to the den. "I came here intending to ruin you," he admitted roughly. "I wanted to buy this farm no matter what the cost." He took out the legal documents that John Morris had prepared. After showing her the contract of sale, he tossed it into the fireplace, and the coals from the previous night burst into flame against the crisp, white paper. "It was all so damned pointless," he said. "All I want is for you to be my wife."

"And I will be," she vowed.

"Even if it means living part of your life in Ireland? We have to bring Devil's Gambit home, you know."

"It doesn't really matter where," she said. "As long as I'm with you."

Zane folded her into the protection of his arms. "I'm not a patient man," he said.

"Don't I know."

"And I'm not about to wait."

"For what?"

"To get married. The sooner the better."

"Anything you want," she said, her blue eyes lingering on his handsome face.

"Anything?" With a wicked smile, he urged her slowly to the floor with the weight of his body. "You may live to regret those words."

"Never," Tiffany whispered as Zane's lips covered hers and she entwined her arms around the neck of the man she loved.

* * * * *

REQUEST YOUR FREE BOOKS!

2 FREE NOVELS
FROM THE ROMANCE/SUSPENSE
COLLECTION PLUS 2 FREE GIFTS!

BOB08R

LISA JACKSON

77282	SECRETS	___ $6.99 U.S.	___ $8.50 CAN.
77202	THE McCAFFERTYS: RANDI	___ $6.99 U.S.	___ $8.50 CAN.
77140	THE McCAFFERTYS: SLADE	___ $6.99 U.S.	___ $8.50 CAN.
77111	THE McCAFFERTYS: MATT	___ $6.99 U.S.	___ $8.50 CAN.

(limited quantities available)

TOTAL AMOUNT	$ _____
POSTAGE & HANDLING	$ _____
($1.00 FOR 1 BOOK, 50¢ for each additional)	
APPLICABLE TAXES*	$ _____
TOTAL PAYABLE	$ _____

(check or money order—please do not send cash)

To order, complete this form and send it, along with a check or money order for the total above, payable to HQN Books, to: **In the U.S.:** 3010 Walden Avenue, P.O. Box 9077, Buffalo, NY 14269-9077; **In Canada:** P.O. Box 636, Fort Erie, Ontario, L2A 5X3.

Name: _____
Address: _____ City: _____
State/Prov.: _____ Zip/Postal Code: _____
Account Number (if applicable): _____

075 CSAS

*New York residents remit applicable sales taxes.
*Canadian residents remit applicable GST and provincial taxes.

HQN™

We *are* romance™

www.HQNBooks.com

PHLJ0608BL